ENTER THE EDGAR RICE BURROUGHS UNIVERSE™

A century before the term "crossover" became a buzzword in popular culture, Edgar Rice Burroughs created the first expansive, fully cohesive literary universe. Coexisting in this vast cosmos was a pantheon of immortal heroes and heroines—Tarzan of the Apes™, Jane Porter®, John Carter®, Dejah Thoris®, Carson Napier™, and David Innes™ being only the best known among them. In Burroughs' 80-plus novels, their epic adventures transported them to the strange and exotic worlds of Barsoom®, Amtor™, Pellucidar®, Caspak™, and Va-nah™, as well as the lost civilizations of Earth and even realms beyond the farthest star. Now the Edgar Rice Burroughs Universe expands in an all-new series of canonical novels written by today's talented authors!

RED AXE OF PELLUCIDAR

EDGAR RICE BURROUGHS UNIVERSE™

The Edgar Rice Burroughs Universe is the interconnected and cohesive literary cosmos created by the Master of Adventure and continued in new canonical works authorized by Edgar Rice Burroughs, Inc., the corporation based in Tarzana, California, that was founded by Burroughs in 1923. Unravel the mysteries and explore the wonders of the Edgar Rice Burroughs Universe alongside the pantheon of heroes and heroines that inhabit it in both classic tales of adventure penned by Burroughs and brand-new epics from today's talented authors.

TARZAN® SERIES

Tarzan of the Apes
The Return of Tarzan
The Beasts of Tarzan
The Son of Tarzan
Tarzan and the Jewels of Opar
Jungle Tales of Tarzan
Tarzan the Untamed
Tarzan the Terrible
Tarzan and the Golden Lion
Tarzan and the Ant Men
Tarzan, Lord of the Jungle
Tarzan and the Lost Empire
Tarzan at the Earth's Core
Tarzan the Invincible
Tarzan Triumphant
Tarzan and the City of Gold
Tarzan and the Lion Man
Tarzan and the Leopard Men
Tarzan's Quest
Tarzan the Magnificent
Tarzan and the Forbidden City
Tarzan and the Foreign Legion
Tarzan and the Madman
Tarzan and the Castaways
Tarzan and the Tarzan Twins
Tarzan: The Lost Adventure (with Joe R. Lansdale)

BARSOOM® SERIES

A Princess of Mars
The Gods of Mars
The Warlord of Mars
Thuvia, Maid of Mars
The Chessmen of Mars
The Master Mind of Mars
A Fighting Man of Mars
Swords of Mars
Synthetic Men of Mars
Llana of Gathol
John Carter of Mars

PELLUCIDAR® SERIES

At the Earth's Core
Pellucidar
Tanar of Pellucidar
Tarzan at the Earth's Core
Back to the Stone Age
Land of Terror
Savage Pellucidar

AMTOR™ SERIES

Pirates of Venus
Lost on Venus
Carson of Venus
Escape on Venus
The Wizard of Venus

ERB UNIVERSE™

SWORDS OF ETERNITY SUPER-ARC

Carson of Venus: The Edge of All Worlds
by Matt Betts

Tarzan: Battle for Pellucidar
by Win Scott Eckert

John Carter of Mars: Gods of the Forgotten
by Geary Gravel

Victory Harben: Fires of Halos
by Christopher Paul Carey

OTHER ERB UNIVERSE BOOKS

Mahars of Pellucidar
by John Eric Holmes

Tarzan and the Forest of Stone
by Jeffrey J. Mariotte

Tarzan and the Dark Heart of Time
by Philip José Farmer

Tarzan and the Valley of Gold
by Fritz Leiber

EDGAR RICE BURROUGHS UNIVERSE™

RED AXE OF PELLUCIDAR®

JOHN ERIC HOLMES

Foreword and Frontispiece by
CHRISTOPHER WEST HOLMES

Includes the bonus novella

JASON GRIDLEY™
OF EARTH
ACROSS THE MOONS OF MARS
BY
GEARY GRAVEL

EDGAR RICE BURROUGHS, INC.
Publishers
TARZANA   CALIFORNIA

Contents

FOREWORD

I AM VERY HAPPY you are about to read the sequel to *Mahars of Pellucidar*. This book was my first experience of an unpublished novel and of my father's writing being rejected. Despite critical praise, *Mahars* had poor sales and the head of the Burroughs corporation was no longer the enthusiastic grandson who helped that book get published. I have always suspected that the title may have worked against it and that *Red Axe of Pellucidar* might have sold more copies in the late 1970s. The book did get privately published in a very limited edition by a fan of Dad's writing. Leaked copies of this manuscript, with many errors, have been available to a few. I hope you haven't spent much money on them because their production and art are not worth it. Now at last we have this lovely edition.

The next couple of paragraphs contain spoilers, but not too many, I hope.

A novel of Pellucidar with Mahars, tyrannosauruses, and a giant octopus is a hard act to follow. Dad did a good job of it, though, and didn't skim on the monsters. Mostly he introduces us to two tribes of believable prehistoric peoples: the Polynesian race that draws upon his knowledge of his Hawaiian childhood, and the mammoth people who are inspired by Edgar Rice Burroughs' wonderful mammoth hunters in the novel *Back to the*

Stone Age. My father also had a beautifully illustrated series by Dr. Josef Augusta and a great painter named Zdeněk Burian from Czechoslovakia. One volume was *A Book of Mammoths*, and this was a favorite of my father's. My favorite was *Prehistoric Animals*, which told the story of evolution in beautiful oil paintings. Speaking of evolution, we are again treated to a panoply of prehistoric monsters in this book, including a mysterious poisonous flying reptile and a creature so huge it is mistaken for a god. Where have I heard of that plot device before?

A couple of differences between this book and the Burroughs novels are the depiction of the heroine and of older characters. Though some of Burroughs' heroines are women of action, not many are the expert archer and fearless fighter that Varna is. Varna accomplishes her own escape from the fortress of the mammoth people and later kills an attacker with a dagger. She is more than just a princess to be rescued but not yet a main character of her own story.

Dad revisits a theme that is popular in Burroughs' works: a false religion that demands much in sacrifice from a primitive people and gives an evil hypocrite power over them. We see this theme used satirically in *Savage Pellucidar* and more seriously in *The Gods of Mars*, and I know there are even more examples I can't recall. This theme resonated strongly with my scientist father, as it did with the science enthusiast Burroughs. When Red Axe must convince Onoloa's brother to aid her, he avoids attacking Tumu's faith directly, but he does attack the character of the priest who represents the theocracy.

Red Axe has a different interaction with the witch doctor of the mammoth tribe, one that is much more optimistic about a symbiotic relationship between science and religion. The doctor in Santa Monica speaking in this scene is, of course, my father. Your author just taught you a little neuroscience using cavemen and witch doctors.

Had *Red Axe of Pellucidar* been published in the '70s, it might have been followed by *Swordsman of Pellucidar*, but what that story would have been we will never know because Dad kept it to himself.

CHRISTOPHER WEST HOLMES

1

DINOSAUR SWAMP

I T WAS A STRANGE GROUP that cautiously threaded its way over the half-submerged fallen tree trunks of the tropical swamp. A brilliant sun beat down upon them from the zenith, for this was Pellucidar, that world at the Earth's core where the sun, hanging in the center of a hollow ball, is always directly overhead. It is a timeless world of tropical immensity, and much of the life that flourishes under the bright, hot inner sun has long been extinct on the outer crust.

The leader of the little band of adventurers pulled himself to the top of a patch of soggy mulch surmounted by cycads and giant ferns. Small lizards scampered out of sight on all sides, some running on two legs, some on four. Giant dragonflies as long as a man's arm darted aside to hover on iridescent wings. From farther ahead in the swamp, invisible in the greenery, there came heavy splashing noises, as if some of the larger reptilian denizens had been disturbed.

Christopher West's clear blue eyes swept his surroundings. There was no horizon. Inside the hollow Earth the distances faded upward into blue, with forests, mountains, lakes, and oceans blending into one another as they receded. In Pellucidar, distance had no end and time did not exist.

West searched both the sky and the adjacent jungle for possible enemies. He was a giant of a man, well over six feet, and his suntanned skin covered a rippling wealth of muscles that proclaimed him to be in peak physical condition. His hair and beard were blond, his sun-bleached hair falling to

1

his shoulders. He was dressed in a short-sleeved khaki shirt and leather shorts and wore stout hiking boots. He had been carrying a pack-frame, which he now slipped from his shoulders with a grunt of relief and lowered to the ground. Strapped to the sides of the pack were a bow and a quiver of arrows, along with a short-handled steel axe. The crimson paint on the blade of this latter weapon had given the man his Pellucidarian name: Red Axe. Around his waist he wore a pouched canvas belt from which dangled a canteen, a first aid kit, and two long-bladed steel hunting knives. In his right hand, West carried a long pole which he used as a staff as he walked. The upper end of the weapon was shod with a broad razor-sharp blade like an assegai or stabbing spear.

The blond American's scan of his surroundings had failed to reveal any potential danger. Less than a mile away, a herd of huge brontosaurs wallowed in the mud, their great necks waving to and fro above the tree ferns. Their presence was reassuring, for it meant there were no large carnivorous dinosaurs in the immediate vicinity. If there had been predators nearby, the gigantic but timid brontosaurs would have retreated into the water of the adjacent lake. Christopher West sighed and turned to speak to his companions.

"It's dry here," he said. "Let's stop and make camp." He waved into the sky to signal the fifth member of their party, as the three behind him put down their packs with exclamations of relief. They were an oddly assorted group. One man was tall and well-muscled, though not so well-built as the leader of the party. His hair and eyebrows were white, although the pupils of his eyes were pigmented light brown, not the pink of the true albino. His skin, once as pale as his hair, was slowly tanning a reddish brown under the eternal sun. Born and raised underground in a city of the Mahars, the dominant race of this world, Elkar was now an escaped slave, a man without a tribe or country. He was dressed similarly to West and carried an identical set of weapons, save for the red axe.

The second man—if man he could be called—was obviously a native of the primitive world of Pellucidar, for his like could be seen nowhere on the outer surface. Tall, slender, and graceful of limb, Mooh-lah was clad only in a leather loincloth. His skin was dark and covered with fine brown hair, as was his face. His skull, however, was obviously human, and intelligence and humor sparkled in his large brown eyes. His most startling attribute, however, was a long prehensile tail, which he now carried curled up over one shoulder. As he shook off his pack, this remarkable appendage reached around to grasp the straps and lower it to the ground.

The last human member of the party was a young woman. Varna of the tribe of Val-an was tall and dark, and the hot noonday sun had burned her skin a dark bronze. Her startling beauty would have attracted attention anywhere in the outer world. Her hair was black and luxuriant; she had tied it back with beaded thongs, so that it hung in a thick, lush rope halfway down her back. She wore a soft leather loincloth and a beaded leather vest that failed to cover her breasts. Long bronzed legs, covered with barely perceptible scars from a life in the wild, ended in soft moccasins. Like the monkey-man, she carried spear, knives, bow, and arrows. These she placed carefully near at hand—no daughter of that primitive world was ever out of arms' reach of a weapon! She turned her gentle eyes to her mate and leader, Christopher of the Red Axe, in time to see him step aside to allow the last of his party room to land atop the hillock.

With a great flapping of bat-like wings, the creature swooped to West's side, alighted, and folded its wings. This was a Mahar, one of the ruling race of Pellucidar. Known as Zed to its human companions, it was a giant intelligent pterosaur, and stood over six feet high, its folded wings ending in sharp points several feet above its body. The reptile had a long narrow head, with huge intelligent eyes and a beak-like mouth lined with sharp fangs. The back of its body was serrated into bony ridges and ended in a long, ridged tail. The feet were short and the talons were webbed. The upper tip of each wing ended in three slender fingers.

Zed turned its head from side to side, regarding West first with one eye and then the other. The man nodded to the strange creature, but turned back to the humans when he spoke. Like all members of its species, the winged Mahar was completely deaf.

"Rest a few moments," said West. "Then we'll see if we can find fresh meat. First I'll call the terminal and report in." His companions sprawled under the cycads and firs, trying to avoid heat and insects, except for the winged Mahar, who perched comfortably in a low tree. The blond giant unpacked a miniature radio transmitter with a directional antenna from his kit. He assembled the apparatus with a practiced hand, aimed the antenna back the way they had come, and soon picked up a tracer signal. One of the advantages of the hollow world, West thought to himself, was that as soon as you got some distance from the transceiver, radio communication became a line of sight matter—much simpler than on the surface. This wouldn't hold if you went around to the opposite side of the inner world, however, for then the small central sun would produce radio interference.

West triggered his set and called into the microphone: "Hello, California base. Anybody home?" The signal was picked up by a receiver fifty miles away, converted into laser beam pulses and projected through a narrow disintegrator hole to the outer crust. In the laboratory of Drs. Kingsley and Moritz in Santa Monica, a technician monitoring the earth probe circuit promptly responded.

West's companions watched curiously as he reported their position to the transmitting station. The cave people accepted the radio as magic, while the reptilian Mahar had enough scientific knowledge to understand the principles involved. Zed had been a research scientist in the underground city of the Mahars from which they had recently escaped. The Mahars did not have the technical ability to duplicate a device like the tiny radio, however. Their electrical apparatus was still in the voltaic-cell stage.

"We're camped on a little island in the swamp," West reported. "Herd of about half a dozen brontosaurus to the west. According to my compass, we're still heading almost due south, following the homing instinct Varna has for the land of her birth." He glanced around. "Looks like storm clouds in the east," he remarked, before bringing the conversation to a close.

"Roger your report. Taped here. Santa Monica out," replied the man on the surface.

West replaced the radio and took a plastic slate and stylus out of his pack. He wrote a note to Zed, using the ideographic characters of the master race's own written language. Writing was the only way he had of communicating with the intelligent pterosaur. The Mahars used a mysterious "telepathic" method of communication among themselves, as well as a crude sign language in order to converse with their gorilla-like servants, the Sagoths. Christopher West had learned the elaborate written language of the Mahars while imprisoned as a slave in the reptiles' underground city of Phuma. Now he quickly informed his weird companion that the humans in the party planned to camp, hunt, and sleep in this area before continuing on. The strange creature nodded once— they had established some signals that did not require writing—and flew off into the blue, circling their campsite in ever-widening circles.

An altercation had broken out behind. He turned to find the beauteous Varna belaboring Mooh-lah with an obviously harmless leaf frond she had stripped from a nearby fern.

"Ho, Red Axe!" cried the tailed one, jumping backward and falling into a clump of cycads. "Ouch! Call off your woman, before she makes me lose my temper."

"What is it now, you two?" West asked with a grin.

"Silly monkey-man," Varna said, taking a final swipe at him with her improvised weapon.

"I only say," Mooh-lah protested from the relative sanctuary of the cycads, "that in a real tribe of gilaks, the shes make the camp and cut the firewood, while the bulls do the hunting."

"It is my turn to hunt!" cried the beautiful cave girl. "Christopher, they went hunting last time. It is time for us to hunt and them to fix camp."

"Crazy female," growled Mooh-lah. "Here—hunt bugs." He threw a clod of wet earth at her.

"Beast!" she cried, trying to sound angry but beginning to laugh. "In the tribe of Val-an, we catch mischievous monkeys by their tails and swing them round our heads!" She returned the dirt clod with interest.

"Oh, here I am, little gilak maiden! Come pull my tail." A cloud of debris burst from the cycads and Varna prepared to rush her tormentor and make good her threat. West stopped her.

"Come, Varna," he said. "You and I will hunt. Mooh-lah and Elkar will gather wood and set up camp."

"Just in time, Red Axe." The monkey-man stood up. "She came close to being strangled by my powerful tail, and then pulled limb from limb." He tossed one more clump of dirt, striking the girl on the rump. She squealed in indignation, started back, thought better of it, and turned away with feigned indifference.

West and his mate picked up their bows and arrows and started across the flat swampland, primitive man and primitive woman setting out side by side into the prehistoric landscape. As always, West carried the axe that was his namesake, and both wore sharp hunting knives in leather sheaths. The twentieth century had spawned him, and it was twentieth-century technology that had precipitated him, unarmed except for this steel axe, into this antediluvian world where the flora and fauna of all the ages of earth's past were mingled together in a fantastic paleontological kaleidoscope. Now he not only considered himself as much a Paleolithic tribesman as his beautiful mate; he gloried in it.

The matter transmitter through which he had arrived in the lost world could not be used to transmit explosives, because any unstable compound tended to blow up as it went through the disintegration-reintegration cycle. This meant that firearms were not among the few amenities of civilization his friends on the outer surface could send him. West had grown accustomed to making his way by the strength of his arm and the sharp edge of his axe. He also had a certain natural talent for leadership. This, along with his size and muscle, had enabled him to escape with his companions from the underground city of the reptilian Mahars.

There were few game trails through the swamp, and those they encountered meandered in circles or petered out in pools and bogs. This mattered little to the beautiful Varna, who was content to wander in the company of Red Axe wherever the hunt took them.

Broad-leafed swamp plants and ferns covered the ground. The cycads and other palms grew in clumps that towered eight to ten feet in height. The wind at their backs carried a hint of coming rain, but for now the noonday sun of Pellucidar still blazed down on their heads. Frogs and giant salamanders sat by the fragrant pools, jumping into the water as they approached. An occasional serpent slipped off into the undergrowth. Clouds of tiny midges rose from the surface of disturbed pools, making the two of them cough and fan the air. Giant dragonflies hovered overhead. The swamp itself was made up of layers of fallen fern trunks and rotting vegetation. Red Axe and Varna crept cautiously through the moss-covered muck, bows strung and arrows notched at the string. They were hoping to come upon some of the little birdlike erect dinosaurs or a large iguana—both were good eating. The inhabitants of the swamp seemed to be exclusively amphibian or reptilian, but there was always the possibility of bagging a waterbird or two. All of these creatures were wary and swift, and the hunter must be ready with arrow or javelin. Varna was the best archer in the party—if they found game, she would be able to bring it down. The two walked slowly and without speaking. The silence was necessary if they were to catch anything, but it was a comfortable silence. They were a couple who understood one another, automatically adjusting their actions to meet each other's needs. One would always hold back, weapon at the ready, while the other probed a clump of greenery or climbed to the top of a moss-covered fallen log. They communicated by hand signals and body movements, climbing stealthily through the thick swamp growth.

They hunted for hours without finding food. Twice they came upon crocodiles—or great beasts that resembled the crocodiles of the outer world. The first rushed splashing into the swamp, and for a long while they could hear the noise of its passage. The second beast was larger, at least eight feet long counting the tapering tail. It opened its catlike eyes and snapped its long-toothed jaws, showing no inclination to retreat as the two humans approached. Red Axe itched to put an arrow into one of those slit-pupiled eyes, but he checked himself. He and Varna withdrew slowly and carefully, watching the beast until they were out of its sight, and then circled around.

"No use disputing our path with him," Varna whispered.

Red Axe replied in the same soft tone: "Look, we're close to the playground of the great *lidi*." Indeed, by climbing on a branch of one of the fallen trees that littered the swamp, they could make out the gigantic brontosaurs. The huge beasts were browsing now, their heads often submerged in the water. One or more of the great long necks was always up, however, the tiny head turning this way and that on the alert for predators.

Varna watched with as much interest as her mate, for the giant reptiles were not found in the mountain hunting grounds of her tribe. She, too, had seen them for the first time when they had started their travels through the great swamp.

The wind blew more strongly now and the rain began to fall, softly at first, then harder. They turned back to their hunting. Around the dinosaur wallow, thick layers composed of hundreds of dead tree trunks piled upon each other formed an almost impenetrable tangle covered with mosses, ferns, and flowering plants. After struggling through this maze for a few hundred yards, they were ready to turn back. The rain was heavy now, the water sluicing off their bodies and soaking their leather clothing.

As the two huddled together in the partial shelter of overhanging branches, a great crashing of tree trunks issued from behind them. To their amazement, the head and neck of a brontosaurus appeared above the brush. The driving rain washed the mud and muck from the gigantic neck and the ridiculous small face at its end. The great creature craned its neck snakelike, looking this way and that, then opened its mouth and emitted a long hooting whistle that nearly broke their eardrums.

"What on earth is it doing?" whispered Varna.

"I've not the slightest idea," West replied. "How did it get behind us anyway? I thought . . ." At that moment there came a long undulating call from somewhere off in the rain clouds. With a great crashing, the shape of another brontosaurus appeared. This beast was even bigger than the first one. Varna looked back over her shoulder and clutched West's arm.

"Look, Christopher." The long neck was sliding back out of sight.

"It's going underground," Red Axe said, straining his eyes to see through the rain. "No, that's impossible. Varna, these dead trees must form a solid mat floating right out over the water. The thing swam under it right beneath us!"

"Watch out—here comes the other one!"

He turned to look. It was indeed a spectacle worth

watching. The second brontosaurus was approaching them in a series of great leaps. West knew the big dinosaurs could move rapidly when they had to—he had seen one pursued by a tyrannosaurus. This great lizard's progress, however, was being impeded, because each leap sent its monstrous bulk smashing through the layers of dead vegetation. It would then struggle out of the resulting hole and hurtle forward in another jump.

"My God, it's coming right at us!" Scrambling through the dead branches, slippery now with rain, Varna and Red Axe sought to get out of the path of the advancing monster. *Crash!* The tangle of branches, mud, and ferns shook with the force of the brontosaur's leap. The long neck craned over them, questing in the rain. Again they heard the searching hooting. This time the other dinosaur answered from somewhere behind them and to their left. The great bulk of the saurian staggered to its feet, the humans dodging as six cycad palms were squashed flat. Gathering its elephantine legs beneath its great gray belly, the giant beast launched into another leap. *Crash! Crash!* The floating mat of tree trunks began breaking up like an iceberg. More palms and tree ferns were bowled over by a sweep of the twenty-foot tail as the beast took off after its quarry.

West was suddenly knocked flat by a flying giant fern. The tree trunks were breaking up, and he would have rolled into the dark waters beneath them had Varna not grabbed his hand and helped him back to his feet. They looked after the vanishing back of the brontosaur in amazement. Clouds of driving rain hissed on the fallen fern leaves and obscured their view.

"What are they doing?" Varna asked. "Are they fighting?"

"Fighting?" Red Axe pondered a moment. "No, I don't think so. The smaller one seemed to be calling the other to follow. They . . ." He paused. "You know what they're doing? They're mating!"

"What?" The girl stared at him. "What did you say?"

The big blond man laughed. "Of course. We've never seen

one of these big fellows behave like this, leaping about like he was a puppy. It's some kind of courtship dance!"

Suddenly the hooting whistle broke out again. They turned to see the two dinosaurs headed back toward them. The smaller beast was only a short distance ahead of her pursuer and the long neck was turned backward watching him.

"This way, Varna—quick!" West cried. "Here they come again!"

Scrambling and splashing, Red Axe and his mate strove to get out of the path of the approaching monsters. The dinosaurs were not moving very fast, but the humans were hindered by the dense tangle of dead branches. They climbed over and through these, heading out now toward the open lake. The smaller brontosaurus—West was sure now it must be the female—came to a halt, and the male blundered into her. Both beasts fell over, smashing all the nearby vegetation beneath the water level.

"What a fate!" West gasped, as he pulled Varna out of a puddle onto a large log. "Crushed by a love-starved brontosaurus!"

"Stop, Chris," the cave girl pleaded. "I want to watch them!"

"I admire your scientific spirit, my dear," said the man, "but—" *Wham!* The two brontosaurs, their necks now twined around each other in a saurian love-knot, had rolled over in the water, striking close to where the two humans stood. The force of the blow threw them both to the ground.

"I guess you are right, after all, Chris," said the girl, regaining her feet. "Let's get out of here!" An almighty tail slapped the nearby water as if to underscore her decision.

The tree mass was fragmenting rapidly, and progress became increasingly difficult. The rain continued to pour down out of the sky as the wind picked up force. Soon the hooting and crashing of the amorous dinosaurs was almost drowned out by the noise of the storm.

Leaping from one clump of smashed driftwood to another,

West looked down into the rain-lashed surface of the lake. A huge reptilian head floated into view like a submerged log breaking from the bottom to rise to the surface.

"Varna, look!" He hugged the wet body of his mate to him and pointed. "The great-granddaddy of all crocodiles." Indeed it was. Disturbed from its slumber by the thrashing of the brontosaurs, the great beast drifted by, while the two drenched humans scrambled to places of greater safety on their tiny island of rotten wood. The monster's head was easily ten feet long and most of its body was still out of sight in the water. Red Axe seized a long, broken branch, thinking vaguely of using it to fend off the huge jaws if the thing tried to come up out of the water at them. He thrust his pole at some nearby sunken trees and the little island of broken wood moved away from the menacing head. As soon as the improvised raft broke free of its entanglement, it began to drift with the wind.

The super-crocodile turned its baleful head and watched the clump of dead trees and its human occupants float away.

"Don't move," breathed Varna. "Perhaps he hasn't noticed us." Indeed, the hideous reptile made no move to follow as they drifted steadily farther away. In a few minutes the rain-lashed water had obscured the beast and West drew a deep sigh of relief.

Then he glanced around and realized with a start that he could no longer make out the shoreline through the rain. The wind was moving the crude raft farther and farther out onto the lake, and the surface of the water was now lashed with good-sized waves. They had no way of controlling their vessel and the storm was becoming more violent.

"Christopher!" cried Varna. "How are we going to get back to land?"

"I don't know, Varna," the man admitted. "I'm not even sure which way it is!"

2
ONOLOA

THE CAVES OF THE HAPU TRIBE were in the walls of a canyon that bordered the sea. At its mouth, the canyon split in two, leaving a spire of yellow rock where the blue waves shallowed rapidly into green tide pools. On either side the land fell away in precipitous cliffs, the surf breaking sullenly at their feet.

A narrow rocky path led from the ledges and cave mouths of the tribe along the side of the cliffs, a hundred feet above the water to a point opposite the spire. There had once been a narrow rock bridge to the isolated peak here, but time had worn it away. In later days, and with immense labor, the tribe had cut and felled huge trees from along the coast and carried them long miles in order to make a narrow footbridge. Below the point where the bridge terminated, the smooth yellow stone was too steep for any ascent here on the landward side. On the opposite side, sheer cliffs overlooked the Place of the Gods.

The yellow stone of the spire had been pierced by the wind close to the top. An enormous cavern, a hundred feet high at the peak and fifty wide at the base where the floor had been solidly filled in, gave a glimpse of the blue sea and the sky beyond, as if one were looking through the eye of a giant fish-bone needle, such as the women used for stitching hides together.

Onoloa stood at the doorway of her brother's cave, and looked out toward the stone spire and its single blue eye.

In the sea beyond, two of the tribe's double dugout canoes floated on the calm water where the fishermen were at work. All the riches of the sea belonged to the Hapuans, brought to them through their worship of the mighty Manu, Lord of the Sea. The young woman bent her head unconsciously as she thought of the god.

She turned to go back into the cave to get her light fishing spear. She had promised her brother's wife that she would go to the tide pools below the cliffs and catch some small fish for dinner. A movement out on the needle rock halted her. A dwarfed human figure descended the path to the bridge. A premonition swept over the girl like a cold wind. She shuddered and then stepped back into the dim light of the cave.

By the time she reached the beach, the image of the figure on the spire had faded from her mind. There were a number of naked children playing on the sand at the foot of the trail. She greeted them only briefly, having decided to go up along the coast to a place where the reef shallows gave way to deeper pools and the fishing was good. She slung her short wooden spear over her shoulder on a thong and set out at a steady trot, her small, bare feet making no sound on the hard-packed sand. The surf broke softly among the corals to her right. On the left, the great cliffs rose above the narrow beach, their rocky faces covered with clumps of clinging greenery. The feathery tops of palm trees overhung the cliff edge, and the noonday sun of Pellucidar beat down fiercely on the slender girl as she ran along the beach. Her long black hair flowed in the wind, unrestrained by anything except a band of shells. But for a necklace, wristlets of more tiny shells, and the narrow strip of tapa cloth encircling her hips, she was unadorned. Her skin was a rich bronze where the eternal noonday sun had burned it. Her deep brown eyes were slightly slanted and her hair was straight and a rich blue-black. Had that race of Polynesian seafarers who colonized the vast Pacific also found their way to the inner world sometime in centuries past? Hapuan legends still told of a rich land to the north where the sun rose and set. Perhaps sometime in the distant past there had been a polar opening to eternally sunlit Pellucidar. In past ages, when the ice caps had melted and the outer surface of the planet was warm, were there open sea-lanes between the distant tropical isles and the prehistoric shores of Pellucidar? If there were, those incredible Stone Age navigators would have found them. Onoloa seemed to be living proof that some ancient odyssey had taken place.

The young woman was little concerned with legend. The premonition that something unusual was about to occur still hung in the back of her mind. She dismissed it as she neared the fishing pools as a natural uneasiness caused by the sight of the Priest of Manu. Until she reached full womanhood, that grim figure would remain a threat to her, for the dark shadow of the great god Manu hung over the life of every young male and maiden of the tribe of Hapu.

When she reached the fishing grounds, Onoloa tossed her loincloth on the sand and plunged into the surf. The wide crescent of golden beach was deserted, but the young maiden was unafraid. Although the water deepened here to eight or ten feet between the great coral heads, there was a reef offshore that prevented the entrance of sharks or the great sea lizards. The canoes of her people patrolled the shoreline for a hundred miles up and down the coast, while the cliffs that bordered the sea protected the Hapuans from the beast-men and monstrous creatures who lived in the inland jungles.

Like all her people, Onoloa swam with the grace of a porpoise. With her sharp wooden spear in hand, she searched the green underwater world of the pools, pursuing and lancing her prey with a skill born of long practice. At last, with three large, fat fish securely impaled on the shaft of her spear, she made the leisurely swim back to shore and climbed up on the beach.

Instantly she knew that there were eyes upon her. Shading her brow from the noonday sun, she scanned the shoreline. Yes! A man stood at the edge of the beach beneath the palms, watching her. Not just a man, a stranger!

The man under the palm tree did not move. He was tall and broad-shouldered, although no taller than many of the men of her tribe. It was his color that startled her, for he was white. Almost like a bleached fish skeleton, she thought— no, that was not fair, for his shoulders and chest were pink and his hair was pale yellow. She could not see his eyes. He was carrying a bow and arrows. Onoloa immediately recognized them as weapons of some sort, but they hung quietly at his knee. The girl wished that her short spear was not encumbered with fish, yet she hesitated to throw away her catch. Perhaps the stranger was alone and not dangerous. Perhaps she could bluff him into believing that the rest of her tribe would be along any moment. Perhaps someone would come along the shore. Why didn't he speak?

"Who are you, stranger?" called Onoloa. "What do you in the land of the Hapuans and the domain of the great god Manu?"

The pale blond man merely stared stupidly at her. Onoloa became angry. She was angry with the man for frightening her and with herself for being frightened. And she was angry with him for not opening his stupid mouth. She stamped her tiny foot in the surf.

"Answer me! Are you an idiot? Are you mad? *Pupule?*"

Elkar shook his head to regain his wits. He had understood only part of what the girl had said to him. Although she spoke the common language of Pellucidar, her accent was different from any he had heard before and there were occasional words from an unknown tongue he could not understand. Her meaning was clear, of course. What kept him tongue-tied was the girl herself.

He had seen someone swimming in the lagoon from the

cliff top and descended cautiously to seek the swimmer's identity. Then this slender maiden had walked up out of the sea. Now she stood with the waves washing her ankles, naked except for a few strings of shells, and the most beautiful thing he had ever seen in his life.

Long, wet black hair framed her soft oval face and clung to her skin down to the small of her back. Her eyes were large and brown, with slightly tipped lids and long lashes. Her nose and mouth were delicately shaped, and when she spoke he could see the flash of white teeth. Her skin, Elkar thought, was the most beautiful brown, smooth, satiny, and still wet with the salt water. Her rounded hips were a little paler, showing that she usually wore some covering around her loins. The rest of her unclad form, however, was as tanned as her face and her slim, flat abdomen.

Elkar continued to stare at her, choked with emotion and unable to speak a word.

"*Ah-weh!*" cried Onoloa in exasperation. "Perhaps the creature is deaf or mute." It seemed to her that she had heard of albinos so afflicted. Elkar looked like an albino.

She walked up onto the beach and stuck her fish spear in the sand, then picked up her brief tapa-cloth skirt and fastened it around her waist. She retrieved her fish and began walking away slowly down the surf line, keeping a wary eye on the stranger. She hoped he would continue to remain frozen under the palms and allow her to get away. But she was not to get off so easily.

"Wait!" cried the man, suddenly realizing she was escaping from him. He did not want to frighten the girl. He stepped onto the hot coral sand slowly, keeping his weapons in hand but letting them trail inconspicuously. His normal facility with words began to return.

"I am not deaf," he said, "but I was struck dumb at the sight of one so beautiful. I thought she must be the daughter of some sea goddess."

Onoloa could not suppress a smile. Elkar dared to come

closer, continuing to keep up a stream of compliments. It took him quite a while to arrive at the reason for his presence on that shell-strewn beach.

"My chief and his mate were swept away by a storm, perhaps blown out to sea somewhere off the coast here," he said. "Have you heard of such a thing? A tall, fair man, taller than I but not so pale. A dark-haired woman, beautiful, but not so beautiful as yourself?"

Onoloa laughed at the blatant flattery. No, she told him, she had not heard of the lost couple, but her people ranged the wide blue sea in their outriggers. If there were castaways in the water, they would sight them. Perhaps the fair-haired stranger should come to the caves of her people and inquire. It took some time for all this to be communicated, for Elkar had been born and raised underground in the city of Phuma, ruled by the super-intelligent reptiles called Mahars. He did not have words for ocean or ship. He had to explain this to the beautiful girl, who seemed uncommonly interested in his plight. Then they had to decide whether it would be safe for him to return with her to the caves of the Hapu.

This latter point was an important one. Even though he had never before been outside of the underground city where he had been born, he knew enough about "wild gilaks"—that is, free men—to realize that they were more likely to murder him at Hapu than to aid him. Onoloa tried to reassure him that strangers were not routinely massacred by her people. She felt a strong attraction for the big pale man and found that she didn't want him to run off into his jungle on the other side of the mountains.

In the end Elkar agreed to accompany his sea-nymph home, mostly because he was already madly in love with her. He tried not to admit this even to himself, much less to the girl. He was persuaded by her assurances, and told himself that he needed information. Her people were apparently seafarers, and it made sense that they might have come across Red Axe and his mate or some sign of them.

Elkar also felt that he had an insurance policy of which the girl was not aware.

He offered to carry her fish, but the slim brown maiden refused, preferring to retain possession of her spear. The oddly matched pair set out along the bright coral sand while Onoloa plied her new acquaintance with questions. Elkar answered her with honesty and a quiet modesty that she was quick to appreciate. He seemed a gentle, harmless man, yet he looked at her with something in his eyes she did not recognize. The young men of her own tribe had never looked at her that way.

"You came through the swamp of monsters?" the girl asked in amazement. "My people have sailed up into the lake hunting the great turtles, but they say the swamp is impassable and filled with giant meat-eating lizards!"

"Indeed it is, or almost impassable," agreed Elkar. "It is quite full of the giant lizards, and although not all of them are meat eaters, many of them are. I have been pursued by a two-footed monster as tall as a tree and knocked unconscious by a single sweep of its tail!"

Around the next turn in the shoreline they came into sight of the high cliffs where Onoloa's people lived and the single spire of somber stone that marked the mouth of the canyon beyond. Half a dozen outrigger canoes were drawn up on the sand, with as many men gathered about them. At the sight of the stranger someone called out, and the tribesmen came running down the beach to surround the pair. They were big, broad-shouldered men with dark brown skin and dark hair like the girl's, and they were armed with wooden spears and heavy war clubs studded with shark's teeth. Each of the older men had one of his earlobes pierced to hold a large white shell plug.

"The *haole* comes as a friend," Onoloa replied to the many queries, using the Hapuan word for stranger. "He is hearthguest at my brother's house." She stepped closer to Elkar and slipped a little brown hand into one of his. Her touch sent a tingling sensation through his whole body as if he had stepped into a breeze. He wondered what it meant.

By the time the two of them had made their way down the beach and up the winding trail that led to the higher cliff caves where Onoloa dwelled, Elkar had had a chance to interrogate a number of native fishermen. None of them had seen any sign of his missing friends.

No one challenged their progress. Most of the men and women carried spears or shell knives, but there were no hostile gestures. Little children ran out to stare, while dogs, to Elkar's amazement, appeared at the cave mouths to bark as he walked past. This was a new species to the man, one he had never seen before. It seemed most strange that these people should choose to share their dwellings with such noisy, vicious-looking beasts!

"Here we are, Elkar, my brother's—oh!" The girl stopped dead in her tracks.

Confronting her on the narrow path was an old man. His hair and scanty beard were white, and his entire body, except where it was wrapped in a blue tapa loincloth, was covered with wrinkles and tattoo patterns in black. He carried a long wooden staff, higher than his head, the top of it carved like a flower with long, slender, open petals. A massive shell ornament of intricate design hung about his neck. As the old man saw the girl approaching him, his face broke into a strange smile. Elkar could see that he still had all of his teeth.

"Aha!" The man raised his hand and pointed a withered finger at the young girl before him.

"*Hapuna! Hapuna Mana!* The Chosen One!" he cried in a voice of triumph. Onoloa recoiled, her face gone pale. Her slim body pressed back against Elkar, and he instinctively put his arm around her shoulders.

The ancient apparition approached, chuckling in his thin beard. Leaning on the carven staff with his left arm, he reached his right hand out toward the girl and touched her forehead. She recoiled against Elkar's body, then stiffened and stood motionless as the old man's fingernail traced some symbol on her brow.

This performance completed, the strange figure pushed past them on the narrow path and went hobbling off down the cliff toward the ocean. After staring after him for a moment in amazement, Elkar turned to his companion.

"Onoloa, what was that about?" he asked. His question was not soon to be answered, however, for a crowd of tribesmen burst from the nearest caves and rushed to the girl, touching and patting her solicitously while they jabbered away at great speed. Once she was among them, they managed to separate her from her newfound friend and lead her off into a nearby dwelling. Elkar soon found himself standing almost alone on the rocky trail.

The tall blond man gazed down the long cliff trail, studded with the entrances to the tribal cave. Many of the stalwart brown people stood still, looking up at the site of the recent commotion. The cause of it all, the strange old man with the bizarre ornaments and the staff, was making his way along the cliff to where the long, precarious bridge spanned the chasm to the rocky needle. From his vantage point, Elkar could now see the cave that pierced the stony spire, though it had not been visible to him as he had walked up the beach with Onoloa.

"Stranger," said a voice behind him. Elkar turned, half on guard for an attack now that his fair guide had been taken from him. It was a boy, tall and strong of limb, but not yet at his full manhood. He carried a spear tipped with a shark's tooth, but he did not appear hostile.

"Where is Onoloa?" asked Elkar.

"She has retired to the cave of her older brother," the boy replied. "The women must cry over her and start the rites of purification to prepare her for the sacrifice to Manu."

Elkar understood only part of this, for the boy spoke rapidly and some of the words were strange to him. Although almost all the human races of Pellucidar, from the lowliest ape-man to the most highly developed Stone Age barbarian, spoke the same basic tongue, there were local variations in vocabulary and accent that could make communication between isolated peoples difficult. The man from the underground city of the winged reptiles struggled to get more meaning from the words of the youth. The boy was eager to talk, and set about chattering at a fast pace with his new friend.

The god Manu, it seemed, claimed the ritual sacrifices of one of the young people of the tribe at regular intervals. These times were determined by the rise and fall of the tides, though Elkar, who had never seen an ocean before in his life, could not grasp this part of the story at all. The boy, whose name was Tumu, was Onoloa's younger brother. "She sent me out to find you and take care of you," he said. Elkar's heart gave a jump at that. The girl was concerned for him; despite all of her own sudden troubles, she had thought of him! It strengthened his determination to see her through the strange doom that had descended upon her.

Elkar's entire philosophy of life had changed since he had met Red Axe. Formerly he had accepted his own status as a slave in the city of Phuma as part of the natural order of things. He would, he realized, have as easily accepted the sacrifice of this beautiful girl to her tribal god, whatever it was, without questioning. The man from the outer world had altered all of that. Red Axe accepted nothing, challenging man, beast, or idea. He had persuaded the slaves of Phuma to make a mad, hopeless attempt at escape and he had succeeded. He had rescued his mate from ape-men and a man-eating tyrannosaurus and single-handedly stood off a small army of the gorilla-like Sagoths. Elkar smiled a grim smile. Red Axe would never let the lovely Onoloa be destroyed by her own people. As Red Axe's friend, he would do no less. And, he reminded himself, he was still seeking signs of his missing friends. He turned back to the boy and questioned him.

Tumu thought it best they descend the cliffs again and talk to the fishermen who cruised up and down the coast. If there were news to be had of the white man's lost friends, it would be from them. Elkar was unwilling to leave Onoloa's vicinity until he was sure she was all right. The boy assured him that the girl was safe with her family. He drew Elkar into the cave—it was merely one of several chambers—and pointed out the hide-curtained alcove from which women's voices echoed. The pale man was somewhat reassured. He and the boy paused to eat at the family's communal cooking fire, where a sort of perpetual fish stew steamed in a giant clamshell. While they ate, Elkar continued the conversation.

Manu, it seemed, demanded a sacrifice at the time of the low tide.* Smaller sacrifices of animals and fish were thrown to the god at frequent intervals. The boy took him to the cave mouth and pointed out the great stone needle at the mouth of the canyon.

"Beyond the spire is where the god lies in his pool," he said solemnly. "The sacrifices are hurled from the cave rim out over the ocean and the god receives them in his gigantic maw."

Elkar took all this quite seriously. In his own city, it was commonplace for living human beings to be fed to the flying reptiles who ruled them. It was a fate he had only escaped because of Red Axe and his friends.

"At special tides, dictated by the god, or, more probably, by evil old Apu, the high priest, the sacrifice must be a human being," continued his informant. "Sometimes he uses savages we have captured from the jungles, but more often it is a young virgin maiden from the caves. We think old Apu picks them himself—too often they are of families who have offended the old crab in some way."

"How long before Onoloa . . . ?"

"Many sleeps before her family must conduct her, weeping,

---

* Although Pellucidar has a stationary sun, its oceans are under the influence of the outer moon as it circles the globe, and thus experience tides much like those of the outer world, though somewhat gentler. —J.E.H.

across the narrow bridge to the spire of the God. There Apu and the lesser priests will keep her until the time of the sacrifice. They had best not molest her." The young man shook the fishing spear in his fist in helpless fury and his brown eyes filled with tears.

"Ah, my young friend, I feel as you do," said Elkar. "Is there no way we can save her from this terrible thing?"

"It is taboo." The lad's face was a mixture of anger and misery. "If she flees from the tribe, Apu will only pick the daughter of some other family. No, every hand in the tribe would be turned against her. She would have to flee to the jungle. She would be outcast, killed on sight by her own people. The god controls the sea, and the sea feeds us all. The god's will must be obeyed."

Their meal finished, Elkar allowed the boy to conduct him back down the long trail he had ascended so recently with Onoloa. Then, however, he had had the intoxication of her small hand in his. He wondered if he would see her again. There was a heavy feeling in his chest, like a great stone, when he thought that he might not.

"Tumu, has anyone ever escaped from the god?"

"Not once the priests throw them into the water. The great arms are powerful and the god Manu and his children are everywhere. A few ones have run away from the tribe after being chosen. They are taboo and hide out along the coast. Every loyal Hapuan is sworn to kill them—though perhaps a hunter or a fisherman, meeting such a one that he may have known, pretends he does not see, walks by, and looks to the other side."

They reached the beach. Elkar and the boy wandered among the canoes, questioning the fisherman who squatted among them, mending nets of vegetable fibers or cleaning their recent catch. There were more than fifty canoes drawn up along this end of the beach. Elkar had never seen outriggers—or boats of any kind, for that matter. Many of these were over twenty feet long and had sails of woven grasses. As they picked their way among them, new boats came in through the surf to land on the long, bright yellow coral beach.

The fishermen were kindly and willing to help, but none had seen a light-skinned man and a woman on shore or on the sea. They wanted to talk; Elkar had to explain himself and his mission to each new boat crew. He grew tired and discouraged, and finally his young friend drew him down the beach away from the canoes.

"Come," he said, "I will show you the great pool where the god Manu lives. We are not permitted on the rock except during the priests' rites, but I can take you to the edge of the beach in my brother's canoe."

"Good," said Elkar, "but first I must let my . . . my . . . guardian spirit know that all is well with me." To the boy's mystification, he walked out on the wave-smoothed sand, raised his hands above his head, and made a series of gestures, seemingly toward the jungle-covered cliff tops a half-mile away. He returned smiling to his companion.

"Guardian spirit?" asked the boy. "I saw nothing except a big pterodactyl fly down from the cliff and return."

Elkar grinned at him. "The *thipdar* is the special totem of my tribe. Now you must show me how to use the boat—I have never been in one before."

The big pale man knew how to swim and so was unafraid of the water. Under the guidance of the young Hapuan, they got the small outrigger launched through the surf. Elkar was clumsy with the broad wooden paddle, but he was strong and the boy found him quick to learn. They made their way slowly but surely, as the man struggled with lifting and dipping his paddle simultaneously with his companion's, down the narrow river mouth to the foot of the stone spire. There Tumu sprang from the bow to pull the little vessel securely up onto the glistening white beach.

Until he stepped ashore through the waves, Elkar did not notice that the beach was in any way different from the coral sands they had just left. Then he stopped with a grunt of amazement. The sparkling white beach was not sand at all—it was bones! Narrow and rapidly sloping, for here the ocean was deep, the strip of white ran along the seaward side of the great rock for nearly half a mile. Every foot of it was covered with polished bones: ribs, vertebrae, flat shoulder blades, jutting hips, polished arm and leg bones, rounded skulls, and, packed between them, smaller bones, some the digits of larger animals, some the skulls and body bones of smaller creatures. Toothed and toothless jaws and the skulls of great sea lizards and giant fish, fanged crania of the car-nivores of the prehistoric world, the lion, bear, wolf, and saber-toothed tiger all gaped at him. Even a few massively tusked skulls of the mastodon were to be found in that in-credible assembly. And, scattered among them, were hundreds of human skulls, their empty eye sockets turned to the blue sky and the deeper blue of the sea!

"The god Manu does not eat the bones of his victims," remarked the boy; "instead he spews them forth. Since the beginning of the world they have been piling up here, so that the bottom of the lagoon is covered with bones. Come, leave the canoe. Farther down you can see the ledge where the priest Apu stands to deliver the sacrifice."

The smooth, wave-polished bones were hard as boulders under Elkar's feet. He made his way slowly, stopping to gaze in amazement at the glittering rows of teeth in a plesiosaur skull.

High above them, the smooth rock walls leaned outward over the sea and the grisly beach. Below the needle's eye, Tumu said, there was a ledge where the sacrifices were made ready and then cast out into the sea.

He pointed across the quiet surface of the blue lagoon. "There is the abode of the god Manu."

Elkar turned to gaze across the placid water. Then he gave a gasp, echoed by his companion. For a moment something had flashed in the noonday sun near the center of the reef-fringed pool. Elkar had the impression of huge pinkish objects like the petals of some of the exotic flowers he had seen in the jungle. For an instant they curled and twisted about the water and then they were gone.

"Manu!" hissed the boy. "The great god Manu."

3
THE FIN-BACKED MONSTER

THE THICK GRAY RAIN CLOUDS blew away and the surface of the water calmed. The whitecaps died down and the makeshift raft ceased its wild plunging and rocking. Red Axe peered out across the bright blue waters as the clouds cleared away.

"Varna, my love, is that land or a cloud bank ahead of us?"

The cave girl drew the thick masses of her raven's wing hair, which she had spread to dry in the sun, back from her face with both hands. "Land, I think," she replied, "but with mist or low cloud across it."

"Good," grunted the man. "At least the wind is carrying us in the right direction. Let me see if I can make this hulk of dead timber a little more seaworthy and rig up some sort of mast to catch the breeze." They were both powerful swimmers; if the wind and the current brought them close to shore, they could abandon their involuntary cruise.

He set to work with his axe, trimming the raft of unnecessary tree trunks. Varna located a few yards of serviceable vines and they contrived to lash the remaining timbers together. A few of the longer poles were jammed upright into the "prow" of the craft to catch the wind.

Varna went to the stern with an arrow to see if she could spear a fish. The pair had not eaten for a long while. There is no way to measure time in Pellucidar, but the inhabitants use "sleeps" as an estimate of the passage of time. By this method, it had been two sleeps since either of them had eaten anything.

The water teemed with fish, and the girl succeeded in capturing one of them and then building a small fire on a large branch with her flint and steel. Soon a thin trail of smoke and the irresistible odor of cooking rose from the raft. Red Axe ceased his labors on the makeshift mast and joined her.

The fish gave each of them about four bites. Picking his teeth idly with a rib bone, the big blond man leaned back in the branches. The beautiful dark girl looked troubled. She kept scanning the cloud-flecked sky with anxious eyes.

"Varna, what's the matter? We've been in worse situations than this and gotten out."

"Two things bother me, Christopher. I do not know where we are, and the water is salty."

"Salty?" The man moved hurriedly to the side of the raft, dipped a hand in the flood, and tasted it. "Damn! We've been swept out into an ocean."

He gazed about them. Soft cobalt-blue swells rocked the raft. Ahead lay the low landmass or cloud. In the distance, whitecaps grew higher where the wind tossed the waves and above them sat a few fluffy white clouds and the brilliant noonday sun. They were out of sight of shore and the thing ahead looked to be no more than a low island, at best.

"Varna, you really can't tell direction?"

"Christopher, it's so strange." The lovely girl shivered and moved close to him. "I think it is all this water—this is more water than I have ever had between myself and my home. On land, you know, I can always tell in which direction Val-An lies—or any place in the world I have been. Here— here I can feel nothing. Nothing at all!"

Red Axe hugged his mate and kissed her cheek, now salty, not from tears, but from the fine spray from the prow of their primitive vessel.

"Fear not, beautiful one. I have my compass in my belt and the dinosaur swamp and our friends lie somewhere north and west of us, wherever we are. Our problem now is to find land—and fresh water."

Probably, West thought, it was just as well that his mate had lost her inborn sense of direction. They had no control at all over their craft and chances were it was sailing away from anywhere they wanted to go. It was probably lucky that she did not know it. He tried to console himself with this unlikely philosophy while Varna scraped the last of the fire down through the gaps in the logs so that it fell into the ocean.

Looking up, the girl beheld a strange apparition to the stern of the raft. For an instant, she saw something loop up into the air, shining and silvery in the sunlight. She shrugged it off—probably a large fish jumping.

She stood for a moment, gazing out across the waves, her thick black hair streaming in the wind. She was a child of the forests and caves, and the sea was almost unknown to her. She had the acute vision of the tribe of Val-An, however, and she knew that something was following them just beneath the surface. Something large.

"Varna," the man called, "what is it?" He came to her side just as she glimpsed another flash of silver.

"Did you see that?" she asked.

"No, where?" He gave a gasp of astonishment, for the thing appeared again—lifting ten feet above the water, then plunging out of sight into the blue depths.

"Sea serpent!" breathed Red Axe.

Indeed it was as fine a sea serpent as any sailor could wish for when it came to swapping tales with his cronies in a portside bar. High above the waves rose the coiling neck, the jaws opened, and there was a flash of hundreds of pointed teeth. *Splash!* The beast vanished again.

"Look, another one!"

There was a splash on the opposite side of the raft. West unstrapped his axe. The creatures had made no threatening move as yet, but they were obviously of large size. Now glimpses of them were visible on both sides. A great body came close and almost to the surface as one of the long necks arched over the mass of driftwood they occupied. They could make out the thick body and a long flipper.

The creatures were after the school of fish from which the two humans had recently obtained their own meal.

Varna had never seen such monsters before, while on West's world they had been extinct long before man appeared. They both watched entranced as the long necks rose and fell. Sometimes there were as many as half a dozen plesiosaurs visible above the surface at a time. How many there were around the raft they could not tell. Fortunately, the enormous reptiles chose to ignore the fragile craft, for a blow from one of the gigantic flippers would have smashed it to matchwood. Occasionally one would lift its head with a fish still disappearing between its jaws.

The sea was now comparatively calm and the long, ungainly silhouettes of the weird beasts could be seen in the depths beneath the raft. Every few minutes one or more of them would surface briefly, take a snorting breath, scan the horizon with little lizard eyes, and drive down again beneath the waves. Except for the snorting and blowing and the occasional slap of a flipper on the surface, they were silent. Cumbrous as the broad bodies, flippers, and long necks appeared, the creatures moved beneath the water with speed and fluid grace. The tiny head and long neck flashed this way and that like a striking serpent among the schools of fish. The tooth-filled jaws snapped and another scaled and finny denizen of the deep started down a long gullet. Again and again, the head would dart in and out, and then the great marine dinosaur would rise quickly to the surface. Usually just the head and a few feet of neck would protrude for a few seconds while the reptile breathed. Sometimes a great coil of neck would be thrown up out of the waves, only to quickly descend.

It was, West thought, like being surrounded by a pack of submarines. You could catch a glimpse of their activity in the water, and rarely a slender periscope would protrude briefly into the air. Sometimes the periscope would be run up many feet and take a quick look around, only to descend as quickly as possible.

Gradually the number of surfacing heads grew fewer, as the school of plesiosaurs moved away from the raft. The two humans watched them as they faded off into the distance, until finally they could no longer see the arch of those great silver necks above the blue waters. The surface of the ocean to every side was unbroken and the strange beasts were gone.

Beneath the hot sun of Pellucidar, the tiny raft and its passengers crept on across the brilliant blue expanse. Thirst was first a nagging worry and then an ever-present obsession. West and Varna washed their mouths with salt water—even drinking small amounts of it. The former prowled up and down the ten-foot length of their craft, trying to think of something other than water.

The wind was blowing them gently closer to the little rocky island, yet so slowly that the speck in the distant blue seemed to remain the same size. Varna thought there might be a further landmass beyond, but she could not be sure because of the haze and the low-lying clouds.

West searched the mass of driftwood on which they floated, selecting and trimming with his axe a pair of fairly straight limbs for paddles. He worked his "mast" into an open wooden triangle in the prow of the raft, but could think of no way to equip it with a real sail. Neither of them had enough clothes on to make anything that would catch the wind. Despite the presence of the wind and the waves, the speed of the raft seemed to slow to almost nothing.

Thirst became a torment. Red Axe and his mate took turns sleeping while the other kept watch. Each time they awakened their mouths seemed a little drier.

"If it looks like there is water on that rock," said West, "we're going to it if we have to abandon ship and swim."

Varna shook her head. "I can't see trees or anything green

on this side of the island," she warned. "But it does look as if there are things moving on the rocks."

"Seals? Turtles?" Red Axe asked eagerly. The girl shook her head. She could not tell. "Moving shapes—not human—can't tell anything else."

"Very well, we'll try to circle the island as we come closer and get a look at the other shore. I haven't given up on it yet." He picked up one of his makeshift paddles and prepared to guide their ungainly craft as best he could.

Slowly the rocky shore grew closer. The light breeze seemed inclined to carry the raft around the right side of the islet in an attempt to turn the driftwood mass in closer to the rocks.

"Chris, I can see those things moving down into the water. I think they are coming this way!"

"Get your bow ready, darling," the man grunted, struggling with his crude oar, "and let me know if you see any signs of fresh water."

The breeze quickened. Now Varna could make out bulky forms low in the blue water with tall fins cutting the foam.

"They're getting closer. *Oh!*" she cried.

Red Axe turned from his paddling to see what had evoked the exclamation from his mate.

A green monster was trying to climb up onto the raft. The creature was about six feet long, although the hind quarters and the lashing tail were still in the water. Its forelegs were short and stubby, its feet webbed like a crocodile's. The head was too short to resemble any of the large water reptiles of the outer world. The skull was more doglike: short snout, bright yellow eyes, and a wide mouth, now open to reveal a forest of sharp fangs.

The most incredible aspect of the creature, however, was the fin that rose along its back, running from head to base of tail like a huge ribbed sail, twice the height of the beast's stubby body.

The thing emitted a frightful screech as it dug the talons of its forefeet into the rotten logs.

Even as she cried out, Varna sent an arrow into the beast's throat, drew, and fired another into the left eye. The beast threw back its green, scaly bulldog head to scream again. Red Axe thrust at it with the dripping end of the pole he was using as an oar. The reptile slipped into the ocean.

The two humans had only a moment to congratulate themselves, however. The wind continued to drive the log raft past the rocky islet, but now half a dozen of the high sail-fins could be seen approaching them through the water. There was no sign of the creature they had just thrown overboard, and Red Axe made haste to work with his primitive oar against the side of the raft to veer them away from any oncoming reptiles.

"Keep looking for any signs of water, Varna," he urged. "We may have to run a blockade of these sailbacks, but if there's a stream it's worth the risk."

It seemed that the breeze would carry them past the approaching reptiles before the beasts could swim far enough out from the island to intercept the raft. West feared the creatures might overtake them, however, if they kept up their pursuit. It was with relief, therefore, that he saw the great rounded fins turn back toward the rocks as the raft pulled further out to sea. But as they rounded the rocky point toward which Red Axe had originally put his hope of landing, Varna cried out again with warning.

A long peninsula of rock was now revealed. Across the sun-drenched barren beach dozens of the big marine reptiles could be seen moving. Awakened from their basking as the raft came into view, they waddled clumsily to the surf, where they plunged into the deep waters of the ocean and began to paddle powerfully toward the intruders. The great back-fins cut through the water and the heavy, short-muzzled heads rose and fell as the creatures gulped for air while they swam. They were fiercely graceful in their own element, but the two humans were in no situation to appreciate their aesthetic qualities. Red Axe cursed sullenly and tried to swerve his mass of rotten logs out farther from the shore.

For a time the distance between the raft and the swimming monsters seemed to be increasing. Though the sailbacks were coming almost directly into the path of the makeshift vessel, the wind had continued to grow as they rounded the island. Now the waves were curling to a height of two feet and breaking into whitecaps. There was pitifully little he could accomplish with his crude oar, yet Red Axe estimated that the wind-driven raft would escape the creatures, who were fighting both wind and waves, by a wide margin. He kept paddling just the same, and directed Varna to take a short pole and do likewise on the other side. For long minutes they struggled with their oars. The raft was bouncing badly in the choppy water, and West could only pray that his lashing of vines would hold together, for he doubted that the two of them would ever be able to outswim their pursuers.

"Christopher," called Varna anxiously, "they're turning." He left his side of the raft to stand next to her and watch the great fanlike fins cutting through the water. The entire group had turned, like a school of fish might do.

"Varna," he said suspiciously, "can you see anything to the right there? Are they avoiding some larger monster under the surface?"

The girl strained her eyes, lifting her hands to her forehead to shade her brows and hold back the wind-whipped strands of her hair.

"It is hard to see, Christopher, with the waves all splashy and the white foam everywhere, but there seems to be nothing at the place where they turned. Look! They turn back!"

"They're zigzagging," he muttered. "What on earth . . ."

"They come closer!"

Indeed they did. Despite the choppy water and the brisk wind that cupped the tall membranous fins across their backs, the monsters were obviously gaining on the raft. As he watched, they again executed a sharp-angled turn that appeared to head them away from the raft but brought them closer and closer to its line of advance. Much further and they would indeed intercept the raft's course as it passed the island. Another sharp turn brought the tall fins closer again and charging in toward their port bow.

"They're tacking!" Red Axe cried in amazement. "Look at that—they're tacking into the wind! Varna, get your bow. Here they come!"

Crash! The first of the brutes struck the side of the raft. It clawed at the logs with its webbed talons, the green muzzle split in a frightful snarl that revealed yellowed and broken fangs. *Twang!* Varna's first arrow took the beast through the neck. The pinkish-gray maw opened still wider in a screech of pain, and it slid backward into the waves.

Immediately, however, three more fin-backed creatures, each over six feet in length, reached the raft and started clambering up onto the logs. The crazy patchwork craft creaked and groaned and tilted down into the waves. Varna cried out and slipped to her knees on the wet wood. Red Axe struck one doglike green head with the end of the oar, dislodging the creature momentarily, but next instant the end of the pole was seized in the jaws of the adjacent beast. The hissing and snarling was hideous as the creatures tried to crawl aboard the raft to get at its occupants. The weight of the great marine lizards threatened momentarily to sink or capsize the clumsy vessel. As West grabbed for his axe, holding Varna by the shoulder while she regained her feet, he felt the water swirling around his ankles. One of the monsters had been forced back into the water. The other two, one with the broken oar in its teeth, were crawling closer. West tried to get Varna behind him. The image of her bronzed skin and rounded muscular body being torn by those savage fangs filled his mind for a horrifying split second. Then he struck!

A quick rap to the side of the jaw with the flat of his axe turned the beast on the left. The one on the right lunged at him, jaws open. He danced to the side and aimed a terrific overhand blow with the full force of his muscular shoulders behind it. It connected, the blade of the steel axe biting deep into the lizard's skull. The creature screamed in pain and fury, reaching one clumsy taloned paw up at the offending weapon. But the man had pulled it out with a mighty heave of his bulging muscles. Again he struck, this time hewing through the forelimb; thick red blood poured from the wound to swirl in the lapping waves. Another blow and yet another and the axe blade severed the fin-back's spinal cord just behind the massive head. The webbed limbs went limp and twitching, the great dorsal fin sagged to the side, and Red Axe was able to roll the carcass over into the beast on the other side. The two reptiles, one wounded, one dying, slid off the edge of the raft, which tipped disastrously under their combined weight and then slowly righted itself.

He stumbled to where Varna crouched, bow in hand, in the center of the raft. She clung to him as he clasped her close with his left arm, his right hand still clutching the long-handled axe. Primitive man and primitive woman, they stood silent a moment, looking out over the white-capped sea.

The raft wallowed in the troughs, seemingly unable to make headway despite the favorable wind. In the distance, more lizard fins cut through the waters as the carnivorous denizens of the island glided closer to the fragile sanctuary.

"I love you, Christopher," the black-haired girl murmured. "No matter what happens, I love you."

"And I have loved you since the first moment you led me into the sunlight of Pellucidar," he replied. "But we're not done for yet. If we could get this barge moving, we might outdistance them." He turned from a contemplation of the circling sailbacks to the craft on which he stood. The futile tripod of branches still stood in the bow, but they had nothing to put up against it to catch the wind. All the clothing they had now consisted of torn leather shorts. He had used remnants of both shirts to help tie the logs together.

Up over the stern of the raft came the biggest sailback they had yet seen. Climbing clumsily but quickly, it thrust a ten-foot-long body onto their craft, submerging the entire rear half of the raft with its weight. The great ribbed fin stood a good five feet above the beast's back.

Varna notched one of her last three arrows and drew the string back to her ear.

"Wait!" he cried, placing a gently restraining hand on her shoulder. "Let him come further aboard!"

"He'll sink us!" gasped the girl.

"We'll have to risk it," he replied. The giant reptile had already begun its advance, and the two humans had to scramble back out of its way. Red Axe circled to the right, hoping for an opening at the neck. Varna's bowstring twanged and an arrow sank into the fleshy underjaw. The beast paid no heed but turned, keeping its eyes on the moving man. Suddenly the great head lunged and the jaws snapped, missing only by inches as West leaped back. He chopped at the head with his axe, inflicting only superficial wounds. Now he was confronted with a pinkish-gray maw filled with fangs, and a gust of noisome breath as the vicious reptile snarled and screamed at him. There was no opening to the more vulnerable neck and throat.

On the other side of the raft the brave cave girl crouched. She could not see a target worth an arrow, and dared not spend her last two shafts in a futile attack which might wound her mate.

Then, briefly, the monster turned its head to bellow defiantly. The underthroat puffed out and the fierce jaws opened fully. Varna took careful aim, waited a long anxious moment for the bobbing raft to reach the crest of a white-capped wave and pause suspended there, and loosed her arrow. Into the beast's eye it plunged and the roar became a scream. The great doglike head was lowered to the deck while the creature clawed at its face with both forelimbs. West needed no further opportunity. Inviting complete disaster, he rushed to close with his foe on the opposite side from the arrow wound, well within reach of the taloned forepaws. Three swift blows of the keen-bladed axe and the beast was literally beheaded. The entire raft was awash with blood. A spasmodic flailing of the limbs of the dying torso caught the man a blow to the chest that knocked the wind out of him and threw him off the raft into the sea.

Varna rushed to the edge of the raft as he rose spluttering to the surface, still retaining a grim grip on his axe. Unharmed but winded, he climbed back onto the heaving deck of his craft. There he reassured the girl while quickly completing the severing of the giant head, which he rolled overboard. Then, warning Varna to keep a sharp lookout for the next attack, he wedged his axe into a secure place close at hand, drew his knife, and began hacking at the base of the giant back fin.

"Chris, what are you doing? We've got to get that carcass overboard—it's weighing us down."

"Right," the man grunted, "but first I've got to strip this thing off." It was hard work, for the tall membrane was composed of tough lizard skin and supported by slender spines of bone that grew up from each of the vertebrae. Each of these spines had to be cut off close to its base in order to free the entire dorsal fin in one piece. Finally, however, he was rewarded by a flexible fan that was eight feet long and five feet high in the center.

"Now we can roll him off," he gasped. He carried his blood-soaked trophy forward and laid it along the up-rights of his tripod mast, hooking the skin on stick stubs through puncture wounds made with his long hunting knife. Immediately the wind caught in the natural sail and the raft turned and leaped forward, heading now true to the waves and rapidly leaving the tiny rocky island behind.

Red Axe turned to help his mate, and together they levered the gory, dismembered green carcass to the raft's stern and dropped it into the depths.

"I think already the sailbacks are falling behind us," Varna said hopefully.

"Just hope no more are in a position to intercept us," replied Red Axe. "We should make better time running before the wind than they. Now, lord knows what scavengers all that sailback blood will bring, but with luck we will leave them behind." He watched their stern for a while—they were now leaving a distinct wake, one that any denizen of the deep could easily follow, but at the moment there were no shadows in the blue depths. He turned to gaze forward.

"Come up in front of the sail, Varna. There—does that mass below the clouds look like land?"

"Yes, it does, and that is rain. We are being driven toward it. Somewhere ahead there will be water, Chris—I know it."

The big man embraced her, holding her close to his bare, bloodstained chest. Beside them, the ribbed, membranous sail hummed tautly in the wind.

4
THE SKELETON BEACH

THE SURF ON THE APPROACHING REEF made a dull booming sound, rhythmical and growing louder. Wearily, Red Axe raised his head. Weakness and dehydration had brought him to the brink of collapse. It took some seconds for the scene to register on his benumbed brain. The reef made a line of heavy white. Beyond, the lagoon was fairly clear and emerald green. There was a long coral sand beach, bright yellow and backed with palms and heavy undergrowth, and above it reared gigantic gray rock cliffs, festooned with clinging plants and vines and topped with overhanging foliage.

"Varna!" he cried, grasping the girl beside him by the arm. "Varna!"

Crump! The flimsy log raft hit the outer reef with a jar. Varna groaned and opened her eyes. West quickly rose to his knees, holding on with one hand while he hurriedly fastened a thong around his axe and slung it across his back.

"Come on, Varna—the raft is breaking up. Slide off the front into the surf!"

Four- and five-foot combers were breaking on either side of them. Red Axe desperately pulled a loose log from the disintegrating raft and dragged his mate through the water to it. "Hang on to this. Hang on, Varna!"

The next swell took them. On the rise the beach was clear. With over a hundred yards to go, the blue-green crest began to curl over. "Stay flat in the water," he gasped.

41

"Keep flat—the coral is close to the surface!" He applied a little drag with his feet, delaying the driftwood log on the curve of the wave as the crest curled over and a long tube formed and then collapsed. He let the log with its two passengers slide down the crest, where the running foam caught it, lifted it, and held. Away they went, the wind and the spray singing about their ears, rushing across the lagoon on the dying wave, until it gently deposited them halfway up the sandy beach.

"Ooh! Christopher!" Varna gasped, as he helped her to struggle to her feet. Half supporting each other, they staggered up the beach to the line of trees. "How did you do that? That was wonderful!"

"Surfing," he panted. "We've just introduced a new sport to Pellucidar."

"Wonderful!" the girl repeated. "Let's do it again!"

"Later," he said as they collapsed onto dry sand, now safely above the waterline. For a while he lay there, trying to regain some of his strength. Must get up soon, he told himself, must find water or we will die. He roused himself to sit up and scan the beach. Surf, sand, and palm trees. Down the beach between the tree line and the surf, a number of low, black things were moving. He turned his head the other way: there they were to the left, as well. Whatever they were, they had them surrounded. He staggered to his feet and slipped the strap from his shoulder to free his axe. Whatever this new menace might be, he would meet it armed and fighting.

Varna let out a cry. He turned back to her. Out of the sand close to her outstretched hand there appeared a rounded head somewhat smaller than the girl's fist. Two round golden eyes regarded her quizzically. More sand toppled to either side as the creature climbed into view. Red Axe saw a black shell trimmed with green, nearly a foot across, four short stocky flippers, and a diminutive pointed tail. The little beast studied them a moment and then, with an ungainly waddle and an air of completely unconcerned nonchalance, walked carefully around Varna and continued on down the beach toward the sea.

"Look, Varna," the man cried, "they're on both sides of us. There must be dozens of them—no hundreds! Look at them!"

Indeed, the beach was covered with slowly moving black dots for as far as they could see in either direction. As they watched, more of the little turtles emerged from the sand near them, shook themselves off, and waddled determinedly into the surf. Varna plunged an arm into the warm sand where the first had emerged and pulled out fragments of a tough, flexible egg case. "See, Christopher, they are hatching. They are all babies, all of them being born at once."

Red Axe was about to sit down on the beach beside her when another moving shadow caught his eye. This was a faster shadow and it swept down the shoreline parallel to the water's edge, silent and deadly. Then, with a wild screech, a pterodactyl alighted on the beach, seized one of the young turtles in its talons, and took off again with much flapping of its finger-tipped, bat-like wings. Within moments there was another, and another. Fairly large, though not as large as Zed or the terrible man-eating thipdars, with wingspans of two or three feet, the ugly creatures circled and dove to pluck their helpless prey from the sands. A flash of featherless wings gave Red Axe a moment's warning as ugly reptilian talons slashed at his head and shoulders. He ducked, swung his axe over his head, and missed. With a squawk of disappointment, the flying lizard flapped up out of range. In a moment, however, another zoomed in. The man caught it a glancing blow with the axe head and it fell to the sand, stunned.

Undeterred, two moderately sized pterosaurs flapped down over Varna's unprotected head. She cried out, beating them off with her hands and bare arms. With a shout, Red Axe leaped to her defense and stood straddling her body, swinging the great axe above them as the vicious reptiles circled, screeching and attempting to get through his guard.

He knocked another and yet another of the pterodactyls from the air, but now his muscles, weak from dehydration and exposure to the noonday sun, began to ache with effort. Red Axe knew he could not hold the weapon up any longer. With a cry of pain, he fell over Varna's body, endeavoring to protect her head and eyes with his flesh.

Even as he did so he saw a dark shape leap through the breakers on the reef and sweep shoreward, soon to be followed by a dozen more. He groaned. What new menace was this? Crouched on hands and knees above the prostrate form of his mate, he watched the long outriggers reach the beach. Shouting men leaped from them, brandishing spears.

The flocks of pterodactyls flapped up out of the way as a tall, pale-haired figure ran up the sands, dodging both the crawling turtles and the wounded flying lizards.

"Red Axe! Red Axe! Red Axe!" cried Elkar. He seized his friend by the shoulders, helped him to sit, and scooped an arm under Varna's body.

"Water, Tumu, water!"

When the drinking gourd had been brought and the two castaways had slaked their thirst and washed the salt from their faces, they sat with Elkar crouched between them, watching as the men of Hapu gathered baby turtles in nets, chasing away the screaming pterodactyls with wildly waving spears.

"Oh Elkar, were we ever glad to see you!" Varna exclaimed.

"And I also to see you," the big man said with a grin. "You must see these people and their canoes, Red Axe. I am glad I found you in time—only you must help me. We have to rescue a beautiful girl from a terrible death."

Red Axe crouched at the water's edge. Behind him the grisly ribbon of the skeleton beach stretched to the far cliff of the towering needle. The tide was down and there was no wind. The waves of the sea washed gently onto the snow-white bones at his feet, the osseous beach shelving rapidly into the deep green-blue. Red Axe and Elkar peered at the narrow strip of shallow water where Tumu pointed with an impatient brown finger.

"There and there," said the boy, "in the pools that the low tide never quite dries. See? The little ones, the children of the god Manu." He straightened up and looked out across the blue lagoon. "The whole bottom is covered with his children, hundreds and hundreds of them."

The two men watched the tiny flowerlike creatures, only two or three inches high, their slender pink tentacles waving in the eddies of the softly breaking waves. Elkar plunged his brawny arm into the warm water and wrenched one from the bone-crusted boulder on which it grew. The squishy brown stalk turned in his hand, the tiny pink tentacles clinging to the ball of his thumb. With difficulty he pried the thing loose with his other hand and threw it back into the water. Muttering imprecations against the spawn of the sea god, Elkar washed the glue-like slime from his fingers in the salt water.

"They grow larger, do they?" Red Axe asked. When the boy nodded emphatically, he said, "Where?" and his informant gestured out into the lagoon.

"Come," said the big man, handing his weapons to Elkar, "I want a closer look." The boy plunged into the lagoon and Red Axe followed with long, powerful strokes of his brawny arms.

The youth dived and the man followed him into the sunlit depths. The salt water blurred his vision and stung his eyes, but a strange and beautiful world appeared below him.

Living coral rose in miniature hills and valleys, covered with fine, flowing seaweeds of greens, reds, and browns. The crevices and holes in the coral were filled with the ubiquitous white bones, and over them swam schools of flashing silvery-blue fishes. Dotted everywhere were the brown stalks and pink blossoms of the giant anemones, some of them a foot across.

Periodically surfacing for air, the man and his slim brown guide scouted the shallow sea bottom. Red Axe dropped bits of shell into the waiting tentacles, disturbing a little bright orange fish who floated unafraid within range of the miniature monster. The pink petals seized the tidbit, coiled round it, drew it to the center of the tentacular circle, and slowly stuffed it into a waiting maw where a beak-like mouth opened greedily.

When the man tried to herd some of the smaller fishes toward the anemones, however, they warily dodged the carnivorous flowerlike creatures—all except the little orange fish, who would actually settle down on the pink tentacles with impunity.

Surfacing a final time, Red Axe swam slowly back to the shore, where he sat thinking in the sun until his skin had dried.

"Come on," he said to Tumu and Elkar, finally getting to his feet. "Back to the mainland."

"You have a plan, Red Axe?" asked Elkar.

"Maybe the beginning of one. Tumu, what are those little fish who dare to swim in reach of the children of Manu?"

"The *wiki-wiki* fish," said the boy, smiling. "That little fellow has no fear of being eaten. Long ago he and the little new Manu agreed to be friends. He is the bait that brings the bigger fish within reach of Manu's many arms, and as a reward he is protected by all of Manu's children."

"Like your priest yonder in his stony spire," grunted Elkar, "he leads the helpless to their doom!"

"Ay, perhaps. Perhaps the old man is a wicked wiki-wiki fish grown to human form, since the great god's appetite can no longer be satisfied by fishes alone."

"How long, Tumu," asked Red Axe, "have the priests of your tribe been feeding the great Manu?"

"Oh," said the boy, gesturing at the bones on which they trod, "since the beginning of time. How many skeletons do you see before you?"

"These too?" asked the man, stomping on the great hollow skull of a mastodon.

"Sometimes the hunters trap or kill such beasts in the jungles beyond the cliffs," Tumu replied, "or the outriggers battle the great killer lizards of the sea. Then the carcass is brought back and cast into the arms of Manu to thank him for our good fortune and to let him grow great and strong. But if the hunting and fishing is bad, then a young man or woman of the tribe is thrown to Manu to appease his anger and once more solicit his aid in the fishing." The youth said all this with absolute conviction. Elkar made as if to reply, but Red Axe caught his eye and shook his head in negation.

"There are hunting trails up to the cliffs, then?"

The boy nodded. "Yes, but too narrow and steep for the big lizards or the long-nosed hairy ones to find their way down. Sometimes one of the wild dogs or a *tarag** finds its way to the beach, and then the whole tribe turns out to hunt it down."

By the time the three had beached Tumu's small canoe and made their way up the cliff trail to the caves, they could hear a wailing and crying from the cave of Kee-ah, the boy's brother. Tumu ran ahead and parted the curtain of tanned cowhide that partly obscured the entrance. A flood of grief-filled female voices answered his inquiries. Varna had followed him inside. As Elkar and Red Axe paused, alarmed but reluctant to intrude, she exited the cave and came to join them.

"The priests came for the girl Onoloa," she said. "They have taken her away."

Elkar's face was, if possible, even paler than usual. His jaw muscles worked and his voice was thick and choked.

"They have killed her!" he grunted, then corrected himself. "No, they cannot have had time to throw her from the needle, as we have just returned from the beach of skeletons."

Varna laid a hand on his arm. "As I understand it, they

---

* Saber-toothed tiger.

will wait until the water in the lagoon gets as low as they think it will go. Then the entire tribe will assemble in the cave on the pinnacle and watch as she is thrown to her death. It will not be right away, Elkar. She still lives, but old Apu will keep her prisoner in the rock."

A gleam of desperation came into the man's eyes. He had not slept since the recovery of his friends from the distant seacoast, sitting awake in the cave after the others had dozed off, racking his brain to think of some way to rescue the beautiful girl who had been torn from him almost as soon as they met.

"Red Axe," he said, "let us rush to the cave in the rock needle. There cannot be many of them and they will not be expecting an attack. We will kill them all and flee up the cliffs with the girl."

"Elkar, old friend," said the American, "the only way out of that place is the bridge, and the path we now stand upon, which runs past many cave dwellings of the tribe. We are only three—four with the girl—and we cannot fight our way through five hundred Hapuans."

Elkar sighed and shook his head.

"Besides," Red Axe went on, "there may still be a possibility of using my plan, but we will need to work fast. Varna, will anyone from the family be allowed to visit her? Can we get a message to her in some way?" The girl shrugged. He pushed her back toward the cave. "Try to find out, talk to some of the older women—maybe they will know. And send Tumu back to us. We have a lot to do and it will take time. Hurry."

The information they obtained from the boy and the rest of the family was reassuring. Tumu was sure that it would be at least five sleeps before the low tide. He pointed out a group of coral heads close to the reef, visible through the crystal-clear blue waters, which he said would project above the waterline when the tide reached its ebb.

"Then will all the outriggers of my people be lined up

upon the beach," he concluded, "for the channel through the reef is too shallow at the time of Manu's feeding for the big fishing canoes to get to the open ocean. Only after he has been fed does he permit the water to rise so that his people may fish again."

The group withdrew down the beach to discuss their plans. Red Axe's first problem was to convince young Tumu to help them. The boy had still not guessed their intent.

"But if you cheat the god of his prey," he gasped, "he will send away all the game fish and then set the great sea-dragons against our outriggers! All of our people will be killed or die of starvation, the caves will stand empty, and the dead bodies of the tribe of Hapu will lie withered in the sun!"

"Oh, nonsense, boy," said Varna. "The big beast does not control the ocean or its creatures. There will be plenty of fish for your tribe."

Red Axe stopped her. "I don't think this is the time to try to convert the boy to atheism," he said. "Listen, Tumu, you have said that the priest Apu is a cruel old man?"

"Aye, Red Axe—and that one hates my sister and my family. We are too successful, and too many fine shells and ivory tusks adorn the cave of Kee-ah and the caves of his brothers and cousins."

"Then it is very likely you yourself may be sacrificed next?"

"Aye," said the boy sadly. "I had thought of that."

"Or your friend Elkar, since he is a stranger?"

"I had wondered about that, as well," the youth replied, "but decided that Apu had made up his mind to demand Onoloa, the youngest and fairest one from our cave, and even the arrival of strangers could not change his mind."

"Then we are all in danger?" Red Axe pressed him. Tumu nodded. "We must trust you, Tumu, and we need your help. If we succeed, you are welcome to come with us when we escape. You would like to see the rest of Pellucidar?"

"Yes," he agreed, "for if we do this thing, I cannot stay here and watch my tribe die."

"They will not die," the man assured him, "but they are very likely to sacrifice you in your sister's place. Now, do you swear to be faithful to us, to aid and protect us, and not reveal our plan to Apu, whether we succeed or fail?"

"I will swear," the boy replied, "by my family name, since I cannot swear by the great god himself. May shame and an evil death befall me if I do not keep my word." He paused. "Likely you would have killed me if I had not agreed to help you anyway."

Red Axe smiled grimly. "I must admit the idea briefly crossed my mind," he said, "but I would have found some other way, for you have been fair and honest with us."

Tumu smiled back at him.

"Good," the man continued. "Now in my land we seal a partnership like this by clasping hands—using the right hand, which is usually the one that carries weapons." They all solemnly clasped hands with the young Hapuan, who then gave a sigh of relief, as if some great weight had at last been lifted from him—as indeed he felt it had.

"Tell us, now, what we must do," he asked.

"All right," said Red Axe. "We must start immediately. I think we have a chance, but it depends largely on speed and luck."

Red Axe and Tumu went on up the beach to the fishing grounds, while Varna and Elkar returned to the caves and gathered fishing spears, gourds, a small net, and Elkar's bow and arrows, before joining them. No one challenged them, and after a reasonable length of time the four returned, although with only a meager catch.

Onoloa's sister was allowed to visit the prisoner and take her something to eat and drink. To his continued discomfort, Elkar was not allowed to see her, and although he had sent along an urgent and ardent message, it had to be verbal, and he did not know if the woman would deliver it.

"Fortune favors us so far, my friend," comforted Red Axe, as they watched the distant figure of the woman crossing the narrow bridge into the priest's sanctuary. "At least we know she is still alive."

Elkar sighed and turned back through the hide curtain into the cave. The fire warmed a central room that was illuminated by a few streaks of sunlight through the entrance. The man of the household was absent, but Tumu and three younger children, as well as two old women and the family's wolflike dog, gathered at the fire with Varna and the two male strangers for a meal consisting of thin cakes of some sort of baked bread and the ubiquitous fish stew. Afterward, Red Axe and his mate urged their anxious companion to bed and he finally fell into an uneasy slumber, awakening frequently from dreams in which he seemed to be falling from a great height into the sea.

"Christopher," whispered Varna, when the two of them had retired to the narrow sleeping niche assigned them, "do you think we can make this work?"

"I don't know," he replied.

"You are worried, I can feel it." The woman ran her fingers over his hair and down across his shoulders.

"You're damn right I'm worried!" he replied, swearing in English for lack of a fitting Pellucidarian equivalent. "The whole plan has too many weak spots in it. One of the worst just occurred to me during our last meal."

"What is that?"

"The girl. Suppose she doesn't want to be rescued? You heard Tumu, and we've had a much better chance to brainwash him. He thought it might be a duty to be sacrificed so the god would protect and reward his people. Suppose Onoloa feels that way? Suppose she gets our message and spills the plan to Apu? Where will we all be then?"

"I got to know her a little before the priests took her away," Varna whispered. "I don't think she would knowingly put another in jeopardy—particularly not her brother."

"Good, I hope you're right."

"Yes, so do I. But then . . ."

"But then what? Is there another problem?"

"Yes," the girl whispered. "What if we get her rescued and safe and it turns out that . . ."

"That what?" he urged.

"That she's not at all in love with Elkar."

"Good lord, I'd never thought of that."

"No, you wouldn't," she giggled. "You men always assume . . ."

"Well, you fell in love with me when I rescued you from the Had-Bar."

"Indeed? What makes you think so?"

"Oh-oh? Why this, of course."

"Oh, that."

"Yes, and this."

"Oh."

"Well?"

"We'll let Elkar find out for himself."

5
SACRIFICE

THE WIND RUFFLED the bright lagoon where the dark coral heads, some glistening with whitened bones, now protruded above the surface. Farther out, the top of the reef showed black against the blue of the ocean. The tide was too low now for the wave to break over that living barrier, and the inner lagoon was almost mirror-calm.

Varna and Tumu managed to slip away when the tribe began to gather for the ceremony, but Elkar and Red Axe, conspicuous by their size and coloring, were caught up by the throng coming down the cliffside path. All the able-bodied members of the Hapuan nation seemed to be seeking the causeway to the needle's eye. Red Axe noted this with relief, for part of his complicated rescue plan depended upon there being no guards at the canoe moorings.

The Hapuans, normally rather cheerful and talkative by nature, were quiet and grim. There was little talk and the group shuffled along at an appropriately funereal pace. The two haoles were jostled and pushed to the chasm's brink. The narrow wooden span across the gap was made of whole logs, cleverly interlocked and fastened with wooden pegs. The wooden section was only a dozen feet long, the original rock arch having survived as two massive stone piers, one on the face of the cliff, the other protruding directly from the mouth of the cave that pierced the great spire. Here the rock spread out into a wide comfortable ledge, but across the dizzy chasm the crowd was forced to travel one by one.

There was neither guard rail nor handhold, and Red Axe was thankful that the wind was not blowing. A hundred feet below, a thin trickle of water ran down the sandy floor of the canyon to the quiet sea. Thick marsh grasses lined the streambed, though the steep, yellowed sides of the rock needle itself were without greenery.

On the other side of the bridge, Red Axe and Elkar were relieved of their weapons and the coil of rope Elkar carried across his shoulder, and allowed to enter the cavern. The Hapuans, however, retained their spears and shell or bone knives. The walls of the great cave were carved into intricate *tiki* gods, with the flowerlike motif of Manu the sea god dominating. The crowd pushed through the passage to its end, where there was a wide ledge looking out over the lagoon.

To the left and right the ledge narrowed against the sheer cliff of the needle. On one side stood the old priest, Apu, staff in hand. A full-length cloak of brilliantly colored feathers covered most of his scrawny body. Before him, at the edge of the breathtaking drop to the pool below, was the girl, Onoloa. A pair of tree trunks had been set upright into the ledge, carved like the cave walls into leering demon faces. The slender form of the maiden was suspended between them, each wrist secured to a post. Her bare feet still touched the ground, but she drooped between those grotesque guardians, her long black hair streaming down over her face and her bare breast. She was clad only in a narrow strip of tapa around her hips and her posture was that of resignation. Behind her stood the haughty old priest and six of his acolytes, the latter armed with great ceremonial war clubs topped with human skulls. Red Axe had never seen the girl before; his heart went out to her in her beauty and despair. He heard Elkar, close behind him, give a gasp. On the other side of the ledge, more priests began a slow booming on great wooden drums.

The crowd of natives, packed onto the ledge and extending back into the cavern behind them, prevented the two strangers from getting close to the girl. Somehow she sensed their gaze upon her, however, and raised her head. Her eyes met Elkar's and her shoulders stiffened. Slowly she nodded her lovely head just once. Elkar sighed again.

"She did it!" he hissed in Red Axe's ear.

The big man grunted. "Now if it will only work," he whispered. "We know it is effective on the little ones . . ." His voice trailed off as the men and women around him began to chant. Several were pointing into the lagoon and others were pressing forward from behind them to see down into the water. The two outsiders let the crowd around them force them back against the rock wall at the mouth of the cavern.

Below them, the surface of the calm, reef-fringed pool began to seethe with motion. The American suppressed a gasp as he looked down. The thing was unbelievable! Fifty feet across, at least, the long, fleshy red tentacles waving and crawling in the air. In the center of those horrid pseudopods, a ghastly birdlike beak, three feet across, could be seen opening and shutting rhythmically. Even as he watched, the entire wriggling mass pushed itself up out of the water, rivulets streaming off the tentacles as it rose several feet above the surface. The drums quickened and two priests stepped forward to the cliff edge and raised giant conch shells to their lips. An eerie hooting whistle echoed over the lagoon.

The priest, Apu, raised both his arms, holding his staff above his head. The drums and the chanting hushed, as the monster below sank back into the waves. Apu began his harangue to the tribe. He had a clear, carrying voice, much greater in volume than one would predict from his puny size.

The high priest addressed himself mostly to the god, asking him to continue to reward and protect them, to fill their nets and carry them safely over the waves. In return, he promised that as each generation of his tribespeople grew up, the most fair would be presented to Manu in tribute. Red Axe thought he felt a stir in the crowd, as if the old man's theology was not without opposition, but no voice was raised against him.

The drums rolled again. Behind Apu, the priests parted and a small figure was led forth. A sigh went through the rapt crowd on the ledge. A child! Somewhere close to Red Axe and Elkar a woman let out one heart-breaking, despairing cry and was hushed, then dragged unprotesting back into the cave. The evil old man lifted the child in his arms—it could not have been more than four or five, and stepped to the brink. Every eye was on him now. The drums increased their tempo.

"Manu!" he cried, "Manu, great god of the sea, your people offer you their own flesh and blood!"

He cast the child out over the lagoon. The water was lashed by the eager reaching pink tentacle. The child's body was caught by the fleshy, obscene petals and passed from one to the other, inward toward the center. The beaked orifice gaped, then closed over its prey, cutting off the death cry of the doomed child. Red Axe felt sick, his stomach churning with revulsion. Elkar's fingers dug into his shoulder.

"God," muttered the blond giant to his companion. "This awful thing has to be stopped! That man . . ."

"Onoloa," hissed Elkar. "What it your idea doesn't work, what if . . ."

"We do the best we can, friend," replied Red Axe. "There is always—revenge."

The monster had finished the last scarlet tidbit. The pink petals waved randomly in the breeze. Apu began a singsong chant to his god, and the tribe joined in. The drums boomed on. Only the two strangers stood frozen with the horror of the last few moments. From the back of the great cave came, faintly, the sound of the grieving mother, weeping for her lost one.

The ritual was rising to its climax. Red Axe felt a thin film of nervous sweat break out across his forehead. He wiped his face with the back of his hand. Should he have gambled the lives of his entire party in a mad attempt to defy the age-old customs of this otherwise hospitable people? After all, what business of his was it what gods they worshipped, or how they worshipped them? Too late now, he thought. As usual, he had plunged headlong into danger and then had second thoughts about it afterward. It was the same impetuosity that had brought him into the inner world in the first place.

Two burly subpriests put their skull-headed staffs into holes in the rock so they stood upright and advanced on the pillars where the Hapuan girl hung like a fly in a spider's web. They unfastened her wrists and dragged her to the brink of the cliff, the conch shells wailing. Apu's voice rose to a scream as he worked himself up into a religious frenzy. He gestured imperiously with his wand of office. The two men shoved the girl forward. She struggled a moment, teetered on the edge and then fell into space. Elkar cried out and his friend grasped him across the chest as he sought to rush forward.

The girl recovered herself in midair and straightened out into a shallow dive. The great god Manu had retreated to just below the surface of the lagoon, and her slim brown body came into immediate contact with the pink, petal-like tentacles as soon as she hit the water. She sank and then rose slowly, facedown in the water. Perhaps she was stunned, Red Axe thought. It was a long drop; the force of striking the water must have been terrific. The slimy tentacles rose on either side of the girl's body and enfolded it. The rest of the creature's head, or top, rose to the surface, and the vicious, beak-like mouth once again became visible. It was already open, anticipating. The tentacles did not close, however. They circled, touched, withdrew, touched again, and pulled away. The girl stirred, seeming to rouse from her shock. She looked about and slid, half-swimming, still prone, across the great flowered disc. More tentacles rose before her, touched her body, and withdrew. As a slow moan of disbelief rose from her watching tribe, she glided to the edge of the fleshy mass and dove cleanly into the water a few feet below. Out of the corner of his eye West saw a slim outrigger, dark against the brilliant blue-green of the shallow lagoon, round the corner of the beach below and pull rapidly toward the fugitive. She saw it also and struck out strongly for the craft. On the canoe three figures bent vigorously to the oars. In the prow, Tumu shouted encouragement to his sister. Behind him, Varna and Moo-lah bent their oars, the monkey-man kneeling in the center of the narrow craft, his long tail curled up over his shoulder.

"Manu!" The voice of the high priest of the sea god cracked with emotion.

"Manu!" Red Axe bellowed. "Manu refuses the sacrifice!"

"Manu!" cried the blood-mad fanatic to his god. "Kill the blasphemers! Kill! Kill!"

"Let's get moving, Elkar," hissed Red Axe. "Fast!" They pushed their way through the stunned crowd. A few men tried to bar their way, but the American pushed them aside, muttering, "Taboo, taboo! Manu refuses the sacrifice! Apu fails his god!" The bewildered tribesmen allowed them to pass.

No one seemed to know what to do. The high priest was still screaming hysterically, his voice ringing within the cavern. The two men reached the edge of the crowd. Here the mother of the dead child lay in a huddle of grief on the sandstone floor where several other women tended to her. God help me, thought Red Axe, could I have saved him too? There was no way to know.

Elkar's bow and arrows, the coil of rawhide rope, the steel axe, all lay at the mouth of the cave where the narrow span of stone and wood bridge began—but here there was a guard. A big burly man with the skull-topped staff of a priest, he barred the way.

"Taboo!" he cried. "It is taboo to leave the eye of the needle until the god Manu has finished with the sacrifice."

West took one quick look behind. So far there was no pursuit.

"Grab the weapons, Elkar!" He closed with the priest, hitting him once on the jaw with all the weight of his powerfully muscled body behind the blow. The man went down, KO'd with a single punch. They ducked out onto the narrow, unguarded logs. Here Red Axe paused to fasten one end of the rope around his waist. He handed the other end to Elkar, and took his axe from his friend's hands.

"To the other side, quick," he instructed the other man. "Onto the cliff and then hold on to the rope!"

Without looking to see if his companion had obeyed, he examined the ancient construction of the bridge, locating the joining where the logs sagged a bit. The tree trunks had been notched together and a long wooden pin driven through them. A few strokes with the keen blade of his axe and the entire structure began to give way. With a cracking and snapping of the wood the log span bent beneath his feet.

On the ledge, Elkar braced his body and took up slack on the rope. His friend outweighed him by a number of pounds and he knew that it would be touch and go if the big blond American fell. The bridge began to collapse. Red Axe held the supporting rope in his left hand, taking a few loops around his wrist, then clambered farther up on the logs as they gave way beneath him. Reaching back with his right hand, he continued to hack away at the weakened joint until it suddenly sagged downward. Quickly he clambered up the rope to his friend's side, just as a shout came from the other side of the chasm. Looking across the now-broken and dangling span, he saw the ancient priest, surrounded by the amazed and outraged tribe of Hapuans.

"The curse of Manu upon you!" shrieked Apu, gesturing with his staff. He muttered to his followers, pointing at the wreck of the bridge, but no one rushed to attempt the crossing. Angrily he repeated the command. Two young stalwarts started out onto the sagging logs. The span swayed and creaked.

"Manu will have vengeance! The curse of the god Manu is death!"

Red Axe could not resist the opportunity to reply, although he knew it was pointless to argue with the madman.

"Manu refused the sacrifice!" he shouted. "No more innocent victims need be thrown to that overgrown sea slug of yours, Apu. No more children need die to keep you in power!" Elkar tugged at his arm. He would have continued to hurl epithets at the priest, but now a shark-tooth-studded spear flashed across the intervening space and narrowly missed his neck to clatter against the rock wall behind him.

"Quickly, Red Axe, we must get away to the beach," the pale man urged.

"Manu will destroy you!" cried Apu, "Manu will have his revenge!"

"To the Molop Az with you and Manu both!" West shouted, invoking the fiery sea upon which many of the inhabitants of Pellucidar believed their world floated. Two more spears flew toward him as he turned to run. The climbers on the broken bridge had succeeded only in bending it still further under their weight; it looked as if it might topple at any moment.

The two men raced down the long rocky path, past the now-vacant caves of the tribe.

"You were quite right, Elkar," Red Axe said to his friend, not slackening his pace. "Those spears were getting too close for comfort. In my country we have a saying 'sticks and stones may break my bones, but names can never hurt me.' Unfortunately, I had no spears to throw back at that murderous priest. Perhaps we should have tried a few of your arrows."

"No time, no time, Red Axe," the other urged. "The others must be all the way to the beach with Onoloa." The trail zigzagged before them down toward the beach.

Behind them there was a sharp cry. They looked up to see that the wrecked bridge had given way, sending one of the bold tribesmen plummeting to his death on the rocks below.

"That will keep them busy for a while," muttered Red Axe, as they hit the sand and Elkar sprinted ahead to the canoe landing. Moo-lah and Tumu were just putting the narrow outrigger onto the shore. Elkar ran to lift the graceful form of the native girl out of the boat in his arms and carry her to dry ground, while Varna leaped over the prow to join her mate. They gathered around the rescued girl, who now stood, one hand still resting on her devoted knight's shoulder.

"Onoloa," said Red Axe, "you don't know how glad we all are to see you alive."

"I never believed I would live," the girl replied, "no matter how much stinking fish oil my brother's wife smuggled to me to rub on my body. I smell like last week's garbage left out in the sun!"

"But it did work, Onoloa," Elkar broke in. "The monster thought you were a little wiki-wiki fish and let you go."

"I must confess," Red Axe told the girl, "that we had no idea whether it would work. The little creatures accept the wiki-wiki fish, but we couldn't be sure that Manu would accept you. Anyway, the smell is a small price to pay for your safety."

The group was so busy congratulating themselves that they ignored the chants and curses from the tribesmen stranded on the top of the needle. More dangerous, and also unnoticed, was the great form looming up through the waters of the lagoon. It was Varna who happened to glance up over the heads of the men. Her face turned pale and an involuntary scream was wrenched from her throat. Red Axe turned to confront a sight of such unbelievable terror that for a moment even he was transfixed by his emotions. Twenty feet high it loomed above them, its great slimy base undulating across the sand, the gray, scarred, and knobby skin streaming with water from the lagoon.

The fleshy pink top was almost out of sight, the thing so close now it towered over the terrified humans, its gigantic shadow engulfing them as the top of the thing began to bend downward.

The great god Manu had pursued his lost victim onto the very shore!

6
ESCAPE

THE MONSTER SEA ANEMONE moved by protruding part of its base, like a fleshy snail-foot, and drawing the huge ungainly body after it. Great wrinkles and rolls of slimy tissue formed around its barrel as it started to bend forward. Red Axe doubted that the creature could reach its tentacle top all the way down to the ground where its victims crouched in terror and amazement—but it might fall in the attempt, crushing them with its ponderous weight.

He looked around at his demoralized little force. Onoloa was frozen with fear, her lovely face gone pale. Poor Tumu had fainted or collapsed and lay sprawled on the sand beside the beached outrigger canoe. Elkar, Varna, and Mooh-lah looked ready to run. Red Axe himself was little better off than his followers. For a moment there was no sound but the squishing of the oceanic monster, and, faintly in the distance, cries of excitement and triumph from the tribe of Hapuans stranded in their rocky spire.

"Elkar, take the girl!" he shouted. "The rest of you, run! Down the beach! Get moving!"

The American rushed in at the base of the towering creature. The body was rough, covered with knobs and clinging bits of seaweed. It looked impregnable. The protruding, slimy foot, however, appeared softer and more vulnerable. He chopped at it with the axe, hacking pieces off the pseudopod, cutting through to the sand below. The thing stopped moving for a moment, then retracted its injured member. An eerie,

63

screaming whistle resounded up and down the beach. It echoed off the cave-packed cliffs, redoubling its volume until it seemed to split the eardrums. Manu cried out in pain!

Elkar lifted the brown-skinned girl in his arms and backed away. Pink tentacles flailed over his head as he ducked and ran, stumbling in the soft sand. Varna struggled to get the boy to his feet. Not ten paces away, the gigantic anemone turned on its axis and started forward again, wet gray flesh sliding out over the beach and rivulets of sea water running down its sides.

"Mooh-lah, help me," Varna gasped. They lifted Tumu between them and half dragged him away from the creeping menace, crouching as they moved to dodge the massive tentacles. Red Axe struck again and again. The monster slowed, but still came on, its injuries too small to deter the huge bulk from its purpose.

"Christopher!" cried Varna. "Run! Leave the canoe!"

Indeed, just then one of the creature's tentacles, lengthening beyond his expectations, seized the outrigger beside Red Axe and lifted it into the air. The petal-like things played with it a moment, found it inedible, and dropped it. The canoe fell to the sand on its prow and then toppled into the surf. More of the pink members swung down toward the injured base of the thing.

"Christopher!" screamed his mate again. The live, ropy things were sweeping the yellow coral sands on either side of the spot where he stood.

Red Axe turned to run. A soft, sticky, wet tentacle touched him on the left side, the tip curling swiftly around his body. He heard Varna scream again, followed by a shout from Mooh-lah. The pink mass lifted him up into the air.

Red Axe chopped desperately at the pulpy thing with his axe. He felt his legs grasped by eager hands as Mooh-lah ran to his aid. The glue-like secretion of the member kept it adhered to his body and left arm, as the keen steel axe blade severed the top of the tentacle. He staggered on up the beach to join his companions, the tailed man at his side. The eerie whistle of the giant anemone pierced their ears; looking back, they could see the monster still in ponderous pursuit. Red Axe tore the fragment of pseudopod from his flesh, the slimy adhesive drying to a stiff sheen on his bare skin. Elkar still held the limp form of the Hapuan girl in his arms. Varna clutched her mate.

"Christopher, when I saw that thing grab you and lift you up . . ."

"Close call, my darling. Let's get the hell out of here." Red Axe picked up the still-unconscious form of the boy, hung his axe at his belt, and slung his human burden across his broad shoulders. The little band of fugitives started down the beach at a trot, soon leaving the clumsy monstrous form of Manu the ocean god whistling and lashing his tentacles on the shore behind them.

Elkar knew of only one place where the shoreside cliffs were scalable, and that was the lagoon where he had first met Onoloa. Before they had run that far, however, the girl struggled in his arms and asked to be put down. After a quick discussion, she led them into the palm jungle that bordered the beach, where they found a hidden path upward. Access was gained only by climbing a leaning coconut palm that brushed the cliff with its cylindrical trunk some fifteen feet above the ground. The ascent was not that difficult, especially now that Tumu had also fully recovered.

Though narrow, the trail above that point was easy to follow, and soon they were above the tops of the feathery palms. Here they could look back to the caves of the Hapuans. The huge form of Manu was returning to the water of the lagoon, the hot, dry sand and the strain of supporting its massive weight out of water having proven too much for the creature. There was great activity visible around the top of the spire where the tribe was marooned.

"They'll lose no time getting started after us," the American grunted.

"But it is not far to the wild lands above, Red Axe," said the boy, who was standing next to him. "And hunting parties do not go into the realm of the great beasts."

Red Axe turned back to the ascent, but in a few paces the path came to a dead end. Above was sheer rock cliff, festooned with vines that hung from the crest some thirty feet over their heads.

Onoloa only laughed at his obvious puzzlement. She and Tumu showed the others the hidden handholds chipped out of the rock at irregular intervals, now overgrown with moss and tiny ferns, but still deep enough to take a sandaled foot. Tumu scampered to the top and waited while the rest of the party caught up with him.

The forest grew thick up to the cliff's edge, tall palms and ferns mingling with the sturdier hardwoods. Thick-leafed vines and creepers covered the tree boles and hung down the face of the cliff, their dark green leaves taking advantage of every spot of sunlight.

From here they had a clear view of the emerald lagoon behind them and the bright blue ocean beyond, where it faded up into the misty distance. Manu had retreated beneath the waves, but frantic activity continued on the needle's eye.

"They'll soon have the bridge fixed, or find a way to the ground with ropes," observed Varna, shading her keen brown eyes with her hand. "We'd best be moving off."

"*Faugh!*" muttered the tailed man. He spat over the cliff. "Pursued again! Traveling with you, Red Axe, is like being always in front of a stampeding herd of *tandors*."

"Moo-lah," said his friend, "you know I would not make you travel with us if you wish otherwise. We all know you can go more quickly through the jungle than we."

The monkey-man looked long and seriously into the big man's face before he broke into a grin. "What, and miss all the fun?" he said with a laugh.

Red Axe grinned back and gripped Moo-lah by the shoulder. "You are a true and brave comrade," he said.

"Ha!" Moo-lah replied. "And who in all my race has ever seen anything like that great walking potato-worm from the sea? Wait till I tell my grandchildren that tale!"

"All right, Elkar, which way to the camp?" Red Axe asked.

The tall pale man pointed down the cliffs across from the cave village of Hapu. "Past the lagoon where Onoloa and I met."

"There is a path my people use to get through the jungle to the open wild lands on the other side," said the Hapuan girl. "It will be faster going there. There are few game trails in the jungle itself."

Red Axe nodded in agreement. "Good. You and Elkar lead the way. Here, we must give you some weapons." The three humans had retained their bow and arrows. The tailed Mooh-lah had lost his, but was armed with a steel-bladed spear, as well as an axe and a knife. Elkar strapped his own steel hunting knife around the girl's slim hips and Tumu gave his sister one of the two ivory-headed fishing spears he had brought on his adventure. The group moved off down the barely discernible hunting trail at a slow trot.

The adventurers carried their spears and bows at the ready, but they encountered none of the dangerous carnivores of this prehistoric world. The undergrowth was full of lizards, most of them less than a foot long, some running on four legs, some on two, who scuttled out of sight as the big humans blundered past. There were clouds of flying insects, and, among the ferns, some spiders as large as a man's hand crouched in their webs, waiting for the colored butterflies that filled the air where bright beams of sunlight penetrated the jungle roof.

The path was not usually wide enough for two to walk abreast. As a result, Elkar and Onoloa had little opportunity for conversation. When the group stopped to rest they whispered together, but on the trail the common sense of the wild dictated that they move in silence.

"Apu will persuade the warriors to follow us," the girl

confided on one of the short breaks they permitted themselves, crouched around a tiny stream that flowed through
the jungle to tumble down the guardian cliffs and into the
sea somewhere behind them. "He will never let me escape,
not after imprisoning me in the needle's eye and then trying
to kill me by throwing me to . . . to . . ." she began to shudder.
Elkar put his big hands on her slender brown body and drew
her head to his chest. She clung to him briefly, soft and
yielding. "He will never touch you again," the man whispered.
"Not while I have strength to lift my hand." The girl turned
his head so that she could look up at his face, keeping her
cheek and breast pressed close against his body.

"No one else would have risked his life to save me," she
said. "I feel safe now, knowing you are close by." Elkar hugged
her to him, swept with a feeling of pride and protectiveness
he had never before experienced.

A short distance away, Varna was bathing her face in the
stream, crouched on a flat rock that rose above the water.
She glanced up, tossing her thick black hair back from her
face, and saw the two lovers amid the ferns on the other side
of the stream, locked in their embrace. The cave girl's tired
face softened into a smile and she caught her mate's eye and
nodded in their direction. Red Axe smiled back at her.

The path, being a game trail and not a man-made thor-
oughfare, seemed to wander aimlessly back and forth through
the heavy foliage. The band of fugitives was hungry and
exhausted by the time they finally came out of the jungle
onto rolling, green-covered hills. Now they looked out over
open country, mostly lush meadowland dotted with great
trees. Behind them was the belt of green that fringed the
cliffs and behind that the ocean rose into the distance, although the shore was no longer visible. The new country
was filled with game. In the distance were herds of antelopes,
eohippus, camels, rhinoceros-like creatures with sets of six
horns arranged in pairs on their heavy skulls, wild cattle,
and other animals Red Axe could not identify. It was a scene

much like the great plains of Africa he had seen in pictures, except that the grasslands were greener and the beasts even more exotic, and nowhere was there any sign of man.

Varna's bow brought down one of the little horses and the beast was quickly skinned and butchered. They would have loved to stop and make a fire to cook the meat, and also to rest, but the gnawing fear of pursuit drove them on. The meat was cut into strips and eaten raw as they hastened on their way. The rest of the carcass, left behind on the grass, quickly became a battleground for a struggle between a pack of jackal-like creatures and a number of small pterodactyls that circled in from the jungle beyond.

Elkar was still in the lead, and he turned parallel to the jungle belt, choosing the best path he could find with Onoloa's help. After a while, the yapping and screaming of the scavengers faded into the distance behind them. There was a cool breeze coming down from the green hills on the left, and it carried a hint of rain. At Red Axe's insistence, the group was moving at a slow trot.

"Where do we go now?" asked Onoloa.

Elkar peered ahead. "Somewhere up there is our old camp, where Zed awaits us with the rest of our belongings," he replied.

"There is another man?" the girl questioned. "Is he too from your underground city?" She smiled. "Is he as handsome as you?"

The man grinned. "Wait and see. Perhaps more handsome." The girl laughed, swinging her stride to keep up with her companion. She knew there was no man in all Pellucidar as handsome and as brave as her own tall, pale-skinned man!

The party was not to be reunited yet, however—not without encountering new dangers in this hazard-filled land.

The country they traversed was not flat, but cut with innumerable low gullies that often carried streamlets down to the ocean. Red Axe was glad this was so, because the little hills soon cut them off from view of the point at which they had left the jungle, and hopefully would allow them to lose their pursuers.

Elkar and Onoloa had made their way down into one of these little valleys. The grass and reeds were lush and tall at the bottom where there was water, and there was a clump of low thorn trees near the trail. The two had passed the trees and were starting up the slope when a harsh cry made them turn.

Into the trail before Tumu stepped a gigantic bird, one of the fierce hunting fowl of the early age of the surface world. The thing was taller than a man, with huge, powerful legs and talons, and useless diminutive wings. The heavy head ended in a beak over two feet long that was shaped like a falcon's and razor sharp. With this terrible weapon the creature struck at the boy's head, and, though the lad leaped back just in time to avoid it, he felt it tear at the hair of his forelock.

Tumu jabbed at the feathered beast with his spear, causing the thing to give another shrieking squawk. In a moment the vicious bird was surrounded by a yelling circle of humans. The sweeping cuts of that mighty head and beak kept them all at bay. Arrows thudded into the heavily muscled body without result. The creature made a charge at its foes, but they ran nimbly out of the way and were on it again as it turned. Varna finally got a clear shot at an eye as the bird lifted its head for another scimitar-like stroke with the beak, and planted an arrow squarely within its skull. Except for another shrill scream of rage, this too, seemed to have no effect.

Christopher unlimbered the great steel axe that gave him his name. "Keep him busy in front!" he shouted, circling around behind the beast. The others tried to do as instructed, yelling and leaping just in front of the deadly beak. The grass was trampled to the ground and the bird's talons were kicking up a cloud of dust as it made short rushes at the humans. Red Axe closed to strike at a leg, only to be thrown by a mighty kick that sent him tumbling over and over on the grass, half stunned. The bird turned to see what had attacked it and swooped upon him, beak raised for the kill. The American tried to roll out of the way, but came up against a tree stump in the grass. There was no time to get to his feet.

Elkar rushed in behind the monster, swinging his own axe to slash the hamstrings in the massive thigh. The creature fell, screaming defiance, and Red Axe seized the chance to crawl away.

"Christopher, are you hurt?" Varna rushed to his side.

"Just a few bruises, most of them on my pride," he confessed. The others gathered around the kicking and struggling bird, stabbing and chopping it finally into a merciful death.

"When that foot hit you, you actually flew through the air," Varna told him, as Red Axe regained his feet and limped to Elkar's side to clasp his hand in solemn thanks. The partially dismembered *phorohacos* was still twitching. The vitality of prehistoric life never failed to amaze West: the creatures simply refused to acknowledge that they were dead!

"Is this overgrown chicken any good to eat?" he asked the exultant group.

"I don't think so, Christopher," Varna replied. "I have heard that they are tough and bad-flavored. If this is a female, though, there may be eggs in its nest somewhere nearby."

"All right," Red Axe announced. "I think it's time we took a break. The Hapuans and Elkar make camp. The rest spread out and see what you can find."

It was Varna, of course, who discovered the nest, but—alas for Stone Age appetites—the eggs were all hatched and the fledgelings long since departed. The group built a small fire and roasted what was left of the horse meat, their spirits undaunted. They felt they had escaped scot-free from Manu the sea monster, and, as for the perils of this new land, the first of these had been bested with relative ease. There was much laughter and talk. Onoloa quickly joined in, her

naturally cheerful and sunny disposition blossoming now
that she was no longer living in the shadow of a frightful
death. Elkar watched her with wonder and growing adora-
tion, nor was the slim brown girl unaware of the way his
gaze followed her around the campfire.

"I think Elkar's problem may already be solved,
Christopher," whispered Varna to her mate.

"Aye," he replied, "or soon will be. But now it is time to
set watches and rest."

Red Axe allowed the group only a short catnap, however,
and soon had them up on the trail again. The rolling hills
on their left gave way to great open grassy plains, swarming
with prehistoric life. In the distance stood purple and snow-
capped mountains. To their right, the thick tropical jungle
belt they had just left screened the nearby cliffs and the
shore, though they knew the ocean was not far. Gleaming
and blue, it rose gently in the far distance, dotted with dark
green islands, to fade into the intense glare of the eternal
noonday sun.

Red Axe and Elkar conferred briefly on their next destination, and then the pale man led the group along the plain,
skirting the thicker jungle as they sought to rendezvous with
the lost member of their party.

"If we keep on along the coast in this direction," said
Onoloa, beating the thick grasses aside with the handle of
her spear as she kept pace with Elkar, "we will come to the
tribe of Pelan. Tumu and I could find shelter there."

Elkar gave her a startled glance. "But surely you are coming
to Val-an, to Varna's tribe, with us?" He had not detected
the twinkle in her eyes, for she had studiously avoided looking
at him. "With me?" he pleaded.

She smiled and he felt a great weight lifted from his
heart. The thought that this beautiful creature might leave
him after everything he had done for her had not occurred
to him.

Onoloa laughed at his perplexity. "Perhaps I had better

stay with you, after all. The Pelanans file their teeth to points and eat human flesh. It is unlikely that Tumu and I would like it there.

Elkar caught her free hand in his. "And I would never let you go!" he whispered fiercely. Her slim fingers squeezed his in answer to his passion.

"Hey," called Moo-lah from some distance behind them, "are you two paying any attention at all to where you lead us? The rest of us are tired of struggling through this thorn thicket. Surely you can find a path?"

The man and the girl looked back to see the rest of the party was, indeed, picking its way gingerly through the thorny limbs of the close-set trees that they had avoided but not noticed. They both laughed in embarrassment.

"I am sorry, Mooh-lah," Elkar said. "I'll try to find a way better suited to your tender feet!"

"My feet are no more tender than yours," the tailed one retorted. "You are tender in the head!"

The path, when Elkar and Onoloa finally regained it, led them wandering in the fringes of the jungle. In the distance, however, the man thought he recognized the trees that marked the spot he was seeking. The trail wound among cycad palms, dark green and low to the ground, and down into a reed-filled marsh. Here the spoor of big-footed beasts was all around them, and sounds of grunting and snorting deep among the reeds betrayed the presence of some of the trail makers.

The little party of humans slaked their thirst at one of the less muddy pools and hastened across the marsh, anxious not to arouse any of its inhabitants. Red Axe, bringing up the rear as usual, was just congratulating himself on their luck, when, with a long series of rumbling grunts, several denizens of the swamp stepped into the trail behind them.

For a long moment the man and the lead beast regarded each other. Probably, West thought, the same kinds of thoughts were crossing the animal's mind as preoccupied his own. What is it? Is it dangerous? Is it liable to attack? Perhaps even: Is it edible?

The creature was large, gray, and rough-skinned like a rhinoceros. This resemblance was enhanced by the presence of horns, although no self-respecting rhino had ever borne so many. Three pairs of horns adorned the long snout: one pair above the little piglike eyes, another at mid-muzzle, and a final duo above the nostrils. In addition, the brute sported long, downward-curving tusks from its upper jaw. The horns were short and knobby, but looked distinctly businesslike, nonetheless. Thick, splay-toed feet supported a heavy body that ended in a scrawny little tail tufted with long black hair. The creature regarded the man intently, sniffing the air, its ears pricked up to catch the slightest sound. Red Axe gestured behind his back for the others to move on. He took a cautious step backward. His bow was ready in his hand, but an arrow in this monster's thick hide would only make him mad.

There was more crashing among the thick green reeds. Another, and then another gray horned head appeared. The first bull sniffed again, swinging his head from side to side. He pawed the ground, trying to make a decision within that tiny brain.

"Everybody ready to run," Red Axe called softly. "Pick out your trees. When we start, scatter. These guys look fast and mean."

The lead bull grunted and pawed the ground some more, kicking up the rich brown loam. He glanced at his herd mates on either side and finally made his decision. The little bristle-tipped tail came up erect and his pupils dilated.

"Run! Here he comes!"

The humans broke in all directions. Behind them thundered the horned herd. The pursuers had the advantage of weight and size in trampling down the heavier clumps of reeds and bamboos. Two of the big beasts came close on Varna's heels and Red Axe and Tumu fell back, yelling and gesticulating to either side to draw their interest. When the ugly brutes turned toward their new tormenters, they fled, leaping over the thick grasses while yelling and hooting in derision. Clouds of insects swirled up around the passage of the ungainly herd, and a giant pterosaur detached itself from the trees ahead and swooped over the heads of the fugitives. Onoloa cried out and ducked as the winged shadow passed over her, but Elkar grabbed her reassuringly by the arm.

"It is Zed, the one we were looking for," he told her. By this time the entire group was among the trees and scrambling into lower branches as the big gray beasts charged beneath. They circled, snorting and blowing, glaring up at the puny humans now safely ensconced above their heads.

"The other man in your party is a thipdar?" asked Onoloa, as soon as she had made herself comfortable some fifteen feet above the ground.

"Mahar," Elkar replied, "and quite as intelligent as a man." The big winged creature settled itself with much flapping in the tree containing Red Axe. "Actually," the pale man continued, "the Mahars believe themselves to be the rulers of all Pellucidar. I believed so myself, once," he admitted, "but that was before I met Red Axe."

7
THE MAMMOTH HUNTERS

T HERE WAS NO WAY TO ESTIMATE how long the little band of adventurers remained treed by the multihorned herd. When their four-legged captors finally wandered off, the sun was still at zenith, as it had been since the inner world was created. The grass and plants at the foot of the trees were cropped down to the ground in a large circle, which was covered with the droppings of the giant beasts. The humans above had trimmed the branches of their trees and built crude platforms that enabled them to sleep. A true Pellucidarian never rolls over in his or her sleep; a careless move like that could drop the sleeper out of the protecting trees and into the jaws of a waiting predator.

Zed had flown some of the equipment into the trees, and the great pterosaur and Red Axe had an opportunity to discuss their recent adventures and future plans. The winged reptile was still interested in accompanying the growing band of gilaks on their wanderings. Sitting on a branch beside the man it had befriended, the creature wrote laboriously on a pad with a ballpoint pen.

"There are too many scientific marvels to unravel, and you hold the key to many of them—the mysteries of sound and of the reception of sound in communication, for example." The Mahars, the most technologically advanced race of the inner world, were all deaf. Zed, a scientist, had made the first study of sound waves in the history of Mahar science, with the help of Red Axe, once a lab assistant in a

neuroscience laboratory on the surface world. The phenomenon of human communication by sound waves fascinated
the pterosaur as much as the apparently telepathic communication of the Mahars fascinated the man.

"When we reach the safety of Varna's Val-an tribe," Red
Axe wrote to his strange companion, perhaps with unjustifi-
able optimism about the challenges of that journey, "we
can start some new experiments for you. We can get small
pieces of apparatus from the earth borer site back there
beyond the swamp, as long as you can fly them from there
to the mountains."

"A good plan," the Mahar wrote in return. "You, at the
same time, can continue to study Mahar communication.
I know you have an interest in that, as I do in human
communication."

The man looked at the reptile, but the huge eyes and
beaked face revealed no emotion he could read. He had
never had any reason to doubt the trustfulness of this creature,
however.

"Yes, ever since the day the electrical spark discharge in
your laboratory back in Phuma caused such consternation
among the Mahars," he admitted.

"Your long-distance communication device also causes
me to react," the pterosaur wrote. "Does it function like an
electrical discharge?"

"No," Red Axe replied, "but both emit long wavelength
energy." He tried to communicate to the reptile a description of the electromagnetic spectrum and the nature of
radio waves. The creature had an unusually brilliant mind,
even for that intelligent race, and was quick to grasp the
ideas the surface man was proposing, despite the clumsiness
of their communication and the man's limited vocabulary
in the written language of the Mahars. West, his own
scientific imagination aroused, was elated to find his original
speculations about the mysterious mental language of
the bizarre creatures who ruled most of Pellucidar might

be confirmed. On the outer crust creatures were known who were sensitive to ultraviolet, infrared, and even X-radiation, but no naturally occurring radio-wave organs had even been described.

The two oddly paired scientists pored over their tablets, the tall, winged beast writing alternately with foot or with its slender wing fingers, the muscular, seminude human, his long blond hair falling about his intent face, sitting beside him, his legs dangling over the circling brutes at the foot of the tree. Varna had to rouse the two from their discussion to eat the last of the dried meat they had carried up into the trees during their escape.

"A few simple test implements would be all we need to measure the radio-wave output from your head," Red Axe wrote, "and a variable transmitter might put me into direct contact with you on your own wavelength."

"It would be an exciting experiment. The Mahar organ of telepathic speech is so underdeveloped in lower forms," Zed replied, automatically including in this category its friend from the surface. It was arranged that the Mahar would fly to the earth borer terminal to pick up the instruments.

"Do you really think you can train me to project my thoughts as you do?" Red Axe asked the pterosaur. "It would please me to be in closer contact with the mind of one I have come to think of as a friend and ally."

"It would please me as well," the creature wrote back. "I have felt friendship for you since you first appeared in our laboratory at Phuma. It is most unusual for one of the superior race to feel any affection for a member of a lower order like yourself." Red Axe smiled when he read this. It was hard for Zed to break its old habits of thought. "But," continued the Mahar in writing, "I do harbor such feelings toward you—perhaps related to the fact that we are male and female."

"What?" Red Axe scribbled on the bottom of the sheet.

"Christopher, what is it? What did he say?" Varna asked, watching her mate's face.

West read the extended missive the Mahar handed him before replying. "Well," he said to the young woman, "I don't know why I'm surprised, but I must admit I am. He says he's a she."

Varna let out a merry laugh. "Oh Christopher, your face looked like it was the most terrible news in Pellucidar."

"It's just a surprise," the man said. Like most reptiles, the Mahar had no visible external reproductive organs, so there had been no reason to think of it as either male or female, but he had gotten into the habit of referring to the creature as "he."

"Listen, Varna," he said, reading from the tablet as Zed continued to write, "it's even more surprising. She says there are no male Mahars at all, and that there haven't been for many generations."

"No males?" the girl asked. "But we saw a whole room filled with their eggs in the buried city. Zed herself said one of the eggs was hers. What does she mean?"

"I can't understand all the details yet," the man replied. "We've run out of words again, but apparently the Mahars have perfected a method of parthenogenesis, a way of fertilizing the eggs without the involvement of a male. All the males of the species died off—or perhaps they were killed—I'm not sure. The artificially fertilized eggs produce only females. The race has been without sex for longer than any member of it can remember!"

"Humph!" Varna grunted, and then her eyes twinkled. "Perhaps that's why she is so anxious to have you learn the mind speech. She probably thinks there's a lot you could teach her!"

"Varna darling, I don't think Zed is really my type."

When the group of humans descended from their treetop refuge to continue their journey, the great pterosaur flew off down the ocean coast to pick up the new radio instruments.

Red Axe hesitated a moment before separating himself from his winged ally, but there was no logical reason to delay getting the equipment. He had to trust Zed's natural caution not to get caught in any trap the Mahars might have set up at the spot where the disintegration apparatus had broken through the crust from the earth's surface. It occurred to him that he might need the creature's help before she could return to him, for there was no way to predict what new adventure he would find in a world inhabited exclusively by ferocious beasts and savage men. As a matter of fact, his next encounter with the strange denizens of the prehistoric inner world was unexpectedly soon.

The way to Val-an lay across the great plains with their herds of teeming game, in the opposite direction from the seacoast. The little band of humans made its way cautiously through the lush green grass, zigzagging to avoid the larger beasts, the towering *megatherium*, looming above the treetops; the herds of *titanotheres* with their short tempers; the gigantic hairy mammoths; the hulking ground sloths, many of them over ten feet high; the giant bears, almost as large; and other monsters too numerous to list.

As a precaution against predators—the saber-toothed tiger, the giant bear, or the winged terror of the sky, the ferocious thipdar—Red Axe angled their line of march so as to be as close as possible to climbable trees at all times. Often they had to sprint to the safety of the trees as one of the other inhabitants of the prehistoric world took exception to their presence. In general, however, they kept on toward a series of snow-capped mountain peaks in the near distance. Somewhere beyond these, Varna's homing instinct told her, lay the hunting grounds of her tribe.

Many miles away, events were transpiring that were to drastically alter the lives of Red Axe and his followers. At the edge of the jungle belt that bordered the cliffs overlooking the sea, a troop of Hapuan warriors stood in perplexed argument. The thirty-odd men, armed with long wooden spears, gazed out over the green, tree-dotted plains with suspicion. Bold seafarers all, they did not hesitate to risk attacking the whale or the plesiosaur from their fragile outrigger canoes, but they feared to set out on what now appeared to be a forced march across open country populated with herds of unknown beasts.

"We have gone far enough." One of the men voiced the common consensus. He stepped forward, tall and muscular, the lobes of his ears adorned with huge shell circles, a necklace of giant shark's teeth hanging low about his brown throat. The arm that brandished his barbed spear was scarred from battles with the monsters of the deep. "Let them go on into the wild country. None of them will survive. I say we return to the caves of Hapu."

"Fools!" cried the old priest who stood among them. "Fools, to defy the will of Manu, lord of the ocean! No fish will fill your nets, no wave will carry you to safety across the guardian reef. The Lord of the Sea will deny his people."

The men muttered uncertainly among themselves.

"We all saw the god refuse the body of the girl Onoloa. If great Manu had wanted them, he could have captured them easily on the beach when they were within his grasp. Perhaps the will of the god is one thing, the cries of an offended priest quite another."

"Who speaks?" the white-haired one shrieked. "Who dares to challenge my word? May the curse of Manu strike you!"

The men grumbled more openly. Finally the tall warrior who had spoken earlier addressed them again.

"Let the priest Apu do what he wishes. My kinsmen and I will return to the tribe now. It is not well that the beaches of Hapu be left so long unguarded." He walked determinedly back down the trail and into the vine-covered shadows of the jungle. About half the group followed him immediately; the others hesitated, some looking at Apu to see what he would do. The old man watched the mutiny with disbelief.

Since he had been a young and beardless youth the spiritual leadership of the tribe had been his. The magnitude of his loss had not yet dawned on him. All his power over his people was being stripped away as each man turned and, without so much as a backward glance, strode off into the jungle. The last three, after a hesitant look at the old man's face, gathered up their weapons and hurried after the rest of the party. Old Apu stood like a statue, leaning a little on his staff. The last man turned and saw him there, the wind from the hills blowing his long white hair and beard around his face, his eyes cold and strong with rage. The tribe of Hapu was never to see or hear of him again. His power destroyed, his people disillusioned and deserting, there burned now within him a new passion. No longer did he crave the power he had enjoyed from his people. Now he craved only revenge, both against the girl and against her companions who had defied and destroyed him. After a long while he turned back to the trail. He was no hunter, as it was not necessary for the priest of Manu to hunt or fish, and their trail was impossible for him to see. The path, however, was obvious here and he followed it, having no idea whether it took him toward his quarry or not.

The game herds were on the move. A vague apprehension seemed to pervade the plain. A herd of giant mammoths milled about, the calves squealing beneath the cows' legs. A number of huge tapir-like creatures loped up from the tall grass and thundered off into the nearest gully where the brush and small trees could be heard splintering and smashing. Red Axe directed his band toward the nearest stand of trees, these being thorned mimosas, and with some difficulty they ascended the rough-barked trunk of the largest of them.

Mooh-lah sniffed the air. "Nothing upwind of us," he reported thoughtfully. "*Ta-ho, tandor, ryth, dyryth,* nothing more," he said, naming the Pellucidarian lion, mammoth, cave bear, and sloth. "Ah, wait!" The monkey-man's nose worked furiously and Varna joined him in sniffing the breeze. "Yes, it is as I feared."

The girl looked at him and nodded. "Maybe they will pass us by," she said hopefully.

"What is it, you two?" asked West, whose nose told him only that a great number of animals were living, digesting, and, in all probability, dying and rotting upwind. "This whole plain is so filled with animal scent I can't pick out any single one."

"Man," said Mooh-lah shortly.

Red Axe grunted in surprise and dismay. He and the other five scanned the grassland for any sign of the intruders, but for a while they watched in vain. West considered ordering them all down out of their refuge and across the veldt. The herd of mammoths had wandered close to the tree, however, and were stamping and muttering only a few paces away. Nervous and edgy, they might easily charge if they saw the humans running away.

"I think there may be more than one party," Varna ventured, turning slowly about the bole of their tree, one slim brown arm encircling it as she tested the air first in one direction, then another.

"In that case, if we try to run we may find ourselves among them," concluded her mate.

"Aye," agreed the tailed man, "and we do not know whether the men we smell are hunters or more of the hunted."

"Ah, I hadn't thought of that."

Mooh-lah's speculations proved wrong, however. Shortly thereafter, half a dozen big mammoths came charging across the plain, and on their backs the American could see human riders, a number of them apparently clinging to the rough coat of each of the beasts. The herd of wild mammoths seemed about to flee when another group of hunters on mammoth-back appeared from the opposite direction and spread out in a thin line as if to cut them off. Before the wild beasts could make up their minds how to cope with this new menace the attack was upon them.

With wild yells the mammoth riders leaped from the backs of their gigantic mounts. Leaving only one or two men behind with their own beasts they rushed upon the wild herd. The big bulls turned to face them, herding the cows and calves behind. The massive hairy heads and trunks tossed and turned, the great curved tusks brushing the ground. The attackers capered about before the herd's defenders, yelling and gesticulating wildly. They were armed with spears and great stone axes that they waved and brandished in heroic display. Red Axe noticed, however, that the hunters were careful to stay out of the reach of the big brutes, and that when a bull mammoth charged, as several of them did, their tormentors were quick to flee from their path.

Meanwhile, the second group had also dismounted and approached the herd from the rear. The attention of the mammoths was entirely directed toward the men in front of them. Now the purpose of this elaborate maneuver became apparent, for the second—and more silent and stealthy—group carried long rawhide nooses. With these, they managed to snare several of the baby mammoths before the herd realized what they were about. Soon wild squeals from the young ones alerted the mothers, however, and the daring primitive hunters were confronted by the enraged cows, who needed no further evidence of ill intent toward their shaggy offspring. Each noose had two long pull ropes attached to it, and the men on either end, by dancing back and forth, managed to elude the attack of the females while maintaining some hold on their captives.

At this moment one of the big bull mammoths trumpeted a mighty scream, and Red Axe turned to see what had excited him. Daring the flailing trunk and flashing tusks, one of the stalwart attackers had rushed in close to the monster and cut the tendons in his hind leg just above the knee. The beast plunged forward on three legs, but his tormentor had fled backward, avoiding the clumsy charge. Immediately another fur-clad savage, this one armed with a long-handled stone axe, closed in on the other side. A swift attack, two overhand blows with the huge axe, and the mammoth was hamstrung on that side as well. The great shaggy beast fell ponderously on its haunches. Now other hunters closed in, long lances flashing in the sunlight, as the mighty beast trumpeted one final crescendo of defiance. Then the great tusked head was down, the killers, dwarfed by the bulk of their prey, plunging their lances again into the carcass. They raised a shout of triumph.

The little group in the tree watched as three more of the great bull mammoths were crippled and dispatched. The scream of the wounded animals made the air hideous. One big beast eluded the first assault and seized his attacker in his trunk, swung him over his head and hurled him twenty yards. Before the injured man's companions could rescue him, the mammoth charged forward and knelt on his body with both forelegs, crushing the life from the broken body.

The bull's triumph was short. A circle of shouting hunters formed about him, scattering before him each time he charged, then closing in again as he paused to rest. It was only minutes before the daring axe-men, rushing in while those armed with lances feinted to the front, had hamstrung the beast and brought it crashing to the earth.

Eight of the big bulls and cows had been killed and four baby mammoths had been lassoed and dragged, squealing, from the herd. The survivors of the herd finally made a concerted charge, carrying the rest of the calves with them in the middle of a stampeding, trumpeting mass of terror, out of the trap and out across the plain. The hunters let them go.

Now the victors danced about the mighty bodies of their kill. Parties climbed onto each carcass in turn, crying boastfully, reliving the triumph.

Red Axe crouched in his tree, surveying the scene of battle and carnage below.

"Mooh-lah?"

"Yes?"

"Do they look like they are about to leave?"

The monkey-man grunted noncommittally, then answered slowly. "Look, Red Axe, they are starting to skin them."

"You're right."

"They're going to be here a long time."

The group in the treetop settled themselves to wait. The mammoth hunters went slowly about their work, skinning the great fallen beasts with flint knives and butchering them. Three large fires were built and haunches of meat were roasted. Chunks of cooked meat were distributed to the working parties and to the men guarding the tame mammoths a short distance away. To the distress of the treed companions, the odor of roasted meat filled the air. Red Axe felt himself becoming not only hungry, but also thirsty.

"Varna," he whispered, "how long do you think we can stand it without food or drink?"

"My stomach feels very empty already," the girl replied, "and the dried meat is all gone."

There were, however, parties of the hunters on both sides of the trees now, and descending without observation was obviously impossible.

"We've got more important problems than your woman's stomach," whispered Mooh-lah from the branch above.

"Nothing is more important than my stomach," hissed Varna. "What's bothering you, monkey-man?"

"The scavengers are beginning to gather," said Mooh-lah. "Beyond the mammoth herd I can see the *jaloks** moving in the heavy grass. And I guess you hungry ones have been watching your stomach and not the sky."

Red Axe looked up. There were always flying creatures

---

* Hyaenodons.

visible in the Pellucidarian blue, but his tailed companion
was right. The air above them was filled with circling winged
creatures: carrion birds, flying lizards, and pterodactyls of all
sizes, drawn by the slaughter on the ground. The hyaenodons
that Mooh-lah had referenced were no threat as long as the
party stayed in the trees, of course—nor was West sure they
would attack an armed band of humans on the ground. The
flying creatures, however, were already starting to settle in
the uppermost branches of the thorn trees.

"Down into the lower branches," he hissed. Fortunately
the foliage was thick enough to shield them from the
mammoth hunters. Tiny pterodactyls, about the size of
sparrows but with ferocious teeth, flashed in and out of the
grove and flapped in the faces of the humans as they descended cautiously to the lower levels. The vicious little
reptiles screeched and whistled as they flew by, and Red Axe
could only hope that they would cease their unwelcomed
attentions as soon as they all stopped moving about. Onoloa
cried out suddenly. Elkar reached her first. A foot-long
purplish pterodactyl had seized her arm and sunk its tiny
fangs into her shoulder. The big man plucked the flying devil
from his loved one's flesh to wring its neck.

Red Axe crouched on the lower branch, peering through
the leaves at the men on the plain below. None of them
seemed to have heard the girl's cry. Several of the mammoth
carcasses had been stripped now and abandoned by the
hunters. Clouds of the flying carnivores—bat-winged, partially feathered, and fully pinioned scavengers—descended
as soon as the men left, and in places the dead mammoths
were hidden by the moving swarms of birdlike creatures.
The sound of their screaming and squawking had drowned
out Onoloa's cry.

Now the larger flying reptiles were descending, some with
wingspans of up to six feet. Three larger pterosaurs drove
the smaller scavengers off the carcasses. The pterodactyls
avoided the large fires, however, where most of the hunters

had now gathered. Red Axe and his companions were now forced to sit silently and watch while the men below gorged themselves on roast mammoth, occasionally swatting away the more aggressive of the flying reptiles.

"Good lord," grunted West, "it looks like they will never finish." Some of the mammoth hunters remained around the fires eating, but many of them now gathered on the freshly skinned hides, and, with a few remaining on guard, fell asleep. To the distress of the six in the thorn tree, the group chose the grassy slope right in front of their hiding place to nap. Over the carcasses of the slain animals the scavengers continued to alight in an almost continuous stream. From the plain beyond came the barking and howling of the four-footed carrion eaters, but the broad-shouldered hunters took no notice.

Red Axe settled himself as comfortably as he could, wishing they had chosen a tree unencumbered with thorns. He and Varna straddled a branch and he cautiously leaned his bare back against the tree trunk, avoiding the barbs with which it was irregularly covered. The girl slumped against his chest. Mooh-lah crouched on the same limb beside them, patiently watching the men on the ground. Despite the heat, discomfort, and his hunger and thirst, Red Axe dozed off.

He was awakened by something falling with a crash into the tree. Onoloa cried out. Mooh-lah was up in an instant, bare knife blade in his hand.

"How . . . ?"

"Something lands above. One of the flying creatures." The tree shook. "Must be a big one," the tailed man observed coolly.

There were shouts from the ground. Apparently whatever had landed in the tree had attracted the attention of the mammoth hunters.

"Here they come," whispered Varna. "They're sure to see us if they come under the tree." There was more squawking and commotion from the upper reaches. Red Axe peered upward. A twisted shape fell from the greenery, glanced off their tree limb, and fluttered to the ground amid bits of broken branches. Mangled, bloody, with smashed wings, it was the remains of one of the larger pterodactyls. The tree continued to shake. Elkar's voice cried out in warning and one of the strangers on the ground shouted a question which they did not heed. Then, sliding down the tree trunk, its wings folded along its back, came one of the ugliest denizens of Pellucidar that West had ever seen. The creature's body was four or five feet long and four taloned feet grasped the tree. It descended headfirst and the long tail coiled sinuously around the limbs above. The head was lizard-like and pointed at the snout. Great, round golden eyes gleamed lidlessly and the slit-shaped pupils widened and narrowed with the beast's emotions as its glance slid over the three humans.

"Red Axe!" Elkar's voice sounded urgently from above. "Cry out if it attacks, and we will try to pin down its hind-quarters with our spears."

The monster seemed to hesitate, torn between pursuit of the fallen pterodactyl and these strange new creatures in the tree.

"Don't move," warned Mooh-lah. "Maybe it will pass us by."

"Good God," said Varna softly in English, and then added in Pellucidarian, "I hope so."

The green-gray apparition paused in its descent at the junction of tree trunk and branch. The three humans confronted it, balancing on the thick limb. Under the beast's chin a yellow fold of scaled skin pulsed in and out. After what seemed to the American an eternity of waiting and watching those inhuman eyes, the beast opened its jaws. The gums and palate were pale pink, as was the long, forked tongue that slithered out as if testing the air in their direction. More terrifying, though, were a set of foot-long fangs that descended from the upper jaw as if hinged back against the roof of the mouth. As these fearsome weapons swung down and forward into position, a swollen gland at the root of each tooth exuded a drop of heavy liquid, like honey, which ran slowly down the deadly white length of the fangs. Red Axe felt his heart skip a beat, but he was the primitive chieftain of his band, and his mate stood behind him on the tree limb.

"Ready, Elkar," he called calmly.

The monster made a hissing sound and came at him, bringing both forelimbs around and down on the limb. West swung his axe in a carefully controlled blow, severing one of those deadly appearing incisors close to the root and sending it flying out into space. There was a crashing above as the three on the branch overhead attacked the hind quarter of the flying lizard. Varna knelt, strung her bow, and, shooting around Red Axe's legs, put an arrow through the beast's palate and the side of his head.

Elkar's cries grew more furious. Whatever he was doing seemed to penetrate the reptilian brain, and the creature turned to go back up the tree toward its tormentors. Red Axe closed, striking at the junction of head and neck, trying to sever the spinal cord.

Elkar's voice cried, "Watch out!" A furious, thrashing snakelike coil fell from the leaves above and encircled Red Axe's chest and shoulders. The force of the blow staggered him, and he stumbled and fell from the tree.

The branches below caught him for a moment, then broke off close to the tree trunk. Bending with the weight of man and lizard tail, it formed a leafy, thorn-studded incline, down which the man and his opponent rolled gently to the grass. The living tail was still coiling and uncoiling reflexively around him, but its strength was weakening and Red Axe was able to strip the thing from his body. Regaining his feet, he cast the ghastly, writhing appendage onto the ground.

"Ho! Well done, stranger."

Over a dozen fur-clad hunters had gathered around him. The speaker was barely five feet tall, broad of chest and shoulder, his dark brown hair pulled back into a pigtail decorated with a knotted thong. He was barefoot and clad only in a wide breechclout. A necklace of carved ivory beads hung about his neck and he carried a six-foot axe with a flint blade. Dark brown eyes surveyed Red Axe from under bushy eyebrows that met over the bridge of a flat wide nose. The man grinned, revealing a set of wide-spaced yellow teeth. He gestured with his free arm. "Here comes the rest of it," he chuckled.

Red Axe whirled. The beast had reached the ground behind him. Its tail had been lopped off to a bloody stump, one fang had been cut away, it was bleeding from several axe cuts, and two of Varna's arrows were still sticking out of its neck. Despite this, the monster seemed less daunted than enraged. The ugly pink maw gaped to reveal the remaining poisonous fang, as, hissing with fury, it rushed at its enemy. West scrambled unsuccessfully in the grass for his axe, rising at the last moment to sidestep the beast's attack.

The dragon creature turned, its purplish wings now half spread, slit pupils dilated with fury and pain from its wounds. The man was still empty-handed. The creature clawed the ground. Wings flapping, it began to rise clumsily in the air, hissing all the while like a steam kettle. Beneath its talons, the dismayed West saw his axe buried in the thick green grass. Farther up the slope the mammoth hunter sensed his consternation.

"Ho, Yellow Hair!" he shouted. "Methinks you'll need a weapon. Catch!" He hurled his great stone-bladed axe like a massive javelin almost straight at the astonished American. Red Axe caught it by the thick wooden haft and a moment later the monster was over his head. He dodged the flailing claws and ran out from beneath the beast as it strove to crush him to the ground. Turning, he swung the flint axe at a wing, tearing the membrane. The primitive weapon was longer than his own, but the shaft was well balanced and the black blade had been chipped to a razor sharpness.

Red Axe turned and circled beneath his opponent, trying to keep out of reach of those poisonous jaws. The leathery wings flapped and beat as the beast twisted and turned in midair to get at him. It was still bleeding from the amputation of its tail, but its vitality seemed unchanged. Again and again Red Axe slashed at the limbs or wings without effect. He could hear shouts of encouragement from his own followers, as well as from the mammoth hunters. A rough-clawed forepaw seized his shoulder, but he pulled away as the injured head struck downward. Running beneath the monster he swung upward with the axe. Catching the breastbone and then carrying his blow down into the abdomen, he ran under the creature while holding the axe above his head, slashing through the tough lizard hide. Entrails spilled out onto the ground. West jerked his borrowed axe free, ran beyond the tailless rump, and turned, weapon still at a double-handed guard. The creature had fallen to the ground in a pool of gore, writhing in its final agony.

By the time the rest of his party had reached the ground, Red Axe confronted at least twenty of the armed but quiet hunters. They were all tough, brown, and brawny, like the one who seemed to be their leader. They wore a variety of necklaces, bracelets, and hair ornaments of carved ivory, but were otherwise clad only in strips of furry hide around their loins.

The first man held out his right hand to Red Axe imperiously. Reluctantly he returned the flint axe. His own weapon, he noted, had already been retrieved by several of the hunters who were now examining it with interest.

"Well fought, Yellow Hair," said the axe owner. "Now your people will yield their weapons and we will take you to the camp of the mammoth hunters."

"Suppose we do not wish to go?" inquired Red Axe.

"Then my warriors will fall upon you with their spears and axes. We will cut off your heads and carry them to our chief, but then he will not be able to converse with you."

The short brown man grinned. "I think you would rather talk to the chief yourself."

Red Axe smiled back. "We have been sitting in the trees so long that if we do not drink and eat we may not be able to talk to anybody, headless or not."

"We have plenty of food," the hunter replied. "Throw down your weapons and we will let you eat." Red Axe looked at his followers.

Mooh-lah grunted. "I'm too hungry to fight, anyway."

Varna nodded. "For once I agree with the ugly monkey-man."

Reluctantly Red Axe let his party be disarmed. After they had eaten and drunk from a nearby stream, their hands were bound loosely behind them with rawhide thongs. They were unceremoniously hoisted onto the backs of several of the big woolly mammoths. The hunters loaded the other beasts with fresh meat and hides, along with the dead man, now carefully rolled in the hide of the mammoth that had killed him.

Each of the squealing baby mammoths was held down by a gang of men so that a thick hide harness could be fitted over its back and shoulders. Straps from either side of this were then attached to shoulder harnesses on two of the domesticated adults, so that the little one walked between a pair of mammoths and could be led or even dragged if he tried to escape.

"They must capture and train the young ones," Red Axe whispered to Varna as they sat astride one of the bigger mammoths, now contentedly pulling up grass by the trunkful and stuffing it into its mouth as it waited for the rest to be loaded.

The leader of the band climbed onto the shoulder of his mammoth—a huge black-haired male—and stood erect, raising his axe above his head. "Ho!" he roared. The other hunters hastened to their mammoths. The driver, or rider, mounted the beast on which Varna and Red Axe were seated.

More bundles of meat and hides were pulled up and slung behind the prisoners.

"Ha!" yelled the leader. With a rolling motion, the herd of hairy beasts set out across the open plain. The animals' backs were broad enough, and their speed slow enough, that riding with their hands bound behind them was no particular discomfort.

"What do you think they'll do with us?" Varna asked her mate.

"They seem to have a sense of fair play," he replied optimistically. "Perhaps we can bargain with them." He hoped that these primitive hunters, like the nomadic tribes of his own world, might live by a strict code of honor, and, once strangers had eaten with them they might be treated with respect.

8
BLOOD OATH

THE MAMMOTH MEN'S encampment was a surprise. Log palisades and fortifications of packed earth surrounded it, and the entrance was through a narrow gate that led between mounded hills of earth lined with tree trunks. Lookouts atop the wall spotted the approaching hunters and cries of recognition and welcome split the air. The party had to enter the gate in single file, the laden pack-mammoths almost touching the reinforced sides of the approach tunnel.

The camp was large and became increasingly noisy once they were inside. Crowds of women and children gathered about and the party moved only slowly toward a cleared area in the center of the palisade. The dwellings were crude, partially excavated hovels with frames over them to support roofs and sides of hide. Red Axe noticed with a start that while some of the framework was logs, much of it was made of ivory mammoth tusks!

The women of the tribe were like the men in appearance. All were short and heavy, none over five feet in height, and their flat faces were vaguely Asian in appearance. In addition to the dark hair on their heads, which they wore in long braids, their limbs and faces were covered with a finer coat of hair, several shades lighter in color. Most of the women and older children wore knee-length smocks of tanned hide as well as a variety of ivory, bone, and stone ornaments. Here inside the camp the people were barefoot. The hard, reddish-brown soil was well trampled by the mammoths, as well as liberally covered with their droppings.

The prisoners and the butchered mammoths were unloaded in the central square of the encampment. Off to one side the body of the dead hunter was gently and reverently lowered to the ground. There a quiet crowd gathered, but no keening or crying could be heard. After a time, the corpse was carried off by what appeared to be the family of the deceased. The group passed close by and Red Axe had an opportunity to see their face—three women, half a dozen children, and a gray-haired oldster. The women and younger children were weeping silently, but the old man and two young boys were dry-eyed and grim-faced as they carried their mournful burden on a litter shoulder high. The crowd parted before them and then closed up behind.

The rest of the mammoth hunters were certainly not silent. Squawking infants and chattering, rotund females crowded around the strangers, questioning their captors and eyeing them with humor and curiosity but no hostility.

Onoloa and her brother were recognized by their coloring as belonging to the "ocean people," but the tall, light-haired males and the statuesque dark female were obviously not familiar, and the tall, slender man with the prehensile tail was a total novelty!

Once again the short, bowlegged leader of the hunting party presented himself. His heavy eyebrows met in a line across his wrinkled forehead. He still clasped the gigantic stone axe with its six-foot haft, and he leaned on this as he contemplated his charges.

"Greetings," offered West. "We're ready to have our hands untied now."

A big grin split the prehistoric man's face, revealing his teeth. "You speak like a bull tandor before his first herd fight," he conceded. "Come now, we will see the great chief."

The great chief was old enough to be grizzled and getting fat, but most of his squat frame was obviously muscle, and he had a certain dignity that was not inappropriate. His name was Mow, and he had only one arm—the left. The other ended in a stump just below the shoulder, obviously the reminder of some past battle, but he wore a robe of bearskin that kept it covered most of the time. Mow ignored the strangers and gave his attention to his captain, who told of their capture in detail. The chief sat above them on a tall chair made of great curving tusks and cushioned with fur. Red Axe looked around as the story was being told. The chief's hall—it was too big to be called a hut—was twelve to fifteen feet high and fairly brightly illuminated by the noonday Pellucidarian sun through a series of smoke holes in the roof. Scattered about the wide dirt floor were the fires that necessitated these smoke holes, and crouching about them were men, women, and children. It was difficult to tell if these represented the chief's family or his retainers. Only later did West learn that the chief had twenty-five wives. Most of these, however, had secondary husbands and appeared to function within the family unit more as daughters and sons-in-law. There were so many terms for family relationships in the language of the mammoth hunters that the American never fully understood them all.

The axe-carrying captain gave a long-winded account of the hunt and his triumphs, with the apprehension of Red Axe and his band as an addendum. The chief now inspected each of the prisoners with interest.

"I demand to know why the warriors of Mow have captured us," said Red Axe, taking a step forward toward the chief's throne. Two burly guards kept pace with him and seized him by the shoulders, one on either side.

"You all appear useless to me," said Mow gravely, hardly bothering to look in the American's direction.

"Good, then we will bid you farewell and continue on our journey."

The chief grunted, but it did not sound like an assent. He leaned forward in his ivory throne. "The males might be of some use working on the walls or in the pits," he grumbled, "but the women are too tall and stringy. Throw the females out."

Red Axe was about to protest when he felt the unmistakable sawing of his wrist fetters with a stone knife. As the rawhide straps fell away, he cried out.

"Wait, Chief Mow, there is one more thing you need to consider!"

The chief shifted his gaze directly toward the younger man. Deep-set under a heavy, overhanging forehead, his eyes were shining black dots. "Yes, what do you mean?"

Red Axe seized the man on his right. There was a gasp from the crowd in the hut. Before the man could act, West had swung him off his feet, around in front of his former prisoner, and slammed him into the guard on the left. They both fell into a heap. Before they could scramble to their feet, Red Axe had disarmed them of their flint axes and stepped back. He took a moment to look behind him. He caught a glimpse of Mooh-lah, a stone knife still clutched in two turns of his prehensile tail, busily cutting the others free. Instantly, however, they were surrounded by a crowd of armed men, brandishing spears, axes, and stone knives.

"Hold!" cried Red Axe, threatening those before him with a captured axe. "Mow, call off your men and we will yield without bloodshed." The younger man was gambling on what he felt to be the old chief's willingness to use people rather than kill them outright and the obvious fact that he and his band were outnumbered ten to one and trapped in the center of a hostile encampment.

Mow roared an order above the din and the room fell silent.

"Speak stranger, before my warriors tear you to pieces."

"Mow is wise," replied Red Axe. "We cannot fight free, but we will take many of his brave hunters with us before we die. Mow needs workers. We will agree to work willingly for him if he treats us as men. Return our weapons and allow our mates to stay with us. In return, we will obey the chief of the mammoth hunters."

"He lies, O Chief," cried one of the men Red Axe had disarmed. He had drawn the flint knife he carried in his loincloth and he brandished it now in his right hand. "They are helpless before the weapons of Mow. Let us cut them to pieces!"

"Talk is easy when you are surrounded by your brothers," Red Axe challenged. "Dare you meet me man to man?" A cry of approval went up from the milling throng of savages.

"Give me back my own knife," the American demanded, gesturing toward the back of the hall where the captives' possessions had been brought. The chief of the mammoth men gestured with his one arm and the strangers' weapons were located and brought before him. He fumbled among them and extracted a belt with a sheath knife attached and threw it to the young man.

Red Axe discarded the stone axe he had been holding and stepped cautiously forward on the hard-packed earth before the chief's throne. He unsnapped the safety strap on the long-bladed steel hunting knife, holding the handle in his right hand and the sheath in his left. His challenger rushed forward, arms wide, his eight-inch flint blade poised for the thrust. Red Axe dodged his first attack and circled, forcing the spectators to draw back and give the combatants more room.

The blond giant had the reach on his broad-shouldered opponent, but the brawny caveman was fast, experienced, and determined. The flint knife, sharp as broken glass, swung perilously close to West's body. Fortunately, there was little science to his attack; it was all rush and slash. West was forced back again and again. He was reluctant to kill his opponent, and had hoped to terminate the bout without bloodshed. The ferocity of the mammoth man's attack, however, seemed to make this objective unobtainable.

The muscular tribesman rushed in repeatedly, trying to

grapple with his elusive opponent. Despite Red Axe's size, the man believed he could maim him with his hands if he could just catch him. The knife seemed less important, especially as the blond man did not seem to be using his. In his eagerness to close with his wary adversary, the mammoth man rushed once too often and too wildly. West hit him a fast sharp blow with his left fist that staggered him and then came up under the shorter man's chin with his right, the hand weighted with the knife, in a vicious uppercut that lifted the stocky body up off the ground and sent chief Mow's champion tumbling unconscious to the dirt. Red Axe stepped over the prostrate body and took the stone knife from the limp fingers.

As he straightened up, Red Axe looked into the eyes of the chief.

"I will not kill him," he said. A gasp of disbelief and astonishment arose from the crowd around him. Mow leaned forward in his ivory seat, staring at the stranger. "He is a brave man and a good warrior," said West, "and I would have him live to hunt and fight for Mow's people again." The chief grunted what sounded almost like an assent.

"Coward!" cried a voice behind Red Axe.

A flat-nosed man with a scar over one eye pushed his way to the front. In one hand he held the long-handled stone axe of the mammoth hunter, in the other a knife of carved bone, broad-bladed and heavy. A half smile distorted his ugly face. "The stranger fears the wrath of the warriors— friends and family of Nota," he snarled. "Let us have him, O Chief, and we will teach him the meaning of fear."

Red Axe looked around the room. The armed savages had closed in upon his friends, and although they had not as yet attacked, the menace in their faces and postures was clear. The chief's face, meanwhile, was impassive, and yet, a moment later, he spoke to the new challenger.

"Mow does not recall that you were family or friend to Nota, Batu," he said. The sarcasm was thick in his voice.

"You know the law: a life for a life. The stranger spares Nota's life; perhaps as Nota's newfound friend you wish to give yours in his place?"

West stood his ground, unmoving. The interplay between Batu and the chief was not clear to him and he did not know how to play his hand. His companions grouped behind him.

"We are all armed, Red Axe," whispered Elkar. "Even Tumu and his pair of knives. Say the word and we'll fight our way out of here."

"Wait a moment and see what happens."

"Nota loses honor by being overthrown by the stranger," Batu insisted. Stepping before the chief's throne, the ugly mammoth hunter turned to address the crowd. "The honor of the tribe is dragged into the mire. Only blood can wash clean again the mammoth tusks that hold up the roof of the chief's hut. If he cannot do it, there are men here who can. I modestly indicate myself!"

There were a few cheers and laughter and some rude noises from the onlookers. Fortunately, at this moment, Nota chose to regain consciousness and sit up.

"Where am I?" he grunted, feeling a lump of bruise beginning on his jaw.

While Batu continued his harangue of the crowd, Red Axe whispered a few instructions to his followers and stepped to the fallen man's side.

"Batu seeks to bring honor to himself by avenging your downfall," he said in a low voice. He lifted the man to his feet. The savage was more alert now, and although he held one hand to his jaw, he listened to what Red Axe was saying.

"Ho, Yellow Hair," he muttered to Red Axe, "how did you knock me down so easily with your hand?"

This is a hell of a time to give boxing lessons, West thought, but it may be important.

"Make a fist, like this," he said, demonstrating. "Now when you hit, use your whole weight and swing the arm out straight, like so."

Nota grunted and then stepped quickly to the side of the gesticulating Batu. He swung a single terrific right to the side of the head, putting the full force of those broad shoulders into the punch. Batu looked stupid for a moment—or maybe only stupider than usual, thought West—and then fell to the ground. The tribe went wild, cheering and laughing. Nota waved his clenched fist above his head and grinned.

"My honor is still safe!" he yelled.

Chief Mow grinned. "You learn fast, Nota," he said. Nota grinned back.

"Let the strangers be assigned to my family hearth," the mammoth hunter requested.

Mow grunted assent. "Do you take blood oath for their conduct?" he asked.

"For this one, the leader," said Nota, placing a hand on Red Axe's shoulder.

"What is happening?" whispered Red Axe to the man beside him. "Watch out, Batu awakens!"

"I take blood responsibility for you," the mammoth hunter answered. "If you do wrong, the chief will punish me, not you." He turned to his recently felled tribesman. "Ho, Batu, do you want to be knocked down a second time?" Batu snarled, but he slunk off into the crowd, which opened to receive him without comment.

"Chief Mow." Red Axe addressed the leader again. The tall, bronzed American, his remarkable blond hair swinging about his shoulders, caught the king's attention. "Nota takes blood oath for me. I take blood oath for all of my people."

Mow considered for a while, his brows furrowed over his deep-set eyes, and then he grunted again. "So be it," he said. "The tall pale man is obviously of your tribe, but why do you claim the ocean people to be of your tribe? Or the strange one with the tail?"

West did not have the vocabulary to answer the question. He turned to Varna, who stood, as usual during any danger, directly behind him, so that she could detect any attack from the rear. She stepped to his side and answered the king of the mammoth hunters.

"We all come from different tribes, O Chief," she began. The old chief eyed her buxom form with obvious interest, not failing to note the stone knife prominently displayed in her right hand. "Red Axe has been chosen to lead us, and we all swear loyalty to him. Each of us he has rescued from death or slavery. Three of us," she gestured to include Elkar and Mooh-lah, "from the city of the Mahars, the other two," and she pointed to the Hapuan girl and her brother, "from sacrifice to the sea god Manu!"

"Who is this woman, Yellow Hair? Does she speak the truth?"

"She is my mate, O Chief, and what she says is true."

"She is a fine woman, though a bit bold," the chief said meditatively. Here comes trouble, thought Red Axe, his grip on his weapons instinctively tightening. "It is too bad she is so tall and skinny," the savage ruler went on, "or I would be interested in buying her for my own household. However, she seems untamed and is not very good-looking."

"Your majesty's opinion may well be correct," said Red Axe politely. Varna hissed under her breath and jabbed him in the ribs. "Fortunately, I like them tall and skinny."

The chief grumbled. Already his mind had turned to other problems of his tribe. "Take them away, Nota," he said, "and bring Yellow Hair back after two sleeps to tell the story of his battles with the Mahars and the Sea People. Until then, keep them close to your hovel."

Nota's establishment could hardly be called a "hovel," but the Pellucidarian term meant more "hole in the ground" than it meant "cave" or "shelter." A flight of steps led down to an entrance ten feet belowground, but the roof was logs overlaid with sod held up above surface level by a framework of logs and timbers. Sunlight streamed through holes in the roof and illuminated an interior of at least three hundred square feet. There were several cook fires and hide-curtained tunnels leading into side rooms for storage and bathing. Nota led them to the largest fire and left them with an older woman and several curious children with instructions that they be fed.

There was a large stone vessel close to the fire, heated by the hot-rock method of taking stones from the fire and putting them into water in the vessel. In this improvised pot was a meat stew. The ex-prisoners were served portions of this in carved ivory bowls and found it delicious. Red Axe was careful to praise the cooking to the old woman who tended the fire, for he knew how a good cook appreciates recognition.

"No, surely," he said, "this can't be mammoth meat. I've eaten mammoth cooked by some of the best and it never tastes this good."

"Ah, it's the seasoning, young sir," she smiled. "The seasoning makes all the difference. Young folks nowadays don't know how to gather and dry the best herbs."

"Well, it's truly remarkable. Don't you think so?" he asked his followers. The food was good, and it was easy to respond in the affirmative. The old woman helped everybody to seconds.

"You look like a fine bunch of hunters," she said. "You bring me some horse—with the bones on, mind you—and I'll show you something really good!"

"Will we be allowed to hunt with the other warriors?" asked Elkar.

"Indeed, sir! You be members of Nota's clan now—and very lucky to be so, from what I hear. But you'll not last long, unless you bring in more food than you and your females can eat. The clan has to remain strong."

"How long have you been here?" asked Varna, shrewdly guessing that the old woman had not been born in the tribe.

"Hai, I was a pretty young girl, fat and hairy—unlike yourself, if you'll pardon the expression, dearie—when Nota and some of his braves carried me off from the Makim tribe in the snow-covered mountains." She sighed heartily. "Everyone knows we mountain girls are the prettiest. Well, Nota and the other braves rode their great beasts far up into the mountains to find and steal me. Ah, but I was worth it!"

"Do you ever want to go back to your own people?" asked Varna.

"No, dearie, not now. Oh, for a while I did pine for them—for the open meadows and the wind in the crags, you know. But now, I tend the fire; I never go outside anymore. I have plenty of young ones of my own to look after, you know. And if I weren't here, who would cook for them and see that all were well fed?" She beamed. "Now, who'll have more?"

Later, when all had been assigned duties in Nota's household and given sleeping quarters—these amounting to a place on the floor of the hall and a great furred skin to sleep on—Varna and Red Axe retired to rest.

"I do not care to remain the rest of my life cleaning meat and tending fires like that old woman," whispered Varna vehemently. "She may be very happy, and if Onoloa thinks it's acceptable, that's fine for her, but I would hate it."

"Nor do I intend to spend my life hunting mammoths and wild horses for a tribe I do not belong to," replied Red Axe. "But for the moment we are all alive and well, and I've escaped from worse places than this."

As they got to know more about Mow's tribe, however, the chances of escape seemed slim. At first none of them were allowed outside the huge hut. Finally, individual members of the group were taken out for hunting or foraging trips. Never, however, was more than one member of Red Axe's band out at a time. The rest of the clan was hospitable, but they made it obvious that those who stayed behind were being held hostage for each other's behavior. In this way, Red Axe, Elkar, Tumu, and Mooh-lah learned how to ride and guide the great tame mammoths. These huge, intelligent beasts were taught to obey a series of verbal and hand signals, as well as to turn, run, and halt at commands transmitted by nudging the beast behind its ears with the driver's knees. When they had become proficient, each man had to pass a test in which he must approach a mammoth he had ridden before and get it to pick him up in its trunk, place him in the "driver's seat" astride its neck behind the great head, and then run the length of the exercise path that circled the encampment.

It was an exhilarating feeling. The great shaggy-coated beasts moved with a rolling, bobbing motion that was difficult to anticipate. Some riders used a harness strap around the neck, the *tandor-tess*, with leather stirrups for the rider's feet. Others merely grasped the mammoth's coat with their bare toes. In either case, pulling behind the ear on one side and thumping on the other with a knee or a fist was a signal to turn. Instructions to slow down, to stop, or to run were transmitted by a series of taps on the head. Red Axe's mount was Ma-Ah, "the Old One," a big, gentle, good-natured beast who obeyed all his commands with an air of patient resignation. Red Axe suspected the animal of being far more intelligent than it acted. At times he caught the little black eyes watching him, and when he would return the stare the big tandor would lower its head, peer at the human a moment, and then turn away as if bored and disinterested.

"Now, Ma-Ah," whispered Red Axe, giving the signal for the final gallop, "quick time back to the pens and I'll go out and cut you an armload of the greenest grass I can find within walking distance of camp!" His gigantic mount stretched its stride and took off around the camp wall as if a pack of tarags was at its heels. His riding test completed successfully, Red Axe was informed by Nota that he was now eligible for the next big hunt.

"I don't know why you are so pleased with yourself," Varna remarked. "It seems that all you men do is get to ride around the countryside pursuing wild mammoths, while Onoloa and I languish here in these huts learning to sew." As a matter of fact, the two women had been hard at work stitching together harnesses, weapon straps, and fur-lined cloaks to be used in cold weather. The tribe of Mow used bone and ivory needles, and thread made of sinew that required frequent knots and wore like iron.

"Have patience, my darling," Red Axe whispered to his mate. "I have some ideas for escape, but it will be important that we are able to steal some of the mammoths and ride them. We are not likely to escape pursuit otherwise."

Varna leaned her dark head against his shoulder. "I trust you, dear. These people are good to us, but I am tired of doing women's hearthside work and teaching their little children the songs of my people."

"If I can gain their confidence," said the man, toying with her hair, "we may be able to figure some way for all of us to be out in the open together. Then all we have to do is steal a mammoth or two . . ."

There were obvious problems with this plan, but Varna did not point them out. And, when Red Axe did get to go on his first hunting expedition, he learned that there were obstacles to their escape he had not dreamed of.

The American was the only one of the strangers chosen for this particular trip. There were twelve mammoths, and Red Axe was the driver or rider of one. The leader of the troop was not Nota, but a younger man of his household and kinship, La-Lu by name.

"You are not of this tribe," said a short, burly man with hair in a pigtail all the way down his back.

"Nay," replied Red Axe, "but I am oath-bound to Nota and his kinship."

"It is well. Those who seek to escape their obligations find only dishonor and death. Which is your mammoth?"

Red Axe indicated the bulk of old Ma-Ah across the pen.

"Get him and bring him over here. I have something to

show you," the warrior said with an unpleasant smile. By the time Red Axe, taking care not to be trampled, had made his way through the crowd of huge beasts, climbed to his perch on Ma-Ah's broad neck, and guided him back, the other man had disappeared. The mammoth stood quietly, picking up bits of straw from the ground and munching on them, while they waited. Red Axe wondered if this were some kind of hazing, in which case he might wait forever and then be disciplined for not joining the hunt, which he could see forming at the far side of the compound. Then he saw the man he had been talking to walking back across the trampled earth. He carried a bundle of sticks bound with hide thongs, about five feet long. The thongs were tied so that all the sticks were gathered together at one end, but the bundle was divided in two at the other end.

"Here, stranger." He tossed the peculiar object up to the man on the mammoth. "Put the dummy in your place and climb down."

By this time several other tribesmen had come over to see what was happening. One of these was La-Lu, the leader of the expedition. Red Axe looked at him to see if he should obey. The savage subchief nodded agreement and gestured to him to comply. Red Axe obediently took the stick bundle and set it upright on his docile mount, pushing the twig-lashed fork over the beast's neck like a man's legs. He then climbed down to the ground. Several of the mammoth hunters nearby also dismounted. The man with the long pigtail placed both hands to his mouth and uttered a piercing cry. The mammoths stirred uneasily, shifting from foot to foot, waving their trunks in the air. Three times the man repeated the shrill sound while the herd became more and more nervous. Then the savage called, *"Kreeg-ah! Kreeg-ah! Trag, tandor, trag!"* Old Ma-Ah threw back his head and trumpeted a warning, seized the man-sized dummy rider from his neck, and threw it across the mammoth pen. Other mammoths reared and kicked their front legs, tossing their trunks into the sky. Red Axe was impressed. He did not need the insistence of the savages that he remember what he had seen. It was obvious that he had not been taught all there was to know about riding the trained tandor!

"So," Varna commented when he told her of the demonstration. "Even if you tried to steal one of the mammoths and ride to escape upon it, any member of the tribe could call out and have you flung to your death!"

"Yes," agreed Red Axe, "so they could. However, I have myself been a trainer of animals, and I saw more than they really wanted me to." He turned a spit over one of the small fires in Nota's great communal hall. The hunt had been successful, although his own part in it had been insignificant, and haunches of antelope were roasting at all the cooking fires. Around Varna's fire gathered all of the strangers, and for the moment they were alone. Nota and La-Lu were moving from fire to fire, speaking to the men. In a few moments they would come their way. Red Axe looked thoughtful.

"All the riders dismounted for the demonstration," he mused, "so all the mammoths must be trained to the same signal—and presumably do not distinguish between stranger and their usual rider. The command to *trag* (throw in Pellucidarian) is a double-edged sword." He used the English word for sword, as the tribes he knew had no such weapon.

"Red Axe!" Nota's voice interrupted, and the blond man turned and stood up. "You and the other two males will go with the clan to hunt the wild tandor herd that La-Lu reports in the low mountains. Eat well and get one more sleep here before you leave. Take all your weapons. Have your women put up smoked meat for you on the hunt. I have spoken."

"I hear, Clan-Chief. We will be ready," Red Axe replied.

"Christopher," whispered his mate, after the two tribesmen had departed. "We are never going to escape by sending all you men off on tedious mammoth hunts. I'm tired of sitting around the house here doing nothing!"

"You heard our chief, woman," said Mooh-lah. "Get busy and make smoked meat for the hunt. Do you want us to be the only hunters without provisions? You have plenty to do!"

"Oh, shut up, you stupid monkey! I'm afraid you'll all go off and get killed!"

Red Axe put an arm around her. "These hunts are carefully planned," he said, "and Nota does not want to lose a single warrior. We are too useful to him alive. Be brave a while yet, and we'll find some way to get out of here." The excitement of the prospect thrilled him, however, even as he comforted his mate. One more sleep and they would hunt the wild mammoth with the weapons of the Stone Age, just as his own ancestors must have done, millions of years ago!

9
THE MAMMOTH HUNT

THE WIND WHISTLED across the open tundra of the highlands. On some of the hill slopes there were patches of thin snow. Low grass and moss covered most of the ground and the trees were stunted, and wind-shaped. Here most of the hunting party was camped, the mammoths widely tethered so they could browse on the scanty growth. Flexible poles, covered with hide and lashed firmly to the ground, made a circle of rounded tents. Overhead, wind-driven clouds obscured the nearer mountain peaks and sometimes threatened to blot out the sun.

The guardsmen were muffled in bearskin robes, their feet protected by thick furry buskins laced up to the knee. Still they shivered and stamped their feet, their breath frosty in the filtered sunlight.

"A curse on the heads of Mow and his crazy hunters," said Elkar, leaning on the eight-foot-long, flint-headed lance he carried. "Only a madman would come to this crazy country where the water turns hard on the ground and the tops of the puddles are like stone! I prefer to hunt in the warm plains below."

"Somewhere," said Red Axe, pausing beside him, "there should be a pass through these mountains and down the other side. We're going to need to find it, if we are ever to get the women and escape from here."

"*Faugh*, my blood will turn to stone from the cold before we get out of these hills," the other man continued to grumble.

"Why do Mow and Nota think there's anything to hunt here anyway? No self-respecting animal would live in such a country!"

Red Axe grinned and picked up his own spear. "Come, on, keep moving. It will keep your feet warm. Around the camp again, we're getting behind."

"My feet will never be warm again," the big man whined. "Ho! What is that?"

A faint cry sounded from the hills ahead of them and to the left. They strained their eyes, but could see nothing.

"Up that gully, perhaps," said Red Axe. "What do you think it was?"

"Man, I think," said his companion.

"*Hallooo*—the guard!" cried Red Axe. An answering cry came from the far side of the camp and another from one of the tents where the hunters who were not out scouting had gone to warm themselves and sleep. Within less than a minute, six of Mow's warriors had rushed to join them— some only partially clad for the chill windy weather, but all armed to the teeth.

"What do you see?" demanded the leader, an older, graying, scarred hunter named Kor. Elkar pointed and was about to speak when another shout came from the distance and two men debouched from the little canyon and ran on down the slope toward the encampment.

"It is Barak and one of his band," said one of the men quickly, "and what is it that pursues them?"

"Ryth!" cried several of the others. Elkar and Red Axe stared in amazement at the great brown beast that lumbered into sight behind the two mammoth men.

"It's a bear," said Red Axe, using the English word, "but it's more the size of a freight train!"

"Come on, you two," bawled Kor. "Muka and Tulak, back to the pickets and get your tandors. The rest of you come with me!" Without a moment's hesitation, he ran up the hillside toward the fleeing men and the onrushing monster.

As the primitive hunters reached the mouth of the gully, the two fugitives rushed among them. Both were weaponless, and one man, a huge gash running the width of his shoulders, was half supported by his companion. Quickly Kor arranged his men in a semicircle facing the cave bear. Now that reinforcements had arrived, the men who had been fleeing turned and stood behind the line of hunters as their pursuer came up.

On closer examination, Red Axe had to modify his original estimate of the animal's size, but only slightly. The beast that rushed toward them with a rolling gait was a good eight feet high at the shoulder, the highest point of the body as it approached on all fours. The thick tan fur was smeared with blood across the chest and forepaws. The ryth was wounded in one shoulder and there was a gash in the scalp that had nearly sliced off an ear, but it was easy to see that most of the gore that covered it was not its own. Great white-fanged jaws slavered open and the beast snarled as it reached the circle of the Stone Age men.

"Throw!" shouted Kor, launching a stone-tipped javelin. Four more missiles followed in rapid succession, and then the gigantic bear was among them. Ancient man had played out this same savage drama on the glacial plains of the Ice Age, thought Red Axe, the modern man turned primitive. How often had the prehistoric beast confronted these puny little howling bipeds, only to find that they carried pain and death in their hands?

The mammoth men had each retained one spear or flint axe and with these they closed upon their foe. One sweep of a giant paw sent a man tumbling head over heels on the snowy ground. The man merely rolled over and over and then climbed back to his feet, unhurt. The others thrust and jabbed, trying to inflict a fatal wound. Surrounded, the bear sat back on its haunches and reared upright to its full height, towering at least twelve feet above the ground. While the other men circled warily, keeping out of range of those huge paws, Kor stepped in and swung his long-handled axe, the favorite weapon of the mammoth hunter, for a neck blow. The beast parried the stroke with a backhanded sweep of a forepaw, knocking the weapon from the hunter's grasp. In a split second the monster had seized the man in both forepaws and crushed him to its chest.

Red Axe could imagine the pressure of that incredible grip. Kor's spine and ribs would crack in a moment. He dropped his lance and picked up the unfortunate man's fallen axe. Praying he could avoid hitting the trapped tribesman, he stepped close to the giant bear and swung the razor-sharp stone edge against its upper arm. Three blows smashed bone and nerve, leaving the forelimb partially paralyzed. Elkar shouted at him from the other side of the animal. He stepped back, threw the axe, haft foremost, to his waiting companion, and bent to pick up his fallen spear. The movement saved his life, for the bear, identifying its tormentor immediately, dropped the mauled but still living body of Kor and leaned forward. Balancing on the ruin of its left forefoot, it swung the right in an arc of death over Red Axe's body. The clawed limb passed so close that the fur actually brushed his back gently as it went by.

The beast recovered but now had to use the good forelimb to support its weight. Elkar hewed away at the elbow as if it were a tree, drawing attention away from the two men to the beast's left. The ferocious head turned toward the new attack. Red Axe grasped his spear in both hands and stepped up close to the injured paw. Quickly he slid along the chest wall with the point of his weapon, felt the sharp flint slip between two ribs, and thrust. The beast reared back and screamed, but Red Axe had the brief moment he needed, before the shaft of the spear could be torn from his grasp by the bear's upright posture, to plunge the length of the weapon into its chest and pierce its heart. The mammoth men scrambled back out of the way, two of them dragging the limp form of Kor between them. The giant cave bear roared his defiance once again, swayed, and fell with a thud that shook the earth. The men on mammoth-back, rushing to reinforce Kor's handful of warriors, sent up a shout of surprise and admiration. Red Axe confronted the blond Elkar across the great fallen head of the dead bear, the blood-smeared axe still in his hand. They both grinned.

"Well struck, old friend," he said to Elkar.

"Well thrust, Red Axe," the man replied.

"It seems Mow was right, there was something to hunt in this frozen land after all."

"So it seems. Let us hope that we have killed it and that there are no more."

The medicine-man had treated Kor's wounds with a poultice of leaves and bear fat, bound his left arm to his side, and wrapped the mauled chest and shoulder with strips of soft doeskin.

As he approached, Red Axe thought that he would have preferred a few shots of penicillin. His first aid kit, however, was back in the main camp. Besides, the medicine man would undoubtedly disapprove of using an extract of bread mold to treat his patient. "He'd probably tell me the magic was all wrong for bear wounds," he said to himself, then added aloud: "Kor, I am glad to see you sitting up with your soul still in your body!"

"I am glad to see you, Red Axe." The tough old warrior grimaced with pain as he tried to turn. He indicated a spot beside the small fire in the center of the tent. "Sit. I heard it was you who broke the ryth's arm and released me. I am grateful. I thought my time had come to join my ancestors in the hunting grounds beyond the sun."

"It was no more than any of your warriors would have done," said Red Axe, pleased at the old man's praise.

"Nay, it was a brave act and saved my life, providing my ribs and my hide will now heal. Kor does not forget. You have made a new friend, Red Axe. You have need of friends, stranger, for you have enemies among the tribe of Mow."

"That I know, and I fear them not."

"You are a brave man. Do you know that a voice speaks against you at the Place of Singing Stones?"

"Singing Stones? What do you mean, Kor?"

"Far from here, stranger, but close to the fortified town of Mow's people, there is a place where the rocks cry out—or, as the shamans say, they sing. Yet here, I am told, a demon voice calls out your name."

"Strange. How would the demon know my name?"

"Kor does not believe in demons." The man patted his injured shoulder gently with his good hand. "Only those who come armed with tooth and claw. There are enough of these in the wide world that we need not seek the insubstantial kind."

After Kor and the other wounded man had rested, Mow summoned them all back to the permanent camp. Meanwhile, the other scouting parties kept coming in and reporting, and finally news of a small herd of wild mammoths arrived. The chief sent for several of his more experienced hunters, and, among them, Red Axe.

The American was surprised to be called to this council, but Mow greeted him by name and commented to the others on his proven bravery and leadership. The one-armed chief then launched into his plans for the upcoming hunt. The two men who had been pursued by the bear had found a likely cliff toward which the wild herd was to be driven. Assignments were then handed out and Red Axe found himself responsible for a work party of twenty men.

"You do not get to go with the drive," he told Elkar when the meeting had broken up and Mow's lieutenants scattered to find their groups. "We have the dubious honor of improving the trap."

"Aha," said Elkar. "The men have been saying you would be made a subchief after the killing of the bear."

"Well, don't envy me too much, for most of what we will be doing is digging," replied Red Axe.

The plan Mow and Nota had envisioned was simple. The hunters, in two groups mounted on tame mammoths, would locate the wild herd and drive them to the edge of the cliff. Here they would be either slaughtered or driven over the cliff and killed. This plan depended, of course, on the ability of Mow's mammoth men to drive the wild beasts wherever they wanted. Nobody seemed to doubt this, however, so Red Axe decided it must be a common method. The herd he had seen attacked had been driven, but not far, for the presence of the young calves had made the beasts turn and fight. Their present quarry was a herd without calves. Was it already past the calving season? Could there be such a thing as a season when the sun hung eternally overhead in perpetual noon?

Essential to the hunters' plan was a cliff to which the beasts would be driven. The unfortunate scouts attacked by the cave bear had found a cliff, but it was inadequate. Guided by the uninjured survivor of the scout group, Red Axe led a party of twenty men and five mammoths to the site. They came to the base of a high bluff, and Red Axe and the scout climbed to the top. They passed a deep cave in the rock, the bear's den, and here they found the scattered bones of the other men on that ill-fated reconnaissance. The scavengers of the wild had already picked them bare and dry.

Red Axe inquired as to the customs of the mammoth hunters concerning their dead, remembering that he had seen one dead man brought home to his family. The scout nodded.

"Surely, Red Axe, your tribe must believe that proper disposition of the body is necessary to achieve admission to the eternal hunting grounds beyond the sun?"

"Tribes differ in this regard where I come from," explained the American. "Though you are right, all have some way for this to be done. How is it with your people?"

"We must gather up these bones," said the warrior. He stood, spear in hand, looking down sadly on the smashed and dried relics of his companions. "We must carry them back to the main camp to be burned by their families and the ashes must be scattered at the Place of the Singing Stones."

"Ah, I have heard of this place."

"And the guardian spirits have heard of you," replied the savage. After that he would say no more, and after a while Red Axe forbore to question him further.

"Get three men and a few hides to package up the last of your friends," he said, "and I will lead the mammoths up the gentler slope yonder to the new campgrounds."

Indeed there was space aplenty where the huge mammoths could, with care, ascend to the top of the bluff. Of course, this made the top of it anything but a trap for the wild herd soon to be driven hither. Mow's simple solution to this problem was to dig out the slope until it was in fact an unclimbable precipice. Red Axe's job, which he now contemplated with some dismay, was to dig it out.

Elkar came up the slope to his side. "No self-respecting mammoth is going to fall down that," he remarked as he clambered over the edge.

"Right," said Red Axe. "It's our job to see that they do."

"Your first orders, then, Chief?"

"Pitch camp at the end of the valley, away from the base of our cliff. Where are we going to find trees?"

"Trees? In this frozen waste?"

"Send me the scout when he's through picking up the remains of his fellows. We need logs of some kind."

Fortunately, the scout remembered a few stunted trees no more than two miles away. Red Axe took a working party and two mammoths to get them, leaving the other men digging frantically at the hillside with sticks.

In a narrow gully he hewed down a fair-sized pine tree. He had to do it himself. The savage flint axes of the tribesmen were too delicate for this kind of work, and the flint would dull or shatter. It was an easy job for the steel axe blade, but he preferred not to trust the weapon to anyone else.

The mammoths managed to carry his log and a bundle of smaller branches back to the bluff. After a meal of bear meat, he worked out a way of lashing the shorter branches at right angles to the heavier log to make a giant rake which could be hauled up the hill by mammoths, set tooth deep in the earth by hand, and then dragged down with rawhide ropes. It was slow and tedious, but it beat digging the dirt out with pointed sticks and carrying it down in animal skins. Before three sleeps had gone by they had created Mow's cliff—sheer, undermined, and forty feet high. By the time this was done they had eaten up all the bear meat and anything else the men had brought with them, and still seen no sign of the mammoth drive and the wild herd. Red Axe detailed a fourth of his men out to hunt. He dared send no more; the drive might appear at any time and Mow would be depending on him to be ready.

The men kept watch, collected firewood, and huddled in the tents to keep warm. There was a fall of light snow. They kept the fire in the tents low, burning mammoth dung, so that they were always warm for the men not keeping watch, grazing the beasts, or hunting.

Elkar and Red Axe were huddled in one of the tents over the steaming dung fire, watching a game of *ka-po*, played with pebble counters and a parallel series of holes dug in the dirt. One of the men went to his bedroll and brought back a set of carved ivory beads for counters—each one hand-carved from a mammoth tusk to resemble a tiny face.

Red Axe asked to see the pieces and admired them, turning each bead to the firelight. One of the men chuckled. "Show the strangers your carving collection, Ru." Ru demurred, but his tribesmen insisted, with much laughter. Half blushing, half defiant, the man finally produced a small skin pouch and emptied it on the ground. There were three ivory carvings, each nearly the size of a fist. They were rounded and delicately carved. Red Axe turned them over in his hands. This bump was probably the head, he thought, although the features of the face were absent. The tapering "handle" represented the feet, so this pair of bumps must be . . . He grunted in surprise and the men around the fire let out a shout of laughter. The thing was feminine—no, on closer examination, it was graphically female. But grotesquely, grossly out of proportion. No woman, not even one of the short, fat, rounded women of Mow's tribe, was built like that!

Then Red Axe realized what he held in his hand. His primitive friends were very like the cavemen of western Europe, and once in a museum he had seen a series of carvings similar to the three Ru had taken out of his carrying pouch. The learned description in the museum case had speculated that the artifacts were part of a fertility cult or ritual and referred to them as "Venuses."

"Every thirty sleeps Ru carves a new one," a man was saying. He picked them over. "I'll buy this one, Ru, the one with the freckles on her—" He finished with a Pellucidarian word Red Axe did not know. He could guess at the meaning.

The little female carvings were passed from hand to hand, admired and laughed over, and—except for the one desired by the man who had spoken—finally returned to Ru. The prospective buyer bargained with the craftsman and finally obtained the carving for a promise of four fresh animal hides and any tusks he might obtain in the present hunt. Red Axe watched him carry off his treasure with a chuckle.

Waiting in the hot, smelly hide tents began to wear on the men's nerves. Arguments over gambling at ka-po broke out. Food was scarce and tempers were short. When a messenger finally arrived from Mow, everyone was delighted just to have a break in the monotony.

"We are close now," the man reported to a hushed crowd of hunters around the fire in the largest of the tents. "The herd moves slowly. There are several big bulls and they are always stopping to challenge us."

"How many in the herd?" Red Axe asked.

"The fingers of my left hand three times."

"Fifteen," said Red Axe.

"He cheats, Red Axe," said one of the men, laughing. "He is missing a finger—it's less than that."

"Twelve, then," the big blond man agreed with a smile. "How soon?"

"Soon, soon," the scout replied. "I had to ride my mammoth hard to get here. Now I must go back to guide them."

"Eat hot food first," urged the American, "and I will send another mammoth with you. Elkar and Ru will go. You others stand by to man the cliffs. Double the watch—we don't want to miss them in the snow."

The meeting broke up quickly.

The sun was overcast with cloud when the sounds of the mammoth drive, the shouting of men mingled with the occasional trumpeting from the enraged beasts, reached the waiting hunters on the cliff.

Red Axe had distributed his forces in two groups. The plan depended upon crowding the gigantic creatures to the cliff edge where they must fight at a disadvantage or plunge to their deaths. If the herd managed to turn and run parallel to the cliff top they might quickly elude pursuit and escape. On one side of the cliff, the ground was rocky and fell in jumbled gullies—not an appealing route of escape for their quarry. Here, however, Red Axe posted five men and two tame mammoths. The other end of the cliff was more troublesome. There was little underbrush, and a gentle slope led rapidly down to the safety of the plains below. There the American concentrated his major force—thirteen men and two mammoths. As the sounds of the approaching hunt grew closer, he turned to the man nearest him.

"The light of the sun is dimmed by the cloud. Let us hope the tandors can see us."

"Hai, Red Axe, we have torches." The man next to him called to one of the mammoth riders, who rummaged in the saddlebags attached to the side of his shaggy mount and produced bundles of dried wood, one end soaked in pitch or tar. Red Axe sniffed.

"What is this stuff?" he asked.

"Burns well," the hunter told him. "Oozes up out of the ground at the Place of Singing Stones."

"Yet another reason for me to see the Place of Singing Stones," mused West. It was some sort of petroleum deposit. Perhaps if developed . . . . He shook his head. This was no time to consider the impact of the combustion engine on the Stone Age culture of Pellucidar.

"Red Axe, do you have your fire maker?" the torchbearer asked. Red Axe fumbled in his pocket for the old-fashioned flint-and-steel igniter he had had sent from Santa Monica, California. In a minute they had a torch ablaze. The flame was a lurid yellow in the dim light and a long plume of black smoke curled over their heads.

"Run quickly and light torches for the others," Red Axe directed. The herd of mammoths was already visible coming down the slope that led to the cliffs. A shout went up from the pursuers as they saw the torches and knew they were close to their goal. The harried mammoths trumpeted nervously, swerving from the yelling savages on their left. The blazing torches, the cries, and the brandished spears and axes of Red Axe's men daunted them momentarily. They hesitated. The hunters behind sent up a howl and harried their rear. Trumpeting rage, the trapped herd crowded forward. There was a squeal of terror as two of the great mammoths tumbled over the cliff, and the men sent up a shout of triumph.

Victory, however, was not to be that easy. The great shaggy beasts milled about at the cliff edge. In a few moments they might attempt a charge and escape. One-armed Mow, standing now on the head of his great mammoth Ara, surveyed the gloom and gave quick orders. Tribesmen moved to reinforce Red Axe's position on the left flank, where a breakout seemed most likely. Tired from the long hunt, their fatigue readily apparent now that they had reached their goal, the men and mammoths moved slowly through the fog and new-fallen snow. Meanwhile, several of the bull tandors had discovered Red Axe's little band of torch-waving gilaks. The shaggy heads lowered and the great looping ivory tusks swept the ground. A big bull trumpeted once, rolled his trunk up out of harm's way between his tusks, and charged the line.

Red Axe saw him coming, moving swiftly but ponderously, swaying from side to side with each giant step. He was a magnificent specimen, fifteen feet high with great curving tusks and legs like tree trunks. Each step shook the earth as he bore down on the hunters. How many times, West wondered, as he stood rooted to the ground by an emotion akin to buck fever, had his own ancestors relived this scene? How long had it been carried in his genes, lost to memory except as a vague dream, to now come tumbling back to him as he gazed on those reddened eyes, those ivory tusks, that furry trunk?

"Red Axe, look out!"

The sweep of the beast's head brought the great ivory tusks whistling through the snow. West was thrown, bowled over to one side. On came the great feet. To avoid being trampled into the snow and rock, he rolled—directly into the path of the onrushing monster! In a moment, the black furry trunk had found him, coiled around him, and lifted him into the air.

The mammoth's trunk encircled his waist and Red Axe found himself drawn close to the great head, staring directly into those red, enraged eyes. About him he heard cries of encouragement, shouts of advice. The creature made no attempt to crush him within the coil of its trunk. Instead, he slowly and deliberately raised the man up over his head. In a moment, Red Axe knew, he would be thrown like a bundle of sticks, to land broken, wounded—perhaps dead. Where would the nerves of the coiling trunk muscles come out of the skull? As the lethal serpent of a proboscis tightened around him, he gauged his spot and swung the razor-sharp axe that had never left his grasp. Dark red blood flew and smoked in the cold air. The mammoth had him almost overhead now. Then the trunk loosened and uncoiled, and he fell onto the blood-soaked shaggy pelt over the animal's forehead. The beast trumpeted its pain and fury, a horrible gurgling that sounded as the wounded trunk filled with blood. Red Axe swung up over the head and into the soft saddle behind the skull and the ears. The animal reared to throw him, as screaming cavemen bore in upon them on every side, fast-cutting six-foot flint axes slashing the tendons on the rear legs. The beast crumpled and fell upon the blood-soaked snow. Shouting barbarians leaped upon the tandor with lances, seeking its heart. Red Axe, clinging to the shaggy coat with one hand and his weapon with the other, rode the beast down to its death, then stepped lightly from the carcass as it lay quivering on the ground.

Later, when the entire herd had been pushed over the cliff and the mammoth hunters had gone among them to administer the final *coup de grâce*, Elkar found his friend at the cliff top, gazing again at the gigantic body of the great bull tandor.

"Yet another wingbeat away from death, Red Axe," said Elkar to his friend, using the Pellucidarian equivalent of "a close call." The tall blond man nodded.

"For me, but not for him," he replied, pointing to the huge dead beast. "He was fighting for his life, Elkar. I could see in his eyes that he knew. I am almost sorry that he had to die."

"So am I," said Elkar, "because now we have to skin him."

10

THE PLACE OF SINGING STONES

OW AND NOTA'S HUNTING PARTY feasted, tended the wounded men, and butchered the dead mammoths. The skins and fresh meat were packed for the trip back to the tribal camp, then the largest of the skulls was cleaned and strapped to the back of one of the other pack animals. The other tusks were carefully extracted and loaded, and finally the camp was struck, tents and paraphernalia were packed, and a weary party of hunters started the long road down out of the foothills to the lush green plains visible below.

Mow was generous with his praise of Red Axe's part in the hunt. "Nota does well to accept you into his family, Yellow Hair. You have fought the ryth and the wild tandor. You stand too tall and you are an ugly color, but you are a brave man and a mighty hunter. Mow welcomes you into the tribe." He hugged the embarrassed American to his hairy brown chest with his one good arm.

"Good, Chief," said Red Axe, when he had gotten his breath back. "Now does that mean that I and my people are full-fledged members of this tribe, and no longer prisoners?"

"Not yet, my son. That honor follows a war party, the slaying of an enemy of the tribe, and the ritual of the Singing Stones." He slapped the blond giant on the shoulder. "Be of good heart, though, for Mow sees you as fated for that honor, and destined to be his son."

Red Axe thanked the chief as politely as possible, then

sought his own mammoth, Ma-Ah, and the party assigned to him in sullen silence. It was all very well to be an honored slave, but his free spirit was galled to be a slave at all. The trip back was slowed by the heavy loads carried by the beasts—and by many of the men, who walked burdened with packs of meat and hides. Whenever the party camped, Red Axe took the opportunity to ride off alone with Ma-Ah and train him. Soon he felt he could manage the beast as well as any of the experienced tribesmen.

Mow conducted the march back with the same military care that he had displayed in the initial outward hunt. The mass of loaded mammoths and most of the warriors proceeded in a group, but far-flung scouts and outriders guarded the flanks and kept him notified of possible dangers ahead.

On his turn to ride flank guard, Red Axe and his shaggy mount loped along over the low hills, sometimes in sight of, sometimes hidden from, the main column. Faintly, he could hear the men's voices, but mostly his ear caught the sigh of the wind over the rich veldt. They were back down to warmer climes, now. The grass was thick green and four feet high. There were clumps of heavy trees, many of them thorned acacias like the one in which he and his friends had been trapped by the mammoth hunters so long ago. He stretched out flat on the top of the mammoth's great brown head. The grazing herds of antelope, the giant sloths, a herd of woolly rhinoceros: all moved to avoid the great mammoth. Farther ahead, trees darkened the brighter green of the plain. In the dim distance, toward camp, lay the blue of the sea, now invisible due to cloud and haze, but not the horizon, for there was no horizon. Red Axe turned on his back and gazed up at the stark black and white of the snow-capped mountains they had left behind them. Small in the distance, but still big enough to see clearly, a great winged shape, a thipdar, glided below the mountain peaks. Hunting, thought Red Axe, as he watched the reptilian monster circle on the wind, watching for prey beneath. The pterodactyl turned again, then hovered briefly, the leathery bat wings folding as it fell in a sudden dive and disappeared from view. Long moments later, he saw it reappear above the nearer hills and treetops, wings beating frantically to carry its weight upward, a small limp form clutched in its mighty talons.

On marched the great mammoth, its rolling gait eating up the miles. As the party neared the tribe's hunting grounds, the herds of game grew thicker and more exotic. Great-horned stags; long-necked camels; tan and black bison with curved horns; tiny red horses only a few feet high; huge, fierce, wingless birds; packs of giant hyenas; massive land tortoises with shells six feet across; small horned dinosaurs; and a pack of ape-creatures that scurried sullenly out of their path. Baboons, Red Axe thought, until he noted with a start that all the larger males carried sticks they obviously used as clubs. He watched them carefully as the hunting party moved past them. Their flat, bluish faces stared back at him from the brush, the heavy brows drawn down in frowns of disapproval. Far ahead he could hear the coughing roar of a lion, the answering snarl of the saber-toothed tiger. When he thought it safe, West thumped his heels under Ma-Ah's ears and they rumbled off on their way, leaving the enigmatic beast-men behind.

"Whatever happened to evolution in your world, old fellow?" Red Axe whispered to his mount. "You and Mow's people, now, ought to be neighbors, but those strange characters back there in the grass . . ." He leaned forward between the big shaggy ears. "And the dinosaurs—the thipdars, the Mahars themselves, should have been dead a million years ago or more. Of course," he added, looking up in the direction of the blazing, bright sun of Pellucidar, "it is hard to say years in a world where there are no years, there are no days . . . ."

The hot noonday sun of Pellucidar glared down on his head. It was still shining, directly overhead, when the hunting party finally reached the fortified camp.

"Did you miss me, Varna?"

"Of course. It seemed that you had been gone forever. Then, when I heard the shouts of the stockade guards and knew that you were back, it seemed as if you had just left me." She pillowed the soft fragrant mass of her raven hair against his chest.

When the meat and hides and trophies had been distributed, the dead mourned by their families and extended kinships, and the traditional feast of welcome consumed, Mow announced to the great delight of all attending that after two sleeps there would be a ceremonial march to the Place of the Singing Stones.

Red Axe sought out Kor, whose ryth-inflicted wounds seemed to be healing almost miraculously.

"No, Red Axe, I do not think any harm is plotted against you now," the old warrior confided. "The messages of the Singing Stones are hard to interpret. Go and see—I do not think it will be a trap, for you and Elkar are too high in Mow's favor." He grunted and shifted his scarred arm with his good hand. "Would that I were whole again and could go with you."

The blond man smiled. "I, too, wish you were well. But fear not, you have already been of great help, and if things get tight I still may need all the friends I can get."

Kor grinned. "Your reputation as a warrior has spread throughout the camp. Don't worry—your people will be safe here."

Though Red Axe was allowed to go to the Place of Singing Stones, the rest of his party was not. It was a long trip, conducted with pack mammoths, one of whom carried a trophy skull, tusks and all, from the recent hunt. About fifty tribesmen made the pilgrimage, comprised mostly of warriors, but including quite a few older women. There was one older man, his straggly hair tinged with gray, whom Red Axe had not seen before. Polite inquiry revealed that he was a medicine man, one who read omens and healed the sick.

He was a taciturn individual, however, and the American's attempts to draw him into a discussion of comparative religion met with surly grunts.

When the party camped and he was not on guard, Red Axe did succeed in getting some of the group around the campfire to tell him something of their destination. Even this, however, did not prepare him for the appearance of the place.

The area was volcanic and close to the sea, although they approached by a well-worn trail from the landward side. The ground sloped up, so that the seacoast was hidden by a black lava ridge. They passed several pools of the black tar that the men of Mow's tribe used for torches. The grass and weeds died out, the broad trail now leading up between masses of broken black rock. A trick of the wind brought the sea breeze from the ocean; laden with moisture, it condensed about the lava ramparts into eerie streamers of mist. The mammoths were left with a guard, and, after Mow had sent a scout to the top of the ridge to return with the news that no other tribes occupied the shrine, the group began its ascent in silence. The mammoth skull was carried along by a party of six men. Soon Red Axe began to see similar trophies on either side of the path, offerings apparently dedicated to the spirits. The skulls of mammoth, *brontotherium*, and *baluchitherium*, the biggest of the great plain mammals, stared at the silent procession with sightless eye sockets.

The Place of Singing Stones was used by several nomadic hunting tribes in the area. Mow did not wish to encounter any of his rivals under such circumstances, so a party of armed men stayed behind to guard the beasts of burden and to cover a possible retreat. Mow and the medicine man proceeded up the trail, Red Axe and the others struggling along behind, taking turns helping with the great skull. The cold, wet mist muffled any sound, and condensed in big drops on their exposed faces and as a fine dew on their furry garments.

At the top of the ridge the party halted. The chief and his shaman had walked out on a spit of black rock to the left of the trail's termination. They stood on the rim of a shallow crater, nearly two hundred yards across. The crater floor, only a yard or so below their feet, was bare reddish soil. Across it blew the mist, thicker now that they had reached the top. On the far rim, sometimes visible, sometimes hidden in the blowing curtains of gray, stood a dozen monoliths. Black, upright, like jagged teeth in the crater's jaw, they loomed tall and menacing in the half gloom, silhouetted against the light. The wind, blowing constantly now from the distant sea, and still carrying a salty fragrance that bespoke its origin, whistled and moaned through the upright rocks like a damned soul crying for mercy. The Singing Stones did indeed sing—and a more mournful dirge Red Axe had never heard.

The cavemen stood in an uneasy group, the cold, wet wind sweeping over them to leave them drenched and miserable. Out on his stone pulpit, the medicine man raised both his arms in supplication to the wind and the rocks, and began a long howling chant in a booming voice. Mow the chief stood sullenly behind him, holding his fur robe around his stocky form with his one arm.

Red Axe could make out little of the prayer of the medicine man; despite his forceful delivery, the wind carried most of it away from the audience, and the whistling and sobbing of the air blowing through the towering black rocks drowned out the words. At an appropriate point, however, the shaman turned to the group and screeched, "Behold the offering!" At whispered instructions from his neighbors, Red Axe helped to raise the great mammoth skull, curved tusks and all, above their heads. Apparently the others knew what they were waiting for. They stood there, the heavy skull held at arm's length above them. Then, to Red Axe's amazement, the wind seemed to howl "*En-fir*," the Pellucidarian word for accepted or completed. The sound was weird and inhuman, so much like the meaningless wailing that had been present since they had topped the rim of the crate that he could not be sure he had actually heard it. The medicine man cried a command and the trophy was lowered.

One of the men said, "Come along now, back down the trail with it—and be careful!"

The skull was carried back over the crater rim. The offering apparently having been accepted by the gods, it was placed in line at the top of a row of similar trophies, which extended down the lava-covered slope until they disappeared into the mist.

Their task completed, the mammoth hunters turned and climbed back up to the crater's rim. Here they found that the women had unrolled an animal hide, exposing to the chill wind its contents: slabs of meat, yams, bulb-like roots that looked like onions, and a number of stalks of the sugarcane that grew on the green plains near their home. These offerings, also, were accepted, the eerie howling of "En-fir!" across the desolate waste of rock making the hair on the back of Red Axe's neck prickle like it was trying to stand up. Much as he disbelieved in the supernatural, the bizarre setting, the wind, the mist, the dimly seen black monoliths—all conspired to produce in him that most basic of human emotions: fear of the unknown.

"Nonsense, it's just a trick of the wind," he muttered to himself, hardly aware that he was speaking aloud. "Easy to see how Mow's people came to believe the place is inhabited by evil spirits," he continued, now keeping his thoughts to himself. "If ever a place deserved to be haunted, this is it! Listen to that wind howl! There must be some trick of the rocks that makes it sound like a human voice. I suppose that would be the only word it mimics. What an uncanny coincidence, that the rocks should answer the old faker's prayers! I suppose he's learned to word his requests so that the answer is always appropriate."

The medicine man called instructions to the women.

They folded their offerings in the fur robe and carried it out into the crater, chanting as they went. Red Axe watched them, as did all of the men, as they proceeded out across the bare floor of the dead volcano, the mist concealing their figures as they reached the far rim. The medicine man began a new chant as the wind died down, although the mist still darkened the sun.

"A blessing from the spirits of the air, a blessing from the spirits of the earth . . . ."

He went on, intoning his hymn to the primal deities of this primitive people. Dimly through the mist, they could see the six women returning. They had left their offering on the far side of the crater. As they came closer, the watchers could see that they had covered their faces with some gray pigment or ash. As they walked along, now a solemn group in single file, their faces had a masklike, or even corpselike, appearance. As the women ascended the rocks and passed between the waiting men and down the trail out of the crater, walking silently and slowly, the wind rose in a howl of farewell behind them.

Now the men began a solemn chant. Mow and the priest descended from their rock pulpit and walked out side by side across the crater. The wind quieted, the mist turning to a fine rain. The men chanted on, the rain saturating their long hair and running in slow rivulets down their faces. Silently, Red Axe waited with them. He was part of the tribe, an unwilling recruit, perhaps, but reluctant to disturb or question their religion.

When their song was ended, the short, stocky warriors of Mow huddled in the wind and rain, some turning their backs to the ever-present wind, and waited patiently for their leaders to return. Invisible now in the rain, the Singing Stones still wailed their eerie music.

How long they waited, Red Axe did not know. The tribesmen were impassive, stoic. He was chilled and stiff, however, by the time a stir in the group told him the two men were returning from the shrine. When they had climbed the gentle slope from the floor of the dead crater, Mow stopped directly in front of the American, looking up into his eyes.

"Red Axe, my son, the spirits of the Singing Stones want you."

"What?" Red Axe's mind was still numb from the cold and the waiting. "Want what?"

"It is the ritual," the chief replied. "He who would be accepted into the tribe must receive the blessings of the spirits."

"Tell me, O Chief Mow," Red Axe replied, "what it is that I must do." I should have known there would be some sort of initiation ceremony, he thought. I want the status of full membership in the tribe so I can get Varna and Onoloa out of it. There obviously is some sort of ceremony I have to go through. Probably they put all the young boys through something like this to prove their manhood. Isn't there an African tribe where each young man must kill a lion single-handed? Perhaps this is what Kor meant?

"You must go to the Place of the Singing Stones," said Mow, pointing with his one arm across the crater to the now-invisible standing slabs of black lava. "You must go alone. You must wait there until the spirits have spoken and given you your message from the all-ruling Lord of the Sky."

"Very well, O Chief, I am ready."

"Good, my son. Leave your weapons here. Nota, bring a wolf skin." Red Axe surrendered his steel axe and knife—not without some trepidation—and saw them rolled into a bundle and placed beside the trail in the rocks.

"You will go alone," said the medicine man, speaking directly to Red Axe for the first time. "You are to wait at the foot of the place of worship. When the spirits are ready, they will speak to you. You must wait. You may sleep, but you must not eat or drink until the message from the spirit world has come."

Red Axe nodded with understanding. It was a vigil that

by its very nature, and influenced by the mystery of the place, the addition of hunger and thirst, and the expectations of the superstitious tribesmen, was bound to produce visions. These could then easily be interpreted, perhaps by the medicine man, as a personal message from the spirit world. Well, if that was all that was required, he could easily pass with flying colors. He would think of some appropriate "message" to receive and then, after a reasonable time alone among the rocks, walk back and join the party!

Mow's next command was to the men on the crater rim. "Back to the tandors! Red Axe goes to the Singing Stones for spiritual enlightenment."

There was muttering among the tribesmen, "So soon? He has not been with the tribe longer than one hunt."

"The spirits of the Singing Stones have spoken!" cried the medicine man, gesturing threateningly at the disbelievers. "Red Axe the stranger is called! No man shall question the voice of the stones!" The men turned, stumbling in the wet rain, and marched single file down the trail.

Mow stepped close to the American. "Go with a stout heart, my son," he whispered. His arm groped forward from under his bearskin cloak, pressing to Red Axe's side a razor-sharp flint dagger six inches long. "The spirit voices call you, Mow has heard them. Mow believes in the spirits of the stones, just as his father the chief before him, and his father before him. But Mow would have the yellow-haired one return to the tribe."

"Uh, thanks, Chief." Red Axe managed to surreptitiously slip the weapon into his waistband.

Mow stepped back and said loudly, obviously for the benefit of the shaman and the others who still lingered on the windswept rocks, "Go now to your ordeal, Yellow Hair! When we reach the tribal camp, Mow the chief will send Kor and other warriors on the trail to meet and escort you back to the hut of the great chief." He ceremonially clasped Red Axe on the shoulder with his hand, and then, sweeping his fur cloak around him in truly regal fashion, turned and marched off, leaving Red Axe almost alone. Almost—for the witch doctor remained, crouched in the rain, silently watching. Obviously, he was going to stay until he had seen Red Axe on his way to obey the will of the gods. This also meant that Red Axe had to give up his half-formed notion of taking his weapons with him, ritual or no ritual. With a silent shrug, the blond American started down the slope to the floor of the crater. By the time he reached the other side, the watching figure had been hidden by the mist and rain. Ahead, the Singing Stones softly whistled an eerie note.

The rock became warm underfoot as he ascended the far side of the crater, and Red Axe saw steam coming up from cracks in the hardened lava. Not all the mist, then, was the sea breeze. The subterranean fires of the volcanic crater still smoldered below, and trickles of ground water, finding the molten rock in the depths, were driven forth again as jets of steam.

The Singing Stones themselves were awe-inspiring. Great black teeth on the edge of the volcano, they jutted flat-topped, an even half dozen, oddly angled and awry in the wind that hummed through them like the cries of a million lost souls.

Just below the crater rim, other monoliths had fallen inward, making a jumble of ragged black blocks like steps leading to the surviving titans. Here one flat, table-like slab, ten feet across, had been used as an altar. Remnants of leaves, flowers, and grain were still scattered across it, but of the bundle of meat and hides Mow's women had brought here there was no sign. Perhaps it had been thrown over the far side of the crater.

Red Axe was neither superstitious nor particularly religious, and yet, as he stood there in the gray gloom before those monstrous singing rocks and listened to the ageless voice of the wind howling in that lonely and deserted spot, he could feel a form of kinship with the primitive men who worshipped there. If ever a place was sacred to the elemental spirits of the earth, the wind, the stone, the underground secret fires, it was the Place of the Singing Stones.

He leaned both brawny arms upon the altar stone. The rock was warm, but an involuntary shiver ran over his body. At that very moment the whistling of the wind changed.

"Red Axe!"

West lifted his head in amazement.

"Red Axe!"

The deep eerie notes came again to be carried far out across the deserted crater. Was he hallucinating? Did the lava rock and thermal air and volcanic hot spring know his name?

"Red Axe!"

It could not be. Drawing the slim stone knife Mow had surreptitiously slipped to him—and now perhaps he knew why—he leaped up the rocky wall to stand between two of the stones, looking down on the far side of the volcano. The black lava fell in a sheer drop a hundred feet to jumbled broken rock below, where jets of steam from the hidden hot springs leaped and played like fountains. No sign of life, no habitation, not even a stunted tree or fern was visible, until a mile down the slope where the raw lava left off and the green began again.

There was no sound now but the wailing wind, no shape but the moving fog and steam. The man stood motionless. The yellow hair blowing back from his head, he crouched knife in hand, a fur-clad savage facing the eternal mystery of the supernatural.

The basic instincts of his ancestors, imprinted on the very shape of his brain, raised the gooseflesh along the back of his neck and down his muscular arms. His heart pounded in his ears as his blood pressure rose to charge the fighting muscles of his limbs with oxygen. His pupils dilated as he sought through the fog for any sign of an enemy. All was empty, lonely, as if the nearest human being was miles away—as indeed he had every reason to believe. But now the wailing ghostlike voice came again through the mist.

"The stones say death! Death to the yellow-haired stranger!"

Something stung his face, settled across his chest and left shoulder. Looking down he saw a plaited leather rope tightening across his body. The noose yanked him from his feet. As he fell on the wet black rocks, there appeared out of the swirling mist a figure of nightmare: huge, blank-eyed, the head bulky and the limbs elephantine, eight feet tall but vaguely human, it bounded across the slippery rocks toward its fallen victim.

Red Axe cried out—but not in fear. A single slash of Mow's dagger cut the restraining hide lasso from his body. Then with a leap he was on his feet, dodging the first attack of the weird monster of the rocks. Black and rocklike itself, it turned as Red Axe slammed into it. He seized and ripped the giant wickerwork-and-hide mask from the shoulders. A human face confronted him, its mouth open in terror and rage. A short stabbing spear held in one costumed hand flashed out. The blond giant sidestepped and caught the arm. The stone knife slashed through the bulky mammoth-hide sleeves, deep into the attacking arm, and the man screamed. Red Axe slammed his fist into the side of the man's head and yanked the spear from his nerveless grasp. He kicked the attacker into a crack in the lava rock, where the other lay gasping, nursing his wounded arm. Red Axe circled cautiously, waiting for more monster figures to appear out of the gloom. All was silent, save for the moaning of the wind and the harsh breathing of the wounded man.

"Stay there," he ordered, "or I'll run the spear through your treacherous heart!"

The American traced the leather rope to its end, where it lay quiet and unraveling on the rocks. Then he worked his way cautiously down the line of stone monoliths, expecting to find behind each one another costumed attacker. There was no one. He circled back, still wary, to where his defeated foe lay. The man was unknown to Red Axe, but perhaps he could be persuaded to talk. Here, however, the American was betrayed. Several large, jagged lava rocks had been hurled into the crevice while he lay helpless. Red Axe pressed a hand to the man's chest. He was dead.

11
RESCUE PARTY

HEY LEFT HIM ALONE, to walk back." Varna's dark eyes flashed with fire, her full lips curled in scorn. "This is the kinship, the courage, the bravery, the manhood, of the tribe of Mow, to leave a man alone and helpless in the desert."

"Not in the desert," soothed old Kor, standing his ground as best he could, "but in the sacred place of the spirits, at the request of the voices of the rocks."

"Nonsense!" dismissed the dark-haired beauty, bringing gasps of outrage from the onlookers in Nota's hall. "At the request of the witch doctor, more likely. And now what is to become of him—are we to wait here until the thipdars have picked his bones?"

"Nay, girl, calm yourself," the man replied, shifting his healing arm. "I will take the trail myself with a group I have picked—and with Red Axe's own mammoth Ma-Ah, whom he trained himself. We'll have him back to you, blessed by the magic of the spirits and unharmed."

Varna's ire began to dwindle. "Your spirits are not those of our tribe. It is hard for me to understand the ways of another people. At least you will take Elkar and the monkey-man and young Tumu . . ."

"Ah," said Kor, relieved that the argument seemed over and anxious to be reasonable, "that will be possible. A man who goes to receive the message of the rock spirits should

139

have the warriors of his own clan go to meet him and escort him back to the tribe."

"It is well," said Varna. "Go do what you must to make ready. The women of Nota's household will prepare food for their men to carry with them." Smiling at the wives and children around the central cooking fire, she took Kor's good arm and escorted him to the entrance of the building. The others reluctantly returned to work, only to be distracted once again by the voices of the pair raised in a new argument at the doorway. They turned with interest, but Varna hushed the man, and the rest of their discussion was held in low tones so that the group around the fire could not make it out.

When the men left the building, Varna and Onoloa went to the door with them. Onoloa volunteered to carry the meat and extra weapons to the stockade gate, and the men accepted. Varna bid them a quick good-bye and went back inside. At the cook fire, she spoke to the old woman who ran the household, picked up two empty water gourds, slung them over her shoulder, and left the hut through another door.

The spring from which the entire camp drew its water lay in the opposite direction from the stockade gate, where Varna wished to go. She was an unfamiliar sight on the dirt street, and dared not wander openly through the camp.

She walked reluctantly to the spring, filled her vessels, and took a somewhat roundabout way back, which brought her to the palisade wall. For a moment, there was no one in sight. Varna dropped the water gourds and unwound the rawhide rope she had concealed by wrapping it around her body under her hide dress. In two throws she had lassoed one of the sharpened stakes on the wall fifteen feet above her head. Quickly she swarmed up the rope, and with some difficulty swung one leg over the wall between the sharpened timbers. At any moment she expected to hear an outcry below her as she was discovered by some tribesman. She dared not even take time to look out from her high perch to catch sight of Kor and the promised mammoths at the main gate. She hauled up her rope, made sure it was secure, dropped it over the other side, and slipped down the outer wall to freedom. A moment later, the rope abandoned, she was crouched in the grass not far from the main gate and its watchtowers. At the gate, Kor and another man held three mammoths. They stood talking easily to a group of figures, in which Elkar's pale head made an identifying beacon. Varna watched for a moment, then gave the high-pitched cry of a hunting bird, much like a giant hawk, which patrols the skies over Pellucidar. Several of the men at the gate turned toward the sound. The birdcall came again, with Varna now lying flat in the grass on her back, whistling as loud as she could.

There was a shout from the gate guard. A spear shaft swung in an arc and a man went down. The three mammoths started off down the trail at a run. Smaller figures ran beside them, clutched at the long shaggy fur, and climbed to the quaking backs and shoulders. Varna jumped to her feet and ran to where she could intercept the mounted party. Mooh-lah, clinging to his mount's long hair with toes and tail, leaned down close to the thundering feet as the beast came beside her, and held out a hand. "Here you go, gilak-she. Your bow and arrows are already stored aboard."

Varna swung up and climbed to the back of the galloping tandor. "Did you have trouble back there at the gate?"

"Only a little," Mooh-lah chuckled. "The guard was somehow not deceived that Onoloa was another young man like her brother. It was necessary for Elkar to knock him down and he began yelling, so then we had to knock him out—in fact we may have damaged him quite a bit."

"They will pursue."

"Of course. They would have done so anyway, when you were found missing. Why worry about it?"

Why indeed, the girl thought, filled with the delight of

sunlight and the fresh breeze coming across the open veldt—
that and a sense of urgency concerning the fate of her man.

After a few miles, Kor slowed the shaggy mammoths to
a walk. The camp was now out of sight among the green
hills. "They will not set out after us immediately," he assured
the party. "First they will discover everything that happened—then Mow will probably send Nota and the men of
his family to see that we come back."

"Will Nota punish us for running off?" asked Onoloa.

"Not if you come back."

The women exchanged significant glances. Varna, at least,
had no intention of returning to virtual slavery in Mow's
walled camp. There was no reason to share this with the
well-meaning old warrior—at least not yet. Kor set a steady
pace with the lead tandor, the others following in single file,
since the width of the path did not allow them to ride side
by side. To each member of the party he assigned an area of
surveillance—front, right and left flank, rear, with two
charged to watch the skies for flying reptiles. The herds they
passed were all harmless grazing creatures, however, and only
a few birds and small pterodactyls flew overhead. The great,
green, tree-studded plains were free of large predators, and
the smaller ones stayed out of the way of the mighty tandors.

When many miles were behind them, they stopped at a
stream to eat and drink. Kor gave them little time to rest,
however. The mammoths were allowed to graze for only a
short while before he called the little group back to their
mounts. "It is better that we reach Red Axe before Nota and
the others catch up with us," was all that he would say. He
kept the party moving from then on, allowing only brief
halts to rest and feed their mounts and themselves.

Vigilance had to be maintained at all times on the trail,
for the party was too small to put out scouts. Kor would
not let them sleep on the move, although it would have been
easy to do so while lying on the rolling backs of the shaggy
mammoths. Tumu and Mooh-lah dozed when they dared,

risking a tongue-lashing from their leader when he caught them. Kor's policy paid off, however, and it was Tumu who caught sight of something moving among the hills to their left and softly called the older man's attention to it. The mammoth hunter gave a grunt of dismay. He had them stop and made the humans drop off the mammoth's backs so they would be less conspicuous. He himself lay prone on his mammoth's back and studied this new threat. Finally, he too slid to the ground.

"*Horibs*," he said quickly. "A small party, but not for us to fight. There may be more. Nota follows and he will not be surprised, even though these must be scouting the path we ride. Better we get to Red Axe's side quickly. There may be a war party of these about."

"What are they?" demanded Varna. "In my tribe's hunting grounds I have not heard of such, nor did I see anything yonder when you called to us to halt."

Kor shook his head, "Lucky your tribe, woman, that does not know the attacks of these creatures. They are like men, yet are not men. They hate gilaks and kill them—usually on sight. Sometimes they capture one alive, but that is worse, for they only carry him or her off to be tortured to death. They ride a giant lizard, something like a *slizak*. In fact, they themselves look much like slizaks."

Varna contemplated a manlike creature that looked like an iguana and decided that she did not care to meet one.

"Now," Kor went on, "we continue forward—on foot for a while—to make the tandors look like a grazing herd." They inched their way along, leaving the trail to wander through the thick grass of the Pellucidarian veldt, weapons in hand—Varna with an arrow nocked to her bowstring—until Kor deemed it safe to remount and proceed at their regular pace.

It was not long before signs of pursuit appeared. Little liking the description Kor had given them of the Horibs, Varna at first thought hopefully that it might be Mow's tribe. Whatever was moving behind them in the grass, however, was not the big chocolate brown hulks of mammoths—it was green. Brief glimpses were all they were afforded, as the party to their rear was obviously trying to avoid detection. Kor urged them on, over the next low rise, through a stand of vine-covered trees and down onto the trail. Once back on the trail, he sent the other two mammoths ahead at top speed, while he and Elkar took up the rear, watching for their mysterious pursuers. The shaggy tandors were rolling along at a run, but it was not long before the creatures in the rear made an appearance. Elkar gasped in surprise.

There were two kinds of beast on their trail now—both lizards. The mounts ran close to the ground on four squat legs, their long snouts questing in every direction as slender gray tongues flicked the air. They moved with remarkable speed, and their riders—for each monster carried two humanoid figures on its back—quickly spotted the fugitives and sent their reptilian steeds dashing in pursuit.

Elkar brought forth his bow and let fly an arrow. He did not have Varna's skill, and was shooting from the back of the moving mammoth; the shaft went wide of its target. The lizard riders took evasive action, however, leaving the trail and entering the high grass to either side.

"They will try to flank us," Kor called ahead to his party. "They carry lances and will run at the tandors' sides. Stay alert!"

Here the grass and underbrush grew thick and high as a man's head. The trail, never more than a footpath, was narrow enough so that the greenery brushed the lumbering mammoths on both sides. Overhead was only clear blue sky and blazing sun. Elkar could hear no sound but the thudding of the mammoth's feet and the swish and slap as they forced their way through the brush. He called anxiously to Kor that either their pursuers had withdrawn or they were moving noiselessly. That worthy did not turn from his anxious surveillance of their flank. "They move like the lightning," he warned, "and the big tandors make too much noise to hear them."

A moment later the underbrush cleared somewhat to the right and Tumu called out a warning. Suddenly the lizard riders appeared on both sides, leveled bone-tipped lances, and charged the last tandor in the line. Elkar's arrow went wide again, while Varna's took one attacker in the shoulder, causing him to drop his lance. The incredibly swift lizard rushed in on the mammoth's left flank and the wounded rider leaped to its back, clinging there with both hands as the other rider wheeled his beast and raced off into the brush. Simultaneously, the reptilian mount carrying the second pair of riders struck the other side of the mammoth, one lance striking deep into the hairy chest. The tandor squealed and bucked. Elkar kept his hold with difficulty, dropped his bow, and groped in his belt for a knife or an axe. The hideous creature clinging to the mammoth's hide hissed through half-open jaws and clawed its way up the heaving beast's left side at him. Elkar's fingers closed on his knife hilt, the foot-long steel blade shining in the Pellucidarian sunlight. As the wounded mammoth wheeled to strike at its tormentors, Elkar could hear Kor swearing briskly, a number of the mammoth man's oaths being totally original to his ears.

Holding on to the heaving back of the great beast with his bare toes and his left hand, Elkar grappled with his bizarre opponent. The lizard man seized his knife arm in a cold, clammy grasp. The pale man pulled loose and lunged forward to thrust the blade closer to the unblinking reptilian eyes. The face was snakelike, with the addition of small ears and a pair of horns on the forehead. The scales of the face were mottled green and gray, the soft underside of the neck white, where Elkar could see the pulsations of the arteries. The slit pupils were dilated now, as the knife withdrew, only to thrust again and again, plunging into the side of the neck. Blood spurted over the man's arm and shoulder. The Horib clung another moment, its fanged mouth open, the pointed tongue flickering in and out. Then the monster's grip relaxed. "Curse you, gilak!" the snake creature hissed, as it plunged to the ground beneath the mammoth's trampling feet.

Elkar felt Kor's good hand grip his belt and pull him back across the shoulders of their shared mount.

"What was that thing?" he gasped, still stunned by the apparition.

"Horib, I told you. Lizard man." Neither of the mounted lizards were now in sight. Elkar got their mammoth under control again. The other two tandors had circled back to their aid, the three wheeling beasts trampling a swath of flattened greenery. "Back on the trail," Kor called to the others. "Keep going—there may be a larger party not far behind."

The Pellucidarian mammoth runs with a pace that eats up miles. The big, shaggy brutes can keep it up for long periods of time—although time cannot be measured in the inner world. So it was that Varna and her companions knew only that they were tired and hungry when they finally burst into the open at the foot of the black, lava-covered hill that led up to the Place of the Singing Stones.

Kor called out to the lead tandor to halt. Too late! The three had emerged into a crowd of a dozen mammoths; in an instant they were surrounded by hairy brown warriors with spears. Kor's distress was obvious, and Varna guessed at once that these could not be members of Mow's tribe. They greeted the arrival of the newcomers with cries of surprise and hard laughter. In an instant they were menaced on every side by flint-tipped spears.

"Tribesmen of Mow!" cried a short, brown-skinned warrior with a bushy black beard. "The gods of the stones send us tribute!"

"Horibs pursue us, you idiot!" yelled Kor.

"Who's on guard?" the leader shouted to his men. "Ung— up on that hill! Some of you knock down these strangers and tie them up. Gently now—don't damage the shes!"

Onoloa and Tumu were dragged from their mount's back. Varna and Moo-lah on the lead mammoth, and Kor and Elkar bringing up the rear, put up such spirited resistance, however, that the mammoth men finally resorted to lassoing them with cleverly thrown rawhide nooses and pulling them down.

The leader of the strangers looked them over, prodding Varna and Onoloa with a fat finger through their bonds and laughing when they cursed at him.

"Leave these two down here with the rear guard," he said, scowling at his followers, "and see that no harm comes to them—understand?" The chief glanced around suspiciously. "Probably all nonsense about the Horibs," he said, "but we leave ten men here to guard. Ung—you stay in charge."

"Huh," grunted Ung. "Stay behind, guard the women, don't touch them, don't get to see the sacrifice. Why me, Chief? Why always me?"

"Always you," yelled the chief, "because if you don't do what I say, I club your head to a pulp! Understand?"

"Ung understand, Chief," muttered the man bitterly.

"You are crazy to tie us up like this," spluttered Kor. "We are of Mow's tribe and he will avenge us. Besides, there are Horibs behind us. Untie us and we will help you fight."

The chief kicked him in the ribs, knocking the wind out of him so he could not speak. "Pick these up," he directed a few of the warriors, "and carry them up to the altar stone."

Elkar had little opportunity to see the skull-decorated path that led to the crater's rim, for he was slung over the squat back of one of his hairy, smelly captors and carried with his feet and legs bound together, his arms bound to his sides. His head hung down the man's back, his pale blond hair dragging on the rocky ground. At the top, the three of them were unceremoniously dumped on the ground. They had a glimpse of the mist-filled crater and the distant monoliths, and heard the wind shriek and whistle among the rocks, as if evil spirits did indeed dwell there in the black lava rock.

The tribe's witch doctor ascended the narrow ridge of rock to one side, the chief and warriors watching expectantly as he launched into a long chant. Elkar strained futilely at his bonds. Kor, lying next to him, saw his face. "Do not despair, lad," the old hunter whispered, "Mow will avenge us most terribly."

"I don't want to be avenged," hissed Elkar, "I want to get my hands on that gloating brute before he touches Onoloa."

The chant stopped. The fur-clad savages listened expectantly and Elkar ceased his efforts to rub the rawhide thongs against the rocks beneath him to listen also. Among the wails and whistles of the wind he heard the sobbing voice of the spirits of the Singing Stones.

"Bring. Bring the sacrifice."

Once again the trussed captives were lifted to brawny shoulders and carried, down into the shallow crater and then across it, to be laid on the altar stone, side by side. Elkar felt his hair prickle on the back of his neck. Whence came the eerie, echoing voice?

The witch doctor drew a razor-sharp dagger of jagged black flint from his girdle and stepped to the stone. He grasped Elkar's long hair, pulled back his head, and laid the cold blade against his throat.

"Receive, O Spirits, the fresh blood of these strangers. Receive their souls into the sacred stones as their blood soaks into the ground. Grant us our prayer." The knife slid across Elkar's throat to the pulsating jugular vein and the great carotid artery beneath it.

"*Hold!*"

12

CONFRONTATIONS

HOLD! THE SPIRITS OF THE SINGING STONES reject your sacrifice. Do not kill these men!"

"Uh?" The witch doctor gazed up at the looming black stone monoliths in open-mouthed stupefaction.

"Leave! Leave the sacrifices. Cut their bonds and leave them here. The Great Spirit will deal with them," wailed the eerie voice.

The cavemen whispered together, hesitating. The chief seemed suspicious, the medicine man genuinely awed. The little group of tribesmen were obviously amazed and terrified. Turning his head, Elkar could see the consternation spreading through the party. He made a quick decision. What the supernatural forces of the Singing Stones wanted of him he did not know, but the intentions of the medicine man were obvious and involved his instant death.

"The spirits will swallow us up!" he cried, only partly feigning the fear in his voice. "Run before they descend upon us!"

The eerie voice answered him, but the words were not in a language Elkar knew. "Tell them not to throw you into the briar patch!" The tone was still sepulchral, but the unfamiliar words made his heart leap. The voice continued, now in the common speech of the gilaks, or human races, of Pellucidar. "Yes, leave quickly! The sacrifice is accepted and your prayers granted, but to be present when the spirits of the stones suck the living souls from the men will drive you all mad!"

The tribesmen bolted. The chief and the tribal wizard hesitated for a moment, until a low moaning from the rocks broke their nerve and they followed. In a moment the mist had closed around the bound captives. The murmur of the retreating men's voices and the sound of their feet on the lava faded.

"It's a strange way to die," whispered Kor. "I wish they had cut our bonds. I would like to meet the spirits with my hands free."

"Do not worry, you shall," Elkar replied. "Rescue is close at hand."

They waited. The wind sang in the rocks. Something stirred on the ridge above them. A dim figure moved in the mist, knife in hand. Elkar hissed between his teeth.

"Red Axe! I knew it must be you!"

"Ho, Red Axe," greeted Mooh-lah, "are you not glad we came to rescue you?"

"Old friend, I would be glad to see you under any circumstances." His knife severed the bonds on the man's hands.

Elkar interrupted: "Red Axe, these men have Onoloa and Varna captive at the foot of the hill."

"What!" The blond American hesitated, then turned to Kor. Bending over the man, he cut the thongs that bound his wrists and ankles. "Kor, who are these men? Do you recognize them?"

"Aye, Red Axe. This is the tribe of Rognar. Rognar the chief it was that the spirits spoke to, even now."

"Good, the spirits must speak again. Follow me." Without waiting to see if they obeyed, the big man climbed up between two of the central stones and let himself down into a narrow hole in the rocks, sliding feetfirst out of sight on his back. Elkar, first to follow, found himself in a wide cave. After a few yards, an opening in the roof of the cavern provided a view of the sky and the mist overhead.

Glancing about in the dim light, he made out the remains of a fire, a profusion of furs and food, and Red Axe's personal weapons. Standing against the wall of the cave were three bulky, empty suits of hide armor with detachable headpieces in the form of hideous bucket-shaped masks.

"Where—" he began, but his friend seized him and clapped a hand over his mouth. Placing his mouth next to Elkar's ear, Red Axe whispered urgently, "Do not speak! This is the voice of the spirits, and any sound here is carried outside to the crater. Warn the others!"

Elkar stood at the bottom of the entrance chute and held a warning hand to the lips of each man as he entered.

Red Axe advanced to the center of the cave and opened his mouth. For a moment the four listeners heard him hum, then the curving walls threw back the sound, doubled and redoubled until the bowl-shaped cavern vibrated with it. The blond American filled his lungs and they saw his mouth move. A deafening sound filled the cave and wailed like a banshee out through the open roof and across the crater.

"Rog . . . nar . . . bring . . . me . . . the . . . women!"

The humming died away. Red Axe repeated his message twice, then returned to his guests.

"Do not speak," he whispered. He turned to search the cave for weapons, choosing a stone axe, knives, and three flint-tipped spears, which he distributed among them. Gathering his axe and bow he led them up the lava chimney to the surface.

"So, Red Axe, you were that terrifying voice of the spirits," began Elkar.

"Yes, and doubtless many before me." Red Axe replied. "The voice of the spirits of the stones must have been an ancient, if not too honorable, profession. I killed one such, though I think several others escaped me. Now, we must divide our forces. There is a path to the left that runs around the crater's rim. Kor and I will go that way and see if our friends are obeying instructions. Elkar, you take charge here. Station yourselves out of sight behind the Singing Stones. We may be able to trick them into giving up Varna and Onoloa—but if not, we will fight for them."

The mist obscured the crater floor. Kor followed Red Axe along a barely perceptible path—usually just a series of flatter black lava stones—below the rim. They could see nothing moving out in the crater itself.

"The bastards have probably gone down the trail to the mammoths by now," Red Axe hissed. "How did they come to get their hands on you and the women in the first place, Kor?"

The mammoth man explained in a few sentences.

"How many are there?"

"Two tens at a guess—maybe a few more that we didn't see."

"Damn! And us with only five and the two women held prisoner. I hope I can think of something."

"You will, Red Axe," said Kor confidently. "You saved all of us singled-handed."

The American grunted and held up a hand in warning. They had circled to the opposite side of the crater. Cautious stalking took them to the rocky defile that led down to the plains below. It was empty. The two men listened as the wind blew puffs of mist through the gully below them. Faint voices could be heard from downhill, none from the crater to their right.

"They've gone down to the mammoths," whispered Kor. "What now? Shall we go back to the cave of the spirit voices and wait?"

"I don't trust them," said Red Axe. "From what you've told me, they have already broken the taboo or truce of the holy place by attacking you. I think we had better climb down and see what they are about. I wouldn't put it past this Rognar to mount his mammoths and ride off."

"Good," said his companion, "but move with care. They will have guards."

The warning was well taken, for as the two men came into view of the tramped open space where Rognar's men and his dozen mammoths still milled about in confusion, they heard voices raised in sharp dispute. As Red Axe had predicted, Rognar had ordered his party to mount and flee. He was opposed by the tribal witch doctor who apparently urged obedience to the voice of the Singing Stones. The two squared off, facing each other in the clearing, while the rest of the party gathered about their leaders to listen. Behind the men and their two beautiful captives loomed the brown hulks of the patient mammoths. Here the mists had blown clear and the crisp hot sun of Pellucidar blazed down on the rocks. Rognar's voice was raised and he fingered the huge stone hunting axe in his hands. What further sacrilege he might have committed will never be known, for at that moment there came a new interruption.

At the far end of the clearing from the rocks where Red Axe and Kor watched, the trail to the Singing Stones wound off between low green hills to the lush plains below. A new party now rode up this trail.

"Ho!" cried the leader of this group from the neck of his mammoth. He raised his axe above his head. The watchers could see that he was missing his right arm.

Rognar's tribesmen turned to the newcomers in some consternation. Hanging his axe down his back by a rawhide thong, Mow dismounted from his mammoth and, weapon once more in hand, advanced toward the disputants in the human circle before him. To the chief's rear, five more mammoths crowded into the clearing. Brandishing axe and spear, their riders climbed to the ground.

"What does Rognar do with my people?" cried Mow. "Does the tribe of Rognar break the peace of the sacred Singing Stones? Let the shes go. Where are the four men who accompanied them?"

Rognar had fallen back a few steps at Mow's bold advance. Now he glanced from side to side as if reassuring himself that his men outnumbered Mow's

"Mow had best watch his tongue," he snarled, "or he too may find himself on the altar of the Singing Stones with his throat cut!"

"What?" the one-armed chieftain cried. "Have you dared to sacrifice my men? Only blood on the ground will avenge this deed, Rognar!"

The next moment, all was confusion. Mow tried to close with his opponent, but Rognar withdrew behind a screen of his own men. Mow advanced, whirling his heavy axe about his head. His own tribesmen rushed to cover his back, and the chief became the point of a wedge trying to drive into the milling mass of his enemies. There were cries and the clash of weapons. Mow's axe battered two men to the ground. Rognar shouted confused orders and his group began to give way, backing toward the path to the crater of the Singing Stones.

"Kor," whispered Red Axe, "go quickly across the crater and bring the others." The mammoth man clambered over the rocks, dropped into the path, and vanished up it.

Mow's attack had been halted, and behind the melee Rognar was organizing six of his men and lifting the bound bodies of his female captives over the heads of the combatants. Strangely, neither side made any attempt to use their mammoths as weapons. As the warriors joined the fray, they climbed down from their mounts and left them grazing or shifting peacefully from foot to foot, swinging their hairy trunks from side to side. The men would then gather their weapons and fling themselves into the battle with ferocious war cries. Several cavemen had been put out of action on both sides, although as yet no one appeared to have been killed since Mow's first assault.

Rognar and six tribesmen, four of whom were carrying the women, turned and started up the trail to the crater.

"To the stones with them!" cried the chieftain to his men. "These will die before we'll turn them over to old One Arm." But as the group rushed up the stony path, there leaped to the ground before them a new obstacle to Rognar's plan. Towering over his opponents by a foot to a foot and a half, his teeth bared in a fighting grin, Red Axe barred the path.

"No man shall pass!" he cried. "Release the captives and surrender to Mow!"

"Demons of the Fiery Sea!" cursed Rognar, from the rear of the group. "Who is this one? Cut him down!"

Two willing tribesmen rushed to do their chief's bidding. The path was narrow, with steep irregular walls of lava rocks rising six to ten feet on either side. They could approach together only with difficulty. The steel blade in the blond giant's hands flashed in the sunlight, smashed to slice off the stone head of an opposing weapon, and reversed its flight to sink into the torso of one of Rognar's followers. The smaller man, holding the wooden shaft of his headless axe in both hands, tried to fall back, but his doom was upon him. Red Axe had heard his mate threatened, and his only thought was to reach her side. The red-painted axe head slashed through the useless parry of arm and weapon handle and sank into the man's neck. The next instant Red Axe had wrenched it free and turned to defend himself against two more attackers.

A quick upward swing blocked a murderous axe cut to his head. The force of the blow jarred his arms and spine. Then, with a heave of his great shoulders, he threw his opponent back against the rocks. Varna's bound body had been dropped into the path. Red Axe advanced. Placing one foot over her so that he stood astride her helpless form, he turned to face his enemies, his face still a ferocious mask of rage, and his body in a half crouch. He held the great axe at guard across his chest, the steel blade dripping blood on the black lava stones.

"Come on, Rognar, come and die!"

Rognar and his remaining guard hesitated and drew back

from this horrifying apparition. For a moment there was almost complete silence in the narrow defile, except for the harsh breathing of the battlers and the clear shouts from the glade below.

"Rognar, Rognar!" called a voice from the lower end of the path. "Stop the combat. Mow will parley!"

"Withdraw," said Rognar, his eyes still studying the face of Red Axe, his new nemesis. "Leave the other girl. We will see what the old fool wants." The party of mammoth men descended the path, leaving the bodies of two of their comrades along with the bound captives. In a moment, Red Axe had dropped his weapons, drawn his knife, and cut the wrappings of rawhide on the wrists of Varna and Onoloa.

"Oh, my warrior," breathed his mate, placing both her arms around his neck, "I never doubted you were here, but you did appear at the most opportune moment!"

"And you?" asked Red Axe. "Are you both unharmed?"

"Unharmed, insulted, angry," replied his beautiful mate, "and worst of all, disarmed. I wish dearly for a few arrows and my own bow." She glared down the trail at the retreating Rognar.

"Wait, my love, let us see what Mow plans to do," answered Red Axe. "Besides—" But he was interrupted by the sound of running feet on the trail above them. He swung Varna's body behind him with one hand and picked up his bloodstained axe with the other. In a moment, however, he and the girls cried out in recognition as Kor, Elkar, Mooh-lah, and Tumu pounded down the trail to join them. Elkar swept the slender brown Hapuan maiden up off the ground and crushed her gently to his chest.

"Elkar, Elkar," she whispered, "Mow has come to save us."

Below them in the glade, Mow and Rognar, each surrounded by a knot of followers, confronted each other across an open space where lay the corpses of three of their followers.

Mow looked up as Red Axe and his followers appeared

on the rocks to Rognar's rear. A grin split his wide ugly face. He boldly assumed that they were allies, despite the fact that he had been pursuing them as fugitives from justice. Calmly he pointed out to Rognar that he was now almost evenly matched, and that as violator of the tribal taboos, he was clearly in the wrong. Rognar was not quick to yield, however. It was plain to him that his force still outnumbered Mow. Although most of his men had been wounded, Mow's small group had not fared much better, and Red Axe's reinforcements, while formidable, were poorly armed and included the two women, whom he discounted.

Mow challenged the other chief to a duel of single combat to settle the dispute. His followers sent up a cheer and Rognar's men turned expectantly to the tribal leader. His reluctance was obvious, but he had not risen to leadership of a tribe of cavemen without combat, and he was still fresh, while Mow was already weary from fighting. Rognar selected one of several long-handled stone axes offered him by his men and stepped forward. The opposing groups fell back to give the combatants room to wield their axes.

Rognar took his weapon in both hands and rushed his opponent, raising the axe for a great overhead blow. Mow was not there when it struck. The wily fighter had sidestepped. Unable to get his left-handed weapon into striking position he threw a body block into his opponent, knocking him off balance, and circled for an opening. Rognar regained his balance in time to parry an axe blow with the shaft of his own weapon.

"Red Axe," whispered Varna, "my bow and the other weapons lie in that bundle behind the men on the right and close to the mammoths."

"Very good. Our whole group will move closer. You slip that way, get the bundle, and return at once to the trail behind us."

Thwack! Thud! There was another exchange of blows between the two chiefs. This time Mow blocked Rognar's swing and then made contact with him. Though only the shaft of that deadly axe struck across the other chief's ribs, the sound of cracking bone was clearly audible to the silent group of watchers. Rognar fell back three paces, but kept his feet, regaining the initiative with a driving attack that Mow dodged and blocked with difficulty. Meanwhile, Varna stealthily secured the weapon bundle. She paused a moment to select her precious bow and quiver before moving to return to her companions. It was at that point that one of the Rognar tribesmen turned and saw her bending over the stag-hide bundle with the bow in her hands. He stepped toward her.

"Varna!" called Red Axe anxiously. The girl looked up. Inside the ring of combat, Mow sidestepped another rush, and swung a one-handed riposte that glanced across his enemy's shoulder blades and knocked him to the ground. Mow stepped up and raised his axe over his head.

Just then a shout broke out. *"Horibs!"*

Five of the great mounted lizards burst into the clearing, three coming from the trail and two over the rise of the nearest hill behind Varna. The mammoths began a chorus of trumpeting. Mow called out for the cavemen to fall back to the rocks at the entrance to the crater trail. In doing so, he turned his back for an instant on his rival chieftain, who had lost no time in regaining his feet. Then, to the watching Red Axe, it seemed that all hell broke loose. The reptilian Horibs raised a shrill cry and charged, half of them rushing the riderless mammoths and only three the retreating gilaks. The man confronting Varna grabbed for her with both hands. The girl dropped the hide bundle and came up with a steel-bladed hunting knife in her right hand. She hit her attacker dead center, just below the breastbone. The full length of the blade went into him up to the hilt, severing his aorta. At the same moment, Rognar swung a roundhouse blow with his long-handled axe from behind Mow's back. The stone head of the weapon took the tough old chieftain in the right temple and threw him sideways onto the ground.

13
IN THE NICK OF TIME

"*TANDOR, TANDOR, VAHA!*" Rognar and several of the men cried simultaneously. "Mammoth, mammoth, kill!" The nearest Horibs rushed into the mass of cavemen on the backs of their *gorobors*, or giant lizards, their long bone-tipped lances impaling two of Rognar's men. One of the mammoths plucked a Horib from his mount in a curl of trunk and threw him across the clearing to smash into the lava rocks over Red Axe's head. Varna left her opponent on the ground, still kicking feebly, and raced to join her mate, as the mass of the mammoth men fell back before the assault. The big brown mammoths were squealing with fury. One had been speared by two lances on the first assault and had sunk to his knees. Red Axe saw that the retreating cavemen were leaving Mow's unconscious body in the path of the oncoming lizards.

"Kor! Elkar! To Mow, quickly—we must carry him to safety!" His little party surged forward. Hissing with rage, one of the Horibs leaned from the side of his reptilian mount to strike at Red Axe with his lance. The big American deflected the blow with his axe. The snakelike face of the creature loomed only a foot from him, the lidless eyes with slit pupils gazing into his own. *Thunk!* Suddenly an arrow jutted from the creature's chest; the Horib pitched forward onto the ground before him, the feathered shaft protruding between its shoulder blades. Red Axe took no time to look back; he knew there was only one archer of such skill within

159

a hundred miles of the Singing Stones, and that Varna had reclaimed her bow.

The trumpeting tandors, trunks rolled up between their tusks, bucked at and gored the big lizards on either side. Dust and confusion covered the movements of the three friends as they located Mow and lifted him across Red Axe's broad shoulders. As they turned to retreat, a gorobor caught sight of them. The giant reptilian beast of burden revealed a new weapon, as a six-foot-long tongue lashed out, glanced off the unconscious body of the chief, and encircled Elkar by the neck. Yanked backward, the man lost his balance and stumbled, dropping his spear. Burdened as he was with the body of Mow, Red Axe was relatively helpless, but Kor was equal to the occasion. Dropping the axe he was carrying, he drew a flint knife from his loincloth and slashed at the tongue until he had cut it completely in two. Greenish blood gushed from the wounded member and the gorobor drew back. The three dashed to safety under the clawed feet of the monster as Varna's arrows flickered over their heads.

At the entrance to the narrow rocky defile, the cavemen had bunched together, and then turned to fight for their lives. Varna, Onoloa, and Tumu had climbed the rocks commanding the trail on the left, and from this vantage the beautiful maiden from Val-An plied her bow. Three of the giant lizards were trying to get at the defenders, the other two being engaged by the mammoths. The great triangular reptilian heads with their fearsome fangs and lashing tongues kept the mammoth men at bay, while the Horibs' long lances stabbed at them again and again.

Red Axe was able to push through the melee with the other two guarding his back. Mooh-lah and Tumu joined him, one on either side, and helped force a path through the press to place the senseless body of Mow the chief on the trail above the conflict. Then Red Axe turned back to the battle. Rognar was keeping well to the rear and out of danger, but his men and Mow's were fighting like cornered rats. The gorobors had knocked down three of them. Even as they watched, a hapless caveman was seized by one of the big lizards and dragged screaming back down the trail.

Red Axe and Elkar pushed their way to the front. Axes swinging, they closed on the head of the reptile closest to them. The Horib riding the beast attempted to fend them off with his lance, but Kor and several of Mow's men grasped the shaft of the weapon and tried to wrest it from him. In a moment the creature was dragged from his perch just behind the shoulder of the gorobor and battered to the ground, where willing hands made short work of him. The now-riderless giant lizard withdrew from its enemies, its long tail lashing the ground. The remaining Horib turned his mount when he saw that he was in danger of being surrounded. One of Varna's arrows caught him in the back. He nearly fell, but had regained his balance when a thrown flint axe crashed into the side of his head. He toppled off the lizard, which ran down the trail, its long purple tongue flickering in and out of its mouth with anxiety. The furious mammoths saw it coming, and, encouraged by shouts from the men, two of the bulls charged the beast, one on either side. The great ivory tusks gored into its ribs and lifted it off the ground to be dropped again, still kicking and squirming. The furry mammoths reared up on their hind legs and crashed down on the wounded beast, each great forefoot like a pile driver, crushing ribs, shoulder blades, and spine.

With a great shout, the men crowded in pursuit. The trumpeting and squealing of the enraged mammoths was deafening. The remaining Horibs, still on their mounts, showed signs of lost morale and turned to flee. Red Axe and Mooh-lah found themselves at the forefront. A flick of the long gray tail of the nearest lizard came close to knocking them both off their feet. West axed a hind leg. The creature turned and lashed out at him with that incredible purple tongue. As the coil of moist, slightly warm flesh encircled his raised arms, he pulled back with all the strength of his giant shoulders and broke free, Mooh-lah stabbing at the tongue as it rolled back into the beast's mouth. The Horib on the lizard's back swung his lance in a roundhouse blow that the monkey-man dodged easily. Then the two were inside the lizard-man's guard and they rushed to capitalize on their advantage. Red Axe attacked the shoulder and forelimb of the gorobor while Mooh-lah, jabbing with the spear, kept its rider on the defensive. The Horib hissed obscenities, trying to get a shorter grip on the long lance so that it could be used to parry Mooh-lah's attack. The gorobor staggered and went down, blood gushing from the axe wounds in its smashed right forelimb. The Horib nimbly jumped clear and tried to run for it. With bloodthirsty war cries, the tribesmen of Mow and Rognar rushed after him. Mooh-lah and Red Axe stayed behind to dispatch the giant lizard and then looked about at the scene of carnage in amazement. One of the mammoths was dying in a pool of blood, having been lanced through to the heart. Two of the gorobors were dead. The others had escaped, though even now Rognar's men were organizing pursuit on mammoth-back. Seven men and four Horibs had been killed, and several of the survivors were tending various wounds. Bodies were strewn everywhere. As two mammoths thundered from the glen with armed savages on their backs to pursue the remaining three gorobors, a relative quiet finally settled over the battlefield.

"Red Axe! Kor!" Red Axe turned. To his amazement, he saw that Mow was on his feet. When the one-armed chieftain staggered, Elkar hurried to his side, and the wounded man leaned on his shoulder.

"Someone go after those hotheads on the mammoths and get them back before they are ambushed," ordered Mow. "Red Axe, get some of your people up on the hills to keep an eye out for another party of Horibs—or anyone else. We can't trust these dung beetles of Rognar's to keep a simple guard."

"Aye, aye, Chief," said Red Axe, grinning, "We are glad to see you still alive. I must admit when Rognar struck you down, I thought you were done for."

"I've been hit from behind by better fighters than that," the old chief boasted. "But waste no time, Yellow Hair, and get your lookouts started." Red Axe turned to obey. He found some of Rognar's men who had suffered only minor wounds and took them to the hilltop nearest the glen. Kor organized a party on mammoth-back to recall the pursuers. Elkar, with the help of the two women, moved the more seriously wounded back up the path to the crater. Rognar turned up—unharmed of course—but did not seem to be in the mood to dispute Mow's command of the situation.

By the time West had returned to the main party, the old chief, assisted by Elkar, Kor, and Varna, had divided the remaining men into two groups. The more seriously wounded, with Mow himself and a guard consisting of Varna, Elkar, and Tumu, all of whom were unhurt, took temporary refuge in the rocky trail. All the reasonably able-bodied men, including Rognar, were mounted on the remaining mammoths.

"If we have to fight," Mow told Red Axe, "we will have the advantage of the tandors. I think even the mounts of the Horibs could not climb the crater walls and come up on us from behind, but we should have someone at the top of the path to warn of attack from the rear."

"I will go, Christopher," said Varna, picking up her weapons. "Onoloa and Tumu can come with me."

Mow started to object, but his face was pale and he propped himself up feebly with his one arm. The man next to him had been speared through the chest by a Horib's lance and was coughing blood. Beyond him was a warrior with a broken arm.

"Right, Varna," said Red Axe. "Be careful." A shout from one of the hilltop lookouts turned him around. "I'll see what that is."

Even as he ran up the grassy slope, Red Axe could see the cause of the disturbance. A great flying lizard had circled over the hill and continued on upwind. Now it turned, and, with a few flaps of its great leathery wings, swooped down toward the two cavemen on the hilltop. They drew back their flint-tipped spears to the throwing position.

"Wait!" Red Axe shouted. "Do not harm the beast! I'll run a spear through the man who tries it!"

When the pterosaur had landed and gravely inspected the scene, it took off a leather pack it had been wearing, extracted a slate and a piece of chalk, and gravely wrote, "The reptiles who tried to evolve into men. A most unsavory species, Red Axe. I hope you have not been occupying yourself entirely with combat."

"Just about," the man wrote in return. "I am very glad to see you again. You were gone a large number of lifetimes of some small creature or other." Red Axe could not remember the Mahar symbols for long and short time intervals. In a timeless world, the intelligent race used a clumsy system of biological clocks in which a short period was the life span of a tiny fly that died immediately after laying its eggs and a long time was the life of one of the Mahars themselves.

"I had to wait for your friends on the surface world to find all the things we needed," wrote Zed. "And then I had to find you."

"How did you accomplish that? We are nowhere near our original line of march."

"No, but my ancestors found food by circling in the sky and perceiving small animals moving on the ground." Zed clacked her beak in a manner Red Axe knew indicated amusement. "Your hair, my friend, is easy to see from the sky, and there was enough movement here to catch the eye of a mere fledging just out of her egg. I knew that if there was sufficient disturbance and confusion, you would most likely be in the middle of it. And you were." The creature finished this message with a flourish of her wing fingers and handed it over to the human to read.

Red Axe smiled, hoping the other would know what it meant. "Did you see any large body of Horibs in our vicinity?" he queried. The Mahar made a negation sign with her wings, and the American gave this news to one of the mammoth men, who was watching this interchange with amazement, and told him to carry it to Mow. Then he and the Mahar unpacked the electronic instruments the pterosaur had carried from the communication terminal. One of these was a transmitter on the home-base frequency. Red Axe called the surface laboratory and reported in, beginning to relay the story of his most recent adventures to his anxious friends in California. His story was interrupted when a messenger from the glade below ran breathlessly up to tell him that he was urgently needed.

Red Axe looked at the caveman's paled face. "What is it?"

"Mow the chief is possessed by a demon."

"A demon?"

"Aye, an evil spirit has seized him and he falls to the ground kicking and jerking and frothing at the mouth."

Red Axe hurried to the scene, Zed the Mahar flapping in his wake. The old chief lay senseless on the ground, Elkar bending anxiously over him. A hasty examination showed only the terrible bruise on his temple where Rognar's axe had hit him.

"What do you think, Red Axe?" asked Elkar. "Will he die?"

"I need advice before I can answer that, and the radio set is up on the hilltop," West answered. "Have two men make some kind of a litter and carry him up there. Did Varna bring my first aid kit? Good, find it for me." He ran back up the hill to the transmitter.

"Hello, Santa Monica base? I've got an emergency. Call the Medical School on the phone and get me a neurological consultant—this man is in a coma."

In a few minutes Red Axe was able to relay a description of the problem to the editor of this narrative.

"The diagnosis is obvious, West. Your man was hit on the head and knocked out. Then he had a brief lucid interval, followed by a return of unconsciousness and convulsion. He has a fast-developing intracranial hematoma—a blood clot on the brain—and probably arterial bleeding."

"But, Doctor Holmes, what am I going to do for him? This is a tough, but admirable old bird, and I'd like to save him."

"You need to open his head and extract the blood clot."

"But I can't do that! I've had no experience at all with that kind of surgery," gasped Red Axe. "Besides, my first aid kit has only a few tools for sewing up wounds, and nothing for making holes in a man's skull!"

"Then I'm afraid he's likely to die," sighed his consultant, "unless you can get him back to the disintegrator for transport to the surface."

"Impossible—it's hundreds of miles across wild and hostile territory swarming with prehistoric monsters that you wouldn't believe. Even on mammoth-back we couldn't make it in time." Red Axe cursed under his breath. He sat on the grass, Mow sprawled in front of him. The unconscious man's breathing was regular but his face was pale."

"Do you want us to get a neurosurgeon on the line for you?" asked the operator in Santa Monica.

"Negative," Red Axe replied. "Hey, wait a minute! Didn't Neolithic European man do some kind of skull trepanation? Where's that witch doctor? Is he still alive?" One of the cavemen nodded his head. "Good, then get him up here!"

A few minutes later Red Axe watched while the medicine man of Rognar's tribe, who said his name was Zarko, examined Mow's head and listened to his urgent expostulation.

"A bad wound," the savage said. "He's not likely to survive. Takes too long to make the sacrifices and pray to the spirits before cutting out the demons."

"No time for that," Red Axe urged. "He must be operated on, cut open quickly, before it kills him."

"I agree," said the witch doctor, "but I cannot risk releasing this demon from his head until the spirits sends me a message that the demon will not attack me or some other member of the tribe as soon as it is free."

"Ah," said Red Axe, "a message from the spirits? I'll get you a message from the spirits." He turned to the transistorized radio set, which had been silent since Zarko had come on the scene, and explained his problem in English. To the witch doctor's amazement, the little black box began to talk back in the strange language. Soon he heard the American address the box with a long, complicated question, and then listened in wonder as the eerie voice said: "Zarko must do what Red Axe asks," in the Pellucidarian tongue—albeit with an atrocious accent.

"No harm will come to myself or these others when the demon is released?" he asked in disbelief. Red Axe turned to the magic box. "No harm will come to the rest? Repeat: no harm will come to the rest." The voice of the spirits replied slowly. "No harm will come to the rest." Zarko had seen ventriloquism. He made Red Axe ask the box to speak again while he held one hand over the American's lips, but the message was repeated with even greater confidence. Zarko nodded his acquiescence. "Get me three sharp flint knives," he demanded.

Elkar hastened to secure the necessary implements. Red Axe conferred with the magic box again. He was concerned that they were about to operate under very nonsterile conditions. Watching Zarko choose the sharpest of the flints Elkar brought him and carefully clean it with a piece of animal skin only deepened his concern. He got out his penicillin and gave the patient a large prophylactic dose of the antibiotic. The witch doctor built a small fire and took several powders from a hide bag he wore at his waist. One of these he mixed with water to make a paste he rubbed over the wounded man's temple, the other he tossed onto the fire where it smoldered to produce a cloud of thick smoke.

Zarko made three quick incisions in Mow's scalp and folded down a flap of skin exposing the bone of the skull. Selecting a flint knife with a rounded blade, he then carefully scraped the live bone in a circle, gradually deepening the scratch until a deep groove loosened a disc of bone two inches in diameter.

Inserting the tip of his stone knife, the witch doctor raised the bone and exposed the brain beneath. Red Axe, watching intently over his shoulder, whistled in amazement at the purplish blood clot revealed on the surface of the protecting membranes that covered the pulsating brain.

"Behold," said Zarko, "the demon."

When the blood clot had been gently removed, the witch doctor withdrew and let West sew up the scalp over the open wound with his twentieth-century steel needles and catgut suture. The American then made a head bandage of gauze from the first aid kit. The patient did not awaken, but his pulse and respiration were regular.

Red Axe cleaned his hands with a little water and fresh grass. He sought out the witch doctor and found him crouched on the hillside a short distance away. Zed joined him and the two of them approached. In one hand the man had a short white tube, and as he held it up they could see that it was a length of bone, probably part of the leg bone of a small antelope, that had been cut at both ends and then resealed with beeswax.

"What have you there?" Red Axe asked.

"I have imprisoned the demon within," said the man with a grin. "Every demon I have treated I have kept captive this way. I have a collection of twice my fingers' numbers."

Red Axe shuddered, but then considered that some surgeons of his own world collected the gallstones, bullets, and other impedimenta they removed from their patients' bodies.

"You did a good job," he said. "Mow seems well."

"He will live," the medicine man predicted, "unless a new demon forms and takes over where this one was."

Very true, thought West, reflecting that the man knew more than he had given him credit for, and that a lot of experience must go into this skill. "I thank you for saving Mow. He is the chief of a rival tribe. We are grateful."

"Oh, that," said Zarko. "Rognar has no respect for the spirits or the place of the spirits. Mow is a religious man. Besides, Rognar struck him unfairly from behind. And then," he raised the bone tube to his eyes and stared at it happily, "it gives me another captive demon and increases my power over the spirit world!"

A good technician, thought Red Axe, but a superstitious fanatic all the same. From down the hillside came a shout. Kor ran up to report in breathless tones.

"Red Axe, it is Tumu. He says that Varna and Onoloa have been captured!"

14
"YOU AGAIN!"

RED AXE'S FIRST THOUGHT was of a raiding party of Horibs. He shouted a warning to the group below of possible attack from the crater rim. Then he raced down the hillside, gesturing Zed to accompany him. A quick council of war followed, with Red Axe, Elkar, Mooh-lah, Kor, and the Mahar participating. Tumu now told his story in detail. The three had been attacked by monsters with great bulky bodies who had appeared out of the mist and snared the two women with nooses. Red Axe recognized the description of the spirits of the Singing Stones with consternation. How many enemies was he dealing with? Tumu had seen two figures and thought there were more. Perhaps the displaced Voice of the Spirits had gone for reinforcements after Red Axe had evicted him? In any case, there was no time to lose.

"Kor, I want you to stay here in command." The old warrior looked disappointed. "I must have someone I can trust at my back if the Horibs attack again. There's no telling how long it will take Mow to recover. We can't trust Rognar, he'd probably knife Mow in the ribs while he was still unconscious.

"You will take the flying monster, surely?" Kor asked.

Red Axe shook his head. "She does not fight. I will ask her to circle overhead and keep you informed of any enemies approaching. Elkar, Mooh-lah, Tumu, and I will go after Varna and Onoloa."

"Then take your mammoth. If you have to pursue the kidnappers, he will travel faster than men on foot."

"Good idea. Elkar, run and get him. Kor, Rognar's men still outnumber you—you will have to stay on the alert."

"Never fear, Red Axe. Rognar will not surprise me like he did poor Mow. I will not turn my back on him."

The rescue party clambered up the shaggy sides of old Ma-Ah and Red Axe spoke in his ear. "Good hunting!" called Kor. The great beast started up the trail to the crater, brushing against the rock walls as he lumbered along.

They dismounted at the crater rim and Tumu showed them the spot where the attack had occurred. Red Axe and Elkar stood waiting helplessly while Mooh-lah searched the ground for tracks. Both city-bred—one in Los Angeles, the other in the underground city of Phuma—neither of them could find a trace on that volcanic dust and rock. The monkey-man crawled about on his knees, spear in one hand, knife held coiled in his tail up over his back. After a while he settled on one area, carefully sniffed the rocks in a six-foot radius, and straightened up.

"Easy, Red Axe," he said, pointing through the mist. "Straight ahead, back to the altar stone where Elkar almost got his throat cut."

"Come, Ma-Ah, old fellow," Red Axe called as he climbed up the mammoth's thick coat to his massive shoulders. "Forward!"

The great beast lurched into a lumbering trot. Elkar jumped for the mammoth's side and held on, then dragged himself up hand over hand. The other two ran behind.

The mist was too thick to see the Singing Stones, although the wind brought their musical wailing to the ears of the anxious pursuers. Fortunately, the mist was not too heavy to prevent Red Axe from getting some view of the old trail a few feet ahead of them. He wondered if they were running headlong into an ambush. No time to consider that, he told himself. The women's captors might already be—*wait*! What was that?

Something was moving along the ground to one side of the barely perceptible trail—something about the size of a man, crawling. A word in the mammoth's big ear brought the beast to a halt. Axe in hand, West swung to the ground.

With a gesture and a few whispered commands, he posted his men to guard the trail, both front and rear. Weapon at the ready, he approached the shape lying prone on the ground in the mist. The creature made a muffled noise that in no way resembled speech. Now that he was closer, however, he could see that it was unmistakably a human being. As a matter of fact . . . he rushed forward, knelt, and cut the bonds and gag from a trembling form.

"Varna, my darling!" He clasped the ebony-tressed head to his chest.

"They couldn't carry us both," she gasped. "There are only two and they are wearing great hulking suits and masks of hide. Onoloa is alive, Chris, but we've got to hurry!"

"Onto the tandor then, quick! Are you hurt? Can you walk?"

"I can kill. Give me a weapon."

"Up you go. Tumu, give her your bow. They are somewhere just ahead, and I think I know where."

The party's arrival at the altar of the Singing Stones was heralded by an outburst of eerie moaning and whistling from the giant wind instrument itself. The situation, however, was exactly what they had feared.

The bound form of Onoloa lay on the altar stone. Over her bent the grotesque masked figure Red Axe thought of as the Spirit of the Singing Stones. On either side of it were other figures, similarly garbed and armed with rawhide ropes. Varna drew arrow to bow as Elkar rushed forward with a growl, spear in hand. The masked monstrosity yanked the girl's body half upright and they saw the flint knife at her throat. For a moment no one moved.

A low laugh rang out. "So, Yellow Hair, we meet again!"

Red Axe slid both legs over the left side of Ma-Ah's neck,

preparatory to dropping to the ground. One grotesque gloved hand pulled Onoloa's head up by her long black hair while the other flourished the knife. "Stay on your beast, Yellow Hair! Do not move, any of you, or the woman dies!"

"Release her," Red Axe called, "and we will let you go. Harm her and you will be slowly cut to pieces and fed to the thipdars."

"The gods decide!" shrieked the Spirit of the Singing Stones. "They let you escape, but only so that you would deliver into my hands the rightful bride of Manu."

"Bride of . . . what does he mean?" hissed Varna.

"I'm afraid it's only too obvious," Red Axe whispered. "Can you get an arrow into him if he lowers that knife?"

"I can try," she replied.

"The priest of Manu is a helpless old man," Red Axe cried loudly, "and the power of Manu is nothing here, so far from the sea. I do not believe the tentacles of the sea god can stretch so far. You must prove to me who you are!"

"Then behold the helpless old man who once more defies you!" The figure behind the altar released Onoloa's hair with its left hand and reached up to pull off the cylindrical hide mask, revealing the wrinkled brown features and white hair of Apu the high priest. Onoloa gave a muffled shriek through the gag that covered her mouth. Apu cast the mask aside.

"You again!"

"Aye, Yellow Hair, Apu is not so easily defeated as all that."

"Yes, and what do you propose to do now? If you kill the girl, we will kill you—you are outnumbered. If you don't kill her, we will stand here until your arm wearies of holding the knife at her throat."

The priest of Manu was not dismayed for a moment. "You may have caught me off guard once, Yellow Hair, but not again," he crowed. "There are more passages into these rocks than you have found, and I will surely escape from you. The tentacles of Manu stretch across the world!" He pulled the slim form of the girl off the rocks, and, still holding her by the throat with one hand, reached down to cut the ropes around her legs and ankles. He then backed away from the altar. Keeping Onoloa between himself and his enemies, he forced her to move with him, step by retreating step, the razor-sharp flint knife poised at her throat. A quick command brought the two other masked men to his front to shield him still further.

"Drop your weapons, Yellow Hair!" snarled Apu. "You and the she." Red Axe tossed his axe to ring against the stones. "Drop your bow," he whispered to Varna.

"Good!" cried the old man. "Now off the mammoth, quickly, quickly." The two slid to the ground. They found themselves standing next to Elkar, who crouched, rigid in his fury and frustration, his steel knife in his hand, his eyes fixed on the priest and his victim.

"Send the beast forward to the altar," called Apu. Red Axe slapped the side of the great mammoth and shouted to him. The tandor advanced directly onto the altar stone.

"Pick up your bow, Varna, quick," whispered Red Axe, "before he can see us!" The mammoth's bulk blocked their view of the priest. Varna retrieved her weapon, and nocked an arrow to the string.

"Yellow Hair," called the piercing voice of Apu, "we will leave the girl unharmed. You must let us ride off on the beast. We will turn him loose somewhere on the great plains. I will take only my two followers . . ." His words were drowned out by the humming and whistling of the wind among the standing stones. "Let us pass in peace and we will leave the girl. Do you agree?" They could now see that the two bulky, masked, and costumed figures had climbed up the mammoth's tusks and onto his neck. They were clumsy in their weird suits, and one was half dragging a second figure behind him.

"I agree, Apu," called Red Axe, "but leave the girl unharmed!"

"Done!" cried the old man, scrambling to Ma-Ah's

shoulders with remarkable agility. He stood on the mammoth's back while he readjusted his mask over his head. His voice was oddly muffled. "Stand back now, let us pass!" he cried, as he turned the mammoth about. In a moment the shaggy beast had passed and disappeared into the mist that now filled the crater like milk in a bowl.

Elkar let out a cry and ran to the altar stone. A limp, unbound female figure lay across it, unmoving. As he seized the slender form, the long black hair fell back from the woman's face. Her throat had been cut from ear to ear.

"Fiends!" cried Red Axe. "After them, quickly!"

"Red Axe," cried the distraught Elkar, gazing at the form he still supported in his arms. "It isn't her!"

"What?" A quick glance confirmed the fact. This woman had been older than Onoloa. "He's still got her!" Red Axe gasped, "Is she dead?" Referring to the woman on the altar.

"Yes," said Elkar, more shocked than horrified, "but where did she come from, where is Onoloa?"

"Inside one of those suits," Red Axe guessed. "This woman must have been one of Apu's followers. This was her reward for loyalty. Elkar, he's still got her! She's still alive, man—come on!"

Tumu, Mooh-lah, and Varna joined them as they ran back into the mist-filled crater. "No need for tracking, Mooh-lah," Red Axe directed. "There may be secret ways onto the crater, but there's only one large enough for a mammoth. He's got to go back down the way we came up." He snatched up his axe. "Follow me."

No trace of the fugitives and their captive did they see in the thick mist, as they ran back down the trail over which Ma-Ah the mammoth had just carried them so swiftly. Varna, trotting lightly, paced her mate.

"Why do you think he carried her off?" she asked.

"Onoloa? He thinks he must sacrifice her in some way to Manu to win his religious powers back again—or something like that." Another thought dawned. "He never meant to kill her here. He's taking her back to the ocean to throw her alive to that thing."

Varna gasped, a sound of horror and agreement. They ran on in grim silence, the other three close at their heels. At the crater's rim the mist cleared, but there was still no sign of the beast they pursued. As fast as possible, Red Axe led his band of rescuers down the rocky path, past the glaring skulls of the big game animals set up in tribute to the Spirits of the Singing Stones by worshipful tribesmen. As they burst into the glade below they found their quarry—finally at bay.

Ma-Ah, big and powerful as any of the mammoths of the tribe of Mow, confronted three similar beasts, armed riders on their shoulders, who jostled and pawed the dust before him, effectively blocking the trail out of the glade.

"The agents of the Spirits of the Singing Stones are not to be questioned by ordinary mortals," cried the old man, gesturing imperiously. "Out of our way, we obey the will of the gods, whose curses will fall upon you if you hinder us."

"Nay, ancient one. I do doubt everything I am told, and twice if it comes from a stranger." Red Axe and his group were amazed to see Mow, leaning his truncated shoulder over the supporting shoulder of Kor. The chief gestured with his right hand. "Tell us how you came upon Red Axe's tandor and where you are going."

At this point the pursuers rushed from the narrow trail. "Elkar! You and I to the mammoth!" Red Axe burst into a sprint. "Varna, get an arrow into him, if you can!" The American and the Pellucidarian leaped at the big beast's rump. Climbing hand over hand to reach the back of the startled beast they had, perforce, to drop their weapons. Elkar reached the back a second before Red Axe pulled himself over the mammoth's hip. Apu was seated astride the beast's neck. Behind him lay one of the two costumed "spirits," but the costume was askew and the figure lay slumped over the mammoth's back as if unconscious. Not so the second. Bare hands and feet clutched the fur as this second opponent crawled toward Elkar. Behind the fantastically painted mask glared human eyes, and one hand groped at the midsection of the costume, pulling out a foot-long ivory knife.

The masked man lunged at Elkar, the knife taking him in the shoulder. The pale man was forced to release his hold with both hands to seize his opponent. Apu yelled and the prone figure cried out weakly, as the cavemen shouted encouragement from the ground.

The old priest took in the situation at a glance. Red Axe and Elkar could not get at him so long as his minion held the way up the mammoth's spine, but he was surrounded by enemies.

Red Axe, now astride the familiar back of his beast, clasped Elkar's legs to give him support. The two men crouched before him battled now for possession of the knife. The mammoth swayed and shook under them. Over Elkar's shoulder, Red Axe saw Apu produce that black flint knife again and turn around toward his prisoner. He raised his voice in an ear-piercing shout.

"*Ma-Ah! Tandor! Trag, tandor, trag!*"

The old mammoth squealed in recognition of his voice. Up came the mighty trunk like a hairy gray serpent, up and over the head. It encircled the high priest around the shoulder and the neck. The stone knife went flying. Ma-Ah held the writhing body of the man aloft a moment, then sent it hurtling through the air, over the heads of the astonished mammoth riders in front of him, to fall screaming to the earth fifty yards away.

"Down boy! Steady Ma-Ah! Good boy!" Red Axe called, attempting to calm the bucking mammoth before he knocked Onoloa onto the ground.

Elkar, blood streaming from his wound, got both hands on his adversary's knife arm and yanked him off balance. With a wrench of his powerful shoulders he pulled the other man, clumsy in his masquerade suit, loose from the mammoth's back and knocked him to the ground with a body block. The masked man hit the ground with a thud and lay stunned.

Elkar crawled to Onoloa, who lay still bound. By now Red Axe had calmed his excited mount and found the sheath knife in his own belt. They cut the girl's bonds and lowered her, still stiff and numb from the rawhide binding of her wrists, gently to the ground. Elkar lifted her in his arms and carried her up the hillside to where Mow still stood with Kor's support.

"My thanks, O Chief, that I find my mate still alive," Elkar said solemnly.

Mow grinned as Red Axe came up to join them. "Good. Now, Kor, Red Axe, get the guards back on the hilltops. Elkar, start the men breaking camp. Is your mate well enough to ride? Good. Red Axe, recall the flying dragon from the sky. Once everyone is fully armed, you will lead the march back to camp."

Red Axe looked at the old chief in astonishment for a moment, then grinned. "It is good to see you back in command, Chief Mow."

"If I were not in command these fools would have let those so-called spirits ride off with a perfectly good mammoth and a woman of Mow's tribe," he grunted.

The survivors of the Battle of the Singing Stones mounted their mammoths. There were only five of Mow's party and eight of Rognar's, counting the two chiefs, plus Red Axe and his six people, the Mahar, and the captive "spirit" who turned out not to belong to any tribe known to the others. Rognar proposed to kill him, and Mow offered to adopt him into his tribe, an offer the poor wretch eagerly accepted. For all his tough constitution, Mow tired quickly and Kor and Red Axe insisted on making camp before they had gone very far. This gave the American and his followers a chance for a council of war. After a while they went in search of Kor, but found Mow propped up against a pile of hides, a fresh bandage around his head, chewing on a strip of dried meat.

"Red Axe, you look like you have something to say," he grunted.

"That's right, Chief, and I think you already know what it is."

"Good, say it then, in few words."

"Some of my people are leaving with me when we get in sight of the camp," Red Axe began. "We will ride that far with you so that Rognar does not act up again. Elkar, his mate Onoloa, and the lad Tumu ask permission to stay with your tribe. They have no tribe of their own. My mate Varna and Mooh-lah, the monkey-man, have their own tribes. We will go to them. The Mahar will go with us, and we will take Ma-Ah, the mammoth."

Mow glared at them while he finished his meat. "What if I refuse?" he asked, wiping his greasy fingers on the grass.

Red Axe smiled. "You cannot count on Rognar to back you up. With the Mahar, I outnumber you. Do you think Kor or the others will attack me if you order it?"

"I will not order it," said Mow. "I accept the big white-hair and his mate and her brother gladly. He is a good warrior. Ride with us to the camp of my tribe. Rognar is to be kept prisoner until my head is healed. Then we will fight again. This time I will not turn my back to look at Horibs. Ride with us, and we will supply you with food and weapons for your journey and allow you to go your way in peace. Mow keeps his word. I have spoken."

And so it was that Rognar was held prisoner in Mow's camp. Red Axe and Zed broadcast a report of their adventures and their intention to ride off into the mountains. Ma-Ah was hung with saddlebags containing the radio gear, extra weapons, and food, as well as Red Axe's first aid kit. The three bid farewell to Elkar, Onoloa, Tumu, Kor, Nota, and all of his household who had turned out to see them off, as well as to Mow the chief. Ru presented Varna with a necklace of ivory beads and Red Axe with a small figurine. Red Axe conferred in writing with Zed and the great pterosaur took wing and soared up into the bright Pellucidarian sunshine. The sun-bronzed blond American, his beautiful raven-haired mate, and the tailed Mooh-lah climbed up the mammoth's harness straps onto his broad back.

Red Axe spoke into one of the tandor's big ears and the mighty beast turned and started off across the green upland plains of Pellucidar. The group at the gate of the fortified camp stood and watched until the great bulk of the mammoth faded into a dot against the purple and green of the distant mountains.

ABOUT JOHN ERIC HOLMES

JOHN ERIC HOLMES (1930–2010) was the first writer after Edgar Rice Burroughs to pen an authorized novel set in Pellucidar, the world at the Earth's core. He was also the author of the Buck Rogers novel *Mordred* as well as several short stories. He is perhaps best known for having written the popular 1977 *Dungeons & Dragons Basic Set* (also known among D&D players as the "Holmes Basic Set"), which introduced an entire generation to the world of fantasy tabletop roleplaying games. In 1993, he was honored with the Lifetime Achievement Award from the Edgar Rice Burroughs Chain of Friendship (ECOF).

EDGAR RICE BURROUGHS UNIVERSE™

JASON GRIDLEY™
OF EARTH
ACROSS THE MOONS OF MARS

TRANSCRIBED BY GEARY GRAVEL

BASED ON GRIDLEY WAVE TRANSMISSIONS RECEIVED AT THE OFFICES OF
EDGAR RICE BURROUGHS, INC.,
TARZANA, CALIFORNIA

EDITOR'S NOTE
THE END IS NEAR...

IT IS NO LONGER A SECRET that here in Tarzana, California, at the offices of Edgar Rice Burroughs, Inc., we recently discovered a curious apparatus in a locked drawer in Mr. Burroughs' old desk. The device was a Gridley Wave transmitter-receiver, and with it we have been communicating with other worlds, just as the great author did in the first half of the twentieth century when he made contact with such legendary figures as David Innes and John Carter.

In the back pages of the book *Carson of Venus: The Edge of All Worlds*, one such transmission appeared, which I transcribed from my own communications with Jason Gridley himself, the discoverer of the Gridley Wave. "Pellucidar: Dark of the Sun" opens the Swords of Eternity super-arc, an epic cycle of tales that begins in early 1950 in the inner world of Pellucidar. There Jason Gridley and Victory Harben plumbed the ruins of the buried Mahar city of Mintra, seeking an ancient tablet in the archives of Pellucidar's former reptilian overlords in the attempt to "jump-start" the Gridley Wave, which had mysteriously ceased to be, both in function and as a principle of physics.

If you have read Win Scott Eckert's ERB Universe novel *Tarzan: Battle for Pellucidar*, you already know the story of how the eleven-year-old Victory encountered the Mahar queen Tu-al-sa at the dead city of Mintra. That is why Jason Gridley and his goddaughter returned there in 1950, for Victory remembered having seen records in the timeworn archives of the Mahars indicating that the intelligent

185

reptilians knew of the Gridley Wave, and had knowledge concerning it far beyond Jason's and her understanding. But when Jason and Victory attempted to reactivate the Gridley Wave, their experiment generated a distressing result: the extinguishing of Pellucidar's once-eternal noonday sun. Victory appealed to Tu-al-sa for help, but when the Mahar queen adjusted the settings on their portable Gridley Wave set, a beam of energy reflected off the face of the darkened sun and spawned a maelstrom-like vortex that swallowed Victory whole, appearing to hurl her out of our reality, perhaps to a dimension beyond our own. After a brief confrontation with Tu-al-sa and her Sagoth bodyguard, Jason followed Victory through the vortex, only to emerge upon an alien world and to be seized soon after by a mysterious force that hurled him from world to world via a strange means that resembled the method employed by that deathless Virginian, John Carter, to cross the interplanetary void between Earth and Barsoom.

Shortly after I transcribed that tale from Jason Gridley, I began receiving transmissions from Victory Harben detailing her own adventures after she entered the maelstrom. It seemed that the same mysterious force that had seized her godfather also seized Victory and began to hurl her unbidden through spacetime. Two of Victory's world- and time-hopping adventures were recorded in the stories "Victory Harben: Clash on Caspak," as retold by Mike Wolfer and included in the back pages of *Tarzan: Battle for Pellucidar*, and "Victory Harben: Stormwinds of Va-nah," as retold by Ann Tonsor Zeddies and included in the back pages of *John Carter of Mars: Gods of the Forgotten* by Geary Gravel. Interestingly, Jason Gridley appears in the latter novel, having been hurled to Barsoom by the strange effect.

And now once again have we have heard from Jason Gridley, who has related the story you are about to read, which has been transcribed by the aforementioned Mr. Gravel. It is an astonishing tale that picks up directly after

Jason's translocation from Barsoom to . . . well, if you read on you will discover soon enough exactly where his wayward travels have brought him, and into what trouble he has landed this time.

The story that follows will be the penultimate in the Swords of Eternity super-arc, which concludes in my own novel, *Victory Harben: Fires of Halos*. In the latter, we shall learn in Victory's own words the answers to the many questions and enigmas that have cropped up during the course of the super-arc, such as: Why did the Gridley Wave fail? Why did Jason and Victory's experiment extinguish Pellucidar's sun? For what purpose did Tu-al-sa hurl Victory through the maelstrom? What is behind the teleportation effect that has seized Victory and her godfather? Why did Carson Napier find the corpse of a green Martian on Amtor and Suzanne Clayton find a group of dead Wieroos in Pellucidar? What is the odd auroral effect sometimes witnessed by the crew of the O-220 at the polar opening leading to Pellucidar? What is the nature of the violet aura that the Va-gas warrior Ren-ah-ree perceived swirling around Victory? What is the meaning and significance of Victory's ritual tattoo? Who is the mysterious angelic being named Lahvoh, who are her hungry masters, and why is she tracking Victory through the angles of existence? Is there a common thread weaving through all of these bizarre questions, and if so, what is it?

But Victory Harben's epic narrative is a tale for another time and place. For now, let us pick up the super-arc with Jason Gridley and see down what unexpected twists and turns it leads him . . .

Christopher Paul Carey
Director of Publishing
Edgar Rice Burroughs, Inc.

JASON GRIDLEY OF EARTH: ACROSS THE MOONS OF MARS

A Tale of the Swords of Eternity Super-Arc

WAS STARTING to get the hang of it.

It was by no means an easy process, even with the instruction I had recently received from a seasoned practitioner of the art. Indeed, there was something inherently problematic in trying to master *not* performing a particular action before you had ever learned how to perform it. Imagine being coached to resist the urge to put away overheads from behind the service line when you'd never even held a tennis racket.

The action in this instance had been called by many names, long before its existence was proven. I had first heard it described as *teleportation*, an interesting coinage that combines the Latin root *portare*, meaning "to carry," with the Greek prefix *tele*, "distant." I confess that in my younger days I had given little thought to the concept, relegating it to that catchall of as yet unexplained phenomena that includes water dowsing and clairvoyance.

This all changed in my early twenties when I developed an interest in amateur radio, a pleasant enough hobby that would go on to profoundly influence my outlook on the unexplained. While searching for some means of eliminating bothersome static in ordinary radio transmissions, I stumbled across an extraordinary electromagnetic undercurrent in the ether itself, a phenomenon we who have since learned to employ it have dubbed the Gridley Wave for the sake of

189

convenience, yet which shares few properties with the radio waves heretofore known to science. This discovery not only opened my mind to all manner of possibilities I would once have dismissed as incredible—it forever altered the course of my own life.

In fact, it was ultimately responsible for landing me here in my current situation: perched on the deck of a grounded flying machine on the planet Mars, as I used the Gridley Wave to broadcast an urgent SOS on behalf of John Carter, Prince of Helium and Warlord of Barsoom—the very same person who had given me a crash course a few days ago in fending off the unknown forces that were even now attempting to snatch me from this world and hurl me through the void to who-knew-where—while simultaneously keeping the pistol and dagger that hung from either side of the harness-like affair that passes for formal attire in this place from inadvertently knocking over the latest incarnation of a Gridley Wave transceiver that sat humming beside me on the deck.

But let me back up a planet or two.

I had been orphaned at a young age, having lost both mother and father to the Great Influenza Epidemic of 1918 when I was not quite fifteen years old. My parents had left me with a sizable income, for which I was most grateful, as it allowed me the freedom to do what I wished with my life. They had also instilled in me an insatiable curiosity that ensured said life would be interesting—if not always safe or sane!

At the onset of my twenties I was fresh from earning my Bachelors of Science from Stanford and casting about for a vocation in which to put it to good use. Fate stepped in when I purchased a home in Tarzana, a small village located in the San Fernando Valley of California, not far from the ranch of the illustrious author whose most famous creation had given the hamlet its name, and with whom I soon became fast friends. Indeed, he was at my side when, while tinkering with my newly discovered wave, I picked up the first signals of a distress call from Pellucidar, that storied land that lies at the hollow core of the Earth—and that until that moment I had believed to be the product of my new friend's hyperactive imagination.

I had grown up reading about the primeval world of Pellucidar, as well as of Mars, the dying planet known to its inhabitants as Barsoom, and the fabulous African jungles through which prowled Tarzan of the Apes. Once I adjusted my mind to the idea that the dreaming child who had accepted each word from Mr. Burroughs' typewriter as unvarnished truth had been much closer to the mark than the hardheaded young man who scoffed at the gullibility of his younger self, it was only a matter of months before I found myself departing Tarzana for a trip to the Earth's core in the company of none other than the eponymous ape-man himself.

It was in Pellucidar, battling for my life through a world of primordial monsters and bestial men, that I discovered my true vocation. Along the way, I also found Jana, the Red Flower of Zoram, a high-spirited young tribeswoman from the Mountains of the Thipdars who became—after a sometimes rocky courtship—the love of my life. Resisting the urge to pursue my freshly minted career as an adventurer, I brought my new wife back to the surface world and settled into the roles of inventor, husband, and, following the birth of our son Janson, father. It was a comfortable life, but a relatively uneventful one, and I was as enthused as my homesick mate when circumstances required us to return to Pellucidar. Feeling truly at home again, we stayed on beyond the crisis that had required our journey, while years went by on the surface. No measurable time at all elapsed beneath the stationary sun at the Earth's core, of course, for when there are no days or nights by which to mark its passing, Time itself does not seem to exist—or at least so I have been assured, both by the esteemed Pellucidarian polymath Abner Perry, and by the still-youthful face I see in the mirror some half a century after my birth.

I had gone back to the surface world once again half a dozen year later to enlist the help of my goddaughter and fellow scientist, Victory Harben, in figuring out why the Gridley Wave had abruptly ceased functioning. In the course of our investigation, the two of us had encountered a formidable representative of the reptilian Mahars that had once ruled Pellucidar, watched the tiny inner sun abruptly go dark like a burnt-out lightbulb, and seen the appearance out of nowhere of an unearthly purplish vortex that promptly swept Victory inside. I had leaped into the maelstrom myself in an attempt to retrieve her, only to be immediately separated from her and sent hopping on my own path from one world to the next. Since then I had had but two goals: to reunite with my godchild, and to halt my headlong caroming about the universe so that I might return to my wife and son back home in Pellucidar.

My latest otherworldly transit had landed me in the middle of a desperate battle for freedom in a captive realm beneath the surface of Mars. Having managed to linger on the Red Planet long enough to finally escape the subterranean prison with the aid of the Warlord, I found myself temporarily at rest, yet feeling the ever-mounting thrill of current along my nerves that told me I would soon be powerless to postpone my unconventional departure from this world. Now it was time to utilize the second part of the tutelage I had received from John Carter and see if I could finally break my tiresome habit of showing up naked and unarmed at each new port of call.

The swift Martian sunset had arrived not long after I completed my assigned task of sending out a message via the restored Gridley Wave to my friend's allies scattered across Barsoom, and I had ceased the mental exercises I had been practicing to keep myself from being spirited away. Preparing to give in to the inevitable, I was staring up into the star-strewn sky as I followed the Warlord's instructions to visualize in as minute detail as I could muster my own body, currently arrayed in the barbaric accoutrements and weapons I hoped would accompany it on this latest journey to an unknown destination.

It is surprisingly easy to be distracted when one is on an unfamiliar planet. My eyes chanced to stray to the horizon, where they were drawn to a brilliant object just cresting the hills. Following its perceptible ascent into the heavens, I recognized it with a small thrill as one of the pair of hurtling moons that adorned the night skies of Barsoom. From its nearness and the speed of its ascension, I knew it to be Phobos, called Thuria by the locals. Aware that I should be bending my efforts toward precise inward visualization rather than sightseeing, I nonetheless found myself quite unable to break the hold exerted upon my will by this object of romance and mystery, and sat gazing helplessly upward as the electric tension in my body mounted to a crescendo.

I heard a sharp snapping sound and experienced a moment of extreme cold. The next thing I knew I was somewhere else.

2

I lay sprawled on the ground, blinking in the bright sunlight at the edge of a great forest. Tall trees, each trunk a different brilliant color, thrust up into the cloudless sky above a carpet of scarlet grass.

I got slowly to my feet, noting with some satisfaction that I was still clad in my Martian harness and silks, and that my weapons hung at my sides. Recalling what little I knew of Barsoomian flora, for a moment I believed I must have been transported to some other location on the same world—something that had never happened to me before. Yet when I turned to peer behind me I beheld a most amazing sight: beginning about half a mile from where I stood, a gleaming plain of what appeared to be solid gold stretched off into the distance, while above the far horizon hung the great, dim curve of what looked very much like the planet Mars.

Could my latest transit have brought me to Barsoom's nearer moon? During my recent sojourn on the Red Planet, John Carter had told me of the enigmatic American woman who had appeared out of nowhere just in time to save him from probable death at the bottom of an ancient well in a dead city. Something had impaired Betty Callwell's memory and the knowledge of her true identity had only begun to return to her a short time before she abruptly vanished again. The last time John Carter had seen her, she too was staring up in fascination at the moon Thuria, and he had speculated that she might somehow have been transported there. Now I wondered if that had been my own fate. I knew full well that Thuria—or at least Phobos—had been identified by earthly astronomers as an irregularly shaped chunk of barren rock a mere seventeen miles from one end to the other, yet when John Carter had journeyed there in a borrowed space-ship, he had found himself on a world that seemed every bit as large and spherical as Barsoom. He told me of the theory that supposed some sort of "compensatory adjustment of masses" between Mars and its two moons, such that anyone traveling from the surface of the parent planet to one of its satellites would—along with his vessel and belongings!—miraculously undergo a gradual diminution in size during the voyage, to arrive there in precisely the same proportion to the tiny moon as he had enjoyed on the planet below. Sharing his incredulity at this bit of hand-waving pseudoscience, I had joined him in favoring another hypothesis he cited—this one positing a field of unseen energy surrounding one or both Barsoomian moons that acted as a portal through which one could travel to another planet entirely. This latter theory seemed even more likely now, as my own transit to Thuria appeared to have been accomplished instantaneously, with no gradual shrinkage of my body—but then, how would I know if I had shrunk?

I found the golden plain fascinating and briefly contemplated striking out across its gleaming expanse, which stretched before me to the limits of my vision. Whatever its actual composition, however, the shining surface appeared to be utterly smooth and devoid of features, and I did not fancy plodding along for hours—assuming I could get more than a few yards onto it without slipping and falling on my dignity—with no guarantee of finding water or food. I turned back to the forest, by comparison a known quantity, even though made up of trees never known on Earth. Of course, it was not the trees themselves, but the unknown entities that might be lurking among them that I must factor into my decision.

I made up my mind. My right hand resting lightly on the butt of my radium pistol and the other not far from the hilt of my dagger, I entered the silent forest.

After a few steps it occurred to me that I was walking with the same lightness I had experienced during my visit to Barsoom. An experimental leap carried me up a good thirty feet into the air, confirming that wherever I had landed, it was a planetary body with roughly the same gravitational pull and air pressure as Mars.

The going was fairly easy, the trees being widely spaced with very little undergrowth between them. In terms of unknown entities, I walked for a good while without seeing another living creature—though the first examples I finally came upon more than made up for that scarcity with their unusual appearance. Imagine a bored deity in his celestial workshop, assembling new animals out of the odds and ends left over from the creation of more familiar beasts, and you may be able to envision them. At first glance, I assumed the little four-legged things sitting at the edge of the shallow pools that ringed the base of many of the trees were rodents. Not knowing how long I would be allowed to linger on this world, I crept closer to see if they might be something I could turn into a stew if the need arose, only to find that they were thickly scaled like fish and beaked like birds—the latter comparison becoming more pronounced when one of them caught sight of me and, unfolding the pair of feathered wings lying along its back, fluttered up to regard me with grave suspicion from the nearest branch.

It was several hours before I became aware of the sensation of being watched. This vague feeling was soon reinforced by a soft rustling sound, first to one side, then behind me, then from both sides simultaneously, sometimes accompanied by small tremors of movement along the lowest tree limbs, though I could never discern what caused them. It did not take long before the conviction that I was being deliberately toyed with had become maddening, and I finally halted long enough to make a show of drawing both pistol and dagger before proceeding on. If someone insisted on playing a game of cat and mouse with me, I wanted them to see that this particular rodent was equipped with a not inconsiderable set of fangs.

The sun had been near the zenith when I entered the woods. During my trek it had declined considerably, and shadows now gathered at the base of the trees. John Carter had pressed upon me one of the handy pocket pouches most Barsoomians wore fastened to their harness. In it was a small radium hand torch that would have allowed me to push on throughout the night, had I not already covered so much ground that I was feeling the need for sleep. Concerned that my unseen stalkers might be waiting for the onset of darkness to mount an attack, I was somewhat comforted to note a definite decrease in the occurrence of those unsettling rustling noises as the light dimmed. Perhaps my tormentors were also in need of some rest.

I chose an open glade that afforded good visibility in all directions in which to make my camp, using my dagger to dig a shallow pit in the soft earth roughly equidistant from the surrounding trees, and then gathering armloads of fallen branches and dry leaves to fill it. In addition to the torch, a mirror, a magnifying glass, about two weeks' worth of concentrated rations, and some other odds and ends, my pocket pouch contained a small Barsoomian fire-making device the size of an earthly cigarette lighter, though operating on different principles. Soon I had a respectable blaze going. After an undistinguished supper of two tasteless food pellets, I curled up on a patch of soft grass close to the pit and, hoping that whatever sorts of wildlife roamed the night on this world would prove as wary of fire as their earthly counterparts, allowed my eyes to drift shut.

I am by nature a light sleeper, a predisposition only amplified by my adventures in the perpetually hostile environment of Pellucidar, where unforeseen perils can take a man down in the blink of an eye. It seemed I had just closed my lids when I was roused by a soft thumping sound, as of something dropping lightly to the ground from one of the nearby trees. This was followed a second later by a similar noise—then another and another. By now I was sitting up, my fingers reaching for my pistol only to discover nothing in the holster, while my other hand fumbled at an empty scabbard. I looked around, squinting in the flickering orange light cast by the embers, but I could make out nothing but trees and shadows in all directions.

Then I saw the eyes.

Several times the size of human eyes and gleaming with a greenish phosphorescence, they closed in around me in eerie silence, halting just beyond arms' length to form a ring of glowing orbs. The strangest aspect of this terrifying vision was that I could discern no bodies in the murky shadows, nor even any heads supporting the things—only the great unblinking orbs themselves!

I counted a dozen of the uncanny apparitions, each seeming to hang independently in the empty air at a height of about six feet above the forest floor. Before I could do little more than gape at the fantastic tableau there came a soft, hissing cry, followed by the sound of rapid movement, and suddenly I found myself the target of a number of unseen, yet powerful limbs. I fought back in fierce desperation, striking out wildly against my assailants until something hard cracked against my skull and all went black.

Some hours had evidently passed by the time I came to, and a rosy dawn was beginning to permeate the forest, causing the varicolored trunks to glow in a hundred different hues. I was trussed up securely in several coils of strong vines and suspended between two of my captors, each grasping one of the taut lines affixed to my bonds on either side at shoulder and ankle to form convenient handgrips as they bore me along at a brisk pace. I hung facedown and all but immobile in my vine cocoon, but by craning my neck I could see in the growing illumination that the beings that had attacked me were definitely no longer invisible.

I focused my attention on the creature to my right, as his form was most clearly illuminated by the pale light.

Moving with a feline grace that belied his pronounced muscularity, he appeared quite manlike from the neck down. A close examination of what lay above brought forth details more suited for a nightmare, for his head was by far his most remarkable feature. The skull was shaped much like a man's, but that was where the resemblance ceased. Starting at his forehead, a two-inch strip of stiff yellow bristles ran back along the center of his scalp to the nape of his neck, reminding me of the horsehair crests affixed to the helmets of ancient Greek hoplites, while his ears were very small and set higher and farther back on the skull than those of a human. Sensing my gaze upon him, the object of my inspection turned me an emotionless glance, and the mystery of the great eyes floating in the darkness was partially solved, for but a single large orb occupied the center of the fellow's forehead. The eye, which appeared to be lidless, was about three inches in diameter and composed entirely of a greenish-yellow iris, the pupil set vertically as is the case with a cat. Fantastic as it was, the cyclopean eye was not his most alien feature: below a wide and flattened nose reposed not one, but *two* mouths! It was a toss-up as to which of them was less appealing. The uppermost orifice was small and round, appearing as little more than a toothless pucker, while the lower was much larger, a wide, lipless maw whose great sharp teeth sprouted directly from the skin of the face to confront the viewer with a perpetual ghoulish grin.

Like his fellows, he was barefoot and bare-chested, his only covering a leathern kilt-like garment secured about the waist by a belt fastened with a gem-encircled gold buckle. Later I learned these kilts were often temporarily discarded during hunts, as what I had taken for invisibility was actually the result of an inborn ability on the part of my captors' skin to perfectly match the color of its surroundings in the style of an earthly chameleon. This amazing display of camouflage was not a constant condition, coming into play only when the Masenas—for that is what they called their race— either felt themselves threatened or chose to move in stealth to threaten others. Indeed, as the daylight increased, I could see that the creatures' hairless hides were now a uniform tawny brown wholly unaffected by the variegated coloration of the vegetation through which they marched.

Being lugged along like a steamer trunk is not conducive to accurate time measurement, and I cannot say how many hours elapsed as we made our way through the forest. My several attempts at communicating with my bearers had been met with stony silence, and I confess that after a while I found myself nodding off for brief periods—not surprising, considering my interrupted night. Dusk was coming on when we arrived at a wide clearing where a much larger group of Masenas had established a campsite. My heart sank to see at least thirty other warriors in addition to the dozen of the party that had captured me. I was deposited none too gently on the forest floor, not far from five other prisoners, all of them cat-men and all trussed up from thigh to shoulder in the same heavy-duty vines. I was the object of some initial curiosity on the part of both captors and captives, leading me to wonder if they had ever seen a human being before. As the novelty of my appearance wore off, I noticed that the prisoner farthest from me continued to examine me most intently, nodding vigorously whenever my gaze met his and emitting small mewing sounds from his pursed upper mouth, which seemed to be the one reserved for communication. Figuring that friends of any stripe could prove useful, I returned his nods and grinned my most ingratiating grin, though I was not at all certain how he might interpret the expression on the face of one so different. He evidently did not want to be observed fraternizing with one of my ilk by those in charge, for he quickly broke off his attempts at colloquy whenever one of our captors came near.

We were given water, but otherwise ignored as the tribe prepared the camp for the coming night, a procedure I observed with interest. There was an unusual type of towering tree common to this section of the woods that produced lightweight pods ranging in length from five to eight feet. I watched as the cat-men used the sharp claws on both hands and feet to scurry up the trunks and pluck dozens of them. These they piled one upon the other to form a circular, waist-high kraal around the campsite, with wooden stakes swathed in some yellow mosslike material driven into the ground at intervals between them.

Peaceful and near silent during the day, the forest came alive after dark with the frightful roars of a great menagerie of unseen beasts, at which time the mossy stakes were lit ablaze from a small central fire. Then, their sharp claws extended—for these were the only weapons I ever saw them use—a dozen cat-men patrolled the periphery of the campsite in alternating shifts throughout the night.

One can get used to anything, and some hours into the cacophony of shrieks and howls I passed into a fitful slumber.

The next day I discovered that my experience of being carried like a valuable parcel between two of the warriors had been a one-time occurrence. I was roused at sunrise and hauled roughly to my feet, after which the vines that bound me from shoulder to ankle were removed and refastened in an abbreviated fashion to keep my arms firmly secured to my sides in the manner of the Masena captives, while leaving my lower body free so that I could walk on my own. After that we prisoners were tethered one to another by six-foot lines and prodded single file along the trail.

This routine was to become an index for the next several days of our journey through the forest. Every evening the party would halt at a new campsite and our keepers would unceremoniously shove us to the ground. Without my hands free to break my fall, I soon became adept at tucking my chin into my chest as I toppled, while twisting my body as much as was possible in my bound condition in an effort to minimize the accumulation of bruises. Shallow wooden bowls of water were set on the ground by our heads, such that we had to contort our necks in order to lap at them with our tongues, a practice at which my fellow prisoners were much more skilled than I. Although our captors apparently wanted us to arrive at our unknown destination still breathing, they did not seem overly concerned about the state of our stomachs, for the rations they vouchsafed us in addition to our bowl of water could only charitably be described as meager. Due to the waning sunlight and the often haphazard positions of our bodies, I was unable to see what the other prisoners were offered for their suppers, but my own allotment consisted of a double handful of uncooked tubers and edible leaves tossed carelessly near my head. After we dined we were left to rest through the night, with roving guards regularly checking in on us. At dawn we were hoisted to our feet, once more tethered together, and marched out along the forest trail until near sundown, when we reached the new campsite chosen by the handful of scouts who had ranged on ahead of the main body.

When we made our camp on the second evening, the gregarious individual who had expressed a fascination with me was deposited just behind another, larger Masena, making it impossible for us to establish eye contact. The third evening commenced with the two of us again at opposite ends of the row of captives, and our communication was once more limited to an exchange of nods and grimaces. When we were thrown to the ground at the end of the following day, however, I found myself lying directly adjacent to my would-be interlocutor for the first time. As our guards sauntered off to fetch us the night's feast, we turned our faces toward one another and the cat-man immediately commenced speaking to me in low but urgent tones.

You can imagine my surprise when, unlike our captors, whose own conversations over the past few days had sounded more like the disputations of obstreperous house cats than human discourse, my neighbor addressed me in sounds I could recognize as actual words—albeit completely unfamiliar ones.

His single great eye narrowed when I replied disconsolately in my own tongue that I was very pleased to finally make his acquaintance, but hadn't the faintest clue what he was trying to tell me.

To my profound astonishment, the next words from his upper mouth came in strangely accented English! "This you understand?" he inquired in a soft voice.

"I do! I do!" I emphasized my assent with a frantic nod, the only movement I could make above the waist while my bonds remained tight.

"It is good!" he whispered. "I had thought never to see you again." This seemed a peculiar statement, considering we had only begun exchanging our mutually incomprehensible pleasantries a few days earlier and, being securely bound and almost constantly guarded as we were, neither of us could have been expected to get up and wander off in the time since. "It is fortunate my mind has sharp claws for snaring words—even ones as absurd as these!" he went on. "Tell me, my friend: were you struck on the head during your capture? Is that why you have forgotten all that I once taught you of the *Aahma-mas* tongue?"

When I inquired after the meaning of the unfamiliar word, he translated it as "Milk-Face," one of the epithets his people commonly applied to the native human inhabitants of this world—all of whom, I was to learn, were endowed with bone-white skin and blue hair. It turned out the cat-people had a great catalog of descriptive terms they employed to refer to my human brethren, most of them based on what they perceived as our sad deformities. The least pejorative of these included *Mraa-owa*, or "Many-Eyes," a condition that they deemed grotesque, but less disabling than *Hsa-khaa*, or "Missing-mouth." As is so often the case, it was all a matter of perspective; I knew that my new friend considered my solitary mouth every bit as weirdly unnatural as I found the one great eye he sported in place of my two smaller ones, for he was unable to imagine how a lone orifice could encompass the various functions of speaking, drinking, mastication, and armament provided by the Masenas' pair of highly specialized organs.

I was pondering his puzzling inquiry about a blow to my head, while formulating a question of my own concerning his surprising mastery of the King's English, when the gentle breeze that had been blowing through the camp since our arrival reversed its course. Instantly the cat-man craned his neck toward me, his nostrils dilating. "What is this?" he cried in a hoarse whisper. "You are not John Carter!"

When I acknowledged the truth of this observation, the cat-man readily admitted that all pale-skinned male humans looked much the same to his people, the only distinguishing attribute that John Carter—and now I—displayed being the heads of black hair we possessed in marked contrast to the blue-thatched native population. It might have taken my companion considerably longer to realize his error had Carter and I not emitted noticeably different scents.

Figuring that introductions were now in order, I identified myself as Jason Gridley of Earth, after which my fellow captive gave me his own name, Umka, and the name by which this planet was known to its inhabitants: Ladan.

With these formalities out of the way, Umka told me that he had been leading a small party of warriors from his tribe on a mission to scout out unexplored territory when they had been set upon by members of this hostile roving clan and overpowered, with only himself surviving. Nodding toward one of the perimeter guards, who was slowly approaching our area in his rounds, he warned me that if our captors overheard us talking to one another they would most surely separate us.

"Then we must make the most of our opportunities to confer and pose as model prisoners in between," I said softly. "The more often we two can put our heads together, the sooner we may plan our escape!"

A deep purring sound issued from the back of Umka's throat. "It is *good*!" he said in a fervent whisper, his toothless upper mouth stretching sideways in what I could only interpret as a grin of anticipation.

Our brief conversation was interrupted when the night's server appeared and tossed a handful of the all-too-familiar raw vegetables onto the dirt by my face. A very different entrée was dropped not far from my companion's head, and I finally saw what was considered a balanced diet for the captive Masenas: one of the rodent-bird-fish things from the forest pools lay lifeless between us, its neck obviously broken. Umka regarded the little corpse with ill-concealed loathing.

"They seek to degrade us by giving us naught but dead meat to consume," he growled. "It is a terrible insult! I am tempted to go hungry rather than continue to afford them the satisfaction of watching me choke down another's kill. It is worse for you," he added, eyeing my own serving of scattered plant matter with disgust. "They do not even give you real food! Perhaps you would like to eat this sorry thing?"

Gazing dubiously at the feathered wings, the hard beak, and the scaly skin, I declined the cat-man's generous offer with thanks. Lord knows I had dined on worse in Pellucidar, but so long as I still had the concentrated food pellets with which I hoped to eventually supplement my daily allotment of tossed salad, I was glad to allow him the main course, and reminded him that it was imperative he keep up his strength if we were to have any hope of escape. Though obviously greatly bothered by the idea of ingesting food he had not dispatched himself, Umka proved himself a pragmatist at heart. Uttering a snarl of resignation, he twisted his neck to the side, snatched up the little morsel, and with a few savage bites of his lower mouth made a meal of it, even to the scales and bright feathers.

Ever on my mind since the night of my capture, the prospect of escape seemed more firmly within the realm of possibility now that I had found a confederate, and I began to take stock of my resources. Our captors had confiscated my dagger and radium pistol, which currently hung trophy-like from the belts of the two who had originally borne me along the trail and now served among the ranks of those who guarded the campsite at night. From my assessment of the Masenas' level of technology I was fairly certain that he who carried the pistol had no idea of its function and probably considered it no more than a fancy club. Luckily, following a cursory inspection of its contents, which they must have deemed harmless gewgaws, they had left my pocket pouch hanging from my harness. Thanks to the vines that encircled my torso and bound my arms tightly to my sides, I could not access it, but I had a plan in mind to ensure that this would not always be the case.

My whispered communications with my new ally were

of necessity confined to that period every evening when we were thrown to the ground and left to consume our respective rations while our captors gathered by shifts to have their own raucous meals at the other end of camp; Umka informed me that this involved the release of the many small animals they had captured along the trail during the day, so that each member of the band might stalk and devour his own supper as was proper. Fortunately, we had lately been pushed to the earth in the same order we were tethered together, so he and I typically ended up next to one another. After being prodded along from dawn till dusk in such fashion as benumbed both mind and body, the only sounds the various mewing and purring noises exchanged by my captors, I soon found myself eagerly anticipating this brief exchange of information at the conclusion of each leg of the journey, much as one might look forward to the newest installment of a serialized adventure in the comics section of the daily newspaper.

The other four Masena prisoners, all from tribes either unknown or unfriendly to Umka's people, had shown little desire to communicate with either of us, and I had not paid them much mind. One evening about ten days into the journey the largest of them was abruptly led off amid loud protestations to the far side of the camp. Soon we heard a wild thrashing emanating from that direction, combined with a hideous din of yowling and shrieking sounds that continued on for several minutes before suddenly ceasing. I was horrified when Umka explained to me in the silence that followed that the hunters had grown tired of small game, with the result that there would now be one less captive to swell the homecoming feast when we reached their village. Having assumed until now that our fate was to be enslavement, I shared his deep revulsion at the appalling revelation that the members of our captors' tribe practiced cannibalism.

Umka cast a further pall upon my mood when he reported that during that day's trek through the forest he had overheard a discussion of a scout's report of another small group of Masenas camped four or five days up ahead. Our captors were confident that by striking in stealth they could obtain several new prisoners with little trouble. Because of this, there had been increasing calls among the tribesmen to devour more of their current stock.

"I am sure it is my people come in search of me," he said morosely. "They will stand no chance against a surprise attack by this many. These monsters will gorge on their flesh and cure their hides for drumheads."

As much sympathy as I felt for the unsuspecting warriors of Umka's tribe, it was our own hides that I was most set on preserving. We could no longer wait for the perfect moment to launch our escape attempt. Accordingly, we spent the remainder of our unguarded time before we were brought our dinners—a longer than usual period due to the special nature of tonight's tribal banquet—shaping and refining the plan we aimed to put into action as soon as possible. When the following evening saw a second member of our shrinking band dragged off to provide both sport and sustenance for our hosts, it was plain the time had come.

When we were roused to our feet each morning in anticipation of that day's march, it was customary for one of our guards to remove and then reapply the knotted vines that bound us tightly from shoulder to thigh in case they had loosened overnight, while another stood by to prevent any attempts at escape. As is often the case with repetitive chores, the process had soon devolved from one of precision into a more careless exercise. Outwardly a picture of docility, over the past several days I had begun surreptitiously cupping my right hand against my thigh when it was freed and then pressing it slightly outward at the last minute, which made the vines appear taut from the outside while providing me with some maneuverability in the vicinity of my pocket pouch.

That evening Umka inched his way close to me as soon

as our guards had deposited us on the ground and hurried off for their share of our unlucky comrade. Maneuvering himself about, he employed the prehensile toes of one foot to tug the pocket pouch down from where it protruded below my bonds and the sharp claws of the other to sever the leather cord that attached it to my harness. He then delivered it to the fingers of my right hand that I was now able to extend between two turns of vine.

Our plan almost went awry from the start when one of our habitual guards, apparently among the first in line to sate himself at the horrific banquet, returned long before expected, casually stepping over me to sprawl facing us against one of the pods making up tonight's barricade, and using the edge of my own dagger to groom sticky clots of blood and other matter from his chest. I had been on the verge of employing my Barsoomian fire-starter, which emitted drops of a concentrated fluid that allowed one to apply a flame to a very small area. Given enough time unobserved, I believed I could use it to burn through the outermost layer of the sturdy vines in which we were enshrouded, with my earthly muscles taking over from there, and we would be out of the camp before anyone was the wiser.

I racked my brain for an alternative and soon hit upon a new plan to buy us some time. I had positioned myself on my side with my back facing the guard. Stretching as if to counteract a charley horse in my leg—a practice I had begun a few days earlier so that it would not seem out of the ordinary—I pulled my knee up to steady the pouch while I burrowed within, soon emerging with the small radium torch. These ingenious devices have a movable ring near the tip by which the width of the beam may be precisely controlled. At its widest setting, the torch can bathe a large area in white light; the narrowest produces a small dot of great intensity whose path through the air is nearly invisible. Working with excruciating care, I managed to adjust the ring to the desired setting. I then uncapped the torch and

used the tightest beam to play a small but brilliant white
dot over a pod lying halfway around the perimeter of the
campsite. After half a minute, during most of which I held
my breath in anxiety, our guard happened to glance toward
that area of the camp. Out of the corner of my eye I saw the
cat-man straighten on his log, then lean forward to stare at
the dancing point of light, following its motions as if mes-
merized. When he turned to alert the nearest of his fellows
to the weird phenomenon, I quickly shut off the beam. There
ensued a prolonged bout of meowing and hissing, as our
man tried unsuccessfully to convince the other warrior of
what he had seen. Aiming carefully, I moved the torch to
focus on the ground nearer to the center of the camp and
turned it on again. This time the other guard saw it, and
bidding our custodian to remain at his post, rushed off in
that direction, beginning to chase after the tiny dot as I sent
it racing back and forth. Before long, others were drawn
from around the campfire to join in.

Unable to resist the lure of the erratically jumping dot,
our guard finally rose to his feet. He stepped carelessly over
my body, his great eye fixed on the scene of the commotion,
as he headed off to join the others, who were now raising
quite a row in their attempts to apprehend the mysterious
point of light. As he passed over me I saw the firelight reflect
from my dagger, which he had tucked back into his belt
when he got up. On a sudden impulse, I signaled with my
eyes to Umka, who grasped my intention immediately, rolling
forward with as much force as he could muster into the
distracted man's ankle to bring him crashing down between
us. At once I hurled my body over the stunned cat-man's
head to muffle his cries, bearing down on his windpipe with
my bound arm until his desperate struggles began to lessen,
while Umka flung himself across his torso, twisting his own
body around to where he could stab at the man's throat
repeatedly with the sharp claws of his feet. It was a gruesome
way to go and anything but fair play, but I sloughed off any

feelings of guilt by reminding myself that this fellow would most likely have been at the head of the table when it was my own turn to provide dinner. The frenetic action at the center of the campsite had de-escalated into noisy confusion once I had been forced to deactivate my distraction during the struggle, but no one had yet thought to investigate the status of the prisoners. Now I once more uncapped my torch, this time training the small dot on the other side of the camp and sending it flashing wildly about until the mob caught sight of it and raced off in that direction.

Thrusting the corpse over onto its back, Umka was able to use his dexterous toes once more to relieve the guard's belt of my stolen dagger, which he then pressed up against my partially freed hand. I dropped the torch on the ground between us and grasped the knife in my fingers as Umka turned his back to me. I commenced sawing frantically at the tough vines that bound him, and in less than a minute he was free, at which time he took the knife from my palsied hand and performed the same task for me.

I hesitated as we turned to exit the camp, seeing the desperation writ on the countenances of the two remaining captives, who had followed the entire incident in mute amazement. With Umka already beyond the pod barrier and hissing his strong disapproval, I stooped and sawed quickly through their bonds as well. The freed duo staggered to their feet and off into the woods without a word, discarding their kilts as they fled and instantly becoming nearly invisible as their hides took on the appearance of the nearby foliage, while I hastened in the opposite direction. I hurdled the barrier with ease and caught up with Umka just as shouts of outrage rang out behind us and it was obvious that we had been spotted.

The sketchy trail the tribe had been following paralleled a broad river. This was where they obtained their daily drinking water, and it had, after some prolonged persuasion on my part—and a very reluctant acceptance on Umka's—

figured prominently into our escape plan, especially once I reminded my friend that my unfortunate lack of skill when it came to blending in with my surroundings would make me an all-too-easy target. With our upper bodies still half-paralyzed by days of immobility, and half the tribe in hot pursuit while the rest fanned out into the woods after the other two prisoners I had freed, Umka and I managed to stumble the several yards down to the riverbank. Thinking us cornered, our pursuers yowled in triumph and slowed their pace to the creep of a stalking predator. It was then that we did the totally unexpected: we leaped into the swiftly moving current.

This was an act that Umka had assured me the cat-men would view as tantamount to suicide, for Masenas as a species have an instinctive terror of being immersed in water. Once my coconspirator acknowledged the necessity of using the river to ensure our escape, I had gone over that portion of the plan with him in great detail. However, with our rehearsals necessarily limited to verbal descriptions, I truly had no idea how he would react on opening night—when he actually came into contact for the first time with the cold and frightening reality of fast-moving water.

I felt a surge of relief when Umka, his entire body vibrating with distaste and apprehension, nonetheless forced himself to go limp as I had instructed him, and permitted me to wrap my enervated arm around his upper torso and tow him along with me while I used my legs to strike out through the swift current for the far side of the river. I noticed beneath the shafts of ruddy Marslight that a thin translucent panel analogous to the nictitating membrane of some terrestrial animals had slid horizontally over Umka's eye upon contact with the water. Urged on by the cries of our erstwhile captors, who crowded the near bank and screeched imprecations at us through the darkness, I said a silent prayer that my inert burden would exercise sufficient willpower to keep sheathed the claws that might have slit my own throat, and kicked with all my might. I knew that I would be thoroughly exhausted by the time we reached the opposite shore, and hoped our pursuers would think us quickly drowned and let it go at that.

Exhausted or not, the first order of business once we dragged ourselves from the water was to find a place where the predatory beasts that range the nighttime forests of Ladan could not reach us, and Umka informed me that this meant climbing high into the nearest tree. Now it was his turn to assist me to safety, as his night vision and the razor-sharp claws he boasted on all four of his extremities enabled him to scale the smooth vermilion trunk he had chosen with much more facility than my relatively ineffective human fingers and sandaled feet.

During our long nights of captivity, I had glimpsed from my position at ground level the fearsome creatures that emerged at sunset to skulk beyond our various campsites only as vague but menacing shadows. Now that I was able to scrutinize them from a different vantage as they roamed the forest floor below our lofty perch, I again noted the unlikely amalgamation of familiar features into something wholly bizarre that seemed to be a hallmark of animal life on this world.

Umka swore to me that none of the predators would be capable of climbing high enough to reach us where we crouched shivering in the juncture of two broad branches. Well accustomed to this parade of grotesques, he delighted in directing my attention and the wide beam of my radium torch to several of the more interesting specimens below. Among them were monsters that would not have seemed out of place in the prehistoric jungles of Pellucidar, including a heavyset reptile whose large skull surmounted by a distinctive bony neck frill would have made it a dead ringer for the examples of protoceratops I had routinely observed at the Earth's core, had it not been for the sharp claws and massive canines that marked this variation as a carnivore.

One of the more repellent denizens of the nighttime forest was a slinking monstrosity about the size of a Russian wolfhound, whose naked, scabrous hide, six jointed legs, and inward curving, high-arched tail gave it the look of a giant scorpion, with the unwelcome addition of a horned lizard's saturnine countenance weaving atop its serpentine neck. At one point a delegation of bipedal creatures covered with russet-brown fur and constructed along the lines of earthly gorillas gathered quietly at the base of the tree, their elongated snouts ornamented with a pair of wicked-looking eight-inch tusks in the manner of the African warthog. These wart-apes, as I came to think of them, stood blinking up in the light of the torch in such a way as to suggest disgruntled homeowners rousted out of their beds by some disturbance in the neighborhood. Despite my companion's reassurances that we were completely safe in our perch, I found their almost human expressions unnerving and quickly switched off my light.

The predators battled noisily among themselves throughout the night, the survivors returning to their respective lairs shortly before daybreak. We quickly clambered down from our refuge and gathered heaps of leaves and dead branches that I set alight with my fire-making tool, so that we could finally warm ourselves and our still-damp garments before the welcome blaze.

We had plenty of time to talk now and we put it to good use as we moved briskly eastward through the forest during the relative safety of the daylight hours, when only the fish-bird-rodents and a few other harmless herbivores were likely to be afoot. Umka told me of the bitter enmity that existed between the forest-dwelling Masenas and the various human nations of this world, and of his tribe's recent decision to relocate to a place far from their foes' centers of population. It was while on a scouting expedition for that purpose that he had been captured by our cannibalistic former hosts. He regaled me with tales of his adventures fighting alongside John Carter during the Warlord's visit to Ladan some years ago, while I acquainted him with some of my recent similar experiences on Barsoom. I had been under the assumption that Umka had picked up his extensive knowledge of English from his association with John Carter, and was thus taken aback when the cat-man told me he had gleaned only a handful of words from Carter, and that it was his tribe's new goddess who had helped him achieve his current proficiency.

I was not sure what to make of this unexpected statement. Knowing that differing views on religion often served as a flash point for grave and even violent disagreements, I endeavored to keep my expression free of skepticism as I asked him for more details. Something of my inner feelings may have penetrated my neutral facade, for the cat-man quickly clarified that he himself had not for a moment believed the newcomer to be a supernatural being, confiding that when she arrived out of nowhere in the midst of a tribal gathering, speaking in a tongue only he could recognize, he had seized the opportunity to improve both their lots by at once proclaiming her a goddess and appointing himself both her high priest and interpreter. He cemented in my mind the dawning notion that this recently arrived deity must indeed be the elusive Miss Callwell from Brooklyn who had herself crossed paths with John Carter not long ago, when he told me that—like the Warlord of Barsoom and myself—she had pale skin, black hair, and two eyes, adding that she seemed a very wise and benevolent individual, despite being cursed with the physical ugliness characteristic of all humans.

Umka did not speak much about the impending attack on what he presumed was a search party from his own tribe, but he was glumly certain our frustrated former captors would now devote their energies to waylaying them in order to restock their emptied larder, and I knew he wished fervently for some way to warn them before this occurred. He was confident he knew the general whereabouts of his people, for they would undoubtedly be heading westward in our direction, following along the river and camping overnight in many of the same clearings utilized by his original group. The problem was time: even if we ran nonstop along this side of the river, halting for periodic crossings to investigate the likely resting points, there was little chance we would arrive at their location far enough in advance of the cannibal clan to do any good.

As it happened, the second night following our escape we took our nocturnal refuge in a grove of the towering trees that produced the large pods our captors had employed as a barrier. These husks, I discovered upon close inspection, were hollow when split and divested of their seeds, and constructed of a very lightweight but extremely sturdy material. This gave me an idea as to how we might speed up our progress, and after verifying the pods' buoyancy I set to work gathering the same tough vines that had been used to bind us during our captivity and lashed together side by side the two halves of an eight-foot specimen in order to fashion a crude double canoe. Boats were a completely foreign concept to the Masenas, yet the river had already served us well, and it required somewhat less coaxing this time around before Umka agreed to master his fears a second time and brave its swift current. We took to the water and, despite a few hair-raising moments when twists and turns forced us to shoot some respectable rapids (myself manning our makeshift paddles during the worst of them, while Umka lay curled into a ball on the floor of his own pod, eye firmly shut), we struck pay dirt a scant two days later when we arrived at a spot not far from where my companion judged members of his tribe to be gathered—doing so in fully half the time the cat-man had estimated it would take the cannibals traveling overland.

It was the second time we had come ashore during the journey to check for the presence of his tribesmen. This time Umka sniffed the air with a triumphant expression as we drew our canoe up the bank. "I have caught their scent," he announced. "This way!"

The cat-man was fairly dancing with excitement as we threaded our way through the trees toward the little camp-site. "It is good!" he declared when a small clearing occupied by moving figures became visible. "Though I am almost positive I could have persuaded my people not to eat you, this heroic deed will make it doubly certain."

"Eat me?" I grabbed his wrist and drew him to a temporary halt. "I thought you said that unlike the other tribe your own people were not cannibals!"

There followed a brief dissection of the meaning of the word "cannibal," as I learned that all Masenas, including the members of Umka's own clan, dined without compunction on the flesh of human beings when such became available, the unpardonable sin committed by the group that had captured us being that they extended the same grisly practice to their own species—in Umka's eye a sign of the utmost degeneracy. It was with mixed feelings that I followed my friend into the clearing.

Umka was warmly received by the half-dozen warriors in the camp—as was I, once he had brought them to examine our double-hulled tree-pod vessel and explained my role in ensuring our arrival in time to prevent a massacre.

I was surprised to see that the warriors of this small group were accoutred with stout broadswords—albeit ones carved out of lengths of durable hardwood. Despite the wealth of minerals on their planet, the Masenas had not yet figured out metallurgy, the golden belt buckles they used for their kilts being pilfered from the Tarids, the nation of white-skinned, blue-haired humans located nearest to their tribe. Umka told me that this form of weaponry had been recommended to them by the all-knowing goddess and that they had taken to it well, though he admitted most warriors still resorted to their retractable claws and the sharp fangs ringing their lower mouths in exigent situations. Advanced armament notwithstanding, it was plain that even with the addition of the two of us, this small group would have a difficult time fending off the fifty-odd warriors that made up the approaching band, and the decision was quickly made to break camp and head back home. I felt little sense of personal danger in the company of Umka's people as we jogged eastward through the woods—though I admit I found myself keeping an eye on those nearest me for signs of anyone licking his chops in my general direction.

After three days we reached the arboreal village of Umka's people, where I was introduced to my friend's mate, K'mel, who insisted on stroking my upper arms in the pleasant but rather disconcerting Masena gesture of friendship, as well as to the bewildering number of nearly identical small children belonging to the pair, all of whom seemed to derive considerable joy from racing between my feet or attempting to climb my legs as I teetered on the broad branches that served the place as thoroughfares. To my great disappointment, I soon learned that the goddess known to the tribe as *Yumku-mraa-owa-samyu*, or "Most Wise Many-Eyed Woman," had vanished some fifteen days ago, as inexplicably as she had arrived.

High Priest Umka was nothing if not resourceful. That evening, in a ceremony conducted with much pomp in the largest of their lofty dwellings, my friend donned the golden torc that comprised his priestly vestments and officially presented me to the clan as *Yumku-mraa-owa-samyu-sam-tamna*—otherwise known as Brother to the Goddess—come down from the celestial treetops to preside over their spiritual needs until the return of my divine sister. I asked them to call me Jason.

With nowhere else to go until my own next transit, I remained with Umka's tribe, discharging the few duties incumbent upon a deity of the newly devout cat-people, and looking forward to a meeting with the enigmatic goddess from Brooklyn, should she contrive to manifest her immanence once again before I myself was whisked away. Umka was always on the lookout for ways to improve the standing of his tribe, and I assisted him where I could, giving much-needed lessons in swordsmanship and helping to inaugurate the Masena Holy Navy while I bided my time. This last was no easy task, given the species' inborn terror of water, but with the miraculous return of their High Priest as an example of the efficacy of maritime ventures, and the promise of future successful campaigns against their land-bound enemies, we had soon attracted a small group of dedicated volunteers. With little need for ploughshares among this clan of carnivores, I persuaded some of the warriors to whittle their freshly made wooden swords into paddles. Later I exercised my prerogative as founding admiral and personally christened the half-dozen ships that now consti-tuted our grand fleet. These were the *Sari*, the *Korva*, and the *Oak Park*, three sleek little one-man canoes fashioned each from a single pod; the *Lesser* and the *Greater Helium*, composed of two and three connected pods respectively; and finally our flagship, the mighty *Tarzana*, an imposing craft that boasted six of the largest husks: four lashed to-gether side by side and nose to tail, a fifth fastened up front, and one more to the stern. I was very proud of my team of sailors, daredevils all in a species that abhorred immersion in water from birth. Only a few tribe members were willing to take the plunge—occasionally quite literally during their training—and two of our doughtiest seamen were women. My own status among the tribe rose significantly when they were able to emerge from the great river just after dawn one morning to launch a devastating sneak attack with their wooden swords on a campsite of the very clan that had taken Umka and myself prisoner.

One evening several weeks after my introduction to the tribe, I was reclining on the wide branch I favored for my stargazing outside the small but comfortable hut assigned to the Brother of the Goddess. I had by now grown used to the nightly cacophony below and rarely allowed it to intrude on my thoughts, which alternated, as was their wont, between the family that waited for me back in Pellucidar and the fate of my missing goddaughter. I was gazing up at tiny Cluros, Barsoom's further moon, whose plodding course far above its swifter mate frequently brought it into view. All at once I felt a strange and powerful pulsing along my nerves and experienced my vision fading and returning, almost as if the world around me was blinking in and out of existence. This was very different from any of my previous pre-transit sensations. I heard a sudden commotion from the center of the arboreal village, then half a dozen of Umka's kittenish offspring swarmed out of the main building, mewing and squeaking unintelligibly in my direction, followed by the High Priest himself, who called out to me that the goddess was returning. "It is strange," he proclaimed breathlessly, "for she is here and then not here from one moment to the next, as if undecided as to whether she will remain!"

Doing my best not to trip over the herd of kits, I hastened with my friend to the doorway of the lodge in time to see a light-skinned figure materialize in the shadows within. Her dark eyes locked with mine just as the customary electric tingling of transit suddenly swept over me, and I fell helplessly to my knees and into an abyss of impenetrable darkness.

3

I was kneeling on a cold, granular surface.

As usual, I had shut my eyes instinctively at the onset of the unfathomable process. Now I opened them to look about in fascination, staring at a flat horizon that seemed to begin just a few hundred yards in front of me beneath a black sky sprinkled with stars. It occurred to me almost immediately that I had for a second time been transported to the object I had been contemplating directly before my transit—in this case that irregularly shaped chunk of barren rock known to earthly astronomers as the Martian satellite Deimos, but which the Barsoomians call Cluros. Whether the world of my previous stop had assumed the dimensions of Barsoom due to some sort of mystical compensating factor or was in fact a completely different planet sitting on the other side of an invisible gateway, it seemed obvious that neither fantastic effect was in operation here.

The next thing that occurred to me was that I was breathing without difficulty, having not suffered the rapid and painful death from asphyxiation I might have expected upon my arrival in such a place. This meant, of course, that some sort of atmosphere must be present around the slab of rock—a highly improbable condition on this relatively miniscule body. To compound the conundrum, the gravitational pressure I felt as I rose carefully to my feet on the pebbled surface seemed identical to that of both Ladan and Barsoom!

Doubting the evidence of my own senses, I impulsively decided to test my theory just as I had on the previous world by employing my earthly muscles to leap straight up into the air. Sure enough, I shot up easily to a height of some thirty feet or so.

When I reached the apex of my jump, however, a sudden deep chill spread along the exposed surface of my upper body. I reflexively inhaled a deep breath, feeling a stab of sharp pain in both ears, while the inside of my mouth instantly became numb. My stomach darted hither and yon as for a few seconds I seemed to be floating in midair, and I convulsed with limbs flailing, like a drowning man trying to make his way back to the surface—in this case, the very solid surface lying beneath my feet. I drifted downward with increasing speed as I felt gravity begin to exert its full pressure once more.

A moment later I was coughing and sputtering in a heap on the gravel-strewn ground, cursing myself for a fool even as a wild hypothesis was forming in my mind. Once I had regained my feet and a measure of my composure, I scanned my surroundings for a nearby jut of rock whose crest reared high enough that I reckoned it would serve for my next experiment. I had noticed a dry, flaky substance resembling gray-green lichen on many of the nearby boulders, proving that some life at least could survive in this bleak environment. On each of the taller examples, however, there was a point above which the growth was completely absent, suggesting a clear line of demarcation between air and vacuum. I inched cautiously up the slanted side of my chosen subject until I was able to confirm to my great amazement that the band of both Martian gravity and breathable atmosphere extended out no more than two dozen feet from the moon's surface! A cold sweat broke out on my brow as I contemplated my close call: had the gravitic force on Cluros been operating as predicted by the laws of physics, my ill-considered leap would have achieved escape velocity and sent me spinning off into airless space. As it was, only the upper half of my body had momentarily penetrated beyond the mysterious envelope of atmosphere.

The fragile lichenous coating had turned to dust at my touch. Wiping the powdery residue from my skin and garments, I slumped back against the outcrop and surveyed the barren landscape, wondering, not for the first time, if I would ever get used to the constant shuttling from one world to another. My current circumstances could not have been more different from the teeming forests of Ladan. I was all but certain that here there would be no roaring nocturnal monsters, no one-eyed cat-people with a taste for human flesh, no bird-rodent-fish things, no rushing rivers. Most significantly in terms of my immediate future: no food and no water. The grave nature of my predicament was undeniable. Although I had gotten the hang of prolonging my stay for a while in a given location, I had yet to experience any success in voluntarily departing it, and there was no way of telling how long I would be in residence on this barren lump of rock before I was whisked away to somewhere else. As it was, I had had just enough presence of mind to mentally picture myself in my current attire as the transit had begun and thus, to my great relief, my harness, silks, and sandals had again made the journey with me, as had my pocket pouch and dagger. I had, however, consumed the last of my concentrated rations while in residence with the Masenas, and I had no reason to believe the powdery lichen coating the rocks would prove edible. With but a limited span of days before starvation and dehydration would bring a final end to my travels, I could be certain of but a single fact: one way or another, I was not long for this world.

And yet . . .

Ever since I had been snatched from my home in Pellucidar to embark on this wild tour, each of my previous ports of call had found me in situations which, though often perilous in the extreme, had resulted not only in my own survival, but in the opportunity to accomplish during my stay some small good for others. Thus, I could not believe that I had been brought here to this desolate place merely to die.

Perhaps, I told myself wryly, a fabulous oasis of date palms and cool water awaited me just over the near horizon. Squaring my shoulders, I decided to set out and explore my new home in hopes of a miracle.

In fact, the landscape that met my eyes beyond that horizon was strikingly similar to the one in which I had just appeared: an endless field of grayish-tan gravel and dust, dotted with rocks large and small and pocked with craters of different dimensions. I walked at a leisurely pace, having calculated that I should be able to circumnavigate the entire world in just a few hours and seeing no need to exhaust what energy reserves my body still possessed. With little else to command my attention, I made a point of investigating each crater as I came upon it, finding most shallow enough to be traversed on foot, although several were so deep I could not see their bottoms in the shadows cast by the sun. It was as I was passing one of the latter that I thought to catch a flash of light from somewhere far below.

I circled back to peer over the edge of the crater and spied a metallic glint amid the shadows. Turning my hand torch to its widest setting, I shined it into the interior; to my surprise, the entire crater immediately filled with light. I narrowed the beam until I could see a smooth, mirror-like surface lying some thirty feet below the level of the ground. A hundred feet in diameter, the roughly circular disk spanned the crater's interior, completely sealing off whatever might lie below. I played the beam around the wall, discovering embedded in the rock not far from where I stood a vertical series of two dozen metal rungs that could only be meant to serve as stairs. Following them downward with my torch, I noticed below the lowest rung a faint line bisecting the metal disk to the opposite side, where I could make out a pair of bars or tracks set about six feet apart and rising in parallel up to the rim. Encouraged by these irrefutable signs of the presence of intelligent beings, I resolved to descend into the crater for a closer inspection.

I had just placed my foot on the topmost rung when a deep rumbling noise began from within the crater. The metal floor split open along the dividing seam and the two halves began to ponderously withdraw into slots in the wall on either side. The unmistakable sound of voices drifted up from the widening gap.

As hopeful as I was that the inhabitants of this little world would reveal themselves to be a beneficent and hospitable people, the lessons of grim experience bade me hop back over the rim of the crater. I peered down as a metal platform approximately eight feet long and three feet wide and carrying several figures appeared in the wan light emanating from below and rose slowly upward along the tracks on the far side of the crater.

I bounded over to a tumble of good-sized boulders lying not far from the crater and secreted myself behind a pair of closely positioned rocks so that I could gaze out between them without being seen myself.

The platform and its cargo reached the rim. I watched in fascination as two tall and heavily muscled men with black hair and copper-red skin, clad in what looked very much like Barsoomian attire and carrying between them the limp form of a third man, dismounted onto the surface of the little moon. Exchanging what sounded like humorous jibes, the pair set off toward a nearby outcrop whose dual coloration revealed that its peak extended a few feet beyond the band of atmosphere, and mounted the slope with their burden. When they had reached a flat area half a dozen feet below the threshold of space, they grasped the unmoving man by his hands and feet, swung him back and forth a few times to build up momentum, and then with a mighty heave sent him spinning off above them into the vacuum. I watched in horror as the corpse—for if he had not started out in that state, he had surely now achieved it—drifted off into blackness.

The two men sauntered back to the crater and climbed onto the platform. After they had dropped out of view, I returned cautiously to the rim and watched them descend the last few feet into the lighted space below the parted doors. The two halves of the divided disk came to life with a rumble, inching slowly toward one another. Knowing I did not have much time before the way was closed again, I vaulted over the rim and clambered quickly down the rungs.

Having observed little in their behavior to commend them to me, I hoped I would not find the two men waiting as I slipped through the opening scant seconds before the great doors clanged shut above my head. The area into which I had passed was deserted. A band of yellow lights ringing the lower portion of the crater dimmed and went out as I climbed down the continuation of the stairs. A softer radiance

shone from the entrance to a corridor set at right angles to
the tunnel and I stepped inside.

A narrow bar of yellow light ran along the corridor's
ceiling. I moved warily down the hallway, which had a
patchwork look to it, as if it had been pieced together from
many sheets of metal of varying sizes. Here and there the
walls were marked with panels of familiar-looking picto-
graphs. Although I had picked up a fair amount of the
Barsoomian common tongue during my stay on Mars, I had
learned little of its several written forms beyond the ability
to recognize them when I saw them. Adding this evidence
to the appearance of the two men, I was beginning to feel
certain that someone from Barsoom had made it to Cluros
before me. But how?

Large circular panes of glass like the portholes of a seago-
ing vessel were set at eye level in measured intervals on both
sides of the corridor. I peered into each as I passed, finding
most of the spaces beyond them dark. Light poured from a
pair of open doorways up ahead, and I came to a halt when
I glimpsed movement through the window just before them.
I crept forward.

The occupant of the chamber was moving restlessly back
and forth, his gaze turned away from the round window.
He was speaking rapidly as he paced, which caused me to
peer carefully through the glass in an effort to discern who
else was in the chamber, finally satisfying myself that he was
quite alone, and that the constant flow of speech was being
produced by himself alone.

He was a small fellow, no more than five feet tall, and
from his appearance also a member of the copper-skinned
race with whom I had become familiar during my time on
Mars. Although he looked harmless enough, the grotesque
scene I had just witnessed on the surface prompted me to
pause before making my presence known. As I hesitated in
the passageway, I recalled that one of the items in the pocket
pouch I had received from John Carter was a small container

of the reddish-copper cosmetic ointment Barsoomians commonly used on their skin, and which the Warlord himself had employed on those occasions when he found it more prudent to pass for a member of the native red race than to account for the unusual pallor of his otherworldly complexion. Retreating a few paces to where I could regard myself in the shiny surface of the corridor out of view of the window, I applied a thin layer of the substance to as much of my skin as was visible. Then I stepped forward and entered the chamber to stand just behind its pacing occupant.

"Kaor," I said, gambling that he would recognize this universal Barsoomian greeting. The little man froze in his tracks, then whipped around to stare open-mouthed at me.

Martians retain a youthful appearance for most of their extremely long lives. During my recent visit to Barsoom I had seen a few members of the red race whose signs of physical deterioration showed that they were approaching the thousand-year mark, but none so visibly aged as this man. Over the centuries his features had outgrown his face: large ears, a prominent nose, and a wide, yellow-toothed mouth were crowded onto a small round head, while still-sparkling eyes peered from cavernous sockets above knobby cheeks crisscrossed with a mesh of wrinkles. By contrast, the loose, ruddy flesh of his body hung from his bony frame like a suit of clothes several sizes too large. He appeared to be attired in three or more leather harnesses, one buckled on over the other, and each festooned with numerous bulging pocket pouches in addition to the shortsword, longsword, and pistol customarily worn by most Martians. About his scrawny waist was a thick belt studded with half a dozen peculiar-looking medallions. Most notable was the strange covering he wore on his hairless scalp, a close-fitting spider-web of thin wires studded with small gemstones.

"What are you doing up?" he asked me in a high, thin voice, raking me with his small, bright eyes. From the clutter on the floor and table, I judged that the sizable room in which we stood was a storage area. An even more spacious chamber was visible through its side door. Following my gaze, the little man looked over his shoulder at what appeared to be rows of slightly inclined cylinders that disappeared into the shadows at the back of the adjoining room. "I cannot recall your name!"

Taking my cue from his first question, I rubbed the back of my head and tried to assume a drowsy demeanor. "I seem to have misplaced that bit of information myself," I answered in my best Barsoomian. "Might you tell me yours?"

"O-ho! I am Urxo Dandur," he replied promptly. "But surely you must know that!"

"Now that you mention it, it does sound familiar," I said hopefully.

Urxo Dandur had been staring at me with his round head tilted to one side. "I wonder why I cannot read your mind," he said suddenly, reaching up automatically to pat the wire crown affixed to his scalp. "How can this be?"

John Carter had told me that while all Martians possessed telepathic powers and could project and receive thoughts to varying degrees, none had ever been able to penetrate the mind of any of the Earthmen who had sojourned on the Red Planet. Sensing that this explanation of my origin might be received with great skepticism on the part of my excitable host, I quickly improvised another, telling him that I had recently suffered a mild blow to my head and opining that this had jarred my brain in some fashion, resulting in both my loss of memory and a diminution of my telepathic senses. "No doubt the condition will disappear with time."

"Ho! Undoubtedly there has been a malfunction in your sleeping cell. Striking your head on the lid during your unplanned emergence might also explain your halting speech and peculiar accent. Perhaps I should confirm this by a brief surgical examination of the surface of your brain," he mused, his hand caressing the hilt of his shortsword

I took a step back. "That organ seems to be functioning

more satisfactorily with each passing moment," I told him. "Surely I would be of more use with my skull intact."

He continued to regard me thoughtfully for a few moments before dismissing the subject with a shrug. "Possibly, possibly. I shall keep my eye on you to make sure stronger measures are not warranted. For your own good, of course."

To my relief, the old man seemed to have accepted the notion that I was one of the other inhabitants of this strange miniature world. As we conversed, he warmed to the prospect of reacquainting me with the wonders of his domain, declaring that it would please him to view his many great accomplishments through the innocent eyes of one who might as well be newly hatched. I responded with gratitude to this proposal, eager to gain what understanding I could of the place before I revealed my true identity as a man from another world. Urxo Dandur required little coaxing to hold forth at length, and several interesting bits of information immediately came to light—including the fact that "we" had been stranded here on Cluros for some considerable time, and that the labyrinthine habitation in which we stood had once been part of a much larger structure the old man referred to as the *Hastor*, only a small portion of which currently resided alongside the crater through which I had arrived.

I was debating querying my new host about the grisly scene I had witnessed on the surface of the little moon. Having made the decision to keep my origins to myself until I had a better grasp of the situation, I weighed the consequences of revealing that I had recently been above, which I feared would not jibe with his view of me as a recovering amnesiac. On the other hand, assuming the men who had so callously disposed of another by casting him off into the vacuum of space now also roamed the premises down here, might they not pose an imminent threat to both of us?

The matter was unexpectedly resolved when footsteps sounded at my back. Looking past me in mild annoyance, Urxo Dandur raised a beckoning hand. "O-ho! Come in, come in!" he ordered brusquely. "Why do you loiter in the doorway like truculent schoolboys? You must meet my new friend."

I turned around to discover the two burly men from the surface, now joined by a third individual of equally imposing stature.

The newcomers, so alike in general appearance that they might have been brothers, regarded me with expressions ranging from dull confusion to deep suspicion. Ignoring an attempt to speak on the part of the largest, Urxo Dandur performed introductions. "These are my guardsmen," he said, indicating the hulking trio with three jabs of his bony finger. "Otzrap, Otzkor, Otzgung, here is a new addition to our little family. Of course, he has been on the *Hastor* with us all along, but a recent loss of memory has left him quite ignorant of our circumstances. His own name is—" He paused for a moment, then gave me a sly wink. "He is called Verzan Kai."

Martian appellations often involve subtle meanings beyond the grasp of relative newcomers to the language like myself. Urxo Dandur meant something on the order of "Three Million Ideas." As near as I could figure, the names the little man had applied to the three massive guardsmen translated as "Large-Sly," "Large-Strong," and "Large-Stupid," while the title he had invented on the spot for myself seemed to hint at connotations of both misrepresentation and entertainment. None of the guards seemed affronted by his blunt characterization of them, and so I took no offense myself.

While his two companions stood glowering at me, the largest of the guardsmen drew Urxo Dandur to the side and whispered briefly into his ear, to which the old man responded with a wave of his hand and a peevish comment or two. I wondered if Urxo Dandur had now been apprised of what had recently transpired above. If so, he seemed more irritated than appalled.

He dismissed the trio, who departed the chamber after a

few more suspicious glances in my direction and headed to the right down the main corridor, while we started off to the left to commence our tour of this strange place.

Our first stop was only a few paces away, as Urxo Dandur guided me next door to the large space he identified as the sleep chamber. I wondered if this was where I was presumed to have been before the unfortunate incident that had supposedly robbed me of my memory. Sensing that he was watching me closely for signs of recognition, I affected an expression I hoped would convey a dawning familiarity.

"What are these scratch marks?" I inquired, gesturing to a multitude of finger-length parallel lines just inside the entrance that covered the walls from the floor to a height of about five feet.

"O-ho!" He stretched his mouth in a toothy grin. "You have discovered my calendar."

"You—I mean we—have been marooned on Cluros for that many days?" I asked.

"Ho! Days!" The old man erupted in mirth. "O-ho-ho-ho! No, my forgetful friend—each of these marks represents a year since the *Hastor* departed from Barsoom!"

My jaw dropped. I turned back to scan the myriad markings, which I could now see had been divided into orderly groupings of one hundred. "A thousand . . . *years?*" I whispered. For a visitor from Earth like myself, the implications were even more staggering: due to the time required for Mars to complete a single revolution about the sun, each Barsoomian year—or *ord*—was nearly twice the length of its counterpart back on Earth. I did a swift calculation. Assuming Urxo Dandur was telling the truth, this would mean the vessel of which he spoke had left the planet below more than *eighteen hundred* terrestrial years ago!

"A mere nine hundred and eighty-four ords," he corrected me with an upraised forefinger. "One must be precise, Verzan Kai! The smallest miscalculation can doom an enterprise, as exemplified by the sorry fate of the *Hastor*, the first battleship ever to ply the skies of Barsoom."

"And the five of us have been alone all this time?" I asked in astonishment.

"O-no-no-no," he chortled. "I have many other friends here."

I looked around the silent chamber in puzzlement. Other than Urxo Dandur and myself, I spied no other living beings among the rows of what I took to be some form of storage containers.

"Come with me and I shall introduce you!" The little man then led me down the ranks of metal tubes, which he explained had indeed once been refrigerated food storage units, until he had supervised their conversion into sleeping cells that made use of a soporific gas to suspend and preserve the lives of those passengers and crew members of the *Hastor* who had survived the journey to Cluros. Up close, I could make out shadowy faces behind some of the small transparent faceplates attached to the upper ends.

We strolled among the rows, the little man occasionally pausing to point out an individual and note his expertise in a particular scientific discipline. I counted over four hundred of the things, though more than a third lay empty. The tubes also had a cobbled-together appearance, some being much larger or wider than others. Several times during our inspection, I caught Urxo Dandur examining me with sidewise glances; disconcerted, I had the uneasy feeling he was measuring me with his eye to determine which of the vacant cells had once accommodated my six-foot frame.

At length we left the sleep chamber and moved on down the winding corridor.

I got the *Hastor*'s story from Urxo Dandur in bits and pieces as we toured the patchwork labyrinth, with many a long digression about this or that brilliant idea he himself had come up with over the centuries to improve the lot of the somnolent survivors—often at the cost of many precious years of his own life.

The *Hastor* had been Barsoom's first—and, as far as Urxo Dandur knew, only—aerial battleship, a titanic vessel of war equipped with reservoirs of the then newly discovered Eighth Ray, and launched nearly a thousand long Martian years ago when the red race's experimentation in the science of flight was in its earliest infancy. During my recent time on Barsoom, I had received a crash course in the various solar and planetary rays scientists there had learned to collect and confine. These included the Ninth Ray, which, when isolated from sunlight and specially treated, combines with the ether to yield a breathable atmosphere, and the Eighth Ray, also known as the ray of propulsion, which is used to lift objects of nearly unlimited size and weight from the surface of a planetary body. When it was discovered following the ship's launch that a mathematical blunder had caused far too much of the latter substance to be pumped into the *Hastor*'s buoyancy tanks, a desperate effort was made to release the surplus. Tragically, the master valve had become hopelessly jammed. The ship continued to soar ever higher, all too soon attaining a height from which any attempt to blast open the tanks would have caused the mighty vessel to plummet to certain doom below. The *Hastor*, which had embarked on its maiden voyage with a full complement of five hundred warriors, joined by a small crew and a cadre of scientists with expertise in a wide array of different disciplines, was designed to be rendered airtight when necessary in the thin upper atmosphere of Barsoom, with the Ninth Ray synthesized as needed to manufacture both air and water for its passengers. Pooling their considerable brain power, the specialists had devised methods for sustaining the lives of those on board through the accelerated growth of certain food crops that had been brought along so that their reaction to the effects of flight could be studied. Urxo Dandur told me that he himself had perfected the conversion of the refrigeration units originally designed to store perishables into sleeping cells in which the processes of a man's life could be slowed to an infinitesimal rate, allowing him to come forth after many scores of years having only aged a few days. The majority of passengers had been secured within these tubes, with the scientists among them taking turns emerging from their slumber for short periods as their expertise was required—either to tackle the various problems associated with maintaining life aboard the ship, or to explore any avenue that might realize the goal of someday returning the vessel to the planet's surface—while Urxo Dandur alone had remained awake to oversee the effort.

The first real possibility of ending their centuries-long exile had arisen about seventy-five years ago, when the *Hastor*'s orbit had come close to intersecting that of the nearer moon. Once again Urxo Dandur was in the forefront, devising a plan to detach a portion of the vessel and send it hurtling to Thuria, which their observations indicated would be capable of supporting human life. Something went wrong at the last moment, and the makeshift lifeboat was instead flung into a much higher orbit, where it eventually ended up on a collision course with tiny Cluros. Under his careful guidance, so the old man told me, they had been able to maneuver themselves safely to the surface of the little world—and then down into the crater where what remained of the vessel now resided—with the loss of only a few lives. From then on the survivors had worked ceaselessly under Urxo Dandur's direction, ultimately succeeding in rendering desolate Cluros habitable by harnessing both the Eighth and Ninth rays to regulate the gravity and establish a shallow atmosphere belt, after which they had turned their attention to the ongoing work of creating a congenial habitation in which they might live out the remainder of their long lives.

I found the story impressive and moving, if a bit heavily weighted in terms of its emphasis on my host's own contributions to the admittedly heroic undertaking. I reminded myself that egotism in itself was no crime—especially when it had resulted in the preservation of so many lives!

We had continued our tour as Urxo Dandur recounted his saga. I was shown an experimental horticulture laboratory, a chemical manufactory, and finally a large chamber in which both the production of water and the synthesis of mass quantities of highly nutritional foodstuffs had been achieved, the latter based on the formula used on Barsoom to produce the concentrated food pellets carried by most warriors. Several of these areas were locked behind heavy doors; these the little man opened by means of the medallions about his waist, which he explained were electronic instruments of his own devising, some serving the function of keys while others enabled him to control every aspect of the settlement, up to and including the very atmosphere that rendered the tiny moon habitable. An eerie stillness pervaded the place; though spacious enough to accommodate over five hundred individuals, the chambers and corridors of the *Hastor* were occupied at the moment, so Urxo Dandur assured me, only by the two of us and his three guardsmen, with the rest of the survivors remaining sealed in the cells that preserved their lives until such time as they could be welcomed back to a perfected environment.

Most interesting to me of the various chambers we visited was the storage room in which I had first met the little savant. Dyed-in-the-wool inventor that I was, I itched for the opportunity to rummage through the shelves and crates of discarded scientific equipment.

Urxo Dandur had professed to enjoy the company of one who was to all intents and purposes a newcomer to the *Hastor*, and at his request I spent much time in his company in the days that followed.

I soon discovered that I was not the only one with memory issues—whether feigned or real. Most of the time my host's ancient mind, burdened as it was by centuries of near-solitude and duress, still clung firmly to the present day. Sometimes, however, I would engage Urxo Dandur in conversation only to find that it was many centuries ago and he was in the shipyards of the small principality not far from Helium where the great vessel had been manufactured, browbeating me for the malingering assistant he believed me to be. Other times we were preparing for the exodus to Thuria that had never occurred. Brief as they were, I found myself growing anxious during such forgetful episodes, each time hoping the old man would return to our current reality before making some grievous error that would adversely affect both myself and the hundreds of survivors who slumbered under his care.

In spite of his advanced age and occasional lapses, Urxo Dandur ran a tight ship. A stickler for the routines he had evidently established over many years, he had festooned the walls of the *Hastor* with chronometers, and these he used to maintain a schedule of alternately brighter and dimmer lighting designed to mimic the days and nights of Barsoom, as well as to regulate those activities he considered vital to a rewarding existence. He consumed his four small meals at precisely the same times during each twenty-six-hour day, enjoyed two four-hour rest periods in his own sleeping tube—the only one, as he proudly demonstrated to me, that was equipped with an internal mechanism that both rid it of the soporific gas and enabled it to be opened from the inside by its occupant—and conducted thrice daily tours of the habitation at predictable intervals, sometimes accompanied by his three guards, but often quite alone. Although he and his guardsmen were armed with the typical complement of Barsoomian weapons, I was asked by the old man to surrender my lone dagger the day after my arrival.

"Of course, I have complete confidence in your benign intentions, Verzan Kai, yet Otzkor believes it would be for the best if you were to remain weaponless for the time being. We would not want you to accidentally harm yourself while in the throes of another spell of impaired thinking," he told me, hand outstretched.

"Is there a reason you and the guardsmen go fully armed?" I asked. "Are you not already perfectly defended by the fact that you alone control who wakes and who slumbers in this place?"

"Ho-ho!" He gave his toothy grin. "Yet your own wakefulness has proven that the sleeping cells may malfunction and release their contents without warning, while the state of your memory confirms the unknown effects such a process could have upon one's mind. Where one man might find himself afflicted with amnesia, another could fall victim to raging insanity."

He had me there. I could think of no way to successfully plead my case without revealing my own duplicity, and reluctantly handed over my sole means of defense.

"Otzrap will be pleased," he said. "Better to leave matters of defense to the warriors. After all," he added with a twinkle in his eye, "one never knows when they will be obliged to quell the rebellion of a madman or repel an invading force from another world!"

We shared a laugh.

That night I had an idea, and the following day I told Urxo Dandur that I believed surrounding myself with scientific materials might go a long way toward restoring my faulty powers of recollection. After poring at length over his grand chart of the almost totally deserted labyrinthine habitation he had forged from the bones of a mighty battleship, he agreed to set aside a small section of the storage area just off the sleep chamber as my personal living quarters. When he had two of his guardsmen haul one of the empty sleeping cells into the room, pointing out the convenience of having it just a few yards from my table, I humbly asserted that considering the consequences of my recent bump on the head I would feel safer for the time being taking my rest on a pile of unused garments on the floor. I was relieved when he did not insist on sealing me in one of the tubes each night—particularly since he was the only one who currently possessed the means to unlock them. Knowing that he might not always indulge me in this matter, I determined to alter that situation as soon as I could manage it.

With nothing but time on my hands as I awaited my next transit, I occupied myself by going through the bins and boxes of discarded equipment in the storage room whenever Urxo Dandur was resting or otherwise engaged. Noting to my great delight a large number of materials that had evidently been intended for use in internal communication on board the *Hastor*, I began to explore the possibility of repurposing them in a manner that would benefit my new companions in this strange little world. As soon as I had assured myself of the feasibility of my plan, I approached the old scientist with a proposal to construct a device that would enable us to beam a message describing the plight of the *Hastor*'s survivors down to Barsoom, with the aim of securing our rescue. After a protracted pause, during which he seemed to be appraising my very soul with those sunken, sparkling eyes of his, Urxo Dandur smiled broadly and granted me his permission to begin work on my noble goal—a goal I had the distinct impression he did not believe for a moment I could ever attain. Gathering my tools and materials, I got started that very afternoon on the creation of a Gridley Wave transceiver.

It was good to be working again. I had happily lost myself in the project for several hours when I received an interruption in the form of an utterly unexpected visitor.

4

"That looks very complicated. Are you building a motorcar?" a female voice inquired in clear American English from just over my shoulder.

Startled, I looked up to see a young woman dressed in a leather kilt, a profusion of multicolored beads hanging from cords about her neck to drape her upper body. She had long, jet-black hair and skin that was cream-colored with just a hint of olive. Her oval face, the dark eyes bright with curiosity, struck me as the sort you might initially pass over in a crowd, only to be drawn back repeatedly by some ineffable quality of composition and attitude.

"No," I replied. "A transceiver."

"Ah." She nodded sagely. "That was to be my second guess."

I grinned. "Miss Callwell, I presume."

"Yes, although you must call me Betty," she said, extending her hand to me as if we had encountered one another in the Tea Room of the Waldorf Astoria. Unsure as to whether she expected me to bestow a kiss upon them, I briefly clasped her slender fingers and then returned them to her. "I'm afraid you have me at a disadvantage," she continued, "even though my High Priest swears to the members of his clan that you are my divine brother." Her smile was mischievous. "Yet each time Umka has tried to tell me your name, it has sounded quite different from the time before."

"My name is Jason Gridley, which I'm afraid does not roll trippingly off the Masena tongue," I said, beckoning her to sit by me on the bench. "I am pleased to finally meet you! I believe we have some mutual friends on different planets."

"Jason Gridley. Jason . . ." she echoed, her dark brows contracting in a momentary frown. "Now that I hear you say it, it sounds oddly familiar. And yes, I met John Carter not long ago during my brief stay down there. Or is it up there?" She waved her hand first at the floor and then the ceiling to indicate the possible whereabouts of Mars. "I had lost track of my memory back then, although I've since retrieved it. And my own first translocation was to Amtor, which I only learned many years later was the planet we call Venus. By the time Carson Napier introduced himself to me, I had already been there for some time, living comfortably as the goddess of a race of plantlike creatures. Meeting Carson jogged my jumbled memory, but it was only recently that everything came tumbling back."

"You have had a lot of experience as a goddess," I observed.

"I've never applied for the job," she said with a small shrug. "I was in training to be a stenographer when I was first taken. Yet the work is fairly easy and I seem to have a knack for it—until politics get involved, which was where things went sour with the Brokols. I left Amtor in the nick of time—and purely by luck, I believe, as this was when I was still liable to be tossed willy-nilly from place to place."

"I know the feeling," I said. "And now?"

"Now I go where and when I please," she declared. "Well, nine times out of ten. I'm still getting the hang of it."

"Are you serious?" I had gone back to tinkering with the transceiver as she told her story. Now I set aside my screwdriver and turned to face her. "I've only just learned to bring my own clothing and weapons with me, and to delay my departures by a bit. I've definitely had no success wishing myself elsewhere or exercising any control over where I land."

"Ah. I wasn't sure if you were here by choice or not," she said, looking around the cluttered room. "For myself, I'm happy on Ladan for now. I like the Masenas. They're decent folk."

"At least when they're not eating us," I added.

"Oh, I've talked Umka's tribe out of that," she told me. "It wasn't a very hard sell. As it turns out, they find us rather gamy."

"Well, there are definitely places I would rather be than here," I said glumly. I told her a little about the inhabitants of the *Hastor* and their millennia of exile.

"That does not sound at all pleasant," Miss Callwell said. "And the air is a bit stale. Where would you go if you knew how?"

I related the circumstances of my unplanned departure from the place I now called home, and told her of the wife and son I had left behind. "My first duty is to find my missing goddaughter, though I still have no idea how to go about it. Failing that, I'd very much like to return to my family in Pellucidar and let them know I'm all right."

Betty tapped her chin thoughtfully. "I should be able to get you back to your home without much trouble," she said matter-of-factly.

"Really?" She had my full attention now. "What makes you think so?"

She gestured to her unconventional attire. "As you see, I can also carry whatever I want along with me now when I transit—including other living beings." She lowered her voice. "I brought a pair of chickens back with me after one of my visits to New York. I thought it might make a nice change to have fresh eggs in the morning. Unfortunately, they figured out the latch on their cage, so by now they've either been eaten or I've introduced a new species to Ladan. If I can transport a chicken, I don't see why I couldn't do the same for you."

I leaned back, my mind whirling. Could it be possible? "There are several hundred sleeping men who have been marooned on this little moon for almost two thousand Earth years," I told her. "I need to stay here long enough to finish this device in order to communicate their whereabouts to Barsoom. But after that, if you really think it can be done . . ."

"I'm practically certain I can do it. Umka's a lot bigger than a chicken: when I get back to Ladan, I'll practice some with him before—" She paused as if struck by a sudden thought.

"What is it?" I asked.

"I was just wondering if the different ways our transits work would cause any problems."

"What makes you think they work differently?"

"This, for one thing." Betty fanned her hand in the air between us as if shooing away a swarm of insects. "My own body isn't enveloped in a purplish cloud."

I looked down at myself and saw only empty air. "You see a purple cloud around me?"

"I thought it might not be polite to mention it. But you really can't see it?" She leaned back to regard me critically. "It's calm now, more like a glowing aura than a cloud. But when I returned to Ladan and we faced each other in the doorway of the lodge, I saw it rushing about you like a rising wind—and then you were gone. Whatever it is, I don't think it gets along well with my own situation. In fact, I think it may have been your arrival on Ladan that pushed me off that world for a while, just as my return triggered your own transit here."

I was naturally a little skeptical, yet remembering the purple-blue vortex that had swallowed up first Victory and then myself, I could not dismiss her statements out of hand.

As I resumed work, Betty began to tell me something of her experiences after she had parted company with John Carter on Barsoom. She confirmed that, like myself, she had found herself drawn to Thuria, and had been gazing up into the night sky repeating the name to herself when she was suddenly overcome by the familiar sensations of transit. That was where our experiences differed.

"To my surprise, I found myself not on the moon Thuria, nor on the planet Ladan, as described to me by John Carter, but in a most peculiar place that seemed to be the inverse of any of the worlds I had previously visited."

"The inverse? What do you mean?"

"It was very dark and gloomy. At first I thought I had arrived after dusk; then I saw that a far-off band of light stretched all around me in a big circle. I started walking and eventually stepped right out of the darkness and into bright daylight. From there I could see that the land before me curved upward into the distance, just as if I were standing inside a giant snow globe—though it was very hot there, so of course there was no snow—instead of on the surface as one is meant to. Looking up, I saw an even stranger sight:

a huge sphere floating in the air a mile or so above, and on it I could make out forests and rivers, just as if it were a real world. I realized that the darkness came from the great shadow it cast in the light of the noonday sun. With nowhere else to go, I began walking around the rim of the shadow and eventually I met a man dressed in animal skins and riding on the back of an extremely large lizard with an extremely small head. I don't know if you've ever visited the Natural History Museum in New York, but when I went there as a girl they had the skeleton of a giant prehistoric reptile called a Brontosaur, and this is what the creature reminded me of. The man tried to talk to me, but we couldn't understand each other, which often happens on other worlds. I did manage to communicate that I had been looking for a place called Thuria, and he seemed to recognize the name— but the village he conducted me to on the back of his trained lizard was definitely not on Ladan."

It was obvious that Betty enjoyed having someone to talk to, and I had been holding my tongue as she spoke, but now as she paused for a breath I could contain myself no longer. "But I know just where you were!" I told her with excitement. "You were inside the hollow Earth—in Pellucidar, where I started out! You must have appeared beneath the pendant moon that hangs above the Land of Awful Shadow. There's a settlement there called Thuria. I thought it sheer coincidence when I learned that this was also the name by which Barsoomians knew Phobos, but perhaps there was some ancient connection between the two."

"How odd!" Betty said. "Weren't we just talking about Pellucidar? At any rate, the Thurians were nice enough to me, but I got tired of the sun never going down, and after a while I just wanted to get back to a normal planet where I could walk around on the outside and see the stars at night. This time I made sure to hold a clear image in my mind of Thuria—the one I had been staring up at from Mars, that is—and that's how I finally made my way to

Ladan. I met Umka, who surprised me by knowing a little English, and with his help I settled in pretty quickly with the tribe."

"Interesting," I said. "And how did you get your memories back?"

"I had started to have flashes of strange memories at that point, until one night I woke up from a particularly vivid dream to find myself in the alley behind my old house in Brooklyn. Right then was when it all came back to me. Unfortunately, someone else was living in our home and the streets outside the alley looked very different. It didn't take me long to figure out that a lot of time had passed since I had been taken. I borrowed some things to wear from a clothesline and went to the Public Library, where I was able to find a newspaper account of my own disappearance and supposed reappearance—as a dead woman!—a quarter of a century later. My parents had died and all my friends had grown old, even though I still don't seem to have aged a day since I was taken back in 1915—and I was twenty-two then. Everything had changed so much and it was clear that there was no life there for me anymore, though I did have several good meals at the Horn & Hardart's automat before I headed home to Ladan, and I have gone back a few times since, once for those chickens and after that just to hear people speaking English the way I remembered it and to get a bowl of proper clam chowder at a diner. Isn't it funny how sometimes it's the little things you miss the most—like paper napkins or oyster crackers? The last time, which I think coincided with your arrival on Ladan as it happened without my planning it, I was there for a couple of weeks before I could will myself back. Finally it worked again, which was nice because I was getting tired of sleeping in the park." She paused in recollection. "That particular trip didn't end so well, thanks to the angry angel I ran into in the alleyway."

"Angry angel?" I repeated, mystified. Once she got started,

Miss Callwell tended to speak rather rapidly, with frequent detours that sometimes made it a little difficult to keep up with her train of thought.

"Yes! That's how I think of her, anyway. It was nighttime and I had come back to the alley for another try at returning to Ladan. I had gotten used to coming and going from there, and had stashed away some New York clothing behind the loose bricks in the foundation where I used to keep my diary, my favorite jump rope, and a little mad money for the movies. I had just changed back into my Masena wardrobe when I heard this amazing sound like the blare of a hundred automobile horns all at once and a bright purple light suddenly flared before me.

"As I was blinking the spots away from my eyes, I saw a very tall woman in shining armor and a great plumed helmet standing there glaring at me from a cloud of purple mist. She had bone-white skin like the humans on Ladan, but long black hair like mine, and—believe it or not—huge black wings sprouting from her back. She walked toward me and the purple mist came with her. I took a few steps backward in surprise, but she came right after me, all the while babbling away in some weird language. At first I couldn't understand a word of it, but then the meaning began to come through, almost as if I were somehow learning it on the spot. Even then what she was saying didn't make much sense, as she kept harping on 'angles,' and other more nonsensical things, and demanding that I account for myself! I tried to explain in a civil tone that she obviously had the wrong sinner, but she wasn't having any of it. She continued addressing me in a very hostile manner, big wings flapping behind her as she went on about victories and chasing someone and—*oh*!" Her eyes grew wide.

"What is it?" I asked.

"Now I know why your name sounded familiar! It wasn't victories and chasing she was ranting about—it was victory and *Jason*! Maybe it was *you* the angry angel was really after."

"My goddaughter's name is Victory!" I told Betty in bewilderment. "What happened then?"

"Well, she drew this big sword from a scabbard at her side and the next thing I knew it had burst into flame! Really, the whole thing was getting out of hand, so I decided to make another stab at going back to Ladan, and this time it worked! I haven't run into her since—even when I went back a few days later to make sure she hadn't found my diary—nor had I seen a purple cloud around anybody else until I met you."

I suggested we get up to stretch our legs as I digested this latest piece of baffling information. Betty had noticed the rows of sleeping cells in the adjoining sleep chamber, so I brought her over for a quick tour. As much as I wanted to further discuss her bizarre tale, I saw by the nearest chronometer that Urxo Dandur would soon be conducting one of his daily inspections and told Betty that it might be difficult to explain her presence to the high-strung old man. She agreed to return to Ladan, do some practicing on transiting with another person in tow, and come back in a day or two. When I mentioned that I might not always be in this room, she informed me that when she had decided to come to Cluros to look for me, she had first appeared up on the surface, which she thought had a nice view of the stars, but was otherwise quite dull. Now that we had met, however, she said she would have no difficulty tracking me down next time, no matter where I was—thus revealing another ability she possessed that I did not.

We were saying our farewells in the doorway between the two rooms when Urxo Dandur suddenly appeared in the corridor entrance to the sleep chamber.

Unable to see me where I stood in the shadows of a shelf of materials just inside the storeroom, the little old scientist went rigid with shock at the sight of the newcomer. Betty turned at once to face him, signaling to me behind her back to stay in the storeroom. Not sure what she had in mind,

I lingered there reluctantly, prepared to rush out if the old man attempted to do her any harm.

"Where have you come from?" Urxo Dandur shrieked, snatching his radium pistol from its holster and leveling it at Miss Callwell. "And what are you?"

Before I could act to extricate her from this dangerous situation, Betty took several steps away from the storeroom entrance and performed a small curtsey. "Is it not obvious?" she said, addressing him, to my great surprise, in a heavily accented approximation of the Barsoomian common tongue. "I am a testament to the most brilliant mind in the universe."

That stopped him. The snout of the pistol wavered down a few inches. "What do you mean?"

"Do you believe it is possible for someone to appear fully formed out of the void of space?" she inquired.

"Naturally not!" the old man snapped.

"Where else then could I have originated, Urxo Dandur, other than the depths of your own prodigious brain?" Betty asked. "You have often yearned for female companionship, have you not?"

Urxo Dandur frowned, the pistol drooping still lower as his eyes traveled up and down her slim form. "I have."

Betty spread her hands with a beatific smile. "And so here I am, born of the powerful desires of a thinker without peer."

The ancient scientist looked uncertain. "You are exceedingly pale," he observed. "And your command of the common tongue is atrocious."

Miss Callwell gave a demure shrug. "You are evidently a complicated man," she said. "For I am as you have made me."

Just then the rack I had been leaning against shifted slightly and a pair of screws dropped onto the floor, one after the other, with echoing reports.

I ducked further back into the shadows as Urxo Dandur spun around to peer into the storeroom. When he turned back Betty had vanished.

I hastened to the table and was sitting with my head bent over the transceiver when he walked in a few seconds later.

I looked up. "Good day," I said.

He looked around the chamber with a puzzled expression. "Did you not hear me speaking in the sleep chamber just now?"

"No, I am afraid I was absorbed in my work," I replied. "Why? Were you calling for me?"

He gave me a hard stare, then shook his head and left the room. After his departure, I sat for some time considering the wholly unexpected possibility that with Betty's assistance I might actually have a chance of returning to Pellucidar again and reuniting with my loved ones—even if only for a brief visit before I was once again sent on my way.

I had been puzzling for some time over the relationship that existed between the old man and those he called his guardsmen. Noting that he addressed all three interchangeably by the names he had used to introduce them to me, I had never quite figured out which was which—yet they were equally formidable, and I had little doubt any one of them could have crushed the little scientist's round skull in a single gargantuan hand if he so chose. But no matter how he disparaged them, more often treating them like bumbling children than valued servants and flavoring his commands with barbs and ridicule, the three seemed to hold him in high esteem and granted his every whim without complaint. This impression changed the day after Betty's visit.

I was returning to my room after having indulged in an extra helping of food pellets in the deserted refectory when I heard sounds of an altercation issuing from the sleep chamber next door to my quarters. Concerned for the old man's safety should one or the other of his brutish guards decide to deal with him as they had the nameless individual I had seen flung into space shortly after my arrival on Cluros, I quietly approached the connecting doorway and peered within. What unfolded as I watched astounded me.

From what I could overhear, Urxo Dandur had been castigating one or more of the trio for some minor infraction and had apparently ordered them out of his sight and into their sleeping cells—a not uncommon occurrence when they displeased him. His two brother guardsmen already reposing in their sealed tubes, the burly individual who was either Otzgung, Otzrap, or Otzkor was apparently defying the old man's command to do likewise. As I watched, he took a menacing step toward his master, at which point the latter touched his fingers to his temples, his round face creasing in fury. With a great groan of apparent agony, the burly guard clutched his own skull and toppled writhing to the floor. Smiling in satisfaction, the tiny old man administered a series of sharp kicks to the ribs of the fallen guardsman, who wailed piteously all the while as if in excruciating pain—even though any harm Urxo Dandur was inflicting upon his powerful body could be little more than that which a small child might accomplish. Finally the quaking hulk rose slowly to his feet and shuffled with head bowed low to the open tube, where he climbed meekly inside. With a few additional words of reprimand, Urxo Dandur touched the sequence of buttons on the exterior of the cell that sealed the lid. The old man left the chamber through the main entrance, while I moved quietly back from the doorway and returned to my work table, deep in thought.

I have always had a good memory for numbers. Taking pains not to be caught staring, I had made a point of memorizing the sequence of buttons required to both open and seal the sleeping cells whenever the old scientist used them in my presence, thinking the knowledge might come in handy someday should he fall ill or suffer an immobilizing accident. The next day I waited until Urxo Dandur, who had conducted his initial tour of the *Hastor* without reviving his guardsmen, had gone back to his quarters for his first scheduled meal before I stole into the sleep chamber. I moved down the ranks of silent cells to those farthest from the entrance, selected an occupied cylinder at random and punched in the sequence that would open the lid.

The man reclining inside the tube blinked groggily at me for a few seconds before his face tightened into a grimace of frightened apprehension. As his muscles slowly came to life, he attempted to raise his hands before his face in a defensive posture.

I leaned forward. "You have nothing to fear from me. Can you tell me your name?"

He made a soft croaking sound, coughed, and tried again.

"I am Tav Carza, second botanist. Who besides yourself is awake?" he inquired in an anxious rush of words. "Who are you, for that matter, and how have you obtained permission to rouse me?"

"Only one other is conscious at the moment," I told him in answer to the first question. I chose my next words carefully. "It is Urxo Dandur, the man who styles himself the savior of all those on board the *Hastor*, and he has no knowledge that I have awakened you."

Thanks to the many tales he himself had told me, I had at first regarded Urxo Dandur as a scientific genius without peer, a brilliant, if highly eccentric, master of all trades whose super-intellect had almost unaided shepherded his fellows from the brink of extinction to victorious survival. Lately his unorthodox behavior had caused doubts to creep into my assessment, and now my suspicions were confirmed by Tav Carza's immediate response to my characterization.

"That old skeetan, our savior?" he scoffed. "Nothing could be further from the truth!" The *skeetan*, as I had learned during my time on Barsoom, was a small Martian animal whose pilfering behavior might be compared to that of an earthly magpie, in that it takes from others whatever it desires to furnish its nest, creating nothing of its own.

I raised an eyebrow. "Then the band of artificial atmosphere and altered gravity, the conversion of these storage tubes, the food manufactory . . . ?"

"All stolen from the minds of my colleagues and myself," said Tav Carza bitterly. "For centuries he has kept us hostage as little more than his consulting library, awakened from our slumber by ones and twos only to be set to work for a few days on whatever problem is vexing him. In the beginning he would assure us that our efforts were vital in bringing us closer to that day when we might all enjoy the freedom of the ship and its bounty of increased resources. Now he makes no pretense that this is his goal. Once we have given him the solution he desires, we are filed away again like dusty volumes—if we are fortunate—and so we pass our lives in dreams."

At my behest he elaborated on that last, somewhat ominous statement.

"There have been instances where those among us, be they scientist or warrior, have been roused to serve Urxo Dandur, but never returned to the sleeping tubes. During my last few wakings, I have noted a decrease in the number of occupied cells, yet never seen evidence that more than myself and his guardsmen were currently conscious. I believe that for some time the ancient monster and his foul henchmen have been dispensing with those whom he suspects of plotting against his rule."

I told him then of the scene I had witnessed on the surface several days ago, which he confirmed with sorrow was probably the disposal of a particular expert in plant growth Urxo Dandur had planned to rouse after Tav Carza, whose own specialty was soil composition. "That man was a gentle sort, and had not a rebellious bone in his body," he lamented. "Judging by Urxo Dandur's erratic behavior during my last waking, I think he has now begun to mete out the harshest punishment to whomever displeases him—even by the inadvertent commission of some petty impropriety."

"But how?" I asked. "How does this frail old man wield such power over you all? Even his guardsmen cower before him!" I related to Tav Carza the strange spectacle I had observed the previous day of Urxo Dandur sending one of his henchmen to the floor in apparent agony.

"Then you yourself have seen the means he employs to hold this little world in thrall," he responded.

"Have I? I still have no idea how he brought the brute to heel without ever laying hands upon him."

"Why, the power resides in the diadem he wears."

"What!" I was incredulous. I had thought Urxo Dandur's bejeweled headgear an exceedingly odd affectation—but then, he was an exceedingly odd little man. "I assumed it was something he had fashioned for himself to serve as a gaudy badge of office for his role as chief scientist."

"Sadly, no, although he flaunts it in place of a jeddak's crown to remind us of his omnipotence. It is a clever device created by one among us and stolen long ago by the old fiend, who then used it to deliver a painful death to the inventor in demonstration of its power. It was at that moment that he established his dominion over us and all was lost."

Tav Carza went on to describe the means by which the instrument augmented the telepathic powers of its wearer, allowing him to manipulate electrical currents, including those naturally present in the human brain, in such a way as to inflict unimaginable pain—or, should he desire it, death—upon those who displeased him. "Be thankful he has not seen fit to use it on you," he concluded, growing pale beneath his copper-red coloring. "It is the sensation of a thousand white hot needles penetrating one's brain. And that is the dosage he employs merely to punish—not the one that kills!"

I saw by the omnipresent chronometer that we had been talking for some time. Soon Urxo Dandur would embark upon the next of his thrice daily rounds.

"Listen to me, for I must soon return you to your sleep. Much time has gone by on while you have languished here," I told him. "I know for a fact that there are now vessels capable of traveling out of the atmosphere to return safely to the surface of Barsoom. With Urxo Dandur's blessing I am currently constructing a device that will enable me to transmit a message to those below. Once they hear of your plight, I am certain they will waste little time in coming to your aid."

"Then you are not one of us," Tav Carza said. "I thought I detected an unusual quality to your speech."

I decided to take a chance. "Do you subscribe to the theory that there is intelligent life on planets other than Barsoom?" I asked him.

"Of course. We know that beings much like ourselves thrive on—" He broke off, staring at me with narrowed eyes as I lifted the harness straps crossing my chest to reveal a small area where the reddish pigment had been worn away and my own much paler skin now shone through. "I myself was born on Jasoom," I said, using the Barsoomian name for Earth.

Seething with curiosity, Tav Carza plied me with eager questions until I raised my hands. "This is not the time to go into details, as Urxo Dandur may wander by at any moment and he is well equipped to cause trouble with his diadem and his armed guards, while even my dagger has been taken from me. There are issues that must be dealt with before my plan may be realized—and little time in which to do it. My only advantage is that Urxo Dandur knows nothing of my true origin and believes me a harmless amnesiac who has been with the *Hastor* from the beginning."

Tav Carza's face reflected skepticism. "You say he knows you are engaged in this pursuit?"

I nodded. "So far he has been very encouraging."

"You would do well to watch your back while you work," he cautioned me. "There is nothing the old man fears more than the loss of his own private nation, as he has come to view the remains of the *Hastor*. I cannot believe he would welcome the prospect of succor from Barsoom."

"I appreciate the warning, Tav Carza. Know that I will

do everything in my power to effect your deliverance, and that of your comrades."

"You have my undying gratitude," he said, reaching forward to place his right hand on my left shoulder in the Barsoomian way. I returned the gesture. "But wait—you have not told me your name."

"The name I was given on Jasoom is Jason Gridley," I said, "although Urxo Dandur calls me Verzan Kai."

"By my first ancestor!" He broke into an incredulous grin. "The first name is outlandish, but the second even more so!"

"Why, what are its implications?" I asked. My mastery of the Barsoomian common tongue was still spotty in certain areas, and there were many words whose subtle connotations escaped me.

"Verzan Kai means 'Amusing Liar,'" he said. "If Urxo Dandur has named you that, then you may well wonder if you have deceived him after all. It is too bad you must act alone in this."

The notion that the old scientist might be playing me for a fool sent a chill down my spine.

"I do have a confederate, another traveler from my own world," I assured him.

Tav Carza searched the empty room with his eyes.

"She comes and goes," I said. "It is a long story."

Then, after once more swearing that I would do all in my power to rescue him and his fellows from the clutches of the mad egotist that had held them in thrall for so long, I prevailed upon him to lie back down in the sleeping tube. "With a little luck, the next time you open your eyes, it will be to gaze upon those who have come to bring you home to Barsoom!"

His words of fervent gratitude ringing in my ears, I pressed the buttons that would return him to oblivion—at least for the time being—moved quickly up the rows of cylinders, and hurried to the doorway, where I almost collided with the old scientist himself, his three guardsmen looming at his heel.

Urxo Dandur's bright little eyes swept the chamber suspiciously.

"What are you doing in here among the sleeping cells, Verzan Kai?" he demanded.

"I come here often to enjoy the presence of so many superior minds while I attempt to think through the various problems that arise in my work," I replied. "It is foolish, I know, but sometimes I hope the ingenuity of their sleeping brains will augment my own."

"O-ho. Yet Otzgung and I thought we heard voices in conversation as we came down the corridor."

"Indeed you did," I told him with a self-deprecating grin. "For I often discuss my ideas with my keenest critic—that is to say, myself."

"I see." Urxo Dandur allowed himself a frosty smile. "And how is your great project progressing?"

"I hope to have accomplished my goal before very much longer," I replied.

"Very well," he said, and reminded me again that I was to allow him to inspect the device before activating it. "Just in case you have crossed a wire or misplaced a circuit. I do not boast when I say that I possess a keen eye for error."

In fact, I had the transceiver finished within the hour. With my new and alarming insight into Urxo Dandur's character, I wasted no time in preparing the recorded message I planned to send in a repeating cycle to Barsoom. In it, I outlined as succinctly as I could in the Barsoomian common tongue the dire situation on Cluros, with special attention paid to the depredations of the old man who now considered himself the *jeddak*—or emperor—of the tiny moon. I was replaying the communiqué aloud in order to check the quality of the recording when I heard a stealthy noise from the corridor and the doorway was suddenly crowded with towering shapes. I looked up from the transceiver to find Urxo Dandur's three guardsmen glowering down at me.

"Have I not told you all along that he was up to something?" exclaimed the nearest man. "We should kill you now, but then Urxo Dandur would chastise us for robbing him of the pleasure." Always the most excitable of the trio, the man to his rear pushed past him with a guttural roar and reached for me. "By Issus, I *will* kill him!"

"Don't be an imbecile, brother!" cried the third. "Restrain yourself or it will go badly for all of us. Do you wish to feel your brain on fire once more?"

I had ducked swiftly out of the way of the second man's grasp, causing the first man, who had lunged forward to intercept him, to bang his knee forcefully on the corner of the bench. As he cried out in pain, I attempted to dart past the other two, hoping to lead them away from the transceiver and into the spacious sleep chamber where I would have more room in which to engage them. A hand the size of a bear's paw grabbed my harness from behind and a moment later the third man had wrapped his meaty arm around my neck in a choke hold.

"Stop wailing and go fetch the jeddak!" he shouted to his injured brother. "Then we can all be entertained by this traitor's dying agonies." With a glare of resentment, the first man limped out into the corridor.

I thrashed about with all my earthly might in the crushing grip, which was calculated to prevent me from getting my hands on him while he slowly squeezed my windpipe. His strength matched his enormous size and his hold never faltered.

"Let me have him! If anyone is going to choke him to death, it should be me!" protested the second man, dancing frantically about the two of us in search of an opening. As his brother leaned back against the work table to avoid giving up his prize, my hand brushed against the heavy mallet I had been using to reshape strips of metal for my device.

My head beginning to swim from lack of oxygen, I hefted it high and brought it down with all my might on the back of his skull.

There was a moment's stunned silence as the big man's arm fell away from my throat and he crumpled to the floor. The second man looked back and forth between the two of us, his mouth gaping. For a moment he seemed undecided as to whether he should tend to his brother or finish me off. Seeing the sizable dent in the back of the fallen man's head apparently made up his mind, for he whipped out his radium pistol and aimed it squarely at my breast. "Murderer!" he cried. "Now you die!"

Then he made a sudden choking sound. His eyebrows shot up in consternation as he stared down at the bright red blotch widening on his chest. The pistol dropped from his hand and he toppled forward to the floor beside his brother, revealing a triumphant Umka standing over him, both mouths stretched in frightful grins. The cat-man wrenched the polished wooden sword from the dead man's back and bounded over to my side, purring happily and reaching out to stroke my upper arms.

Now grinning myself, I shook my head in amazement and returned the gesture of friendship. "Umka, where on Earth—"

"No, no," he said. "From Ladan! I have been carried here by *Yumku-mraa-owa-samyu* to see my friend."

As if on cue, Betty Callwell came into the room, humming an air I recognized as a popular American tune of some thirty years earlier. The multiple strands of beads covering her breast had been replaced by dozens of iridescent feathers. "I see you got the others," she said, coiling in her hands a length of slender rope with wooden handles affixed to both ends. She clucked her tongue at the red liquid beginning to ooze from beneath the fresh body on the floor and shook the loop of rope in our direction. "My way leaves less to clean up."

I gave her a brief recounting of what I had uncovered since her previous visit, while Umka wandered about the room, examining everything within reach with a look of delighted wonder. "I was getting ready to take the transceiver up to the surface to hide it on the far side of the moon where Urxo Dandur wouldn't think to look once it's been activated," I finished. "Then those three showed up and the cat was out of the bag—so to speak," I added with an apologetic glance at Umka, who gave me an uncomprehending smile from the other side of the room, where he had stepped inside one of the smaller empty boxes and was now attempting to lower himself into its narrow confines. "One of those ogres was on his way to report my deception to Urxo Dandur, while the other two were vying to teach the deceiver a permanent lesson with a stranglehold or a radium bullet, so your timing was impeccable."

"Good! Then my High Priest and I shall return to our flock before the old reprobate shows up and sees you plotting with his faithless brain child. It often takes me a little while to refocus after a transit, but I'll come back to the surface for you as soon as I can," she promised, beckoning to the Masena. "As you see, I've learned how to travel with a companion a good deal larger than a chicken, and Umka has had a couple of trips he'll not soon forget to the alleyway behind my old home on Earth."

I smiled, imagining the cat-man's reaction to the sights and sounds one might glimpse from a New York City alley.

"It was good to see you!" Umka told me as they prepared to leave. "Perhaps we will meet again, if the goddess wills it—hopefully back on Ladan." He leaned in close to my ear. "I have been two times to the world called Brooklyn! I did not care for the smell."

Betty had been inspecting the bloody corpse of Otzgung, Otzkor, or Otzrap.

"Let me save you the trouble of disposing of this one," she said, hooking her sandal under the massive outflung arm.

She motioned Umka to her other side and took his hand in hers.

"Two at once?" I shook my head. "Now I think you're just grandstanding!"

After they had departed I mopped up the pool of blood with a length of discarded cloth. Then I dragged the remaining brother in from the corridor and manhandled the two men into a pair of cylinders at the farthest end of the chamber, arranging the harness of Betty's victim so that the ligature marks she had left around his neck would not be visible through the faceplate should anyone go looking for him. My own casualty was an easier fix, as only the back of his thick skull had suffered any discernible damage.

I was once more at my work table when Urxo Dandur appeared in the doorway half an hour later. He gazed about the room in perplexity. "Where are my guards?" he demanded.

I responded with a shrug. "I have not seen them for some time, though earlier I overheard one saying that you had sent them on an important errand of some sort."

"I have no recollection of doing that today. And yet . . ." Urxo Dandur rubbed his withered cheek with a frown, his fingers toying with the border of his bejeweled headdress. "Strange things have been happening since your awakening, Verzan Kai! If I thought you had any cause to act against me—" He stopped himself with a glance at the wall chronometer. "But I am in need of a meal, and then some rest. Remember," he added in a peremptory tone, "you are not to activate your project until I have examined it!"

"My memory is now perfectly intact," I replied with a smile, earning myself a final sharp glance from the little old man before he exited the chamber.

Spurred on by the events of the past day, I worked on various projects through the night. Early the next morning I notified Urxo Dandur at his breakfast table that I had finally completed my transceiver. He followed me back to the laboratory, where he offered me his hearty congratulations.

"You have labored long and hard on this, my friend!" he told me, his bright gaze fixed upon the gleaming object on the work table. "You must be fatigued. In fact, I insist you rest your eyes for a bit while I admire your great creation. Surely you have no cause to fear a few minutes in the tube while I stand here to ensure that all is well? I will awaken you shortly and then you may explain its workings to me in detail." After a token protest, I let him lead me to the sleeping cell, where I reclined and allowed my eyes to drift shut. As soon as the tube was sealed, I could hear the old man chortle through the tiny holes I had drilled into the underside of the container as part of last night's activity. "Fool! Deceiver!" he cried. "Did you think I would permit you to summon the armies of Barsoom to war upon my nation? O-no-no-no! In payment for your audacity, I shall allow you to languish here for a century or two before I bring you back!" Hearing his retreating footsteps, I opened my eyes a crack to see him standing at the work table, his gnomish features contorted in triumphant glee. I watched in grim fascination as he raised his hands to his temples and narrowed his eyes. There was an ominous crackling sound and a moment later the fragile device exploded into a hundred tiny pieces.

I forced myself to wait until I was sure Urxo Dandur had returned to his quarters. Then I tripped the internal opening mechanism I had installed in the tube the night before while also disconnecting the sleep gas jets, and climbed out. With a rueful shake of my head for the labor that had gone into the instrument that now lay scattered in smoking fragments on the table and floor, I pulled the spare parts box out from beneath the work table and withdrew the genuine transceiver I had hidden there last night before setting to work on my decoy. Wrapping the device in a length of heavy cloth, I made my way without incident through the deserted halls of the *Hastor* to the base of the entrance tunnel. Here I applied my stolen key to the great lock. I felt a bit anxious as the low rumbling of the opening doors reverberated through the underground corridors, hoping Urxo Dandur had adhered to his schedule and now reposed unconscious in his own sleeping cell. With any luck, it would soon make no difference.

With the transceiver tucked carefully under my arm, I mounted the metal rungs and climbed over the rim to stand once more beneath the black, star-sprinkled sky of Barsoom's lesser moon. Betty Callwell was seated cross-legged on the gravel not far from the crater, chewing on a tuber. She rose to greet me and we set off across the pebbled surface. We walked some distance from the crater of the *Hastor* to a small outcrop that was coated with the ubiquitous greenish lichen and virtually indistinguishable from the hundreds of others that covered the lunar surface. Betty looked on with interest as I unwrapped the transceiver and positioned it in a small sunlit niche on the far side of the rocks. I had contrived a solar battery from some pieces of discarded equipment that had once been part of an array used to gather sunlight for the production of atmosphere on board the *Hastor*, and should now allow the device to transmit as long as the sun shone on tiny Cluros.

I flipped a switch to activate the instrument, which emitted a nearly inaudible hum as it began beaming out its recorded message to the great planet looming above the horizon. Betty looked disappointed. "It would be more impressive if there were weird sounds and dramatic flashes of light," she said after a moment.

"You are welcome to add that feature to the Gridley Wave transceiver *you* put together out of spare parts," I told her.

She shrugged. "Given the choice, I'd probably build a motorcar. Now—are you ready to leave this place?"

"I most definitely am," I said.

She held out her hand, then flinched back an inch.

"What's wrong?" I asked.

"It's your purple cloud. It's becoming agitated again, almost as if it's reaching out for me when I get close. If it's truly related to how you make your own transits, I wonder how it will react when I try to bring you with me . . ." Dismissing the thought with a shake of her head, she clasped my hand firmly in her own. "Picture as clearly as you can the place you'd most like to be and your mind should take us there. I had Umka do that on our second trip back from Earth and it worked well."

I closed my eyes and built a detailed picture in my mind of the rustic cottage on the outskirts of Sari, capital of the Empire of Pellucidar.

A moment later I felt a gentle gust of air ruffle my hair. The pressure on my hand had vanished. I opened my eyes.

I was alone on the surface of Cluros.

Recalling Betty's comment that it often took her some time to refocus her thoughts after a transit, I settled back against the outcrop to await her return, my hand drumming idly on the humming Gridley Wave transceiver as I pondered this new and unpleasant stumbling block.

A few minutes later I looked up at the sound of pebbles crunching underfoot only to see Urxo Dandur approaching from the direction of the *Hastor*, his small round face split by a sneer of malicious triumph. I moved slightly, blocking the nook where I had placed the transceiver.

"I am quite angry with you, Verzan Kai," the old man said in his reedy voice. "You have forced me to trek halfway round the world to retrieve what is mine."

"I don't follow you," I told him. "I have nothing of yours."

"O-ho! Every item, every scintilla aboard the *Hastor*—upon this entire moon, for that fact—belongs to its jeddak," he replied. "This is equally true for both its human inhabitants and anything they may produce. Where is the device?"

"Ah. Forgive me for not allowing you to inspect another transceiver after the mysterious accident that befell the first one," I said. "You were resting and I did not wish to disturb you."

"Liar!" he cried, his hand darting to his head. An instant

later I decided that Tav Carza's description of the effects of
the diadem on the human brain was quite accurate, as I
reeled beneath the onslaught of a thousand needles of fire.
Feeling myself close to losing consciousness, I had slumped
heavily back against the rock when I suddenly glimpsed a
pale figure behind Urxo Dandur.

"His headpiece," I said thickly. "Grab it!"

The old scientist gave an incredulous laugh. "Surely you
do not expect to trick me with that ridiculous—"

Betty's sandal made a scraping sound against the rough
ground as she darted forward to clutch at the glowing diadem.
Urxo Dandur whirled about with surprising speed and now
it was Miss Callwell who fell to her knees, crying out in
agony, as the fire in my own brain did not lessen. While the
old man's attention was focused on Betty, I summoned all
my willpower and thrust myself to my feet. Then, lunging
forward with an inarticulate cry, I seized Urxo Dandur about
his thin waist and hurled him up into the air with all the
force of my earthly muscles. I watched him grimace with
shock and hatred as he passed out of the atmospheric field,
his hands stabbing viciously at his control pendants until his
body grew slack and he began to rotate slowly off into space.

I stumbled over to Betty and helped her to her feet. "Are
you all right?" I asked.

"My skull no longer feels like it's submerged in molten
lava," she said with a weak nod. "That's an improvement."

The pain in my own head was gradually dissipating. "Let's
get back inside," I said. "Now that he's gone we have time
to figure this out."

Small glimmers of motion caught my eye as we began
to walk in the direction of the *Hastor*'s crater. I gazed around
in puzzlement.

Betty followed my gaze with a questioning look. "What
is it?"

"I'm not sure," I told her. "Wait—look there!"

All around us the tallest rocks had begun to darken in a

steady wave downward from their peaks, as their pale lichenous coating dissolved into powder. A cold hand closed suddenly about my heart as I recalled Urxo Dandur's spidery
fingers jabbing at the pendants about his waist.

"He's altered the atmospheric controls and the field that
holds the air is contracting around the moon!" I cried as I
grabbed her hand. "Hurry!" We raced toward the crater,
whose rim was barely visible on the horizon a half mile away.
A wave of utter cold seemed to float just above our heads,
and it was quickly obvious we would not have enough time
to make it. We crouched lower and lower still, and then
finally halted in our tracks. *"Go!"* I ordered Betty. "You can
still save yourself!"

With a stubborn shake of her head, she reached out to
clutch at my wrist. "No!" she cried. "It's all in our minds!
Just give me your hand and concentrate—I *know* I can do
it this time!"

By now we had both flattened ourselves to lie prone on
the plain of gravel. A shudder racked my body as I felt the
icy wave beginning to spread across my back. "I surely hope
so!" I gasped. "For we seem to have reached the point of
now or never—"

It was now.

5

I flung up an arm to shield my eyes from the brilliant dazzle
of light. We helped each other slowly to our feet. The sun
sat blazing at the zenith in a cloudless sky. Taking in a great
breath, I filled my lungs with warm air rich with the inter-
mingled scents of a primeval world. Before us lay a dense
jungle, the tangle of vegetation not silhouetted against the
sky, but curving ever upward and away through dim clusters
of mountains and patches of open water in a haze of green
and brown and blue, until all was lost at last in the distance.

"It's gone," said Betty. Color was just beginning to return to her cheeks. Releasing my hand, she took a step back to look me up and down with narrowed eyes. "How interesting!"

"Gone?" I echoed.

"The purple cloud. It didn't come with you."

It took me a few moments to grasp the import of this simple statement. At the same time, I realized that the mild electric thrill I had finally pushed from my awareness after my many transits was completely absent from my body for the first time since that fateful moment I had been sent whirling through the trackless wastes. With this comprehension came a flood of conflicting emotions. Could I finally be free of the curse of eternal wandering, no more an interplanetary Flying Dutchman searching in vain for a port in which to rest? On the other hand, did this mean I had now lost all hope of crossing paths with my errant goddaughter, as she continued to be flung from world to world in her own solitary race through the infinite? This was an outcome I would never accept.

I heard a small noise from behind me. Turning, I saw the familiar cottage I had pictured in my mind scant moments ago on the Red Planet's desolate moon. A thin, bent figure was just backing out of the doorway as he made his low-voiced farewells to someone still within. I recognized him at once—for here in this primordial paradise, who else would be attired in a khaki jacket and breeches, sturdy shoes upon his feet and his spindly legs wrapped in broadcloth puttees, in a defiant display of the enduring trappings of civilization?

"Perry!" I cried, my heart pounding like a triphammer.

The old man whirled around and peered at me beneath his hand. His querulous frown turned to a look of astonishment.

He came hesitantly forward, staring at me as I stood before him in my tattered Barsoomian finery as if I were a heat mirage. "*Jason*? Jason Gridley? Is it you?" He extended his trembling hand in a formal gesture.

I pulled him into a bear hug.

"Abner Perry, you're a sight for sore eyes!" I announced to his bald spot as the old fellow struggled for breath. Finally I relaxed my hold enough for him to gasp out: "Jason! It *is* you! But—but how?"

"Here is the one who can best answer that for you," I told him, releasing my old friend and gesturing to where Betty Callwell stood just behind me.

There was no one there.

"I see." Perry cocked a white eyebrow at me. "I have something on the order of seven million questions for you, young man," he said.

"And I have an equal number for you! But first—"

At that moment a second figure emerged from the shadowed doorway of the cottage and stepped out into the eternal daylight, where she stood in wide-eyed disbelief for only a moment. Then she ran toward us, her long copper-bronze hair streaming out behind, to halt a few paces in front of me.

"I thought I heard your voice, my Jason," Jana choked, her eyes filling with tears. "But after so long I—I could not believe it!"

"Believe it," I said, as I swept my Red Flower into my arms.

About Geary Gravel

Geary Gravel is the author of Edgar Rice Burroughs Universe novel *John Carter of Mars: Gods of the Forgotten*, the Philip K. Dick Award finalist *The Alchemists*, and the novels *The Pathfinders*, *A Key for the Nonesuch*, and *Return of the Breakneck Boys*. He has written several novelizations, including *Hook*, based on the Steven Spielberg film, and *Batman: Mask of the Phantasm*, based on the animated movie. He lives in western Massachusetts, where he worked for decades as a Sign Language Interpreter for the Deaf.

EDGAR RICE BURROUGHS: MASTER OF ADVENTURE

The creator of the immortal characters Tarzan of the Apes and John Carter of Mars, EDGAR RICE BURROUGHS is one of the world's most popular authors. Mr. Burroughs' timeless tales of heroes and heroines transport readers from the jungles of Africa and the dead sea bottoms of Barsoom to the miles-high forests of Amtor and the savage inner world of Pellucidar, and even to alien civilizations beyond the farthest star. Mr. Burroughs' books are estimated to have sold hundreds of millions of copies, and they have spawned 60 films and 250 television episodes.

About Edgar Rice Burroughs, Inc.

Founded in 1923 by Edgar Rice Burroughs, one of the first authors to incorporate himself, EDGAR RICE BURROUGHS, INC., holds numerous trademarks and the rights to all literary works of the author still protected by copyright, including stories of Tarzan of the Apes and John Carter of Mars. The company oversees authorized adaptations of his literary works in film, television, radio, publishing, theatrical stage productions, licensing, and merchandising. Edgar Rice Burroughs, Inc., continues to manage and license the vast archive of Mr. Burroughs' literary works, fictional characters, and corresponding artworks that has grown for over a century. The company is still owned by the Burroughs family and remains headquartered in Tarzana, California, the town named after the Tarzana Ranch Mr. Burroughs purchased there in 1919 that led to the town's future development.

In 2015, under the leadership of President James Sullos, the company relaunched its publishing division, which was founded by Mr. Burroughs in 1931. With the publication of new authorized editions of Mr. Burroughs' works and brand-new novels and stories by today's talented authors, the company continues its long tradition of bringing tales of wonder and imagination featuring the Master of Adventure's many iconic characters and exotic worlds to an eager reading public.

Visit **EdgarRiceBurroughs.com** for more information.

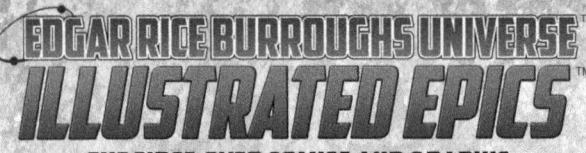

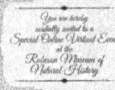

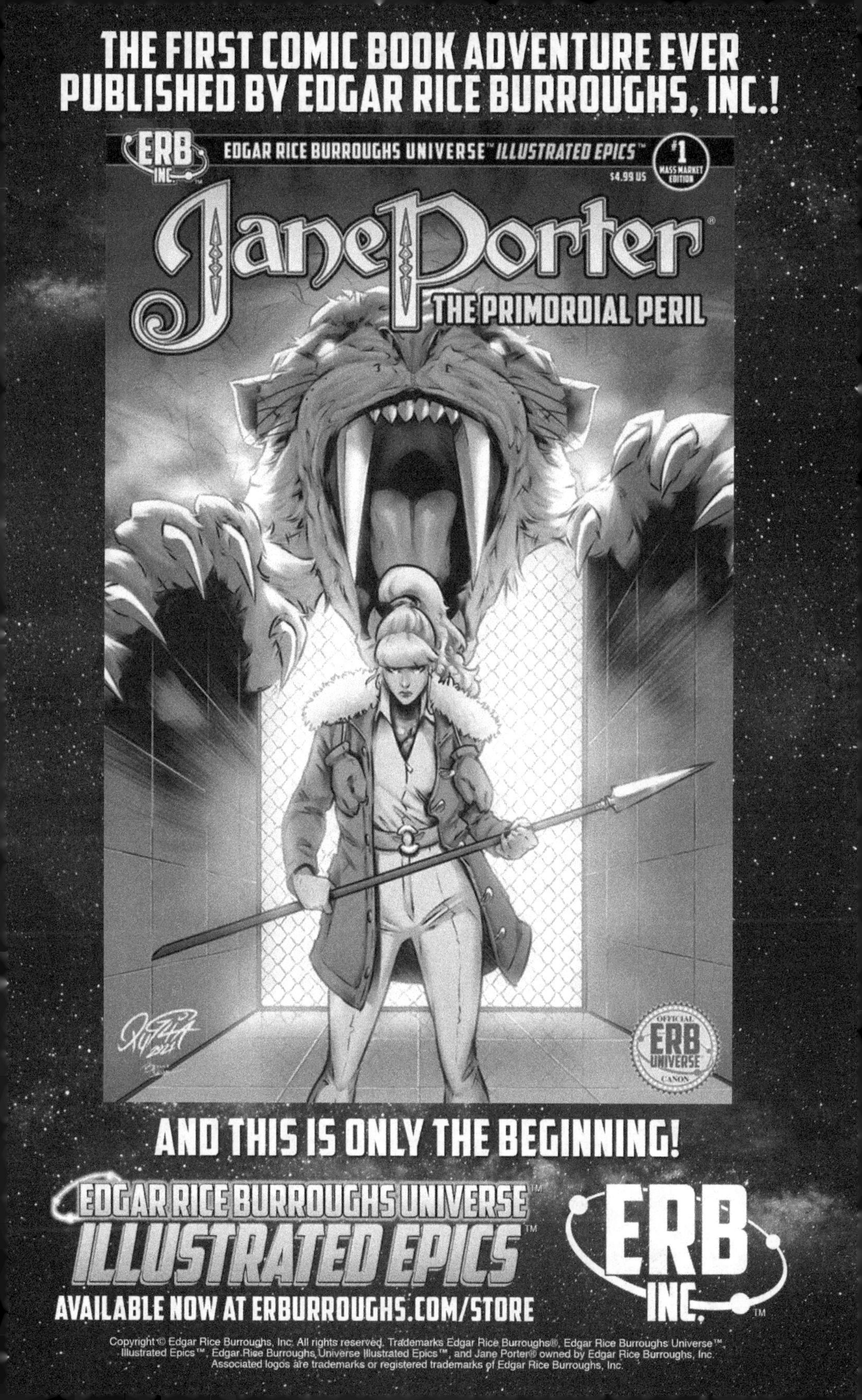
THE FIRST COMIC BOOK ADVENTURE EVER PUBLISHED BY EDGAR RICE BURROUGHS, INC.!
ERB INC.
EDGAR RICE BURROUGHS UNIVERSE™ ILLUSTRATED EPICS™
#1 MASS MARKET EDITION
$4.99 US
Jane Porter®
THE PRIMORDIAL PERIL
OFFICIAL ERB UNIVERSE CANON
AND THIS IS ONLY THE BEGINNING!
EDGAR RICE BURROUGHS UNIVERSE™
ILLUSTRATED EPICS™
AVAILABLE NOW AT ERBURROUGHS.COM/STORE
ERB INC.™
Copyright © Edgar Rice Burroughs, Inc. All rights reserved. Trademarks Edgar Rice Burroughs®, Edgar Rice Burroughs Universe™, Illustrated Epics™, Edgar Rice Burroughs Universe Illustrated Epics™, and Jane Porter® owned by Edgar Rice Burroughs, Inc. Associated logos are trademarks or registered trademarks of Edgar Rice Burroughs, Inc.

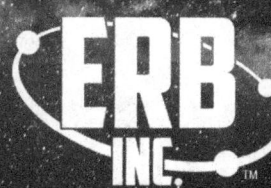

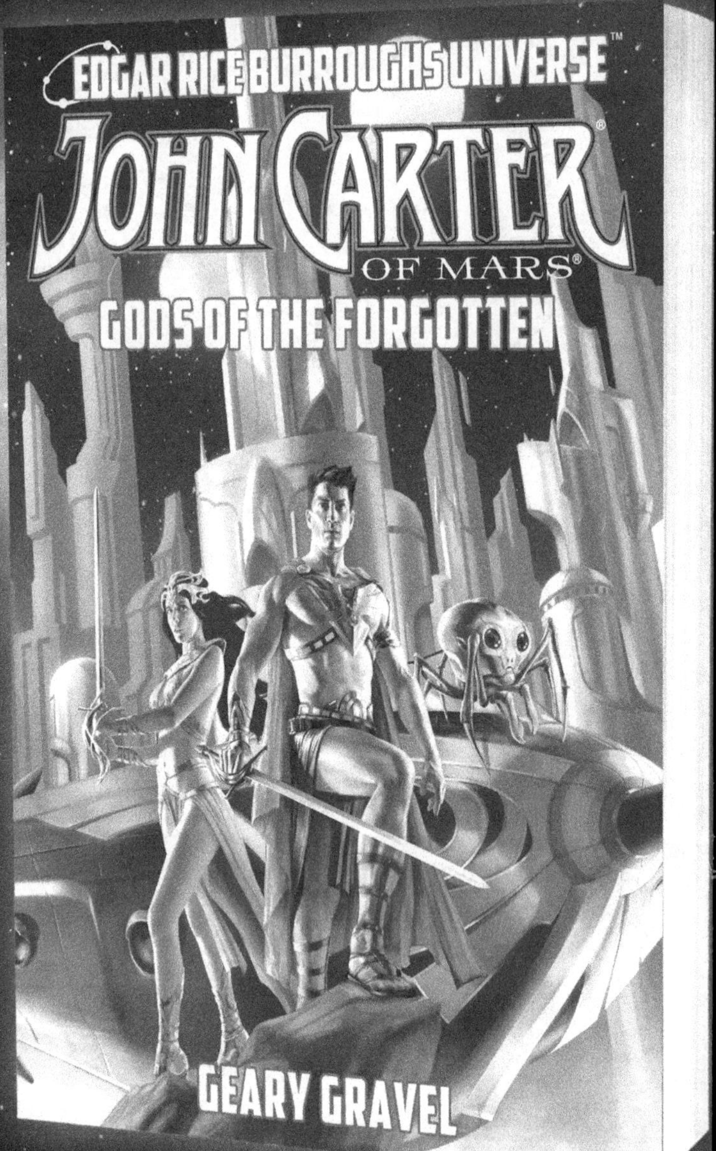

BORN IN PELLUCIDAR® ... MENTORED BY JASON GRIDLEY™ ...
TRAINED TO FIGHT BY TARZAN OF THE APES™ ...

EDGAR RICE BURROUGHS UNIVERSE™

VICTORY HARBEN™
FIRES OF HALOS

CHRISTOPHER PAUL CAREY

AND NOW PITTED AGAINST THE SWORDS OF ETERNITY!

ERB INC.™

COMING SOON FROM EDGAR RICE BURROUGHS, INC.

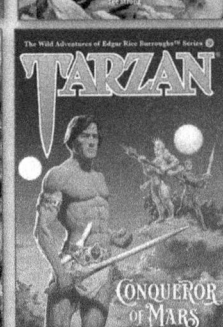

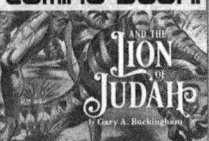

EDGAR RICE BURROUGHS
AUTHORIZED LIBRARY™

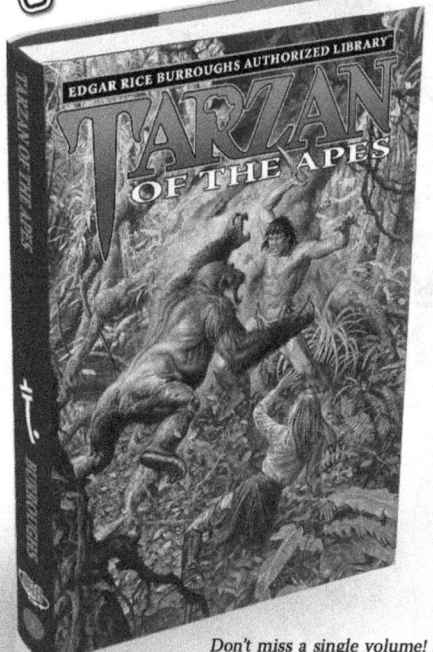

COLLECT EVERY VOLUME!

For the first time ever, the Edgar Rice Burroughs Authorized Library presents the complete literary works of the Master of Adventure in handsome uniform editions. Published by the company founded by Burroughs himself in 1923, each volume of the Authorized Library is packed with extras and rarities not to be found in any other edition. From cover art and frontispieces by legendary artist Joe Jusko to forewords and afterwords by today's authorities and luminaries to a treasure trove of bonus materials mined from the company's extensive archives in Tarzana, California, the Edgar Rice Burroughs Authorized Library will take you on a journey of wonder and imagination you will never forget.

Don't miss a single volume! Sign up for email updates at ERBurroughs.com to keep apprised of all 80-plus editions of the Authorized Library as they become available.

TARZAN OF THE APES	THE RETURN OF TARZAN	THE BEASTS OF TARZAN	THE SON OF TARZAN	TARZAN AND THE JEWELS OF OPAR	JUNGLE TALES OF TARZAN	TARZAN THE UNTAMED	TARZAN THE TERRIBLE	TARZAN AND THE GOLDEN LION	TARZAN AND THE ANT MEN	TARZAN, LORD OF THE JUNGLE	TARZAN AND THE LOST EMPIRE	TARZAN AT THE EARTH'S CORE	TARZAN THE INVINCIBLE	TARZAN TRIUMPHANT	TARZAN AND THE CITY OF GOLD	TARZAN AND THE LION MEN	TARZAN AND THE LEOPARD MEN	TARZAN'S QUEST	TARZAN THE MAGNIFICENT	TARZAN AND THE FORBIDDEN CITY	TARZAN AND THE FOREIGN LEGION	TARZAN AND THE MADMAN	TARZAN AND THE CASTAWAYS
BURROUGHS	BURROUGHS	BURROUGHS	BURROUGHS	BURROUGHS	BURROUGHS	BURROUGHS	BURROUGHS	BURROUGHS	BURROUGHS	BURROUGHS	BURROUGHS	BURROUGHS	BURROUGHS	BURROUGHS	BURROUGHS	BURROUGHS	BURROUGHS	BURROUGHS	BURROUGHS	BURROUGHS	BURROUGHS	BURROUGHS	BURROUGHS
1	2	3	4	5	6	7	8	9	10	11	12	13	14	15	16	17	18	19	20	21	22	23	24

THE JOURNEY BEGINS AT ERBURROUGHS.COM

CPSIA information can be obtained
at www.ICGtesting.com
Printed in the USA
LVHW101132170822
726111LV00004B/41